THE SECRETS OF ROSA LEE

Also by JODI THOMAS

FINDING MARY BLAINE
THE WIDOWS OF WICHITA COUNTY

JODI THOMAS

THE SECRETS OF ROSA LEE

DOUBLEDAY LARGE PRINT HOME LIBRARY EDITION

MIRA®

This Large Print Edition, prepared especially for Doubleday Large Print Home Library, contains the complete, unabridged text of the original Publisher's Edition.

ISBN 0-7394-5732-2

THE SECRETS OF ROSA LEE

Printed in U.S.A.

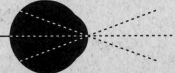

This Large Print Book carries the
Seal of Approval of N.A.V.H.

Dedicated to Connee McAnear,
whose laughter will always live in my memories.

Special thanks to Linda Leopold
for helping me understand roses, and to
Natalie Bright and my fan club
for help and encouragement.

With fall, the wind takes voice in the Texas panhandle. It whispers through mesquite trees and hums in tall prairie grass. When winter nears, it howls down the deserted streets of Clifton Creek after midnight like a wild child without boundaries. But when it passes Rosa Lee Altman's old place at the end of Main, the wind blows silent, no louder than a shadow crossing over forgotten graves.

One

Sidney Dickerson fought down a shudder as she turned up the heat inside her aging Jeep Cherokee and stared at the oldest house in Clifton Creek. Rosa Lee Altman's property. Sidney had lived in Texas for over a year, yet every time she drove down Main Street this one place drew her as if calling her home. In October's evening shadows, the once grand dwelling looked neglected and sad. One of the gap-toothed shutters swung in the wind, making a second-floor window appear to be winking.

I'm coming inside, tomorrow. She almost said the words aloud to the house. *After a year of watching and waiting, I'll finally walk inside.*

The Altman house had been built almost a hundred years ago. In its time, she guessed it had been grand sitting out on the open land by itself, with nothing but cattle grazing all the way to the horizon. Barns, bunkhouses, smoke sheds and kitchens must have sprung up like wildflowers around a rose. A fitting house for Henry Altman, the town's father.

When the railroad arrived a mile away, it had been natural for business to move close to the tracks. Sidney had read that Henry had donated the land for the rail station and the bank, then charged dearly for the lots nearby. The article said he thought to keep a mile between him and the town but, as years passed, folks built along the road from the train station to his mansion, developing Main Street right up to his front yard.

Sidney glanced back at the tattered little town of Clifton Creek. If it had grown to more than five or six thousand, the population would have surrounded the remaining Altman land. But, since the fifties, the town had withered with age and the Altman house sat on a rise overlooking its decline. The train still ran along the tracks but passed the abandoned station without stopping. Nowadays cattle and cotton were trucked to Wichita Falls. Eighteen-wheelers hauled in most supplies. Oil ran in pipelines.

The shadow of the old house reached the windows of her Jeep. Sidney huddled deeper into her wool blazer. She would be forty next week. The same age Rosa Lee had been the year her father, Henry Altman, had died. He had built an empire along with this house. Cattle and oil had pumped through his land and in his blood.

Sidney closed her eyes realizing the old man must have known his forty-year-old daughter would be the end of the line. He'd built the ranch and the ten-bedroom house for a spinster. She couldn't help but wonder if he had encouraged his only child to marry, or had he kept her cloistered away?

Slipping on her glasses, Sidney stared at the house that had been Rosa Lee's so long folks in the town called the place by her name. Wild rosebushes clung to the side walls as if protecting it. Old elms, deformed by the wind and ice, lined the property's north border. The old maid had left the place to the town when she'd died two years ago, but it would be Sidney who would help determine the house's fate.

Demolish or restore? The choice seemed easy, considering its condition. Even the grand white pillars that once guarded the double-door entry were yellowed and chipped. Sidney loved the historical significance of Clifton Creek's founding father's house, but she couldn't ignore how desperately the town needed money. An oil company had made what seemed a fair bid for the land and the mayor had told her the crest, where the house sat, would be the ideal spot for drilling. Sacrificing a house for the town seemed practical, but she couldn't help but wonder if anyone but her would miss the old place at the end of Main.

She flipped open her briefcase on the passenger seat beside her. Beneath stacks of freshman History papers and a file on everything she could dig up about the house, she found a wrinkled old card, water spotted, corners bent. On the front of the card, her grandmother had pasted a recipe clipped from a Depression-era newspaper of Clifton Creek. On the back was one sentence written in a shaky hand. "Never forget the secrets of Rosa Lee."

Sidney fought frustration. How could she remember something she never knew? Once, Sidney had heard her mother say that Granny Minnie had worked in Texas as a nurse until her husband had found a job in Chicago. But, Sidney couldn't remember the name of the town.

She flipped over the card as she had a hundred times before. Two years ago, her mother and Granny Minnie had been killed in a car wreck a hundred miles south of Chicago. Her mother's and grandmother's wills had been standard—except for one item. Minnie had left Sidney a safety deposit key. Locked away, Sidney had found only an old recipe box. An unorganized mixture of forgotten recipes shuffled in with cards and notices for baby showers and weddings that Minnie must have collected over years.

Sidney had looked through the box a few days after the funerals, wondering what had been so important. Why would she have left Sidney, her only grandchild, a worthless box filled with forgotten memories?

This card had to hold the answer. The secret her mother had never taken the time to pass on. A secret her grandmother had thought they must never forget.

Sidney shook her head. She'd taken a teaching job here at Clifton College because of this one card. She had moved halfway across the country in search of a secret she would probably never find.

As darkness settled, Sidney knew she would not sleep tonight. The house waited for her. Tomorrow the mayor's handpicked committee would meet to decide what was to be done about the place.

She smiled, remembering the list of committee members. Like her, most were well-known in town . . . well-known and without influence. It had taken her several days to determine why the mayor had chosen them. At first, she had been honored, thinking he had noticed the articles she'd written about the house in the local paper. But when she'd met with him, she'd known the real truth.

Most folks might only see her as a middle-aged, shy professor, but behind her glasses was a sharp mind. Sidney knew enough about politics to realize that this was an election year, and Mayor Dunley didn't plan to do anything to lose votes. If he decided the fate of Rosa Lee's house, some group in town would be upset. But if he let a committee do it—a committee made up of people connected to everyone in town—no one would contest the outcome.

Red and blue lights blinked in her back window. Sidney glanced in the Jeep's rearview mirror. It was too dark to make out anything but a tall shadow climbing from the police car. She didn't have to see more. She knew who it was.

Sheriff Granger Farrington leaned near as Sidney rolled down her window.

"Evenin', Dr. Dickerson."

Sidney smiled. The man seemed as proper and stiff as a cardboard cutout of the perfect small-town lawman, all starch and order. She might have believed his act if she hadn't seen him with his wife. "Good evening, Sheriff. Is there a problem?"

"No, just making sure you weren't having car trouble."

"I'm fine. How's Meredith?"

A grin cracked his armor. "She's taking it easy. Doc says another month before she'll deliver. I'm thinking of buying stock in Blue Bell. If she eats another gallon of that ice cream, the baby will be born wearing a sweater."

"She craves it, and you supply it."

"Yeah, we're in a twisted relationship. She's a Blue Bell junkie, and I'm her contact." He laughed, then straightened. "I'm surprised you're here after dark, haven't you heard the stories about this place?"

"I heard about them from a few students after I wrote the articles on the house. A madman running through the garden. Chanting in hushed tones drifting through the air, coming from nowhere. Old Rosa Lee's ghost circling the garden, dripping blood over her roses." Sidney laughed. "You believe any of them?"

The sheriff shook his head. "I've never seen anything but kids parking out here on Saturday night. Adams caught some football players smoking pot in back of the house a year ago."

Sidney started the Jeep, guessing the sheriff wouldn't leave until she proved the engine would turn over. He'd given her Jeep a jump twice last winter and, knowing Granger, he'd probably heard about the time one of his deputies had helped her when she'd run out of gas along Cemetery

Road. She couldn't help but wonder if she was on his duty roster. Something scribbled in among the orders, like "watch out for the dingy professor who can't seem to keep her Jeep running."

The sheriff tapped the canvas roof as the Jeep's engine kicked in. "You know, Dr. Dickerson, when you get ready, Whitman will give you a good trade-in on a car. He's got new Cadillacs, but the trade-in lot's got a little of everything."

"I'll think about it." She started to ask one more time if he would call her Sidney. They were about the same age, and he was as close to a friend as she had in this town that welcomed newcomers with the same en-thusiasm as they welcomed fire ants. "Good night, Sheriff."

He touched his hat with two fingers and disappeared back into the shadows.

Sidney glanced once more at the old house. Cloaked in shadows, it looked ro-mantic, mysterious, haunted. She could al-most believe that Rosa Lee, who'd lived all ninety-two years of her life there, still watched over the place.

"Never forget the secrets of Rosa Lee,"

Sidney whispered and wondered what waited behind the solid double doors.

Doors that had kept out the world for a lifetime.

Across town in the Clifton Creek Hotel, Sloan McCormick dropped his leather duffel bag on the tiny hotel bed and growled. He hated sleeping with his feet hanging off the end. At six foot four, it was the rule rather than the exception when traveling.

He also hated small towns with their cracker-box hotel rooms, where neon signs blinked through the thin drapes all night long and sheets had the softness of cheap paper towels.

Emptying his pockets on the scarred dresser, he tried to think of one thing he liked about this assignment. He thought he'd grown used to being alone, but no place made him feel more alone than a small town, and Clifton Creek was a classic. In a town over fifty thousand or so, he could blend in, look familiar enough so that folks returned his smile or wave. But in a place this size, people knew he was a stranger and treated him as such.

"Get the job done and get out." He repeated his rules. "Never get personally involved."

Sloan pulled a pack of folders from his bag and walked to where one of the double lights above the headboard shone. In the dull glow, he went over the list of committee members.

The Rogers sisters would be no problem—he could probably charm them. Both were retired schoolteachers. From what he'd gathered, they were much loved in the community. Though they lived modestly— small house, used van—he was surprised to discover close to eight hundred thousand in their combined savings accounts. A nice little nest egg for the two ladies.

He flipped to the next file. The professor, Sidney Dickerson, would not be as easy to convince. He had listened outside her classroom. Facts, not dreams, would interest her. But, he wasn't sure how to get to her. Dr. Dickerson's interest in the Altman house was far more than mild curiosity. She'd proved that in the half-dozen articles she'd written for the paper.

He flipped to the next member of the mayor's committee. The preacher, Micah Parker, might be convinced "for the good of the community." Sloan had rarely seen a man above thirty so squeaky clean. The private eye he'd hired couldn't dig up a single whisper on the widower, not even in his hometown.

The last two folders belonged to the troublemaker, Billy Hatcher, and the ad executive, Lora Whitman. Both would probably go for money if he offered. Hatcher worked at the lumberyard and did odd jobs around town. Except for one brush with the law, he'd stayed below the radar. Lora Whitman was another story. She appeared to have lived her life in the public eye ever since she was six and had posed for her father's car ads. When Sloan had flipped through the weekly paper's archives, he'd seen several pictures of her. Homecoming queen, cheerleader, fund-raising for one cause then another. Her wedding picture had covered half a page.

Sloan spread the members' fact sheets across the bed. He only needed four to swing the committee. But which four?

He grabbed his Stetson and headed toward the bar he had seen a few blocks away. "Time to go fishin'," Sloan mumbled.

Two

Micah Parker didn't believe in ghosts. He reminded himself of this fact as he jogged toward the edge of town, but there was something strange about the old Altman house. It drew him the way ambulance lights on a highway lured curious drivers.

He caught himself circling past the place each night when he ran. Something must have occurred there years ago and left its impression on the very air—it was not sounds, or odd sightings, but more an emotion that settled on the passerby's skin, thick as humidity just before a storm breaks.

Like most of those chosen for the mayor's committee, he couldn't wait to go inside and have a look. And tomorrow, he'd get his chance. Reverend Milburn had talked him into another civic committee, this one to decide what to do with Rosa Lee Altman's place. As associate minister, Micah followed orders.

Even though a relative newcomer in town, Micah had heard the stories about the old maid who had lived to be ninety-two. She'd lost her wealth—first a section, then a block at a time until nothing had remained in her name but the house and gardens. Some said she'd never ventured beyond her gates. She had had no life outside her property, and folks said no one, not even a delivery man, had stepped beyond her porch.

Micah studied the house as he crossed the street, his tennis shoes almost soundless. Even in the streetlight he could see that weather had sanded away almost all paint, leaving the two-story colonial a dusty brown. The same color as the dirt that sifted through everything over this open land.

Smiling, he waved at the house. It seemed more than brick and board. Some places have personalities, he thought with a grin. If this one had a voice it would say, "Evenin' Reverend Parker," in a Texas drawl.

He slowed in the darkness and stretched

before turning about and heading back through town. The temperature had dropped during his run. Time to get home.

As he stepped into the street, a movement in the gutter caught his attention. He stumbled trying to avoid a collision.

A tiny, muddy, yellow cat, not big enough to be without its mother, curled against a pile of trash the wind had swept in the grate. Its long hair stuck out in all directions, but the little thing didn't know enough to crawl away from the pile of discarded cups and packing paper.

Micah leaned down. "Now, what have we here?" He lifted the shivering pile of bones and hair.

The animal made a hissing sound but didn't fight as he warmed it with his hands.

"How about coming along with me, little guy?" Micah carefully tucked the kitten into his jacket pocket and turned toward home. "I'll share the leftovers from the men's prayer breakfast with you."

The animal didn't sound any more excited about the meal than he was, but their choices were limited. Thanks to his late meeting at the church tonight, his son Logan had already eaten dinner with their neighbor, Mrs. Mac. Micah could go grocery shopping at the town's only store and probably run into half a dozen people he knew, all of whom he'd have to talk to. Or, he could eat out alone and have everyone who passed by look as if they felt sorry for him. Or, he could finish off whatever lay wrapped in the aluminum foil the breakfast cleanup committee had insisted he take. Leftovers seemed the best choice.

When Micah entered the back of the duplex he shared with his seven-year-old son, he lowered the kitten into a basket of dirty laundry and motioned for it to be quiet.

The cat just stared up at him, too frightened to make a sound.

Micah closed the utility-room door and silently moved down the hallway. Sometime during the fifty-year history of this place, someone had cut a door between the two apartments.

He leaned his head into the other apartment and whispered, "Thanks, Mrs. Mac."

"You're welcome," she answered without turning away from her TV. "No trouble."

Micah closed the door connecting the apartments without bothering to lock it, then moved down the hallway to Logan's room. Over the past three years they'd worked out a system. He helped Mrs. Mac carry in her groceries, mowed her side of the lawn and did anything her arthritis wouldn't let her do. She watched over a sleeping Logan while Micah ran, and babysat on the rare occasions Logan couldn't accompany Micah to a church meeting.

Micah carefully crossed the cluttered floor of Logan's room and knelt to pull the cover over the boy's shoulder. He brushed sunny-blond hair away from Logan's forehead and whispered, "We love you, son," as if Amy were still alive and helping him raise the boy.

He backed out of the room slowly, knowing one more day of Logan's childhood had passed.

A little after seven the next morning, Micah checked on his furry houseguest. After crying half the night, the kitten must have licked up all the warm milk in the chipped saucer Micah had left in the laundry basket. The tiny houseguest now lay curled up beside his oldest sweatshirt.

"I want that shirt back," Micah said as he poured himself coffee. He thought of moving the basket to the garage but decided it was too cold. With luck, the cat couldn't jump out and would be fine until he came home for lunch with kitty litter.

"I'll stop by and get some cat food, so consider it a date for lunch." He lifted his cup to the sleeping guest. "I promise not to try to cram any more of the church's scrambled eggs into you." The nuked eggs worked only slightly better than the warmed hash browns. Last night Micah had ended up making a sandwich out of a leftover biscuit and sausage. "I've no doubt you're a Baptist. Any self-respecting Methodist would have downed the eggs."

"Who you talking to, Pop?"

Micah smiled. His son had turned a corner a month ago—calling him Daddy was now too babyish.

Lifting the kitten, Micah faced his son. Logan, thin, blond and full of energy, was a miniature of himself except for one thing. The eyes. The boy had Amy's green eyes. And right now they danced with excitement.

"Where'd it come from? Can we keep it? What's its name? Is it a boy or a girl?"

Micah laughed. "Slow down, partner." He laid the kitten in his son's lap. "I found it last night when I was running. I don't think Mrs. Mac allows pets, but she'll probably let us keep it for a few days until we fatten it up a little and find it a home. I don't know if it's a boy or girl cat, but I do know its name."

Logan wasn't listening. He sat cross-legged on the floor with the cat in his lap.

Micah felt a tug at his heart. A boy should have pets, but after Amy had died, Micah had all he could handle taking care of Logan.

Standing, Micah washed his hands and poured Logan's Cheerios, then sliced a banana into another bowl. "I thought we'd call him Baptist, you know after John the Baptist."

Logan nodded.

"Better wash your hands and eat, son. Jimmy's mom will be here soon." Micah poured the last of the milk in a small glass and set it beside the cereal. Logan never mixed food. Not anything. Mrs. Mac told Micah once that a mother would never put up with such nonsense.

"Will Baptist be here when I get home?" The boy put the cat back in the basket.

Micah tossed Logan a towel to dry his hands and directed him toward the table.

"I'll pick up some food today. We'll be like a hospital and take care of him until someone adopts him."

He didn't miss the pain that flickered in Logan's eyes. For the boy, a hospital was a place to die. First his mother, then his only grandparent. Micah knew he shouldn't have said the word, but sometime Logan would have to understand and learn not to be afraid of words. Words like *hospital* and *cancer.*

Micah reached over and petted the cat as Logan downed his breakfast.

"I'm going to Jimmy's after school, re-member?" the boy mumbled between bites.

"I'll pick you up at six."

"Seven, please. Jimmy's dad's cooking out. Said it's for the last time this year. The grill's going into the garage for the winter. He cooks the hot dogs on a stick and lets me eat them like a corn dog without the bun or anything."

"All right, seven." Micah couldn't blame Logan. His choice at home was usually a kid's TV dinner or fast food.

Jimmy's double tap on the door sounded and Logan was off like a racer hearing the gun. He grabbed his backpack and jacket, slapped a high five on his dad's hand and ran for the door.

Micah scraped the half-full bowl down the disposal and reached for the old leather backpack he used as a briefcase. He knew at thirty-four it was long past time to switch to a briefcase, but the bag he had carried since college still felt right on his shoulder. He hated change. There had been so much change in his life, he clung to the familiar in small ways whenever he could.

"You need anything before I go," he glanced toward the basket, but the cat was sound asleep.

He felt stupid talking to a cat, but it beat the silence of the house. "See you at noon, Baptist."

If he hurried, he'd have time for breakfast at the Main Street Café before the commit-tee meeting. No one thought it strange when a man ate breakfast alone, Micah thought. He'd be safe from sad looks, for once.

With coffee cup in hand, he grabbed his coat and headed toward his car. A blast of sunshine and cold air hit him as he ran the ten feet to the old garage. He tried to hold the coffee and pull on his coat. Brown spots plopped along the walk. By the time he got to his car, the half cup of coffee he'd managed to save was cold. He drank it anyway while he waited for the heater to warm. This time of year, by midafternoon, he'd need the air conditioner. Nothing made sense to him anymore, not even the weather.

He missed the green of East Texas, but he couldn't return. Not yet. When he had moved to Clifton Creek and accepted the associate pastor's position at First United Methodist Church, he'd decided to give his grief a year to mend before returning home. But Amy's memory hadn't faded. In a few months, she'd be gone three years. His heart and body still ached for her. Some nights, he ran miles trying to outdistance the emptiness of his life. Logan was all that gave him reason to breathe most days.

He sat at the edge of the counter at the café, ordered pancakes and strawberry pie and pretended to read the Dallas paper while he tried to figure out when he'd have time in the day to shop. When he'd finished eating, he paid out, speaking to almost everyone in the place.

He elected to walk to his meeting a few blocks away at the edge of town.

Micah smiled and waved as the plump Rogers sisters climbed from their van. He'd become an expert at smiling . . . at hiding . . . at pretending to live.

The Rogers sisters were so short they tumbled out of the Suburban like beanbag dolls. Micah thought of suggesting they drive a smaller vehicle. Since neither had children, he saw no need for six extra seats. But maybe, to them, the van was like some of the old men's pickups around town. Farmers who moved in from their farms wound up hauling nothing more than groceries around, but they thought they still had to drive a truck. Maybe the sisters had needed the van when they'd taught school and had simply become used to it.

"Look Beth Ann, it's that young Reverend Parker," the smaller of the sisters whispered in a voice Micah could easily hear. "He's so handsome it makes me think of changing religions."

Micah fought down a laugh. He certainly wasn't young at thirty-four, and no one but Amy had ever thought him handsome. "Morning, Miss Rogers." He offered his hand to the one who'd spoken. If she'd called the other Beth Ann, then she must be

Ada May. He turned to the other. "Miss Rogers."

Both women smiled, but it was Ada May who spoke again. "You get on this committee, too?"

Micah nodded. As the associate, part of his job was to serve on every committee and charity board that came along. This one didn't seem to require much. They only had to vote on what to do with the old place. He hadn't even gone inside and had already made up his mind. They needed to tear it down before it fell. Micah envisioned a park in its place, maybe with a running track.

"Isn't it exciting?" Beth Ann finally found her voice. "I'm sixty-four and, to my knowledge, no one's ever been past the door of this place in my lifetime. There's no telling what we'll find."

"Mice," Ada May mumbled. "Maybe even rats and spiders. Rattlers, if it's warm enough."

Beth Ann shuddered and pulled a purse, big enough to use for a sleepover, from the van. "We came early, hoping to walk around the grounds before the meeting started. Would you like to join us, Reverend?"

Micah offered each an arm. "I'd love to,

ladies. I planned to do the same thing." He didn't add that he had been early to every-thing for three years.

Stones still marked the path through what had once been a fine garden. Huge bushes of twisted twigs looked misshapen. Micah guessed in spring they'd bloom once more as they had for almost a hundred years. A stand of evergreens along the north prop-erty line blocked the wind and cast a shadow over part of the plants, making them appear gray and lifeless.

Ada May tugged on Micah's arm. "The garden seems to have no order, twisting and turning, but if you stay on the path, you'll make it back to the house. All paths turn back on themselves and lead to the rear of the house."

"Now, how do you know that, sister?" Beth Ann asked from just behind them.

"Everyone knows that," Ada May snapped. "Young folks bring their dates here and have for years. Lovers walk the path at twilight."

"Well," Beth Ann interrupted. "We'll know if it's fact after we walk it. I don't go around telling anything that I don't know to be true, until I check it out for myself. I've heard tell that evil roams these gardens. As a child, I heard of people being chased out of the gardens by a crazy man with long white hair flying like a sail in the wind behind him. But, I don't know that for a fact, mind you."

Both women paused as if waiting for him to say something, but Micah guessed it would be dangerous to come between the sisters. He wondered if any man had ever been brave enough to try. Since they weren't sure where the path ended, he figured neither had ever made this journey at dark when lovers came out.

As they walked along, it occurred to him that he felt as dead inside as the winter gardens that hadn't known a human touch in years. He didn't much care as long as he could hide his feelings from everyone. Like an actor, he'd played the same role so many times that the words no longer made sense.

He couldn't talk about his thoughts, his feelings. Couldn't tell people how much he still missed his wife. Every day. Every minute. It didn't matter. Years had passed since he'd kissed Amy goodbye. All he had to do was stop breathing. Just don't take another breath, and he'd be with her.

But he couldn't leave Logan. She

wouldn't want him to. So he'd go on walking, smiling, pretending, until Logan grew up, and one day he might get lucky and forget to breathe.

As the sisters talked of winter roses, Micah closed his eyes and thought of Amy.

Three

.

"Straighten up, Lora. You look round-shoul-
dered. I swear you've a model's form when
you hold your head up, but when you
slouch, all I see is Lurch from *The Addams
Family.*" Isadore whined. "And hurry up or
you'll be late for the committee meeting."

Lora Whitman pretended not to hear her
mother and wondered if she could special
order an ejection seat for the passenger
side of her next Audi. Sometime during college, she'd become an Olympian at ignoring
Isadore Whitman. Before Lora had hit puberty, her mother had thought her ideal,
dressing her up like a doll and bragging to
her bridge club about the perfection of her
only child.

Then the awkward years had hit and perfection had slipped, never to be reclaimed, no matter how hard Lora had tried to please. Even the night she had been named homecoming queen, Isadore had leaned to hug her daughter and had reminded her how bad her nails looked. While any other mother might have been proud, Isadore had whispered another comment about how fat Lora looked in taffeta.

Lora honked as Old Man Hamm rolled through the town's only stoplight in his rust bucket of a car. For a moment, she visualized him hitting the passenger side of her Audi, sending Isadore into terminal silence. As always, Lora colored her daydream with detail. Blood the same shade of her mother's lipstick. The volunteer firemen trying to pull Isadore out without damaging her Escada suit.

Lora steered left toward the eyesore of a house at the end of Main. Her mother continued to rattle. The plans for what she'd wear to her mother's funeral faded as Isadore began her list of what Lora should do at the meeting. Her mother seemed to believe that if Lora left her sight without instructions she might—even though she was twenty-four years old—wander off the face of the earth.

"I know you think this committee appointment isn't important," Isadore stated as if she had an audience. "But you'll see. One thing will lead to another. You can help decide what to do with the old Altman house. The next thing you know, you'll be moved to some important board seat. Why, in ten years you could be on the town council."

The only goal Lora had was to accumulate enough money to get out of this place. She could see no way that serving on a civic committee would help her accomplish that. But in the six months she had been back handling advertising for her father's car dealership, she'd learned one thing. If she didn't play the game, she had no chance of breaking free. Her father held as tightly to his money as her mother wanted to hold to her.

"Don't park in the dirt." Isadore waved her hand, shooing the car as she might an animal. "There's probably mud."

Lora stopped in the center of the street and threw her silver Audi into Park. "You think you can drive my car home?" She opened the driver's side door with doubts

about her mother's ability to handle anything other than a Cadillac. Lora's ex had
told her she'd picked the car just to anger
her father, but in truth, Lora loved the feel of
it.

Isadore tried not to look as if she were
hurrying when she circled the car and took
Lora's place. "Of course, I can drive this
thing, but don't you want me to pick you
up? I'm just having my nails done. I could
be back in an hour, provided the girl does
the job right. Last time I told her I wanted a
French manicure in another color. I swear
she looked at me like—"

"No." The last thing Lora wanted was to
stand around like a schoolgirl waiting for her
mother to pick her up. "I'll walk over to the
dealership and ride home with Dad."

She heard her mother's "but" as she
closed the door. With Isadore, there was
never an end to conversation, only abrupt
halts.

It frightened Lora to think she might end
up like her mother, constantly harping on
something of no importance. Before the divorce, when Dan wanted to really land a
blow, he'd mention how much she sounded
like her mother.

With determined steps, Lora forced herself not to run as she heard the sound of the window being lowered. At five foot ten, her long legs carried her swiftly to the porch and out of reach of her mother's final instructions. Her high heels clicked across the wood as she squared her shoulders and resigned herself to get this duty over with as quickly as possible.

Lora's car still sat in the middle of the street as she opened the door to the old Altman house and hurried inside.

Air, cold and stale, closed around her. A wisp, thick as a sigh, rushed past. Escaping. She had the feeling she'd be wise to do so, as well. This place, or more accurately the grounds behind the house, held nothing but bad memories for her. She'd just as soon turn her vote in now to demolish the landmark. Anything, even a vacant lot, would be better than having this old mansion shadow Main.

Lora blinked, trying to adjust to the filtered light shining through dirty windows. Dark paneling, rotted in spots. Dusty floors. Silence. She fought the urge to turn and run but remembered her mother probably still waited outside and decided even a haunted house would be preferable company.

The floor creaked when she stepped into a wide hallway with doors on either side. Stairs rose from the back wall of the entry. Huge bookshelves, too large for vandals to steal, lined the corridor as if guarding long-forgotten secrets. A surprising dignity reflected in the room's architecture, like an old soldier still standing proud in the uniform of his youth.

Lora forced another step, telling herself she'd already lived through hell being married to Dan for three years. What else could happen to her? He'd taken everything except her car, and he would have gotten that, too, if it hadn't been in her father's name. Dan had made it necessary for her to quit her job without references. He'd fought until she'd had no option but to do what he knew she hated most—to return home. He'd learned, in the law school she'd worked to send him to, how to cut deep and once he was set up in a practice, he'd cut her out of his life.

Straightening, Lora smiled. She might be down but she was a long way from out. What could one houseful of old stories do to her? She wasn't some frightened fifteen-year-old. She was a battled-scarred divorcée.

At slumber parties when she'd been small, girls had told stories of how old Rosa Lee would kill any man who set foot on her property and cut him up so she could dribble his blood over her roses. In Lora's current state of mind, she didn't consider Rosa Lee's actions all that terrible.

"Hey, lady," a low male voice echoed through the passage. "This the place for the committee meeting?"

Lora fought down nerves as she spotted a kid, maybe late teens, leaning against the banister. Half his body stood in shadow, but nothing about the half she saw looked good. Dirty jeans, worn leather jacket, hair in his eyes.

"It is," she answered. "Why?" She thought of adding, "Shouldn't you be out robbing some quickie mart?" but held her tongue.

He shifted, stepping more into the light. The chain that held his wallet in place clanked against the rivets running along the seam of his jeans.

Lora held her ground. He was a few years

older than she'd thought, a little more frightening. A three-day growth of beard darkened his chin. Angry gray eyes watched her,
studying, judging, undressing her. If she'd
been in Dallas, she would have reached for
her Mace. But Clifton Creek didn't have
muggers, she reminded herself.

"I'm on the committee." He turned, showing more interest in the house than in her.
His hands spread wide over the paneling
and caressed the grooves in the wood. "I've
always wondered what it would be like inside here. One of the guys I spent a weekend in the drunk tank with says his grandfather told him they sent all the way to Saint
Louis for the carpenters on this place. Had
to bring most of the wood out on wagons."

Lora forced her heart to slow. So much
for her mother's idea of it being an honor to
be on one of the mayor's committees. They
appeared to be emptying the jails in order to
fill the chairs.

"I'm on the committee, too," she said
needlessly. No one would be in this old
place at ten in the morning unless they'd
been asked to serve. "I'm Lora Whitman."

"I know who you are." He moved a
scarred hand over the top of one of the

massive hutches, dusting away layers of dirt. "I've seen you around." He didn't look up as he spoke. "You came back after your husband took you for a ride."

Lora shrugged, not surprised even the town's underbelly knew of her troubles. Keeping up with everyone was more popular than sports in this place. But she did resent his comment that made her sound as if she had been no more than a horse Dan had saddled up one day and then turned out to starve when he had gotten where he wanted to go. Which, in retrospect, was accurate.

She straightened, leveling the kid with her gaze. "That's right. He took me for everything, and I had to come back here to work for my father." She had no idea why she was telling this thug her life story. Maybe she just wanted to get the gossip straight for a change. "I was on my way to being an advertising executive with one of Dallas's big five, and now I'm fighting to keep the salesmen from putting their kids in every commercial we shoot at the car lot."

The youth surprised her by saying, "Well, at least you got an old man to run home to. And don't knock those ads. Some folks like seeing the kids. I remember seeing you in a few of your daddy's ads when you were little."

She studied him more closely. "Do I know you?"

"Billy Hatcher." Thankfully, he didn't offer his hand. "I was in middle school when you were a cheerleader your senior year. I liked to watch you jump."

Lora fought the urge to slap him. She tried to picture him as a half-grown boy watching her but had no memory of him. "I don't jump anymore," she snapped.

"Too bad."

He grinned, and she controlled the longing to slug him this time. Much more conversation and she'd be a killer by noon. "Great!" she mumbled, "I'm on a committee with a sex-starved bully." This might prove no more different than her marriage.

"Hello?"

They both turned as a middle-aged woman wearing what looked like a Navajo blanket stepped through the door. "Are you both here for the meeting?"

Billy shrugged, but Lora offered her hand. "Yes," she said, thankful to have someone, anyone, else in the room. "I'm Lora Whitman."

The woman's smile lit her makeup-free face. Her eyes sparkled with excitement behind thick glasses. "I'm Sidney Dickerson, history professor from the college. Isn't this the most exciting thing in the world?" She pulled off the poncho and tossed it over the banister. "I couldn't sleep last night thinking about the adventure we're embarking upon."

Lora caught Billy Hatcher's gaze and realized they had something in common after all. Neither of them agreed with the professor.

As Sidney moved into what appeared to have been the dining room to set up, three more people entered. Lora knew the Rogers sisters and greeted them warmly. They spoke to her as if she were still their student in grade school. Between the two sisters, she'd bet they knew everyone in town. There hadn't been a wedding or a funeral in forty years the old maids hadn't attended. She wasn't surprised when Miss Ada May Rogers took over the introductions.

"Lora, dear, do you know the new Methodist minister?" Ada May motioned with her hand for him to move closer. "This is Reverend Parker."

Lora nodded, knowing anyone not born in Clifton Creek might be referred to as "new." The minister had sandy-blond hair and a lean body beneath his slightly wrinkled suit. She'd guess him ten years older than she, but the sadness in his eyes made him seem ancient. Somewhere in the back of her mind, she remembered hearing he was a widower with a small kid to raise.

Micah Parker offered his hand, reminding her they'd met before at the Labor Day pancake breakfast. Then, to her surprise, he greeted Billy Hatcher warmly before Ada May finished the introductions.

Billy smiled and slapped the preacher's shoulder as Parker complimented the kid on some work he'd done at the church.

Lora tried not to appear to be listening to the men as Ada May chatted with the professor. Glancing at the ceiling, Lora searched for cracks. It would be just her luck that the first day in years someone walked into the house the roof would collapse. The whole town would probably turn out to dig through the rubble for bodies. First, they'd uncover her hand (the one without a wedding band on it) or maybe one leg, all dusty and bloody. One of the Rogers sisters might survive. Of course she would die soon after of loneliness. The town might erect a statue on this very spot to honor the civic-minded heroes willing to serve and die on a committee.

"Are you all right, dear?" Ada May pulled Lora back to reality.

"Yes," she mumbled. "I was just thinking how my clothes are going to get dirty in this old place."

"That's my fault," Dr. Dickerson confessed from the doorway of the room she'd entered. "I only wanted the door unlocked, the boards removed from the windows and little else disturbed." She motioned with her notebook. "Please, would everyone step into the dining room. I did have folding chairs and a table brought in and set up near the bay window so we'd have plenty of light. If we're going to decide the fate of this house today, it's only fitting we do it on the property."

Everyone followed Sidney Dickerson's lead. As Billy Hatcher passed Lora, he whispered, "Take off your clothes and leave

them at the door if you're so worried about
the dirt."

Lora flashed him her best "drop dead"
look and rushed ahead. This was going to
be a fine committee, she thought. Two old
maids, a preacher, a sex-starved thug and a
professor. And me, she thought, the total
failure.

There were definitely levels in hell, even in
Clifton Creek.

Four

A few minutes past ten, Sidney Dickerson had all the members of her committee sitting around a card table. Light shone through the newly unboarded bay window that stretched as high as the twelve-foot ceiling. The wide, planked floor reflected the sun even beneath years of dust. She wanted to close her eyes and spread her hands wide like she'd seen worshippers do on television. *Feel the power!* she thought of saying. *Feel the history.* In her calm, lonely life she'd known only a few times when she'd been so excited.

Judging from the group before her, if she dared do something so foolish, they would turn and run. In fact, none of them looked all that interested in being on the committee.

Billy Hatcher crossed his arms and leaned back in his chair between Lora Whitman and Reverend Parker, who wore a smile that could have been painted on a cigar-store Indian.

Lora Whitman stared out the window looking at nothing.

One of the Rogers sisters had already taken up her crochet, while the other paused with pen and paper, waiting to write down every word spoken.

"Welcome to you all," Sidney began. "Thank you for agreeing to serve on this committee. We're here to study the history of a house that represents the very heart of Clifton Creek. We've been asked to make a few decisions about the future of this building and the surrounding land . . . decisions that will affect not only us but generations to come. We alone will decide if the legend of the fine man who founded this town lives or dies."

Billy yawned.

Beth Ann counted stitches under her breath.

Sidney fought back tears. This house—

that was so important to her—mattered to no one else. No one. Maybe they should agree to take the oil company's money and forget even talking about trying to save an old house.

The preacher checked his watch.

"According to my research—" Sidney knew she had to speed up "—this home was one of the first, if not *the* first, big ranch house built north of Dallas." She glanced at her notes and lectured on. "Henry W. Altman must have been little more than a boy when he rode in and claimed this land. We know he paid cash for the wagon train of supplies and workers needed to build this place, but no one seems to know where his money came from. Probably an inheritance, since there's no record of any Altman family members ever visiting the ranch. He was born in 1878, died in 1950. He fathered one child, Rosa Lee Altman, who never married."

Beth Ann counted a little louder. Her sister elbowed her gently, signaling her to turn down the volume.

Billy leaned farther back in his chair and looked as if he were staring at Lora Whitman's legs under the table. Considering the short length of her skirt, Sidney could only guess at the view.

She lifted her briefcase onto the wobbly card table. Sidney had to do something before someone interrupted her and asked for a final vote. They all looked as if they wanted to move on with their lives. She needed to act fast. "Before we talk about what needs to be done, I want to show you all something I've found. It may be a factor we need to consider."

Pulling a worn book from her notes, Sidney's hand shook. "This book was donated to the library when Rosa Lee died." She beamed. "Though the book is valuable as a first edition, its true value may lie in the inscription. Which, after reading it, I think you all will agree dictates further research on our part.

"It says simply, 'To my Rosa Lee, who promises to love no other in this lifetime. Leave with me tonight. Wait for me in the garden. I promise I'll come before midnight. Fuller, July 4, 1933.' "

Ada May stopped writing. Billy glanced out the window. Beth Ann whispered, "darn," as she lost a stitch. The preacher leaned forward, his smile melted as his body stiffened as if preparing for a blow.

"If this was given to Rosa Lee, then maybe all the stories about her being an old maid who never had a gentleman caller aren't true." Sidney moved around the table, as if circling a classroom. "Maybe there are secrets here to uncover. Secrets the town should know before we sell the land."

"Who cares?" Billy questioned, slouching in his chair. "Secrets about folks long dead are of no interest to anyone."

Lora looked as if she agreed.

Micah Parker stretched his hand toward the book. "May I see that, Dr. Dickerson?"

Sidney smiled, knowing she'd hooked one. "If birth records are right, Rosa Lee would have been twenty-three when she was given that book. My guess is Mr. Fuller would have been from around here, but why didn't he meet her at midnight like he planned?"

"Maybe he did," Billy answered.

Sidney turned to him. "Then why didn't she leave with him if she'd promised to love no other in this lifetime?"

"Maybe her father stopped him," Ada

May chimed in. "She was his only child. Fuller might have been a no-good drifter. If she'd left with him, she'd have been poorly married."

Sidney raised an eyebrow. "A drifter who bought a leather-bound first edition that must have cost a month's wages during the Depression?"

No one seemed to have an answer.

Micah opened the book and ran his fingers over the words. The others in the room didn't have to ask. They all knew the reverend thought of his wife.

"Maybe Fuller didn't show up," Sidney added. "And we have no idea if Fuller was his last name or first, since it was a relatively popular given name a hundred years ago."

The minister studied the writing inside the book. "Why would a man who used such an expensive way to send a note, not show up as planned?"

Lora frowned. "She waited seventy years for a love who never returned?"

"What a martyr," Ada May whispered.

"What a fool," Lora mumbled. "No man's worth more than fifteen minutes, tops."

Reverend Parker stood slowly. He gently

pushed the book across the table and took a step toward the door.

Sidney knew the words in the book had touched him. She saw it in his eyes. The preacher wore sorrow on his sleeve. But would words written seventy years ago pull him into the mystery, or push him away?

She followed Micah to the door, having no idea how she might comfort him or if he even wanted solace. It occurred to her that she'd suffered the greater loss, for she'd never, not in forty years of life, experienced such heartache. At least he'd once had someone promise to love him for a lifetime.

Her fingers brushed his sleeve a second before she heard the sound of a car braking.

She glanced outside. Sunbeams reflected off the bay window. Sidney blinked through crystal-white light a moment before the sun shattered.

An explosion of crashing glass echoed off the walls and bounced back on itself. Sunbeams splintered.

Sidney stepped back, bumping into the preacher. Chaos ricocheted into tiny slivers bouncing and sliding across the floor. She screamed.

Billy Hatcher threw his body into Lora's as

the glass blew around them like a rushing tidal wave. They hit the floor hard, sending folding chairs rattling. Ada May lifted her notebook and huddled near her sister. Glass rained across Sidney's notes, reaching the edge of the crochet square Beth Ann had been working on. Rust-covered metal, the size of a man's fist, tumbled to a stop at Lora's broken chair.

Micah rushed forward. His shoes crackled on a carpet of slivers. "Is everyone all right!"

A chorus of groans and cries answered.

"What happened?" Beth Ann said in a shaky teacher's voice. "Who threw that thing!"

Ada May's sobs grew from tiny hiccups to full volume.

"I don't know," Micah placed a hand on Ada May's shoulder. "All I got a look at was the back of a pickup." He turned to the others. "Is anyone hurt?"

Billy lay curled over Lora. Neither answered Micah's call.

Sydney shook as if someone had hold of every inch of her body and planned to rattle her very bones. "I'm not hurt!" she whispered. "I'm not hurt." She tried to reach for

Billy and Lora, but her legs began to give way.

She looked down at trembling hands and decided they couldn't be hers. "I'm not hurt," she whimpered.

The room faded. She fell into a warm, calm darkness.

Five

Lora Whitman huddled in a corner of the old dining room, her forehead resting on her knees as she tried to calm her breathing. It had all happened so fast. The sound of a car on the street. A rusty oil-field drill bit flying through the window. Glass following the missile like the tail of a comet. Billy's body slamming into hers, knocking her to the floor. Crushing her. Protecting her.

She glanced over at the drill bit still resting on her crumpled folding chair. She'd seen ones like it all her life. The oil rigs changed bits when drilling and the used ones were often thrown in the dirt around the site, or pitched in the back of pickup trucks. This one, all rusty and dirty, seemed harmless now.

"Lora? Miss Whitman?" Sheriff Farrington knelt before her. "You calm enough to give me a statement?"

Lora shoved her mass of blond hair away from her face. "There's not much I can add to what the others have said." Scraped knees poked through the holes in her stockings. "Except I thought it was a rock or a football or something. I didn't know it was a drill bit until later." She stretched out her leg. "I guess it couldn't have been an accident. No one tosses around something so ugly for fun."

The sheriff glanced over at the rusty metal with teeth on one end used to dig into the rock-hard earth in these parts. "It wasn't an accident," he echoed. "There was a note pushed inside the bit."

Lora stretched the other leg. "What did it say?" she asked. She wouldn't have been surprised if it read, *Kill Lora* because the drill point had been aimed right at her.

The sheriff offered his hand to help her stand. "It said, *Let the house fall.*"

Lora managed a laugh. "I guess someone not on the committee wanted to vote.

Funny thing is, I'd have given them my place if they'd only asked."

She stumbled. The sheriff's grip was firm. "The medic said there's nothing broken, but if you want, I could drive you over to the hospital and have them check you out. You'll want to be careful. There's probably glass in your hair." He touched her arm with a light pat as if he'd read somewhere in a manual what to do.

Lora tried to smile but couldn't manage it. "I had my head turned toward the door where Reverend Parker and the professor were standing. Billy hit me and knocked me to the floor before I even realized what happened."

She stared out onto the porch. Billy Hatcher sat on the steps. He'd removed his jacket. Blood spotted his shirt. The medic's college helpers were cleaning cuts along his left hand and face. "When it happened, all I could think about was how angry I was that he knocked me down. I even fought him for a few seconds."

"Don't worry about it." The sheriff smiled. "I'm sure he's not sorry he knocked you out of harm's way."

"How bad is he hurt?" she asked.

"I offered to take him over to the doc's, but he said butterfly bandages are all he needs. He'll have a scar on his forehead worth talking about. The leather jacket protected his arm and back. His hand is bleeding from several scratches but he says they are no worse than what he gets at work. He's lucky."

"No, I'm lucky. That drill bit would have hit my head if he hadn't flown into me." For a moment, her imagination pictured the jagged iron teeth flying into the back of her head. She could almost see her mother leaning over her casket saying something like, "Thank God it hit her from behind and didn't mess up her face."

"Did you see or hear anything that might help me out?" The sheriff broke into her daydream. "Did anyone say anything to you before the meeting? Did you see the truck pull away?"

"Nothing. I didn't even know it was a truck. I'd been watching the clouds a few minutes before. I didn't even notice the traffic." Lora closed her eyes, wishing she could cry. Billy Hatcher had been hurt. Dr.

Dickerson was on her way to Wichita Falls with chest pains. The Rogers sisters were wound up tighter than speed babies. They'd told their story to everyone and were now recounting it to each other. Only the reverend appeared calm. He paced slowly around the room as if looking for a clue everyone had missed.

In fact, he'd been calm since the beginning, like some kind of robot. He'd caught the professor when she'd passed out, dialed the sheriff on his cell, talked everyone into remaining still until help came. She couldn't help but think it strange that a brush with death didn't affect him.

After he'd called the sheriff, in what seemed like seconds, the room flooded with people. Firemen from the station two blocks away, the sheriff, campus cops from the college and the hospital's only ambulance. Clifton Creek might be small, but they could move when needed. She had heard talk that the sheriff ran everyone through drills twice a year in case a tornado hit. Their practice paid off today.

Half the town turned out to watch. Traffic was down to one lane in front of Rosa Lee's old place. If Lora knew them, and she did, most had already made up their minds about what had happened. A few were planning punishment for the villains when they were found.

Through the open door, she could hear Philip Price chanting like a cantor questioning why anyone would want to hurt this group of people. "Who'd want to hurt the Rogers sisters?" he asked, but didn't bother waiting for an answer. "Or a professor? Or the preacher? Or the poor brokenhearted Whitman girl whose husband . . ."

Lora ducked her head. She didn't want to go outside. Somehow, it seemed safer to stay in here. The coolness of the house felt comforting. The dusty smells settling around her seemed strangely familiar. She looked up at Sheriff Farrington. "Why?"

The sheriff shook his head. "Maybe just kids seeing the opportunity to break something. A twelve-foot window in an abandoned house would be hard to resist. Maybe someone who just wanted the house torn down and didn't really give much thought that their note might hurt someone."

"But you don't think so?"

"But I don't think so," he echoed. "There's

no way anyone passing could have missed seeing the committee sitting in that bay window."

"Then why?"

"Someone doesn't want one of you, or all of you, in this house." He stared directly into her eyes. "Whoever threw this meant harm, Lora. To you or to someone at that table."

Lora covered her eyes with her palms, pretending to be invisible as she had as a child. She couldn't think of anyone who would plan to harm her. Phil, the town crier, had been right. Who would want to hurt any of them? The only person she could think of who hated her was Dan, and he didn't want her dead. He only wanted her to suffer. Their marriage, in and out of bed, hadn't worked from the first and he'd blamed her.

"Hey, pretty lady, you going to crumble or fight?"

Lora looked up at Billy Hatcher. He didn't seem nearly as threatening with a bandage across his forehead. "Leave me alone. I'm busy having a nervous breakdown."

"Thought you had more grit, Whitman. Where's that 'Fight! Fight! Fight!' cheerleader spirit?" He leaned closer and whispered, "You mad at me for slamming you to the floor?"

"What do you want? If it's a thanks, you got it." Much as she hated admitting it, she might very well owe this thug her life.

He shook his head and winked. "Wish I'd had time to enjoy climbing on top of you, but in truth, I'll settle for one thing."

"What's that?"

He offered his hand. "Friendship. Looks as if all the committee members may need someone to cover our backs. When my probation officer told me to do some community service, I had no idea it would be so exciting."

Hesitantly, Lora took his hand, convinced that the kid bordered on insane. "Thanks," she answered honestly. "For what you did."

He pulled her away from the wall. "Friends?"

"One condition." She smiled. "Drop the cracks about having the hots for me."

"Mind if I still think them?"

"Not as long as you keep them to yourself."

"Fair enough, Whitman." He lifted his bandaged hand. "How about giving me a ride to Wichita Falls? I'd like to check on the professor." He picked up Sidney Dickerson's glasses. "And take her these."

"The hospital's an hour away. It'll be afternoon before we can get back."

"I know. I figured I'd offer to buy you lunch on the way back. Just lunch, no date or anything like that."

"I don't have a car." Lora watched the preacher fold up the contents of the professor's case, carefully shaking glass from each piece.

Billy dug into his right pocket. "Then you can drive my car, but that means you buy lunch."

Lora thought about what it would mean to go home and listen to her mother, or go back to work and have to recount what happened to every customer who walked in the door. Going to Wichita Falls with Billy Hatcher suddenly seemed like a good idea. "Want to come along Reverend Parker?" she asked over Billy's shoulder.

"No, thanks. I'll see that the sisters get home. Tell Dr. Dickerson I'll be there this evening."

Lora lifted her purse and glanced outside. Her mother poked a manicured finger into the chest of a campus cop blocking anyone from entering the house. Lora couldn't hear what Isadore said but guessed the cop wouldn't hold the line for long under such an assault.

Turning back to Billy, Lora raised her eyebrow in question.

"My car's out back," he said, taking the cue. "Give me a minute to talk to the sheriff and I'll be right there."

Lora nodded and slipped out of the room. The house grew cooler as she walked into the shadows but, as she'd guessed, a hallway to the back porch lay just behind the stairs.

When she stepped outside, the wind greeted her. Leaning over the railing, Lora let her hair shake free. Tiny bits of glass hit the broken brick walk below. She straightened, quickly wiggled out of her torn panty hose and tossed them atop a pile of windblown trash at the edge of the porch.

As she slipped back into her shoes, Lora noticed Billy standing in the shadows behind her.

When she turned on him, he raised both hands. "I didn't see a thing."

"And?"

"And I'm not saying a word, Whitman."

"Don't call me that."

"You got it, only slow down on the rules, I can only remember so many."

Six

Micah Parker quickly found that seeing the Rogers sisters home was not an easy assignment. The pair decided they had to stop several times and let friends know they were all right. With each stop, the story, with all its frightening details, had to be told. And somehow, each time the telling took longer. Micah finally got them home long after noon. He wrote his cell-phone number on the back of an old card he found on the cluttered kitchen table and left them arguing over what to have for lunch.

He dropped by his office, but felt restless. The shock of the morning lingered with him. A renewed reminder of how one moment could shatter all calm. The possibility that someone had meant them harm haunted the back of his mind. He didn't buy the theory that the perpetrators were youths looking for something to break.

The note in the drill bit made it obvious that someone wanted the house destroyed, but who? The oil company that turned in an offer, of course, but they didn't need to frighten the committee into seeing things their way. Near as Micah could tell, everyone but Sidney thought getting money for the land was a great idea. All the company would have to do was wait a day or two to get what they wanted. Only, maybe they didn't think they had the time to wait. But, why?

Micah had a feeling that whoever wanted the house to fall had another reason.

He sifted through his mail trying to think. Nothing came to mind. Signing out for the afternoon, he wrote simply *hospital visit* on the log. He stopped at the grocery store, an independently owned place with the shadows of HEB behind an already-fading new sign that read Clifton Creek Grocery. The produce looked limp and the meat gray, but the people were friendly. He bought milk, sandwich makings and cat food.

"Well, Reverend?" The checker grinned knowingly as she wiggled the bag of kitten food. "You got a cat living with you, now?"

"No, just visiting," Micah answered, hoping he wouldn't have to explain more.

The lady behind him in line, a once-a-month Methodist, chimed in, "My cat won't eat that dry food unless I pour bacon grease on it."

Micah couldn't conceive of a lie to thank her for sharing her knowledge, so he just smiled. The two women didn't need him in the conversation; they continued on about their pets. Anyone passing would have thought they were talking about children and not animals. Micah couldn't imagine getting so attached. His parents had moved around when he was growing up. Extra mouths to feed were not allowed.

He paid out and headed for home. After putting up the groceries, he checked on Baptist. The kitten had finished off the last of his saucer of milk.

"You're looking better, little fellow." Micah poured cat food in a corner of the laundry basket. "That should keep hunger away for a few hours." The kitten jumped into the middle of the food. "Don't waste time blessing it." Micah laughed and wondered if he'd soon be telling stories about Baptist.

He stood, in a hurry to leave. The house always seemed too empty, too quiet when Logan wasn't there. He checked on Mrs. Mac. A game show blared as he opened the dividing door. She waved him away when he asked if she needed anything. He knew better than to hang around talking. She liked knowing that he would be near if she needed him, but she wasn't one to waste time talking when her shows were on.

Halfway to his car, his cell rang.

"Hello." Micah paused, then smiled. "Yes, Logan, I know it's you. What's up, partner?"

Listening, he climbed into his car and started the engine. "Well, if she says it's all right, I guess it's okay with me. Be sure and brush your teeth and go to bed when Mrs. Reed says."

He waited while Logan handed the phone to Betty Reed. A minute later, Micah said, "Thanks, Betty, for offering. It was nice of you." He drove as he listened, then answered, "Yes, I'm a little shaken up. I'm worried about Professor Dickerson. The ambulance took her to Wichita Falls.

They're running tests. In fact, I'm on my way to the hospital now."

Micah paused, trying not to put too much emotion in his voice. "Is it all right if I check in at eight to say good-night to Logan?" He frowned, thinking of how few times he'd been alone since Amy had died. He knew this would happen, first nights at friends', then summer camps and overnight school trips, then college, until finally he'd be fully and truly alone.

"Thanks again, Betty," he managed to say as if she were doing him some kind of favor.

Turning onto the interstate heading toward Wichita Falls, he shoved his phone back into his pocket. The hour passed, as time often did, with Micah lost in memories. Sometimes, when he could stand the pain, he pictured what his life would be like if Amy hadn't died. They would have that second child they'd planned. She would probably be staying home like she always said she would, taking care of babies and working on her master's degree. The house would be cluttered with her projects. She loved to grow things and always had some kind of craft going. She could knit, quilt and uphol-ster furniture better than most of those experts on TV. Once, when they were first married, she'd painted stripes on one wall while trying to pick a color of paint and liked the job so much she painted the other three walls the same way.

Micah blinked away tears. Gentle, loving, soft-spoken Amy. How could God let her die when he and Logan needed her so much? He knew the answer. He'd said the words often enough to grieving families. But, his heart wouldn't listen.

Maybe that explained why the note written in Rosa Lee's book touched him. They were the same he'd said to Amy. *I'll love no other in this lifetime but you.* If Fuller felt them as Micah had, how could the man have stood her up that midnight? Or, had Rosa Lee been the one to turn away? Had she left him waiting?

He forced his mind to think of other things. The sheriff had said someone might have been trying to harm a member of the committee. Who? Not him. He went over the members one at a time, but he drew a blank. Not one seemed the kind of person who made enemies angry enough to endanger someone's life.

Pulling into the hospital parking lot, he

reached in to the back seat for the professor's briefcase. Maybe, if she were awake, he could talk to her about the possibilities. If she found the book from Fuller to Rosa Lee, maybe she'd found other things. She might not even be aware of the importance of her research. Maybe a deep, dark secret lay hidden in the house, and whoever threw the drill bit was warning them to stay away.

When he climbed from his car, the wind whirled around him, trying to lift the briefcase from his hand. The air smelled of promised rain as he darted toward the visitor doors.

A desk nurse told him Sidney Dickerson wasn't back from X-ray but he could wait in a small room to the left of the elevator on the CCU floor. Micah wasn't surprised to find Lora and Billy there. Lora glanced up from her magazine when Micah walked in. Two chairs down, Billy stretched, looking as though he'd been asleep.

"Any news?" Micah asked.

Billy shook his head. "She's been in there for almost five hours and nothing."

"One doctor came out and asked if we were family," Lora added. "I said no. When I suggested I could call them, he said no, not until the tests are all in. I phoned the college to get a relative's number just in case. The clerk said Dr. Dickerson had no listing under next of kin."

Billy stood. "We figure that makes us her next of kin, so we're hanging around. If it's bad news, she doesn't need to hear it alone."

Lora nodded her agreement and offered Micah a cup of free coffee that looked strong enough to be motor oil. "Are the Rogers sisters all right?"

Micah relaxed in the plastic chair between Lora and Billy. "I guess, I left them arguing."

Lora laughed. "They've done that for as long as I can remember. My father mentioned their parents were like that. Never said a word to one another except to yell. He said when they celebrated their fiftieth wedding anniversary no one in town went because fifty years of fighting didn't seem like something to celebrate."

"Strange thing is," Billy added, "I've never known either of them to say a cross word to anyone else. Even when my uncle forgot to put the cap on and oil spilled out all over her engine, Miss Ada May just patted his hand

and told him accidents happen. She wouldn't even let him pay for the damage."

"Do you know of any reason someone would want to harm them?" Micah lowered his voice.

Lora raised an eyebrow. "You buying into the sheriff's idea that someone was after one of us?"

"Not really. Just thinking."

Billy paced the room. "It's just hell-raising. Nothing else. I'd be the one with enemies if anyone in that room had them, and I can't think of one person who wouldn't face me if he wanted me hurt." He sat down as a family of ten came into the room in one big huddle.

Micah's heart ripped. Part of him didn't want to see their sorrow, part knew offering comfort was his calling.

Before he could stand, the hospital chaplain, Bible in hand, hurried into the waiting room and directed the family to one of the semiprivate areas in the back.

A nurse stepped in to tell them that Sidney Dickerson was back in her room, and they would be limited to a fifteen-minute visit every two hours.

"You two go ahead." Micah reached for a magazine. "I'll catch the next time."

"But don't you . . ." Lora began.

"I've nowhere else to be, and it's quieter here than back in town answering questions."

"You've got a point." Lora shrugged. "Mind if I stay? I'm not sure I can deal with my mother."

"No way. You're not staying here," Billy cut in. "We're checking on the professor and heading out for food. I haven't eaten all day."

Lora shrugged at Micah. "I promised the kid a meal if he let me drive his car over here."

They started down the hallway. Micah heard Billy add, "I'm twenty. I'm no longer a kid."

"Well, I'm twenty-four and divorced. That makes me a hundred years older than you." When he said nothing, she added, "Aren't you going to say anything?"

"I promised not to, remember?" They turned a corner and disappeared from sight. "But, I'm thinking it," echoed after them.

Micah tried to get comfortable in chairs that offered little. Why were waiting-room

chairs always the worst? You'd think somewhere, someone would invent a chair that
offered some degree of comfort for all the
people who had to wait.

A tall man about forty wearing a Stetson
stepped off the elevator. He seemed lost for
a moment, then strolled in and took a seat
on the other side of the TV. Micah couldn't
see his face, but his expensive ostrich
boots were visible.

Fifteen minutes later, Billy and Lora returned with lots of details about Sidney. The
doctors thought her chest pains might have
been something similar to a panic attack
and not related to her heart. They would
keep her the night anyway, but they seemed
to think she'd be fine.

Billy mentioned how the professor had almost cried with joy when he'd handed her
the glasses. Once she'd put them on, she'd
demanded to see his cuts. Apparently,
she'd been so blind without them, she
hadn't noticed his bandages.

Though Billy complained about the professor's mothering, Micah sensed he hadn't
minded all that much.

Micah thanked them and suggested they

get home before the rain hit. Lora offered to bring back takeout, but he refused.

After they left, Micah listened to CNN and acted as if he were reading the paper until the duty nurse returned and told everyone waiting that the fifteen-minute visitation was once again open.

As Micah walked out, he noticed the man in the boots didn't stand. Whoever he waited to see must not be in CCU or was too far gone to bother visiting.

Micah found Sidney sleeping peacefully. Someone had combed out her hair and washed her face. She looked better than she had the few times he'd noticed her around town. The prim and proper line she always held had slipped. He couldn't think of anyway to say it but that she appeared more human.

He sat her briefcase where she could see it, guessing she'd want to work if she woke. He couldn't remember ever seeing her when the case hadn't been in her hand.

Leaving, without waking her, Micah walked to his car as the day's fading light glistened off the hood. Nothing waited for him at home, so he decided to visit a book-store. Clifton Creek's rack of top sellers at the grocery was never enough. He liked the little bookstore on Southwest Parkway. All he had to do was tell the owner what he liked, and the man would start stacking up books he'd also love. Micah never drove over to Wichita Falls that he didn't leave with at least half a dozen books.

He'd read all his life. When he'd been a kid, with his parents moving around, he'd learned to escape in books and now they always seemed to welcome him like old friends.

It was almost eight when he left the bookstore. The hint of rain now rode the north wind. Micah sat in his car and called to say good-night to Logan, keeping it short and cheery.

As he drove out of the parking lot, he spotted a pet store and decided to go in. A few minutes later, he was lost in the cat aisle. Toys, cages, beds and food lined the shelves. After an hour, Micah settled on one toy and a children's book for Logan about caring for a first pet. If Baptist planned to stay around for a few days, he and Logan better learn a little about the care and feeding of cats.

When he walked back to the parking lot

he wished he'd brought a coat. Even after three years, he still had trouble getting used to how fast the temperature changed in this part of the country.

Micah drove home, in no hurry to reach an empty house. At least he had a few new books. Maybe he'd read until he fell asleep. Tomorrow was Tuesday, the day he spent most of his time counseling couples planning to marry. Reverend Milburn required anyone married in the church in Clifton Creek to go through at least six sessions. Unfortunately, Milburn never had time to do the counseling himself, so it had become part of Micah's job description. He would also have to attend the Glory Days luncheon tomorrow and teach a biblical history class at the college.

As he pulled into his drive, his cell phone buzzed. For a moment, Micah's heart raced. Logan? Very few people knew or called his mobile number. Most waited until they caught him in his office or at home. What if something had happened at Jimmy's house? What if Logan was homesick?

Flipping open his phone, he made up his mind. No matter what the parenting books say about sleepovers, he'd go pick up Logan and bring him home. Sleepovers could wait a few months or even years, for all he cared.

"Hello?"

"Micah Parker?" A woman's voice yelled into the phone.

"Speaking." He heard loud country-western music in the background. This wasn't Betty Reed, or anyone else he knew. Logan must be fine, probably already asleep.

"I got a problem here, and your number is the one they gave me to call," the woman yelled over the music.

Micah relaxed. Probably someone locked out of the church. Twice last year he'd had to go open the door. Once, Mrs. Beverly had left her purse in the Sunday school room and once, the Ungers had driven off while the youngest one of their seven was still in the church restroom. They had parked in their driveway before they'd bothered counting, and by then the janitor had locked up and gone home. Micah's cellphone number appeared first on the emergency call list posted on the office door.

"How can I help you?" Micah waited for tonight's problem.

"I'm Randi Howard. Randi with an *i*."

He liked the way her voice sounded, thought it belonged with the country music playing in the background.

"I own the bar at the turnoff to Cemetery Road."

Micah straightened. The conversation became more interesting. If she was doing phone soliciting, she'd dialed the wrong number. "I know where it is." He waited for her to continue.

She hesitated. "I didn't know who to call, but one of the old girls gave me your number and name scribbled on a flowery get-well card."

Micah tried to remember where he'd seen such a card. "How can I help you, Mrs. Howard?"

"It's Randi," she said, and he'd be willing to bet that she was smiling. "Just, Randi, Mr. Parker."

He stepped out of the car not noticing the cold. "Randi it is. How may I be of service?"

Randi took a long breath. "I need you to come down here and pick up the Rogers sisters before they start another bar fight."

Seven

Sloan McCormick looked out on the hospital parking lot with the lights of Wichita Falls blinking in the distance. The town seemed fuzzy as if in a fog. Only a few cars remained out front. He could spot his big pickup even five floors up. Trying not to examine too closely the reason he was here, he walked back to the critical care unit doors. Standing in the shadows, he made sure no one dropped in on Sidney Dickerson during the last fifteen-minute visitation of the night.

He leaned against the wall, trying not to look so tall, so obvious. Every time someone opened the double doors, he caught sight of the entrance to her room. Not even a nurse walked near it. No visitor would call now. Not with only ten minutes left.

Still, he hesitated. He had no reason to visit the professor. She'd never met him, and this wasn't the place to talk about a deal his company would be willing to make for the Altman place. But somehow, in the course of his research, Sloan felt as though he had grown to know her. In his line of work, he made it a point to know everyone he might need to persuade. In business, knowledge could swing the deal.

He started to walk away, guessing himself a fool for getting personally involved. Maybe it was time to take the money he'd saved traveling all over the country and start that ranch he kept dreaming about.

Sloan swore. Who was he kidding? Even with this deal, he would never have enough money to stock a ranch with anything but a few chickens. He'd be a land man for the company until he died. He was good at sizing up people, at knowing what made them react, but he'd spend the rest of his days without anyone being able to read him.

A nurse bumped a wheelchair through the door and Sloan glanced up at Sidney Dickerson's door once more. Five minutes left.

The waiting room and hallway were deserted. On sudden impulse, he removed his Stetson and slipped into the professor's room.

Thank goodness she slept. He'd hate to have to introduce himself to her like this. But he needed to check on her condition. He had to know she was all right. Somewhere in his paperwork, she'd slipped from being just someone he needed to win over for the company to a real person. He'd liked the sound of her voice when she'd lectured and the proper way she walked. And, like it or not, he had worried about her all day.

Silently lifting the chart at the foot of her bed, he read through the notes. From what he could tell, she hadn't had a heart attack. Good.

Her age surprised him. He would have guessed her at least five, maybe ten years older. Not that she looked it now without her glasses and boxy clothes, but every time he'd seen her from a distance, she had the stance and walk of someone in her fifties. Now, he learned that he and Sidney Dickerson would be the same age when she celebrated her fortieth next week.

Sloan studied her more closely. She was

tall and what his mother would have called healthy looking, though in today's world she was out of style. In updated clothes, with her hair down, she might look her age. Not his type, he thought, but not all that bad. There was something about her that demanded respect. Not just the fact that she was a professor and seemed intelligent, but more that she was a lady. She was the kind of woman men of all ages opened doors for and tipped their hats to.

She seemed like the kind who should have married and had a big family. He wondered if she'd been one of those who thought school all-important, concentrating on it for so long that by the time she got out, she'd missed her window to marry. Not many men would look at a woman past her youth who had more education than they had. With her height, she'd probably eliminated three-fourths of the men to start with.

"Are you a doctor?" Her voice startled him.

He stared into sleepy blue eyes. "No," he answered from the shadows. "I'm here to take you to dinner." He knew he made no sense, but hopefully she was drugged enough not to care.

"Oh," she mumbled. "That's nice. I don't like Chinese."

He smiled, knowing he was safe. "Me, either. How about Mexican food?"

"With or without onions?"

"Without, of course." He moved closer and noticed her eyelids drifting down. She was fighting to stay awake.

"Can we go, now? I'm afraid of this place," she whispered.

Her honesty surprised him. He wasn't sure what he expected a woman with a doctorate in history to say, but owning up to being afraid wouldn't have been his first guess. "Want me to hold your hand?"

Without opening her eyes, she raised her hand. His fingers closed around hers. For a while, he just stood there, watching her sleep and wondering how many times this woman had ever been afraid. He'd guess she'd been protected all through her life. Even out in the workforce she remained in a bubble, in the unique world of a college campus.

A nurse stepped in to check the machines. He thought of leaving, but feared he might wake Sidney. He didn't want to face any questions with someone else in the room. So he stood his ground beside the bed, his fingers holding tightly to hers, his gaze watching her face for any sign of waking.

The nurse smiled at Sloan. "Visiting hours are over, but if you want to stay with her a little longer, no one will mind. The sleeping pills have kicked in. She'll sleep like a baby until morning."

He knew the nurse guessed him to be the husband or lover. "Thanks," he said. "I'd like to stay a while longer."

Sloan wasn't a man who got close to people, partly by choice, partly because of his job. Staying with someone in the hospital was foreign to him. Strange. As if he were playing a role. Like somehow he'd crawled into another's skin and gotten to feel something real people feel. So much of him had been an act for so long, he wasn't sure there was any *real* left in him. Some days he thought that when he died no one would bother with a funeral. They'd just roll the credits.

He turned Sidney's hand over in his. She was real tonight. Her hand was soft, well formed with short nails and no polish. She would be a no-nonsense woman. The kind who would have nothing to do with him.

"So, Sidney, how was your day?" he whispered, just because it sounded so normal. "I've been worried about you."

Her lashes moved. Blue eyes stared up at him. "You still here?"

"Just waiting to take you to dinner."

"I'm ready to leave. Is it raining?"

He hadn't noticed, but rain did tap against the hospital window so softly it blended with the hum and click of the machines around her bed.

"I'm afraid so." He smiled. "But don't worry, I'll see you don't get wet."

"I'm not fragile," she whispered, closing her eyes once more.

Sloan grinned and leaned closer. "I'd never have guessed you were."

Her breathing slowed as it brushed his cheek. There was something so intimate about the act, almost as if they were lovers who moved near in sleep and were unaware their breath mingled.

Sloan straightened, surprised at his own thoughts. He didn't need to get personally involved with any of the committee. He'd come to check on her, nothing more. Maybe it was because she looked so vulnerable in sleep. Maybe it was because they were really talking. Hell, maybe this job was getting to him.

He should leave. But he hesitated. Not because he needed to know more or thought she might still be in danger.

He simply didn't want to turn loose of her hand.

Eight

Lora Whitman pulled Billy Hatcher's old car around to the back of the Altman house and shoved it into Park. "You sure you want to leave your Mustang here?"

Billy stretched. He'd been asleep most of the way back from Wichita Falls. "Sure," he mumbled as he pushed hair from his eyes. "It's as good a place as any. Safer than in front of my old man's house."

She didn't comment on why he wanted to return to the old place. Maybe, like her, seeing the damage one more time made what had happened to them seem real.

"What time is it anyway?"

Lora rubbed the back of her neck. "About ten, I guess. Maybe a little later."

"I could drive you home, if you like," he said almost as an afterthought. "From the sound of that thunder we might get more rain." He closed and unclosed his bandaged hand.

"I don't mind if I get wet. After today, what could a little water hurt?" She unbuckled her safety belt. "How about walking me halfway? Maybe it will help me relax. I feel like lightning is dancing in me. I'll never be able to sleep after all the excitement. Which doesn't seem to be your problem."

He grinned. "I can sleep anywhere and usually do."

She wished they had talked on the drive back. Billy Hatcher wasn't as frightening as she'd first thought. At dinner they'd shared an unusual conversation. Most folks felt a need to keep up small talk, follow one theme, let the discussion rock back and forth. No such rules bound Billy. He spoke his mind. In a way, it was the most honest dialogue she'd ever exchanged.

"Fair enough. We'll walk." He opened his door. "Thanks for the barbecue, and for driving."

She was glad he didn't add, "because my hand hurts." She noticed him cradling it every chance he got. The cuts ran deep enough to be painful, but to her surprise, she noticed he refused painkillers.

"No problem." She climbed out and caught up with him. "I wish half the new cars on our lot drove as smooth as this old Mustang."

"Yeah. The sheriff sold it to me a few years ago when he bought his wife a new car. The engine was fine. All I had to do was work on the body."

She took his arm to steady her steps as they rounded the back porch of Rosa Lee's old house. Piles of tumbleweeds, broken branches and trash mounded at the corner of the porch. The blackness was almost complete at the side of the house except for faraway flashes of lightning above them.

Lora wasn't afraid, but tightened her grip, fearing she might trip over something in the dark.

"Don't worry," Billy whispered. "There's not that much to fall over back here except your panty hose."

She laughed and relaxed a little. "I was just holding on to you in case you're afraid of the ghost that hangs around this place."

"I've never been afraid of ghosts. Never

seen one wield a belt, or crash a car, or slug anyone. If you ask me it's the living who walk this earth we need to worry about, not the dead."

"You're probably right."

When they passed the side of the house where vines draped most of the windows, he slowed. "Did you see that?"

"What?"

"I thought I saw a light flicker inside the house."

"You'd better not be trying to frighten me." She glanced over his shoulder at the window. A light blinked only a fraction of a second and was gone.

He stopped. His arm locked her hand against him, tugging her closer. "You see that?"

"Yes." She reached in her purse for her cell. "I'm calling the sheriff."

He pushed her into the vines as they watched the pinpoint of light moving slowly across the room.

It blinked again near the front door. Lora couldn't breathe. The good news was that whoever haunted the house seemed to be leaving. The bad news was it was coming outside with them. Visions flashed in her imagination of a battle in blackness against a monster they couldn't see. She would swing wildly, fighting for her life. So would Billy. In the morning, the sheriff would find them both dead. By accident, they'd murdered one another. They'd probably have to wait until a crime-scene photographer came in from Wichita Falls. By then, everyone in town would see her bloody body lying in the mud with vines twisted in her hair and her skirt up. Her mother would be horrified.

"Let's follow them." Billy pulled her forward.

Lora wanted to scream, "Are you kidding?" But yelling would only attract the trespassers. All she managed was a quick nod. She had no wish to trail anyone, but he wasn't leaving her here alone in the vines with creatures already nibbling at her bare ankles.

Billy's undamaged hand slid down to hers as they moved around the corner of the house.

She heard footsteps hurrying across the boards of the front porch. Then a squeal and laughter.

A car drove down Main toward them.

Headlights swung across the yard as it swerved to a stop facing the house.

Footsteps scrambled off the far side of the porch and vanished into the night.

A car door opened, then slammed. "Who's out there?" a man yelled. "This is Deputy Adams. You'd better step into the light right now."

Billy tugged her hand backward, but she stood her ground. She'd never been afraid of the deputy. "It's me!" she yelled. "Lora Whitman."

The shadow continued forward, shining a light in Lora's face. "What are you doing out here?"

Billy reluctantly moved into the light.

The deputy's stance widened. "Who are you?"

"Hatcher," he said.

Lora didn't miss the lack of respect in Billy's voice.

"What the hell are you doing here, Hatcher? Doesn't your probation officer give you a curfew?"

Billy didn't answer.

"He's with me, Deputy," Lora jumped in. "We've been over to Wichita Falls visiting Professor Dickerson, who was hurt this morning. I rode with him, and he brought me back here. My mother took my car home after she dropped me off at the meeting this morning." Lora knew she was rambling, but she didn't like being questioned. After all, they weren't doing anything wrong, she was the one who called him in the first place. They had more of a right to be here than anyone. They were on the committee.

"Well, I guess it's all right." The deputy lowered the flashlight beam. "There's a storm coming in, though. Radio says there might be hail. You both should be getting home."

He turned the light on Billy's face. "You got anything to say?"

Billy didn't move, but she could feel his body stiffen, his grip painful over her fingers.

"One of these days we need to have a talk about your attitude, boy." Adams took one step closer, blinding them with his light. "The sheriff won't always be around, Hatcher. I can smell trouble every time I get within ten feet of you."

"He just offered to walk me home." Lora didn't understand Billy. He made no attempt to be friendly or even civil. No wonder

Adams treated him like a criminal. If he'd tell Adams what they were doing, the deputy would surely back down. "We must be going, Deputy Adams, but you should know that we did see someone inside the Altman house."

Adams turned the light to Billy. "You want to come down to the office and make a report?"

Billy didn't answer.

"No," she said for both of them. "It was too dark to see anything. Now if you'll excuse us, I must be getting home." She should have listened to Billy and never called the deputy.

"I can give you a ride, Miss Whitman," the deputy said formally, as if he just remembered who Lora's father was.

"Thanks." Lora smiled. "But since Mr. Hatcher and I are on the same committee, we've got a few things to discuss. The walk will do us good."

The deputy looked as if he might argue. Adams always thought he knew the right thing to do and didn't mind sharing his knowledge.

"Good night, Officer." Lora pulled Billy along. "Thank you for your concern."

They were half a block away before Billy spoke. "I've never seen old Adams back down like that."

"He didn't have a choice," she answered. "I'm an adult. I can walk down a public street with whomever I want. I can't believe he talked to us like we were kids playing on private property."

Billy laughed. "He's probably having your commitment papers drawn up right now."

"Why?"

"Because you're crazy enough to want to walk down the street with me."

Lora pictured her mother signing the documents. She wished she could be there when someone told Isadore that Lora had left town with a criminal. Her mother would probably shoot the messenger. She looked at Billy and answered honestly. "But we're friends."

"Damn straight," he said. "Friends."

Nine

Reverend Micah Parker circled Randi's bar parking lot twice, unsure what to do. It was almost midnight and this was no place he thought he'd ever be.

He couldn't miss the Rogers sisters' van parked sideways in three parking slots. He had no doubt the call from Randi Howard had been real. The woman who'd phoned him must not have been aware of his occupation, since she'd called him mister and not reverend. Would she have asked him to come after the sisters if she'd known?

He thought of what Reverend Milburn would say if his assistant minister was spotted in the town's wildest bar.

Micah smiled, realizing he didn't much

care. If the Rogers sisters needed help, he'd promised to be there. End of story. He parked next to a huge Dodge pickup covered in mud and got out, pulling his suit coat off. It wouldn't do to go into a country bar looking like a salesman or, he laughed, like a preacher.

When Micah walked inside, familiar sounds and smells greeted him. Smoke, whiskey, sawdust. The whine of two-stepping music that had been born in this environment and the clink of glasses. Raw laughter crackled within conversations carried at full volume.

Memories flooded his mind. His third year of college Amy had miscarried and couldn't work for six weeks. He'd taken on another part-time job so he could stay in school. Sweeping up at a bar had been the only thing that fit into his time schedule. When they'd got back on their feet financially, he'd quit. Micah had been surprised how much he missed the people he'd met and watched every night for months. He'd learned that bar lights reveal layers of truth, like a CAT scan. Weaknesses, dreams and heartaches show up clearly in tobacco-tinted illumination.

His eyes adjusted to the mixture of smoky shadows and twinkling lights along a ceiling covered in beer posters. The place seemed bigger than it appeared to be from the outside. A long mahogany bar ran the length of the far wall. Tables circled round a dance floor on one end, pool tables on the other. Most of the chairs near the dance floor were empty. A group of men played pool. Half of the stools were occupied at the bar.

Most of the men wore Western clothes. A few others looked like oil-field workers who'd put in a full day before stopping by. Muddy boots, Western or Red Wing, were the style. Women mingled among the men. A few looked like they'd lived on murky air way too long, for their faces were pale beneath layers of makeup.

Micah remembered it was Monday night. If this place was like the one he'd worked at, the folks in at this time of night were drinkers, not partiers or fighters. He'd guess they were folks with nowhere else to be and no one waiting for them. They'd finish the night alone with only a six-pack for company.

He noticed a tall woman behind the bar watching him. She had shoulder-length red hair pulled up on one side and an honest face. "You Micah Parker?" She spoke in the same whiskey-smooth voice he'd heard on the phone.

He shook rain from his hair. "I am. Are you Randi with an *i?*" He felt like a paperback detective.

She nodded. "From the way you're dressed, you're not working the oil field or any ranch around, but town folks are welcome here, as well."

"Correct." He thought of introducing himself by occupation, but for a moment, he just wanted to be Micah Parker, period. "I'm the designated driver for the Rogers sisters, at your service."

Randi probably learned a long time ago not to ask too many questions. She pointed toward a beer and raised one eyebrow.

He shook his head. "How'd the sisters end up being your problem tonight?"

"They came in about an hour ago. Appears they had quite a scare today and decided some wine would help them sleep. According to Ada May, they went through every bottle in the house and were still frightened, so they drove over here."

"They come here often?"

She nodded toward a hairy man serving drinks at the other end of the bar. "Frankie said he's sold them holiday wine a few times, but they haven't been in since I bought the place last year." Randi grinned. "One of the guys over near the pool table commented that they shouldn't be in a place like this, being retired teachers and all. Beth Ann hit him with her bag. Before I could get around the counter, they'd landed at least a half-dozen blows on other men standing within range."

Micah fought down a laugh. "I hope no one was hurt."

"No one that would admit it except Shorty Brown. He claimed a crochet needle poked out of her bag and hit him in the eye." She leaned a little closer. "If he'd wanted to press charges I'd have had to call the sheriff instead of you."

"I guess I'd better have a talk with the ladies." Micah tried not to smile. "Where you got them locked up?"

She lifted the walk-through and motioned him behind the bar. As he passed, he realized she stood even with him. It wasn't often he saw a woman his height. In the crowded space, she couldn't step more than a few inches away. He brushed against her as he passed.

Micah kept his gaze steady on her eyes. For a second, their bodies pressed against one another. From the smell of her hair to the softness of her breasts against his arm, he became very aware of her as a woman.

He thought of the bar lights and hoped she couldn't see too deeply into his thoughts.

"I put them in my office with a bottle of their favorite apricot wine," Randi said, as though she didn't notice anything unusual about standing so close to a man she'd just met.

Micah followed her into a small room behind the bar. It had a one-way mirror, so anyone inside could see what was going on at the bar. Papers and notes covered a desk and the safe in one corner sat open. The sisters watched the mirror as if it were a TV. Two empty glasses sat between them.

"Evening, ladies." Randi greeted them with a smile. "I called your friend. He'll see you home."

Ada May giggled. "Evening, Micah. So glad you could join us. Would you like a glass of wine?" She lifted the bottle and re-filled her glass to the rim.

"Yes, do have a drink if you're allowed," Beth Ann added. "You've already seen us home once today. There's really no need to worry about us. I'm still sober enough to drive."

Ada May downed her glass and tried to disguise a burp by coughing. She smiled up at Micah with half-closed eyes and said, "I do love apricots." Suddenly her head hit the desk with a thud. She was out cold.

Beth Ann shook her finger at her sleeping sister. "She's such an embarrassment. Can't hold her liquor any better than our father could."

Micah knelt in front of Beth Ann. "Would you like me to help you get her home? I won't mind. I'm already here."

"You're a fine man." Beth Ann nodded, al-most falling out of her chair. "I may need some assistance. Ada May is no light load when she's out."

A few minutes later, Micah pulled his car around to the back door. Randi guided Beth Ann. As the younger of the two old maids slid into the back seat, she noticed her clothes had gotten rained on and proceeded to take them off. Micah helped the hairy bartender named Frankie half carry, half drag Ada May to the car. Beth Ann had been accurate. Ada May was no light load when she was out cold.

Micah put her into the front seat and turned to Randi, who stood across the car from him. "I'm not driving home alone with one sister out cold and the other stripping in the back seat. You've got to take pity on me."

He must have looked helpless, because Randi shoved wet hair from her face and gave in. "All right, coward." She glanced at the man standing in the doorway. "Frankie, close up for me, would you?"

The man nodded and disappeared.

When she looked back at Micah, she laughed. "I'll go along with you, but I got to tell you, Mr. Parker, you disappoint me. I would have thought you man enough to handle two women at the same time."

He didn't acknowledge her humor as he held the door open. "You ride in the back with the stripper."

She splashed through the mud and climbed in.

Halfway home, Ada May woke up enough to vomit. Twice.

Getting the sisters inside and in bed proved to be a greater chore than Micah could have imagined. Several times, he thanked Randi for coming along. He couldn't have done it without her. Ada May insisted on brushing her teeth before turning in, but she wasn't stable enough on her feet to stand. They all crowded into the tiny bathroom. Micah held her up, his arms locked just below her ample breasts. Randi helped her hit her mouth with the toothbrush.

By the time they finished, Randi and he were both laughing so hard, Micah couldn't catch his breath. They collapsed on a worn couch in the small cluttered living room.

"You think you had a problem with Ada May." Randi slugged him with one of the dozen pillows surrounding them. "You should have tried to get Beth Ann's support hose off."

Micah surrendered. "You win. I haven't put a drunk to bed since my college days, and if I don't do it again in this lifetime it will be too soon." He stood and offered his hand to help her up. They walked out the front door and onto an equally cluttered porch.

Two lawn chairs had been pushed close with a TV tray table in between them. An old, handmade backgammon board rested open on the table. Randi picked up a piece of the game. "Ada May told me tonight that the last thing they do every night is play one game. Whoever loses has to turn out the lights. Sometimes they argue over who won." Randi stared at Micah. "On those nights, the lights stay on till morning."

She tossed the chip to him. He placed it back on the board. "Stubborn women," he said more to himself than her.

"That's why it surprises me they were so shaken by what happened today."

He had no answer. For a few minutes they both watched a car pass down the rain-swollen street.

Randi took a long breath. "I love the rain." She held her hand out to touch a tiny water-fall sliding off the roof.

Micah raised his hand almost touching her hair. Moisture sparkled in it like silver glitter.

She glanced at him with eyes the green of a dense forest. "What?"

"Your hair gets even curlier when it's damp." He hadn't meant to touch it, but the mass was so beautiful, all shiny with red and brown highlights. He let the tips of his fingers brush one curl.

"It's natural." She winked. "All over."

Micah turned his face to the rain. She'd done it again, he thought. Treating him like just any person—like just any man. It felt good and frightening at the same time. Since he'd buried Amy, he thought of himself as a father, a minister, a friend. He'd set all other definitions aside. Now, to be accepted for being nothing more than simply human overwhelmed him. He felt free somehow.

Randi elbowed him. "How about I clean up their place a little? No one wants to wake up with a hangover and have to face all the empty bottles sitting around."

"I'll help."

"No way." She spread her hand out across his chest stopping him from following her. "I think you should find a hose and wash out your car before you take me home. It's too far a drive to hold my breath."

Micah glanced out in the rain. "I'll get wet."

"I'm not riding back with that smell."

"I'll get wet," he repeated.

Randi patted his shoulder. "You'll dry." Then, without warning, she shoved him into the rain.

Micah stumbled off the porch, laughing. He told himself he wasn't attracted to her or any woman, but it felt great to have someone touch him. Just touch him. Not friendly handshakes or polite hugs, but an honest touch.

He dug around in the flower beds until he found the garden hose rolled up neatly beside a rosebush. He did his best to avoid stepping on any of the rosebushes. Everyone in town knew how the sisters loved their roses.

Turning the water on full force, he dragged the hose to his car and pulled out the mats. He hardly noticed the rain. He couldn't remember how long it had been since he'd been so alive. Maybe it was the excitement of this morning, or the way Randi talked to him, or maybe it was just time to start living again. He didn't know. He didn't care. It just felt good.

By the time he got the hose rolled back up in the mud beside the rosebush, Randi stood on the porch ready to go. He motioned for her to climb in and was surprised at how she walked slowly to the car and turned her face to the rain, as if it didn't bother her at all.

When she closed her door, he said, "You really do like the rain."

Randi shrugged. "I've been rained on a lot. It doesn't scare me anymore."

They drove back to the bar in silence. He thought about what she'd said, and what she hadn't said.

The parking lot was dark when they got to the bar. The sisters' van was the only one out front. Micah didn't want this strange time to end, but had no idea what to say. He knew he wasn't likely to see Randi again after tonight.

"You want to come in for breakfast?" She lifted the doorknob. "I always eat when the night's over, then I can sleep until noon without waking up starving."

He hadn't had a bite since before the committee meeting that morning. "I'd love to, if you don't mind? But I warn you, I'm starving."

"I asked, didn't I? I think I can fill you up."

They walked to the back door. She

reached above the frame. "Frankie kept locking himself out and we didn't want to leave the door unlocked, so he installed a latch above the door. Lights flash in the kitchen and my office when this back door swings." She led him down a hallway lined with boxes and mops to a tiny kitchen.

"Of course, I lock it when I head upstairs for the night. We figure only a tall drunk could reach the latch, providing they knew about it."

He wondered if she often told her secrets so easily. Looking around the kitchen he tried to understand her. The kitchen appeared to have been added to the bar in the fifties. Nothing had been updated. The counters were red linoleum, stained and worn through in a few places. Pots and knives hung on the wall behind a stove. The refrigerator clanked out a steady beat. The place was spotless.

"Frankie used to serve hot appetizers years ago, but it got to be too much trouble." She pulled a string on a bare light swinging from the center of the low ceiling. "I keep it open so when I'm stuck here I won't starve." She winked. "A girl can't live on bar nuts alone."

The cleanliness of the place surprised him. There was a wildness about this woman, but there was also an order.

"If you want to dry off, there's a stack of towels by the back door." She combed her hair with her fingers and twisted it into a wild knot behind her head. "How do you like your eggs?"

"Any way but scrambled," he answered thinking of the thousand church breakfasts he'd eaten with scrambled eggs. He heard her banging around the kitchen while he dried his hair in the hallway between the back door and the kitchen. Using paper towels, he wiped mud off his shoes then washed his hands in a big sink that looked as if it would only be used to clean mops. The Rogers sisters' rosebush had torn a two-inch rip in his trousers at the knee, but there wasn't much he could do about it. Since he had no comb, he raked a hand through his hair, hoping he wouldn't frighten her.

Then he laughed. The woman owned the roughest bar for thirty miles around. Probably nothing frightened her. In all likelihood she told him about the back door's latch because she wasn't the least afraid of him.

When he walked back into the kitchen, the smell of steak and onions grilling drifted across the room. She motioned for him to sit before turning back to the stove.

Micah tried not to stare but couldn't help himself. The lean woman in tight jeans and a rain-dampened Western shirt that stopped an inch above her waist was unlike anyone he'd ever encountered. She moved with an easy grace, but everything he knew about her told him she must be made of rawhide.

"How do you know the sisters?" She didn't turn around.

"Maybe I grew up here and they were my teachers?" he offered.

"Nope," she answered as if being tested. "*I* grew up here and they were my teachers. You're definitely a transplant."

"That obvious?"

She grinned over her shoulder and pointed with a spatula. "It's the shoes." When he didn't answer she added, "No man from West Texas wears shoes with tassels. Those are for the big cities like Dallas and Houston. And while I'm at it, any self-respecting working man lets the mud on his shoes dry, then stomps it off."

"Anything else?"

She set two plates filled with eggs and steak on the table. "In my line of work I've learned to read people. You're not married, but you were. Divorced, maybe with a kid, grade school probably. You see him often."

"Widowed. One child, seven."

"Sorry." She met his eyes. "I'm the same. My husband was killed in an oil-rig accident a few years back."

"Cancer took my wife." He wanted to change the subject. "How'd you guess so much about me?"

She opened two beers without asking if he wanted one and sat down across from him. "Wedding band you didn't try to hide. Socks that don't match. No woman would let you out of the house like that."

Micah stared at his socks. They looked like a matched pair to him. But, one might be more gray than black now that he studied them.

"And I sat on a coloring book in the back seat of your car so either you've got a kid, or you're not quite as bright as I thought you might be. A boy, I'd guess, since girls usually don't color Spider-Man."

He smiled. "I made it too easy, Sherlock."

He cut into his steak. "Now for the big question, why did you invite me in? I could be a serial rapist for all you know."

She laughed. "Not with those shoes." She took a bite, then added, "I knew you were safe, first because you were a friend of the Rogers sisters. They're not the types to hang around with dangerous men. Second, you turn red every time I get within waltzing distance. That doesn't sound like a trait a rapist would have. You're safe all right, Micah Parker. Safe as a crosswalk."

Micah wished he could think of a funny comeback, but he was too busy eating. She'd cooked what he was sure must be the world's best steak.

Randi picked at her food. Every time he raised his gaze from his plate, she watched him. He always turned away first. He didn't want to think about what else she'd be able to guess about him.

After finishing his steak, Micah started on hers. She moved her plate toward him without comment. He stopped to take a drink of the longneck, then made himself slow down as he ate the rest of her breakfast. She probably thought he was homeless by the way he consumed food.

"I'm on a committee with the Rogers sisters. Though, I knew who they were. Everyone does."

"The committee that got interrupted by a flying drill bit this morning?" She leaned closer.

Micah nodded. Clifton Creek didn't need a paper. News spread faster than butter on lava.

"I heard a few of the oil guys talking about it, but I didn't pay a lot of attention. When the sisters came in, they wanted to talk about everything but what frightened them." She wrinkled her forehead. "One of the oilmen said there'd been a little interest in the Altman property as a drill site, but no oilman would send a drill bit as his calling card."

Micah leaned forward and lowered his voice. "What kind of interest?"

Randi shrugged. "Just rumors. The men in the bar are always talking about where to drill next. Most of it's speculation and guessing. Since the old house sets on a rise, it would be the prime spot to drill if anyone decided to test for oil below." She studied him. "You think someone was trying to tell the committee something this morning? Or trying to hurt one of you?"

"It could have been an accident. Kids may have found the bit and thought it would be great for shattering windows." He stacked the empty plates and stood. "Maybe they didn't take the time to notice people were sitting at a table on the other side of the glass."

She followed, sipping her beer as he scraped the dishes. "Maybe someone wanted to stop the committee. I don't know who else serves on the panel with you, but the Rogers sisters must have been frightened half to death. They're tough old birds, but I'm not sure they'll be interested in going back into that house. To tell the truth I'm surprised it didn't fall down around the committee this morning."

Micah dried his hands. "It bothers me to think that someone could have been hurt. Really hurt."

She put her hand on his shoulder. "It could've been you." Her words were soft against his ear.

He took a long breath and for once in his life decided not to think, but to act. In half a turn his body brushed against hers and he lowered his mouth toward her lips.

She slowly molded against him, as

smooth flowing as liquid passion. Then, when they were so close, their breath mingled, she smiled. A smile that told him she could read his thoughts.

"I think it's time we call it a night," she said as she stepped away.

She walked across the kitchen. "You know," she said in that low voice of hers. "I was wrong about you, Mr. Parker. You're not safe."

He didn't know if he should apologize or try again. It seemed a lifetime since he'd known the rules—if he'd ever known them.

He thought it best to say good-night. "Thanks for the steak."

"Anytime," she answered. "Nice to meet you, Mr. Parker." The look she gave him said so much more.

"Nice to meet you," he echoed, thinking she was a blast of fresh air in the cellar he'd been living in for years.

Ten

Lora Whitman folded her napkin and tried to give at least the appearance of paying attention to her mother. She should have pretended sleep longer and cut the time at the breakfast table in half. Working for her father was easy compared to having to live with her mother. Luckily, the house was big enough for Lora to have her own wing on the third floor with a study, a bedroom and a small workout area. Her mother rarely ventured into her rooms, claiming the stairs were too much for her.

"I can't imagine how frightened you were, dear. I told everyone how you just couldn't face talking about the accident yesterday. Not even to me." Isadore Whitman finished her coffee. "Of course, you were so worried about that Professor Dickerson from the college who had a heart attack that you rode with the first car leaving for Wichita Falls to check on her." Isadore stopped long enough to spread her lipstick just wider than her lip line. Her own private answer to BOTOX.

Trying to keep her voice calm, Lora corrected, "First, Mother, it wasn't an accident. A ten-pound drill bit almost the size of a football isn't something that just flies into a window. Second, Sidney Dickerson didn't have a heart attack. We feared she had, but the hospital checked her out."

Lora knew she was wasting her time. Isadore lived in a fairy-tale world. Oh, not with giants and dragons, but the kind of make-believe with parties and parades. In Isadore's fairyland, streets could be named Candy Lane just because she bought the only house on the block and daughters grew up and married well. *And never came back home to live.*

"Morning, ladies." Calvin Whitman's booming voice entered the room a few seconds before he did. A large man, he leaned back a little more each year to accommodate his ever-expanding belly.

He patted Lora's shoulder as he passed. "How's my little girl feeling today?"

Lora nodded her hello. She'd always be her daddy's little girl. Unlike Isadore, he hadn't wanted to give her up to marriage and seemed happy to have her back home. In fact, Calvin would be happy if nothing ever changed in his world but next year's Cadillac colors.

"I'm fine." Lora stood. "I thought I'd go in early and see what landed on my desk yesterday while I was out." She was never sure if she truly helped her father's business, or as the boss he simply found work for her. In either case, she didn't complain. Her ex-husband had served her with papers, cleaned out all their accounts and packed her things so fast she hadn't been able to give notice. She was lucky to find work, period.

"This early?" Isadore glanced at the clock. "Don't even think about work yet, Lora."

Calvin helped himself to breakfast laid out in silver dishes along the sideboard. He rattled one of the lids and peeped in as if fearing what might be inside.

Isadore glared at him with disgust but spoke to her daughter. "Aren't you going to have more than coffee, Lora? I know the magazines say you can never be too thin, but you've lost so much weight since the divorce. You look like a coat hanger. If you get any thinner, you'll never catch another man."

To Lora's dismay her father joined the assault.

"That's right, hon." Calvin didn't look up from his food. "Men like their barbecue and their women with just the right combination of meat and fat."

Though Isadore slapped at his arm, he didn't bother apologizing.

Lora thought of telling her mother that she planned to get a doughnut on the way to work, but didn't want to hear the lecture. Isadore had set out the same breakfast for her family all her married life. Lora could go down the neat little silver servers and tell what was in them without opening the lids. Eggs, always in the first. Ham, if a serving fork rested beside the second dish. Bacon if there were tongs. Toast, if butter and jam were on the table. Muffins if only butter sat out. On weekends, pancakes, or if company was there, Belgian waffles. Always served with fruit Isadore bought frozen and never bothered to let thaw before serving.

"I really have work to catch up on." Lora put her coffee cup on the silver tray closest to the swinging door leading to the kitchen.

Calvin set his plate at the far end of the table. "Let her go, dear," he mumbled, giving equal support to *his girls.* "It's a fact, she's got work waiting." He turned his attention to Lora. "I signed on as one of the rodeo sponsors yesterday. Told them you'd give the new president a hand. Real nice fellow running the show this year. Talk is he's planning to run for the state senate next year, so being in charge of the rodeo will get him in front of the public."

Lora wasn't surprised. Her father had always been an easy touch for any fundraiser. He seemed to believe a marketing degree made her an expert in the field.

In the six months she'd been home, she'd talked him into giving Cadillac Cash instead of real money. Some charity would auction off a thousand dollars in Cadillac Cash or have it as their special door prize. The clubs wrote thanking him for the donation, which the business wrote off. He honored the "cash" on any new car. Everyone won and at worst the dealership sold a new car for a few hundred less than they'd planned.

"Is he single, by any chance?" Isadore asked.

"I have to run." Lora moved fast, knowing that if she didn't, Isadore would snare her in meaningless conversation. Her father had already opened his paper. At least he could read while he pretended to listen.

"But—" was all Isadore got out.

Lora grabbed her case at the foot of the stairs and hurried through the side door leading to the garage. She climbed into her Audi, adjusted her seat from where her mother had played with it the day before, and backed out of the driveway as if she were auditioning for a part in a chase film.

At the café near the downtown square, Lora ordered her usual chocolate-covered cinnamon roll and black coffee before she spotted the reverend at the counter, with a worried frown wrinkling his forehead as he read the paper. Yesterday, he'd been all calm and strong. This morning he looked exhausted, as if he hadn't slept at all.

She hesitated. He hadn't seen her. She could grab her food and run. But, to her surprise, she wanted to talk to him. She needed to touch base, make sure he was okay, learn any news. She slid onto the swivel stool next to him and motioned for Polly to bring her order to the counter.

Polly turned away, but her head wobbled back and forth as it always did when she talked to herself about all the extra work she had to do. If friendliness determined tips, Polly would be working for pennies.

"Morning, Preacher." Lora returned his smile as he glanced up from his paper. "How's today treating you?" His eyes didn't seem so sad when he smiled. He blinked as if she'd caught him deep in thought. *Studious. That was the word for him.*

"Morning, Miss Whitman. How are the battle scars?"

She twisted on the stool and showed him the huge Band-Aids covering her knees. "They hardly show under my hose."

He glanced down, then looked away.

"Oh, sorry," she mumbled and straightened.

"For what?"

"Guess I shouldn't be showing my legs to a preacher."

He lost his grin. "Guess not," he answered. "After all, we're not men. Not quite human."

If she could have, Lora would have pulled Micah Parker to her and hugged him. She'd never heard someone sound so miserable in her life. She hadn't thought of it before, but he was right about the way people think of men in the church. Ministers weren't like other people.

Polly delivered Lora's breakfast with a thud. "It's still hot from the fryer, so be careful."

The chocolate sauce bubbled across the top of the round cinnamon roll. Lora took a deep breath. "Chocolate and grease, my two favorite food groups."

Micah's smile returned. "How often do you indulge in this slow form of suicide?"

"Every Tuesday," she answered as she cut off a bite and blew on it. "I came home on a Monday after my divorce. We moved what little I had left into storage, set me up an office next to my father's at the dealership, and I went to sleep in the twin bed I'd slept in most of my life. The next morning I thought I couldn't get out of bed. Nothing . . . nothing would make me want to face this town, this job, my failure."

Micah winked. "And then you remembered." He pointed to the roll.

"Right," she laughed. "My reason to live." She pushed the first bite in her mouth.

Micah folded up his paper as Polly slammed down his oatmeal and wheat toast. "May I have one of those rolls?" he asked politely.

Polly groaned. "Instead of this?"

Micah quickly added, "Oh, no, for dessert. I still want this order."

Polly mumbled something about *break-fast don't have no dessert* as she moved away.

"You're very brave, Preacher. Not many locals have the nerve to change their order once Polly writes it down."

He tasted his oatmeal. "I must be living dangerously lately."

"I'll say," Lora agreed.

As they ate, they talked about yesterday. Neither had much in the way of news, but it felt comforting to rehash the details. They were like veterans in an unknown war.

After Polly delivered his roll, Micah said,

"Sidney's getting out of the hospital today. I talked with the sheriff when I came in and he said Will's driving the ambulance over to pick her up at no charge." He tasted his cinnamon roll and shoved the oatmeal aside. "I really don't know her, but I feel like I do. I'd like to go check on her this afternoon and make sure she's settled in at home, but . . ."

"But it might not look right." She could see his problem. Single minister visits single teacher in her home alone. The town would fill in the blanks. Lora fought the urge to swear. Living in Clifton Creek reminded her of stepping back in time. They might have the Internet and cell phones, but sometimes she expected the theme song from *Mayberry R.F.D* to start playing out of thin air. She handed Micah her business card with all her phone numbers on it. "Call me when you're heading over and I'll meet you there."

"Thanks." He shoved the card into his vest pocket. "You worried, too?"

"In some way we all became a family yesterday. Billy even commented about how we need to watch one another's backs." She shuddered. "I'll be glad when we can vote on what to do with that old house. Give our recommendation to the mayor. Forget about the committee. That old place has years of bad vibes. I've heard stories about it all my life."

"Maybe the drill bit flying was just a one-time, freak thing that happened," Micah mumbled between bites. "It probably had nothing to do with us, just kids playing around. Maybe they wanted the house to fall thinking there would be a park or something else put in its place?"

"Maybe. But if it wasn't?" She pictured zombies running down Main Street all carrying drill bits as they screamed the committee members' names. Horror movies always had a group of people on the monster most-wanted list. "What if someone singled us out?"

"Then we fight." He plopped the last bite of the roll in his mouth and stood.

"Great," Lora whispered as she waved him goodbye. She was going to war with a regiment from the monster appetizers menu and the preacher thought they could fight.

Ten minutes later, when Lora made it to her office, she could still hear Micah's determined words. He surprised her. Weren't *men of the cloth* supposed to be meek? He seemed kind and thoughtful, but meek wasn't a word that fit that minister. Yesterday when he'd removed his coat and only wore a shirt and trousers, he'd definitely been relaxed. Today in his brown suit he looked more official.

As she turned toward the car dealership's set of offices along the back wall of the showroom, Lora wasn't surprised to see a man sitting on the corner of her desk. Her father thought the floor plan of see-through office walls and no doors except on the restrooms made the place look welcoming and honest. Lora thought it more a bother. Anyone trying to sell her anything could camp out in her office until she showed up. Dora, her father's secretary and the unofficial hostess, would even serve them coffee.

She waved at Dora. The middle-aged greeter waved back. Her father's statement about the right combination of fat and meat crossed Lora's thoughts. She shook the possibility out of her head. Her mother would kill her father by slow endless conversation if he even looked at Dora.

Walking into her cage of an office, Lora ignored the young man dressed as if he had just stepped out of a line dance. She put up her purse and removed her jacket. She couldn't miss the width of his shoulders, or his Western clothes right down to his fifteen-hundred-dollar boots and pressed jeans. He wasn't here to try to sell her pencils and caps with the logo of the dealership.

She raised an eyebrow in interest as she shoved her briefcase under the desk. If he needed a car, he would have been waylaid by one of the salesmen before he could make it to her office.

Finally, with everything in order, she faced him. "May I help you?"

His smile seemed calculated. Not too wide, not too innocent. "I certainly hope so, Miss Whitman. I'm Talon Graham. My friends call me Tal." He waited as if expecting her to recognize the name.

Lora had seen his type before. In fact, she'd married one of the tribe. Handsome, well-mannered, high-maintenance, used to getting his way. The kind of man who wanted a blonde on his arm. Trouble was, she'd been that blonde once before and no longer wanted the role.

Since he obviously knew her name, she asked again. "How may I help you, Mr. Graham?"

He stood. "I'm in oil exploration by profession, but I'm here as president of this year's Rodeo Association. I'd like you to help me make next year's rodeo the best Clifton Creek has ever seen."

"The rodeo's nine months away. We don't need to plan advertising yet." She wanted to add that, hopefully, she wouldn't be in town nine months from now, but with what her father paid her, it was a possibility. Also, men in oil exploration weren't known to stay long in one place.

"I know, but it may take some time." He winked. "First I plan to organize a huge fundraiser to improve what Clifton Creek laughingly calls a rodeo grounds. Second, I'd like to get to know everyone in town, or at least anyone who will help." He stood, towering over her. "Your daddy told me yesterday that you wouldn't mind introducing me around. As an outsider, I'll need to move in the right circles fast." He glanced down, seeming almost shy. Almost. "He said you would be at my disposal whenever needed."

Lora swore she felt smoke coming out of her ears. She could almost hear her father telling this man that his poor daughter had nothing to do with her life and would be happy to take him around. After all, divorced women don't have an easy time getting back on the horse.

Talon had the nerve to grin when he added, "So, we'll be seeing a lot of each other over the next few months?"

She'd have to kill *Daddy,* she thought. "I'll talk with my father," she managed to say as she glanced through her glass walls.

He'd finally gone too far, pimping her out to a rodeo. And because Isadore would be impossible to live with as a widow, Lora would have to murder her, too. Maybe she could get a deal when buying double caskets and plots. She saw it all now, the church packed, the funeral procession long and loaded with the newest models on the lot. The coffins would be matching champagne white. Too bad the funeral home didn't have Casket Cash.

Eleven

The afternoon rain drove Billy Hatcher's roofing crew inside. Most of the guys called it a day. Sam Davis and Billy drove over to do cleanup on the window replacement job at the Altman house.

The sky hung low, bringing the shadows of twilight early. Billy heard more than one person say the rain might freeze after sundown. If so, there would be no work tomorrow until the sun warmed everything up. He didn't care. Unlike the others, he had plenty to keep himself busy. Roofing was seasonal work anyway, but it paid well. He figured he had enough put away to last three months in an apartment when bad weather hit. A few inside carpentry jobs should carry him through till spring. If his plan worked, he wouldn't have to move back in with his father and whatever old lady he had playing house with him now.

But until it got too cold, he'd sleep out, sometimes in the country, sometimes in his car. Lora Whitman would have been surprised to learn more than just his car parked behind the Altman house last night. He'd slept there after he'd walked her home. A rich girl like her would never understand that the longer he could wait to get the apartment, the more chance he'd never have to see his old man again. He'd taken the rap for him once and almost landed in jail. He wouldn't do it again.

Billy had missed his class at the Y yesterday because of the trip to the hospital with Lora. He planned to spend extra time tonight to catch up with everyone. The aikido workouts were just one more thing he never talked about at work. He never discussed the classes with anyone except Sheriff Farrington, who'd talked him into starting the martial art. In class, while he practiced, Billy thought of himself as distant from the world, almost as if he were a lost soul floating without any place or past marking him.

As soon as they finished work today, he'd disappear from problems for a few hours. The workout would exhaust him and he'd sleep without nightmares for a change.

Sam Davis unlocked the back door of the Altman place and held it open while Billy carried in a couple of brooms and an empty box. They'd installed new glass in the bay window that morning at the sheriff's request, but they hadn't bothered to clean up. Sam wanted to get as much roofing done as he could before the rain hit.

So they were back, doing cleanup. The dining room looked as it had when Billy left it yesterday morning with folding chairs scattered and fragments of glass everywhere. Only today the clouds brought rainy-day gloom and the house aged in the poor light. The dark wood seemed sinister. The shadows haunted. The hollow spaces lonely.

"Don't understand Sheriff Farrington," Sam said, flipping on the portable work light and setting it in the center of the floor. "If that committee you're meeting with was organized to decide what to do with this house, why not wait until they make up their minds before adding a new window? Glass ain't cheap. We could be tearing this whole place down next week." He bit off a chew of tobacco. "My feeling is most folks in this town wouldn't give a damn if it crumbled. It ain't good for nothing but feeding termites."

Billy ran his hand over the banister, as always feeling the wood as if it could somehow whisper to him as he greeted it. He liked the old house. It was out of place here, just as he felt he was. Billy had no idea what he waited for, but somewhere out there in the future was a chance. Maybe he'd only get one, but when it came he planned to take it.

Sam Davis felt no need to introduce himself to the house. "It ain't like the town's got memories to preserve in this place. Altman might've founded the town, but those who knew him are long gone. Rosa Lee Altman didn't do more than nod at anyone around here. Only person she ever let in was that nurse old Doc Eastland had and I guess maybe the doc visited now and then before he died."

Billy started to work, noticing the light made the slivers of glass sparkle. "Why don't you ask the sheriff? I didn't see the salesman at the lumberyard griping when

Farrington paid for the glass." Billy didn't particularly like Sam Davis, but the old guy was friendlier than most at work. He knew everyone in town and treated Billy the same as he did all those he considered below him in rank. He'd worked for the lumberyard for forty years and made it to foreman of a work crew. Billy didn't see Sam as exactly climbing the ladder, but in Sam's mind he saw himself as successful.

"I did ask the sheriff." Sam leaned on his broom and snorted. "He said the mayor told him to. But if you ask me, it's some kind of trap. Farrington figures if we put new glass in, the fools will come back. He's expecting to catch them, but I think all we'll do is sweep up more glass. The sheriff might catch them if they try something on his watch, but that Deputy Adams couldn't catch a dead rabbit and the guy who comes in from Wichita Falls to take weekend watch isn't much better."

Billy thought of pointing out to Sam that he wasn't the one sweeping up glass in the first place. "Maybe they want this house to look good, it being on Main and all. I heard someone say at lunch that there is more than one oil company in town looking at the land."

Sam laughed. "If it was important to look good, half the buildings on this street would have to go. Willie's feed store hasn't had a coat of paint in thirty years. And don't forget that gas station Dixie Roberts turned into a flower shop in the sixties. She deserted the place to marry some trucker who drove by and honked. Now, ivy grows all over the roof. Realtor couldn't give the place away."

Billy knelt to get a few pieces of glass out of the floor while Sam's voice played on.

"Be careful there, boy. Don't want you getting any more glass in that hand." He moved closer so he could watch Billy work. "If you get hurt on the job, I have to fill out all kinds of paperwork."

There'd be less of a possibility if Sam helped, but Billy doubted that was in the old man's plan. "I'm careful. You ever been in this place before today?"

"Once, when I was a boy not yet old enough to go to school. Miss Rosa Lee wasn't all that old then, maybe in her fifties. She ordered some lumber, big flat boards, delivered to the back door. My father brought it, and she paid him cash."

"What did she need it for?"

Sam frowned. "I don't know. That's been years ago. But I do remember thinking it strange, because my daddy didn't usually take cash at delivery. Folks came in back then and bought the lumber before it ever moved out of the yard. My daddy didn't have the money to make change. He left me sitting on her back porch while he went to get her money."

Sam scratched his head as if he had fleas. "She weren't mean like some folks used to say. I remember. She brought me out a cup of lemonade and talked to me about her roses. I can't think of any one thing she said, but she sure made them bushes sound like they were priceless. Called each one by name, like they were her children or something."

"What did she look like?"

Sam shrugged. "Like an old lady, I guess. I remember she had the palest blue eyes I ever seen. Ghost eyes, I heard someone say."

"What does that mean?" Billy knew he shouldn't keep asking questions. Sam would never start work. But he couldn't help himself.

"I don't know. Maybe it means she sees ghosts. Maybe it means she was one. Haven't you ever heard someone say that about a person with light blue eyes?"

"Nope," Billy answered. "But I haven't been around much."

He was kidding, but Sam nodded as if he agreed.

Billy moved around the room, picking up every sliver of glass. He knelt, noticing the scratch Lora Whitman's chair had left. The fresh scar only added to the thousands already covering the floor. As he progressed to the hallway, checking for any shards that might have slid out the open door, Billy noticed nail holes running in a straight line in front of the stairs. No nails remained, but the holes forever blemished the floor. Whoever had ripped them out had been without skill, leaving marks where a hammer's claw had twisted.

He glanced back at Sam, who now leaned against the door frame. "What do you think of these holes?"

The old man didn't move. "Termites probably. I told you this place ain't good for nothin' else."

"In a straight line? All about two inches apart?"

Sam walked over and took a look. "Strange."

"Why would anyone want to damage this floor? What could they have nailed here in front of the stairs?"

"Beats me, boy, but it's quittin' time. I'm heading home. You want a ride back to the lumberyard?"

"Sure." Billy brushed his fingers against the strange holes. "You want me to drop the key off, Sam? I got to go in and pick up my check anyway."

Sam handed him the Altman house key. "Thanks. That'll save me getting wet."

Billy slipped the key into his pocket then touched the marring in the floor one last time as if to say goodbye.

Twelve

"Please, come in out of this rain." Sidney Dickerson held the door open to her bungalow situated along what everyone called Faculty Row. "Welcome, Lora. Reverend. I can't believe you came to check on me on a day like this." The afternoon sky had darkened to evening hues.

Micah and Lora hurried into the small entryway of the professor's home. He juggled the gift basket he brought the professor while he pulled off his jacket and left it on a bench by the door.

When Micah faced the professor, he noticed the lack of color in Sidney's face, but her smile was warm and genuine. She had been home long enough to take a nap, because the back of her hair flattened to her skull.

Sidney must have read his mind, for she ran her fingers through her mousy-brown curls as she led them to a living area.

Micah glanced around the small apartment. It probably had the same floor plan as the ten others located on the north side of the campus. The bungalows had been remodeled a few years back and were offered to faculty for half what they would pay to rent a similar place in town. It had been a way to attract teachers to a college where the salary couldn't compete with larger schools.

Sidney looked comfortable in her jogging suit and walking shoes. She straightened pillows on the couch as she moved about the room. Micah didn't miss the quality of the furnishings or the collection of art crowded between bookshelves. He had a feeling that all the professor owned rested in the confines of these walls. One framed photograph stood out on the cluttered desk that divided the living area from the kitchen.

"We just wanted to check on you, Sidney." Her name still wasn't comfortable on his tongue, but after what they'd been through, they should be on a first-name basis. "Hope we didn't disturb you."

"I'm so glad you dropped by, but there's no need to worry. I'm fine. I was just relaxing and enjoying the rain." Several potted plants with huge bows were stuffed in corners. Sliding glass doors ran along one wall of the room, with a screened-in patio beyond. The sunroom area was also lined with potted plants, all in straw baskets with big bows.

She motioned them to two comfortable chairs before she sat on a bench by a small fireplace. "I got home a few hours ago and students have already dropped by to check on me. I'm surprised how fast everyone in town knew about the mishap. My neighbor said flowers started arriving yesterday afternoon." She pointed at the largest plant. "The mayor sent that."

Micah placed a basket from the Women's League on the coffee table. "The ladies at my church knew you'd be having more company than usual and thought you could use coffee and cookies." The standard gift appeared more personal with the handwritten note sticking out between a bag of coffee and a tin of cookies.

"Thank you." Sidney smiled with delight. "I'm glad it wasn't flowers. I'll have a devil of a time keeping all these alive. My grandmother and mother had talent for gardening, but I'm afraid the gene wasn't passed to me."

Micah couldn't think of much to say, but thankfully Lora seemed to know all the right questions to ask. While he waited, the women talked of hospital food and how long Sidney planned to take off work. Without being obvious, he studied the small paintings clustered on available wall space. Originals, he'd bet. Nothing too modern. But quality, museum quality, if his three-hour course in art appreciation was worth anything. She must have inherited the paintings, for Sidney's passion was obviously books. Volumes were everywhere, hardback, paperback. Even a tall shelf, circling the ceiling like a border, bowed from the weight of reading material.

Sidney drew Micah back into the group as she laughed, then hesitated. "I had the strangest thing happen late last night. I dreamed a man came into my room and held my hand after he asked me to dinner. I haven't told anyone for fear they'll think I'm crazy, but his visit seemed so real."

Lora moved to the edge of her chair. "Maybe he was real, Sidney," she whispered. "Maybe you have a secret admirer."

Sidney shook her head. "I don't think so. But I can dream anyway."

Micah didn't say anything. He'd had his own share of strange things happening late last night. In fact, Randi Howard had been in the back of his mind all day. He tried to guess at what time she found out he was a minister. Sometime today, someone probably started talking about what happened at the Altman place. After a minute or two they'd mention who was there: the Rogers sisters, Lora and Sidney and a kid doing community service and the preacher. At that point, he could almost hear Randi saying, "What preacher?" in that rich country-and-western voice of hers.

He closed his eyes trying to picture how Randi would react. He'd bet her red hair would fly as she stomped around. She'd probably think about how she talked to him just like he was a regular guy, even flirted with him.

He wondered whether, once she got over

her embarrassment, she'd tell anyone about cooking him breakfast. Maybe she'd laugh about the way he'd almost kissed her. He saw it as no sin, but wasn't sure he wanted half the town hearing about it. Would she tell everyone? Or would she write it off as another drunk trying to grab a kiss at the end of the night shift?

Only he hadn't been drunk. And he wouldn't take their time together back even if he knew it would be announced on the evening news.

"Are you ready, Preacher?" Lora tapped his knee.

Micah realized he'd been lost in his own problems and not paying attention.

"You were staring out at the rain as if you were hypnotized." Lora sounded more sympathetic than scolding.

"Sorry. I was just thinking about something I have to face." He noticed they had already forgiven him before he could think of an explanation. "I guess the lack of sleep is catching up with me."

Both women nodded as they stood. When Micah passed the photograph once more, he asked, "Your family?"

Sidney's smile had a sadness about it.

"Yes. I'm the little girl." She lifted the picture. "That's my mother, Marbree, and that's my grandmother, Minnie, standing beside her. I was an only child of an only child. They were nuts about taking pictures of me, but this is the only one I have of the three of us. My father died in Vietnam before I had many memories of him, and my grandfather died before I was born." She brushed her thumb across the glass in a caress. "We called ourselves the Three Musketeers, my grandmother Minnie, my mom and me."

When she looked up from the photo, Sidney tried to hold on to her smile. "They were killed in a car wreck a few years ago. They were my only family."

Micah opened his arms and Sidney stepped into them hesitantly. He knew there was little he could say that would help. He hugged her gently until she straightened and pulled away, thanking him for his kindness with a nod.

"I'm sorry," Lora whispered.

"It seems a long time ago. I can't believe I'm allowing it to upset me now." Sidney led the way to the door. "I guess it's just the strain of the last twenty-four hours."

They made plans to hold the next committee meeting in Sidney's classroom. Lora complained about the rain and ran to her car. Micah waved goodbye to Sidney and walked to his car that still had the faint smell of apricot wine lingering in the damp carpet.

He started the engine and thought about how Randi had shoved him out in the rain last night because she wouldn't ride back until he'd cleaned up the mess Ada May had made.

Forget about Randi, he thought. He had plenty on his mind already. But, the tall, long-legged bar owner had jump-started his heart. It had been so long since he'd felt it beating, he'd almost forgotten about living. He'd been walking around in the fog for three years and he finally found the door. The only problem was, he couldn't— wouldn't—step out. He'd lived in the fog too long. It welcomed him home. He belonged there.

He drove through rainy streets, telling himself he'd never take Randi up on that offer for another breakfast, but if he accidentally crossed her path again he'd thank her. She'd reminded him he was still alive.

Dropping by the church, Micah unlocked the back door. Reverend Milburn and

Nancy, the church secretary, always left at five, but Micah still had almost an hour to kill before he picked up Logan from Tiger Cubs, so he might as well get some work done.

Logan loved thinking of himself as almost old enough to be a real Boy Scout. Micah knew his son would talk all the way through dinner about every detail of the meeting. After school, the troop planned a tour of the pizza place out by the interstate. All parents were to pick up their sons after six where they could buy a pizza made by their seven-year-old. Logan had promised to save Mrs. Mac two pieces of his, and Micah thought he'd heard his boy say he'd bring the cat a bite.

Flipping on the office light, Micah checked his messages. Nothing that couldn't wait until tomorrow.

He thought he heard the back door bang closed again and decided the wind must have caught it. Next time, he'd be more careful shutting the door when the weather was stormy. Micah continued working. He thought of turning on more lights. The rainy day made his normally sunny office gloomy.

Footsteps moved fast down the hallway. He glanced up. Whoever headed his way made no attempt to conceal their arrival. Micah moved around his desk and took one step toward the entrance to his office.

As if the storm had rushed inside, his door swung open with a pop.

Micah stood face to face, eye-to-eye, with Randi Howard.

Her hair flew wild around her, curly with moisture as it had been last night. She wore a Western-cut leather coat with four inches of fringe hanging off the shoulders. Angry green eyes reflected the lightning outside. Or, Micah reconsidered, the flashes outside reflected the sparks in her eyes. He couldn't be sure which.

Micah took a step backward. One thing was certain, Randi had found out about him. "Now, Randi."

She stomped into the room, her fists rising to her hips.

"I know you're probably embarrassed." He inched backward, bumping into his desk. "But there is nothing to be embarrassed or sorry about."

Before he could think of anything else to say, her hand flew, slapping him so hard his neck twisted.

Never in his life had he been hit in anger.

The shock rattled him all the way to his core. It came so unexpectedly, he didn't think to shield himself. He just stood there, taking the blow full force.

"I'm not embarrassed, Reverend." She said his occupation like it was a dirty word. "But, I'm real sorry." She paced, and it crossed his mind she might be backing away to get a running start next time.

He rubbed the side of his face and tried not to think about how beautiful she was, all fiery and wild. "Sorry for slapping me?" he guessed.

"No." She continued marching back and forth in front of him, her fringe brushing his arm each time she stormed past. "I kind of liked slapping you. But, I'm sorry I let you almost kiss me last night. I couldn't sleep last night wondering what would have happened—no not wondering," she corrected. "Knowing what would have happened if I hadn't backed away." She pointed at him. "And that kind of thing happening hasn't happened to me in a long time. I spent the night thinking I was real sorry I didn't let it happen even though I knew I'd probably regret it come morning."

Micah tried to follow her reasoning, but

was having trouble. Maybe if she'd slow down. Or stopped using the word *happen* like it was some kind of sexual term he'd missed having explained to him. Maybe if she'd stop moving.

She must have rattled something in his brain. He couldn't think straight. "Because I'm a minister?"

"Hell, I don't care if you're a minister."

She stopped, and he considered the possibility that she might try to hit him again. He wasn't sure he was up to turning the other cheek.

"I just don't like being so attracted to a liar."

"I didn't lie to you." Her words hurt him more than the slap. "The subject just didn't come up."

His statement did nothing to calm her. She was off again, a one-woman tornado in his ten-by-ten office. "No, it didn't come up, did it? You just forgot to tell me you were the minister at the largest church in town. You must have known I'd find out. I hear every detail of everything that happens in this town. I could write the confessions of most of these folks before they had time to tell them to you so you must have guessed I'd find out."

"Second largest," he offered. "The Baptists have us beat in numbers. And I'm not *the* minister, I'm the associate minister. Most of my duties are in teaching and counseling." He knew he pushed his luck, but he added, "And Methodists don't take confession."

She didn't look like she appreciated his clarification. "Then, Mr. Associate Minister of the second-largest church, why'd you almost curl my toes with the heat between us? Aren't there enough eligible *Bible-thumping* women around for you?"

Micah smiled. "We don't call anybody *Bible thumpers.* And, yes, there are quite a number of eligible women in the church. None of whom I'm interested in kissing."

She calmed slightly. "Why me?"

"Why not you?" he countered. "You're single. What's wrong with me, a man, being attracted to a beautiful woman like you?"

She jabbed her finger against his chest. "Let me explain something to you, Reverend."

"Micah," he interrupted. "Micah with an *h.*"

She poked him again. "All right, Micah

with an *h.* Let me explain the facts to you. You know when you were growing up and your mother told you to stay away from the wrong crowd?"

"I remember." He smiled, guessing where she headed.

"Well, I'm the wrong crowd." She took a long calming breath. "I own a bar. You run a church. I'm so far into the wrong crowd, I'm surprised we speak the same language."

"So, we're never to speak to each other again?"

She opened her mouth, then closed it. It appeared she didn't like that idea any more than he did.

"We'll just act like we never met, Randi. Like we never talked. Is that how you want it?" He waited for her answer.

When she remained silent, he added, "I don't know if I can lie to myself enough to act as if I didn't connect with you." He watched her. In the stillness, he heard her breathing. "You're the most real person I've met in a long time. Do you know what I mean?"

To his surprise, she nodded once.

"It felt good to just be together last night, even if we were putting two old-maid

drunks to bed and cleaning up their mess."
He waited, then added, "I liked meeting
you. I like being near you."

She shifted, her stare never leaving his
eyes. "Maybe, if we're careful, we could just
be friends. I'd like that. Can't say I've got
many in this town."

Micah leaned on his desk and folded his
arms. "What are you suggesting? Being
friends won't be easy. We don't exactly run
in the same circles."

She sat down, anger disappearing as
quickly as it sparked. Lifting her red boots,
she placed them on the desk and crossed
her long legs an inch from where he sat. "I
liked talking to you last night. I like being
with you. But there can be nothing between
us. No kissing. You and I are both old
enough to know that it wouldn't stop with a
kiss. What I saw in your eyes was a promise. I'm not in the habit of starting something I don't plan to finish. So talking is as
far as we'll be traveling."

"Where would we meet to do this talking?" He couldn't see her walking into the
church socials, and he couldn't make a
nightly stop at the bar. They could hardly

meet for breakfast since he ate at seven, and she cooked after midnight. Walks were out. Everyone in town would see them. Sneaking around wasn't his style. Family dinners didn't seem hers.

"I don't know." She bumped his leg as she swung her boots to the floor and leaned forward. "Maybe we shouldn't, but in a strange way, I don't want to say goodbye to you just yet. The way I see it, we got nothing in common except that we're both bored to death talking to everyone else we know."

He laughed. She was right. Most days, he had the same conversations over and over. Sometimes, he felt as if he could just put his mouth on automatic pilot and not miss a beat. But with Randi, he had to stay on his toes. He had to listen. He had to be present in his life.

"Could I stop by for breakfast after closing some night? I usually run late after I put my son to bed." He couldn't believe he was asking such a thing. All night, he'd thought about how good it felt to talk with her. To be with her. Maybe part of it might be that they were an unlikely pair, but mostly it was her.

Randi Howard was unlike any woman he'd ever met.

"If you'll be honest with me from now on," she answered. "We could give it a try."

"All right, then, I'd better start with the honesty part first. I'm not sure I want to be just friends, but I'll settle for it for now."

Randi stood. She leaned so close he could feel the heat of her body. "Honest enough. But I'd better be straight with you. I don't think I can be any more than just friends to a man . . . any man. I've been burned so many times, I'm starting to look like the poster child for broken hearts. It'll take some time before I can even think about offering more."

"Fair enough." He kept his arms folded. Everything about this woman made him want to be closer to her.

"Eggs over-easy, steak and beer, any night you're interested. The back door will be open if you come by. You can walk through to my office if you don't see me in the kitchen. You know the way." She leaned until her breasts rested lightly atop his folded arms and kissed his cheek. "Sorry I slapped you." She straightened. "But, you deserved it, Reverend."

"Could you call me Micah?"

"Why?"

"I like the way you say my name."

"All right, Micah. See you one midnight for breakfast."

Thirteen

Sidney Dickerson had been dozing in her chair when the telephone rang. She jumped, sending the book on her lap flying across her living-room floor and into the potted plant the mayor had sent.

"Hello?" She noticed the news was on the TV she'd muted hours ago. It had to be after ten.

"I'm sorry, did I call too late?"

Sidney tried to place the voice. "Oh, no. I'm still up," she lied.

"I just wanted to check on you, Professor Dickerson. Make sure you have everything you need."

His voice sounded familiar. But from where? She mentally went down the roll of faculty as she said, "I have everything. Thank you. Everyone has been so kind." She felt like a fool, but she asked, "May I ask who is calling?"

The man laughed, low and rich, like a man who keeps his humor close to his chest. Sidney thought of what Lora Whitman had said about her having a secret admirer. Foolish, Sidney reminded herself as she straightened and waited. Women almost forty didn't have such things.

"Sorry," he answered. "I'm Sloan McCormick. I had a meeting scheduled with you at your office yesterday afternoon, and I'm afraid you stood me up."

Sidney believed him. The department secretary often made appointments for professors during their scheduled office hours. She had no doubt that there would be a note posted on her door or in her box when she returned to work. "I'm sorry. I didn't make it to my office yesterday. Something happened. I assure you it was not intentional."

He laughed again, as though nervous. "I know. I heard about what came up, or should I say *flew in* at the Altman house. Alarming."

"Yes, very." She had no idea what to say to the man. He didn't sound like a student, but people of all ages decide to go back to college. She knew he wasn't in any of her classes. Sidney made a habit of memorizing every name by the end of September. "Would you like to reschedule, Mr. Mc-Cormick? I hope to be back at work in a few days."

"I could." He hesitated again. She heard papers shuffling. "Only, if you don't mind, I'd like to bring you some papers to look over before we talk. I hate to bother you tonight, but time is critical."

Sidney frowned. Maybe he was the father of some student who'd done poorly in her class last semester. She'd never had a parent show up, but it wasn't unheard of at small colleges. "I don't . . ."

"It concerns the Altman house," he added, as if guessing her confusion. "I'm with Russell Wells and Drilling. We'd like to make an offer for the oil rights on the forty acres of land the city owns. We realize one offer has already been turned in. All we ask is that you consider our offer, as well."

"But I have nothing to do with that." She kept her voice formal. This was just a business call after all. He hadn't called to check on her, only about when to schedule a meeting. No secret admirer waited outside her door. "You'll need to talk with the mayor. His office will be taking the bids."

The other end of the phone fell silent for a moment, then he said, "The mayor asked me to speak to you. He said he's leaving all decisions concerning the house and property to the committee. When I tried to hand him the paperwork, he backed away."

She heard McCormick take a long breath and guessed she wasn't the first to notice the mayor had a habit of never making a decision on something that might lose him a vote. If the committee agreed to lease the oil rights on the forty acres, the city could make some money. If they voted to sell the land outright, there would be more money involved. But, in so doing, they'd destroy the homestead of the man who had founded Clifton Creek.

"I'll take it under consideration." She didn't know what else to say. First, the committee had to decide on the house, then second they'd look at who would buy the land. It didn't make sense to her even to think about the second problem until they knew the answer to the first.

"There's no pressure, but we're interested in buying, or leasing oil rights. We're willing to talk about whatever the committee thinks is fair," McCormick said firmly. "As soon as the committee makes a decision I can have an offer drawn up."

"I'll need to talk it over with the other members and, of course, call the mayor." She liked his way of talking, slow and straightforward. She, on the other hand, probably sounded like a fool, all sleepy with no answers.

"Like I said, the mayor doesn't want anything to do with this." His directness surprised her. "There are two drilling companies in town right now, besides the Howard Drilling outfit that bases here. If you give the lease to me, or vote to keep the land and turn it into something else, somebody isn't going to be happy. I just want to get the facts to you. All my company wants is a chance to present our side."

Sidney knew he was right about someone not being happy. She'd sensed it from the first. They weren't just a civic committee, they were the firing squad. No matter what the committee decided, somebody's plans would be shot down. "I understand," she whispered, wishing she didn't.

"Sidney?" The low voice on the other end of the phone said her name easily, like he'd used it before. "Look. Let me help you out a little. I've been in the oil game for a long time. I won't try to talk you into anything. I just want you to know the facts."

"The facts about what?"

"I'm a land man, Sidney. It's my job to do research on who owned what. I've turned up some interesting research on the Altman house and, though it won't help me talk you into selling, I think you should take a look at what I found."

She didn't know if she should trust him. He was probably just trying to persuade her to his way of thinking. The recipe card's message flipped through her mind.

Never forget the secrets of Rosa Lee.

Logic prevailed. "I'll meet with you on Friday, Mr. McCormick. The doctor insists I rest tomorrow."

"Thank you. How about I pick you up for lunch Friday? I promise not to try and talk you into anything."

"All right." Don't start thinking wild things

about a secret admirer, she reminded herself. He only wants to have a business
lunch, nothing more.

"Mexican food. No onions," he added.
She could almost hear the smile in his
words.

Before she could form a question, he
hung up the phone.

Sidney put the receiver down and
frowned. "Interesting," she said aloud. "Very
interesting."

The phone rang again.

"Hello."

She expected it to be McCormick asking
where to meet her, but a panicked Ada May
yelled, "Professor! We need your advice."

"Yes?" Sidney had talked to the two
ladies a few hours ago and they'd seemed
fine, though still shaken by yesterday's excitement.

"Beth Ann thought I should call and tell
you we've gotten three phone hang-ups in
the last hour. Have you had any?"

"No."

"Well, the sheriff told us to call if we noticed anything strange. Do you think the
hang-ups count?"

Sidney smiled. Though they were slightly

younger, the ladies reminded her of her grandmother Minnie, who had once blocked a closet door with every piece of furniture she could shove in front of it because she was certain an intruder hid among the coats. When the police had arrived, they'd found one very hungry squirrel.

"I think the hang-ups count. It wouldn't hurt to call and report them to the deputy on duty tonight. The deputy will probably circle by your house on rounds." Sidney knew the ladies would feel better if they believed they were taking an active role. "I wouldn't bother the sheriff yet. Not with his wife being pregnant and all."

"Oh, of course not. The sheriff should make her his top priority. We know he doesn't have much time to do overtime. He needs to be home. Beth Ann and I plan to help him out with this investigation as much as possible."

"I'm proud of you."

"Thanks." Ada May hesitated. "We're also listing every car that passes our street. I take down the license number and Beth Ann tries to guess the make and model just in case someone's switched plates. I saw that done on *CSI*."

"Good idea." Sidney decided it couldn't hurt. "But don't get frightened. Call me if you need me."

"Thank you, Professor." Ada May said the words as if she considered Sidney their field commander. "We'll be on watch."

"You're welcome. See you Friday at the meeting."

"We'll be there."

Sidney hung up the phone, laughing. She would love to listen in on the next call coming into the sheriff's office.

As she carried her empty dinner glass and plate to the kitchen, the phone rang again. It took her three rings to answer.

"Hello."

The line went dead with a click.

Fourteen

Lora Whitman pulled her Audi behind Billy's Mustang that was already parked in back of the Altman house. She flipped off the lights and climbed out with only the midnight stars to guide her. She'd told her parents she'd planned to go for a drive. And she had. At least a mile stretched from Candy Lane to the end of Main Street where Rosa Lee's house sat back from the road.

She'd used driving to relax since she'd been in her teens and her parents never questioned where she was going. But her father often wondered aloud why she couldn't drive a GM product. He'd given up offering her a Cadillac and she'd given up trying to explain how she just liked the feel of her car.

As she stared at the shadowy house that looked like the perfect setting for a horror film, she remembered the stories of a wild man running in the rose garden, and people hearing chanting that seemed to breathe with the house. Everyone said the madman was the ghost of old Henry, but Lora had never known anyone who had seen him, only people who claimed to know someone who knew someone who had seen the madman.

"Lora?" Billy's voice came through the blackness as she closed the car door.

"Present and accounted for," she answered, remembering how her ex-husband, Dan, always thought he had to know where she was every minute. The habit had irritated the hell out of her. She swore he put a stopwatch on her shower time, and heaven forbid she pause to window-shop.

"Thanks for coming out." When excited, Billy sounded younger than his twenty years. "I wanted to show you something and couldn't get free until now. Hope I didn't wake you when I called your cell. I didn't dare call the house."

"No problem. I've given up sleep." A few days ago she would have brought Mace to meet Billy Hatcher behind the Altman house at this time of night. But Lora had quickly grown to trust him. There was still something about Billy that made her nervous, though, but she couldn't pinpoint what it was. Not a violent streak, as she might have expected, more a calm undercurrent. As far as she knew, Billy Hatcher had little going for him, but nothing bothered him. He seemed to be one of those rare people who was comfortable in his skin. Beneath the rough look were intelligent eyes that missed little.

He took her hand and they moved into the blackness of the back porch. "I could help you with that," he said in easy conversation.

"With what?" She could almost feel the invisible night creatures sniffing at her ankles. Within seconds they'd probably bite deep enough to drain her blood before she could make it back to her car. Lora moved closer to Billy as they walked across the back porch.

"With getting to sleep." He fumbled with a key, then pressed it into a lock. "I know a few simple breathing exercises. The court made me take anger-management classes even though I didn't need them."

Curiosity got the better of her. "Oh, now I understand. It was a case of mistaken identity when you got arrested for whatever it was. Now you're doing penance by serving on the committee."

"Something like that." He laughed and leaned his shoulder against the door. "If you want to know something, just ask, Lora. I'll tell you all about it. Not that there's much to tell. I was in the wrong place at the wrong time with no one to back up my story. My father could have set things straight, but in doing so the cops would have looked his direction next. I guess he figured it was better for me to take the rap as a minor."

She wasn't sure she wanted to know more. "It doesn't matter. I'm sure you learned your lesson and will never do it again."

His laughter brushed her ear. "Not a chance. No lesson learned. Except maybe to stay as far away from my old man as possible. I've got no remorse."

Swallowing slowly, Lora wished she could see more than shadow. Maybe she'd be able to tell if he was teasing her. He didn't volunteer more, and she realized she wasn't brave enough to ask. There were other problems at the moment. She needed to pay attention. The night creatures might be moving closer. She'd always known they were there, hiding in closets and in shadows. As a child, she had held them at bay with screams until her daddy reached her. Now an adult, she tried ignoring them and hoped they'd return the favor.

Standing next to Billy she tried closing her eyes, pretending it really wasn't dark, that she just had her eyes shut. She had no time to think about what crime he had, or hadn't, committed. She had to concentrate on staying alive in the night.

Silence was worse than talking. "I don't need exercise to breathe," she mumbled. "I do it fine."

"Then maybe you need to feel safe where you sleep." Billy shoved the door open and pulled her into the low glow of the work lantern Sam had left. "You're afraid of the dark!"

"I am not."

"Then open your eyes." He moved out of

her reach with a suddenness that left her grasping for air.

She took a deep breath and opened one eye. When she saw it wasn't total blackness, she opened the other eye and relaxed. "I'm no more afraid of the dark than I am of anything else."

Billy lifted the light so he could see her face. "Then, you're afraid of everything, Lora Whitman."

She didn't argue. Billy had known her two days and already guessed more than Dan had in the three years they were married. Her ex-husband never saw through the act. He'd thought her a warrior to fight against. He never saw the frightened child beneath the armor. He never knew his not wanting her had hurt far more than all the battles he'd won in divorce court. And, in the end, she left him angry because she'd given up when he'd prepared to fight. She'd walked away with nothing, leaving him to feel like the loser.

Billy offered his hand again. The bandages had been replaced by a huge Band-Aid that looked almost like skin. "I'll keep your secret, if you promise not to be afraid of me."

"All right." She gripped his hand. How could she be afraid of him? He very well may have saved her life. It didn't take much to figure out that if he hadn't knocked her to the floor, she would have been hit by an oil drill bit three times the size of her fist.

He led her through the back of the house toward the front foyer. Lora refused to even glance toward the bay window where the committee had met.

She rubbed her fingers over his hand. "Why'd you take the bandages off?"

"I couldn't get my hand in my work gloves," he answered. "The cuts are healing. Don't worry about it."

She felt a spot on his thumb where dried blood had hardened but she didn't comment. In a few days, she promised herself, she'd take a serious look at the kid's wounds. If they weren't healing, she'd drive him to the doctor herself.

"I wanted to show you something strange." He knelt at the foot of the stairs. "See these holes in the floor?"

Lora bent over his shoulder. Someone had marred what had once been a fine wood flooring with a row of nail holes. "I don't understand." She ran her hand along the wood.

"I didn't either, but I've been thinking about it all evening, and an hour ago I came up with an answer." He reached around the door facing and produced a long board. "At first I thought someone might have put in carpet, or nailed a rug down. But no one would hammer a rug down with four-inch nails."

"Maybe someone put a gate at the bottom of the stairs, like a child guard?"

"No kids ever lived here."

"Good point." Lora frowned. She was never any good at guessing games. "I give up."

Billy placed the board on the stairs. As it rested on the incline of the steps, the end of the board came to a stop at the holes.

"So?"

"So." He smiled. "When I was a kid—"

"Last year," she interrupted.

Billy ignored her. "We used to build skateboard ramps. Someone hammered nails in the floor here big enough to hold a board in place."

"That's brilliant. Rosa Lee spent her old age skateboarding around the house. Everyone always wondered what she did besides garden. Now we know."

He laughed. "More likely she built the ramp to move something down these stairs that she couldn't carry. And if she built the ramp, she must have had little or no help."

A chill slid down Lora's spine. "Something she had to get downstairs and felt it was worth scarring her floor to move."

"Something she had to move alone," he whispered. "The job's too sloppy not to have been her work. Any kind of workman wouldn't have scarred the floor. I figure they couldn't have been made when old Henry Altman was alive. He cared too much about this place to have left those marks. A man doesn't bring carpenters in to build a place, then scar it."

"Maybe someone broke into the place and used the ramp to haul everything away?"

Billy shook his head. "I asked the sheriff tonight if anyone ever robbed anything. He said no. He said Rosa Lee died of natural causes. A nurse who checked on her twice a week found her in her bed. The nurse reported that it looked like the old lady had passed peacefully during the night."

Lora backed away. "Let's get out of here." Her imagination was already coming up with too many possibilities and she didn't like any of them. If no one robbed her, could her father have somehow trapped her here in her youth? That would answer the question of why she never met the man named Fuller who gave her the book. No, that didn't make sense. Everyone said Rosa Lee tended her gardens every day of her life. She could have just waited until she was outside and then run to the road. If she'd wanted to be with Fuller, she would have found a way. Lora was sure of it.

Billy carried the light and headed back through the house.

Lora stayed one step behind him. He flipped off the work light as they stepped onto the back porch. "Wouldn't want the deputy hauling us in. This time it might not be so easy to talk our way out of a free ride to his office. He's got it in for me, always has. Says he can smell trouble."

"Now who's afraid?" Lora took his hand. "Don't worry. I'll protect you from the big bad deputy."

Halfway down the back steps, they heard

a splashing sound. For a moment, Lora thought it might be a sprinkler hitting the windows, then she realized how ridiculous that would be.

A second later, she smelled gas.

Billy pulled her toward her Audi. "Get in the car and lock the door. Call the sheriff." He shoved her in before she could ask any questions.

Lora saw his shadow turn the corner of the house heading toward the front as she fumbled frantically in her purse for her cell phone.

By the time she finished telling the deputy on duty where she was, Billy was back standing beside her window.

"He's on his way," she cried as she rolled the window down.

"It's too late. Whoever it was must have heard me and took off into the bushes before I could see much."

"What were they doing?" Lora feared she already knew the answer.

"It looks like they tried to set the house on fire. I stumbled over a can of gasoline and someone had stacked dead branches across the front door." He leaned against the car and took a long breath. "If a fire caught, this old house would burn to the ground before anyone could put it out."

Lora heard the deputy's car screech to a halt out front. She climbed from her car and followed Billy.

For once, Deputy Adams didn't ask questions. He just walked around the house, took their statements, and helped Billy pull the brush off the front porch. Then, while they watched, he sprayed the spilled gas with foam from his patrol car fire extinguisher.

Lora watched him drive away, then followed Billy to the cars. "Why would anyone try to burn the house?"

Billy opened his trunk and pulled out a sleeping bag. "I don't know, but I'm sleeping here tonight. I doubt anyone will be back, but I'll camp out on the back porch, just in case."

She didn't try to argue, she only handed him her cell phone. "Just flip it open, press Talk. It will redial the sheriff's office."

He nodded. "Someone seems to be trying to make up our minds for us about this house. Someone seems determined to *let the house fall.*"

"Either that, or someone planned to kill us both." She'd accidentally spoken her fear.

To her surprise and horror, Billy didn't argue.

Fifteen

Micah swept the pizza crusts off the table and into the trash can while he downed his first cup of coffee and tried to wake up. Logan, Mrs. Mac and he had eaten themselves into a stupor last night. When they'd finally made it home with Logan's extra-large pepperoni-and-mushroom pizza, they'd found Mrs. Mac sitting in front of her TV with the kitten, Baptist, in her lap. Apparently, she'd heard him crying and barged through the connecting door to investigate. She'd told Micah that at first she was determined to have him get rid of the thing. But as the day passed, the worthless cat snuggled into her heart. She even swore they liked to watch the same soaps.

Starting Logan's breakfast, Micah realized he'd lost custody of the kitten. Baptist now belonged to Mrs. Mac. He and Logan had visiting rights whenever they liked. It seemed an ideal solution.

"Morning," Logan mumbled through a yawn.

Micah turned to look at his son. He swore sometimes the boy grew an inch overnight. Logan still wore the old T-shirt he always slept in. Micah had made a trip to Wal-Mart and bought pajamas a few times over the past three years, but his son liked to sleep in the shirt. "You're up early." Micah patted down one section of Logan's hair that was determined to look like the world's longest crew cut.

"I want to play with Baptist before I go to school."

Micah touched his finger to his lips, then pointed to the basket that now sat in the open pass-through door to Mrs. Mac's duplex. "He's still asleep. Why don't I help you get dressed and we'll make breakfast. By then, he's bound to be up."

Logan nodded and raised his arms. Micah lifted his son and carried him back into the bedroom. It wouldn't be long before the boy would think he was too big to be carried, but for now it felt good to hold him close. After Amy had died, Micah had walked the floor endless nights with Logan in his arms. Logan would wake if Micah tried to put him down. He seemed to fear he'd lose Micah too if he let go. During those months, Micah had almost learned to sleep standing. But slowly the pain of Amy's loss had turned to memory and the boy slept through the night.

He glanced at Amy's picture on the night-stand as he tossed Logan a pair of socks. She'd been Micah's partner and best buddy from the time they'd walked home from middle school together. He couldn't remember a time without loving her. Amy saw only the good in people. He fought back the lump in his throat. She saw only the good in him.

The words the professor had read from Rosa Lee's old book drifted into his mind. *Promise to love no other in this lifetime,* it said. He and Amy might have never said those exact words to each other, but he knew they'd felt them. So, Micah wondered, why hadn't Rosa Lee left with Fuller that night? If she'd loved him so dearly, how could she not have gone with Fuller? He'd probably never know.

Ten minutes later, Logan was dressed and had picked out his cereal. Baptist stretched and tried to climb out of the basket. As he played with the kitten, Logan said, "I got to have lunch money and an empty bleach bottle for school."

Micah fought down a groan. He thought of telling Logan to inform the teacher that his father wasn't allowed to handle bleach so they didn't have any bottle, empty or full in the house. All true. Micah had ruined half his clothes his freshman year of college and decided stains were better than white spots on his jeans. Somehow, he doubted the teacher would understand.

"I'll ask Mrs. Mac," he said, thinking he'd never make it through the next thirteen years of public school at this rate. The teacher had already asked for baby-food jars, seashells, empty toilet-paper rolls, scraps of felt and glitter. None of which he had lying around.

By the time Jimmy's mother honked, Micah had managed to borrow a half-full container of bleach, pour the contents down the sink and wash out the bottle. He handed it to Logan as his son ran out the door, still chewing his last bite of cereal.

Mrs. Mac smiled from the doorway, the kitten riding in the pocket of her huge robe. "I can't wait to see what they ask for when Christmas rolls around. That's when crafts kick into full gear."

"I'll pick up more bleach for you when I go to the store."

"Don't worry about it. A little hint though. When you talk with that teacher at back-to-school night this evening, ask her to give you a list of what she'll be asking the kids to bring. A few days notice can save lots of panic."

"Back-to-school night is tonight?"

Mrs. Mac laughed. "Logan's been talking about it for a week. If my arthritis would let me go, I would. I always thought those were great fun when my Charlie was growing up."

Micah smiled at the old landlady who somehow had become part of his family. Her Charlie called every Sunday and, thanks to the fruit-of-the-month club, a basket of goodies came like clockwork with his name typed on the card. But he lived in New York and never visited. He didn't allow his mom into his life. He didn't need her. "You do so much." Micah touched her shoulder. "I don't know what Logan and I would do without you." Finding the other half of her duplex to rent had been a blessing to them both.

She waved his praise aside. "That ain't true. If it weren't for you and the boy . . ." She stopped and played tug-of-war with the kitten for her handkerchief. "I'll add the bleach to my grocery order when I call it in. They'll have it ready for you by five."

"I won't forget." Every Thursday, he picked up her groceries, medicine and dry cleaning, and she cooked supper for them all. Usually, spaghetti with the sauce separate for Logan's sake, or fish sticks she'd pulled from the freezer and toasted to a crisp.

It seemed to Micah that she never started the meal until they arrived, then while she cooked, he did all the things on her *these stiff bones won't let me do* list. Mrs. Mac decorated for every holiday, so Micah spent many a night hauling Christmas trees, blow-up Easter bunnies and flags up and down from the basement. Tonight would probably be the three-foot haunted house she put up in her front window for Halloween.

"We'll eat a little early so you'll have time to make it to the school by seven. Wouldn't want to be late."

Micah thought of asking why, but decided he didn't want to know. He'd just wait and be surprised.

That night at exactly seven Micah was surprised. He'd expected the classroom to look like a classroom. When he'd registered Logan in August, he'd seen lines of desks, clean windows and a Welcome sign on the door.

Since then, the room had been taken over by arts-and-crafts elves. When he glanced at another parent at the door, she said simply, "This is Miss Karen's classroom," as if that explained everything.

Children's colorful work covered the walls. In one corner stood a papier-mâché tree with books dangling off the branches. All the light fixtures had mobiles hanging from them and the windows were lined with brightly painted bird feeders that might have been bleach bottles in a former life.

For a kid it must look like a wonderland, but for Micah at six foot, it was more like an obstacle course. He dodged and ducked his way to the front.

The moment he saw Miss Karen, he understood. With heels, she'd be lucky to measure five feet. A rounded bundle of energy, she greeted him with a smile. "Good evening. You must be Logan's father."

Micah took her hand. "Miss Karen."

She didn't give him time to say more. "I'm glad you came tonight. This is my first year to teach, and I'm excited to have Logan in my class. He's a very bright little boy." The next parent closed in behind Micah and, in midhandshake, Miss Karen began to pull him along. "Please help yourself to the cake the kids made today. I'm sure we'll have time to talk later."

Micah nodded and started to say something, but she'd already grabbed the next parent. Logan took his hand and directed him toward the refreshment table. It crossed Micah's mind that he'd need to take speed-hearing to understand Miss Karen.

Logan handed him a piece of cake. "Miss Karen said it's all right to eat it, Pop, even if we don't eat sweets at home. She says it's a special occasion and special occasions are for doing special things."

Micah nodded as he shoved a bite into his mouth and realized he was losing control of his son. After seven years of parenting, it didn't matter what he said. Miss Karen was now the expert.

Two hours later when he carried Logan, fast asleep, from the car to bed, he smiled down at the icing still on the boy's cheek.

"Was it fun?" Mrs. Mac whispered from the doorway.

"Great fun," he admitted.

"I have coffee on if you want some."

Micah tugged at his tie. "No, thanks. I feel like running."

She nodded and said good-night, leaving the connecting door open. On the few occasions Logan awoke, he knew to grab his pillow and head for her couch if his father wasn't in the bed across the hall. To the boy, Mrs. Mac's quarters were an extension of his home.

Fifteen minutes later, Micah ran with the wind. He took the back path down Second Street all the way to Cemetery Road, ran the square around the cemetery, then turned and headed toward Main. As always, he passed the bar bearing Randi's name. Only now there was a face with the name. He guessed Randi would be inside serving drinks behind the bar. He could hear the music as he passed.

He wouldn't stop, he told himself. His day had been too full of Amy. There was no room in his heart for anyone else. He had her memory and their son to raise. That was enough. He didn't need to complicate things.

He made it home without taking time to walk and cool down. He hit the shower, his muscles tired and aching. Bracing himself under the spray, he let the water run across his back until it turned cold. Half-asleep, he fell into bed without bothering to turn on the TV. The pounding of blood still ran in his brain, but his body relaxed.

The wind made a whistling sound where he'd left the window open a few inches. The cold air warned of a freeze, but Micah didn't get up and latch the window. He rolled up in his blanket and told himself to go to sleep as if the demand would make it so.

He lay awake all alone in his bed listening to the clock tick away the minutes. Unbeckoned, Randi filled his thoughts. He wondered what she was doing. Did they close up early some nights? How many nights would she wait up a few minutes after closing to see if he'd stop by?

With determination, he could keep her out of his life. But how could he keep her out of his mind?

Sixteen

Sidney organized papers on her desk. After being out three days, nothing remained in order. She had notes covering the tiny message board by her door and campus mail that would have to wait until Monday to be opened. Thank goodness it was Friday and she didn't have a class scheduled.

A note, obviously torn from a yellow legal pad, slipped from among the others and drifted to the floor. Sidney leaned and picked it up, frustrated because she'd missed it among the others on the more common office memo stationery. She unfolded the long slip of paper, expecting to see a student's reason for not turning in an assignment or a phone number to call to give homework to someone who'd been absent.

All she found was four printed words. *Let the house fall.*

She looked up half expecting it to be a joke someone was playing on her. A cruel joke.

No one waited at her door. No one watched. It hadn't been a joke.

Sitting down in her chair behind her desk, she tried to decide whether or not to call the sheriff. Someone had used the same wording on the note found inside the drill bit. Someone wanted to let her know that he knew where she worked. That he could get to her should an *accident* like the shattered window need to happen again.

She tucked the note into her pocket, telling herself she would not be frightened again. She would not be controlled by fear. She'd always believed she had a strength inside her. A strength she could call on if times got hard. It had helped her get through the deaths of her mother and grandmother. It had shown itself when she'd moved far away from all she'd known. The same strength would help her now. She was not a coward.

Part of her wanted to open the window and yell, "Bring it on," to the world. No one had ever tried to bully her in her life and she decided no one would start now. With determination, Sidney returned to work, shoving the note to the back of her mind.

After scheduling the Altman house committee meeting for three o'clock that afternoon, she asked the department's secretary to call everyone as a reminder. The building would be quiet at that time of day so they should be able to meet undisturbed. On Fridays the whole campus looked like a ghost town. Clifton was a suitcase college, with students swarming in on Monday morning and driving off on Friday. Ninety percent of the student body lived within a hundred miles of campus, so they returned home or to part-time jobs on the weekends.

A door closed several offices down. Sidney glanced at the clock—twelve forty-five. So much for her lunch date. She really hadn't expected Sloan McCormick to show up. He probably found a way around the committee and therefore had no use for her. But, he did have a nice voice. The kind that would have fit a midnight caller. And he had been honest about who he was, or at least she hoped so.

She glanced down at her best wool suit, feeling foolish for taking extra care in dressing for a meeting she wouldn't have. She'd worn her church shoes that were already hurting her feet, and her white blouse with the touch of lace on the collar.

Straightening her glasses, she reminded herself she would be forty in a few days. She should always wear comfortable shoes, her skirts below the knee and little makeup. She was long past waiting for a knight in shining armor to ride up, and she'd never been one to go looking. She may have given up on finding Mr. Right, but she wasn't ready to settle for Mr. Right-Now as some of her friends had.

Swiveling her chair toward the window, she stared out at the campus outfitted in fall. The leaves on the eighty-year-old elms were just beginning to turn. The colors of autumn shone warm and magnificent. Sidney closed her eyes remembering each detail. She took a deep breath and relaxed her mind. All morning she'd been worried about the lunch with McCormick and now it was time to forget about him and think of more important things. She had always been able to organize her mind, set her goals, concentrate on what needed to be done.

"Sorry, I'm late." A low voice shattered her meditation.

Sidney swung around and studied the man before her. Sloan McCormick looked familiar, but she couldn't place him. Tall, well over six foot. Hair a bit too long, with a touch of gray at the temples. A Western-cut suit with boots. Like his name, he was every inch the Texas businessman. He looked as if he belonged to his voice.

She stood and offered her hand, trying, as always, to be sensible. "Mr. McCormick, I presume."

His fingers closed around hers in a familiar touch. "Yes, ma'am."

"Won't you have a seat?" It crossed her mind that he might have been the one who left the note pinned to the board outside her door. He knew where her office was. He had an interest in seeing the house fall. After all, his oil company only wanted the land, not the house.

"I thought we were having lunch." He shuffled his hat between large hands.

Sidney waved toward the extra chair in

front of her desk. "Thank you for your offer, Mr. McCormick, but that won't be necessary. I'm sure we can complete our business in a few minutes."

She watched him closely as if dishonesty might slip out and be noticeable.

He didn't even look at the chair. "It may not be necessary for you, Professor, but I've been on the road to and from Wichita Falls most of the morning. I'd be thankful if you'd take pity on me and allow us to talk while we eat."

Sidney had every intention of standing firm on her choice of meeting location, but she could hardly turn him down when he sounded so sincere. "All right. I'll meet you somewhere."

"I've got my truck parked illegally out front, if you don't mind riding with me." When she opened her mouth to argue, he added, "We could save time by talking on the way."

Sidney realized she would be climbing into a truck with a complete stranger and she should be alarmed. She'd been raised never to take chances but, at her age, maybe it was time to take a small one. Surely serial killers didn't make lunch dates with dowdy professors before they murdered them. "That would be fine," she said. "Only, I have to be back before three."

He held the door open for her as she lifted her jacket and purse from the hook beside her desk. "I'll have you back by then, Professor," he said with almost a bow.

They walked down the hall without a word. His height made her feel small and the way he opened the doors for her surprised her. In today's world with men worrying about always treating women as equals, it was rare to find a man who showed such simple politeness.

He opened the passenger door of his truck and held her arm as she stepped into the cab. Sidney had seen a great many pickups, but none like this. The seats were leather, the floorboard muddy, and the back bench seat covered in rolled-up tubes that looked as if they could be maps. A small laptop rested between them, along with folders and notepads stuffed into what had to be a tailor-made traveling desk between the seats. She didn't miss the fact that one tablet was yellow, just like the note she'd seen earlier that ordered her to let the house fall.

He slid his Stetson into a hat rack behind his head that already held a hard hat and two baseball caps. "The truck stop out by the interstate all right?" he asked. "I hear their Mexican food is good."

"Fine." She'd lived here a year and never gone there. Once in a while, when she forgot her lunch, she'd eat at the snack bar next to the bookstore. When she didn't feel like cooking she'd stop by the grocery and buy one of the box meals, or spoon up a salad from what the grocer called a salad bar, even though it looked more like a salad barrel.

"I'm surprised you don't have a stove and refrigerator in this thing."

He glanced at her a moment as if trying to figure out if she was kidding. "I pretty much live in my truck. It's part of the job. I do have a cooler in the back under the seat, but there's nothing but beer. With some folks, when you're talking oil, you're drinking. My father used to roughneck when he was young. He said since coats could be dangerous around a rig, the colder it got, the more they drank in the early days."

Sidney nodded as though what he said sounded logical.

For a man who insisted on a meeting, Sloan didn't have much to say. He backed out of the loading zone slot and turned toward the interstate. She watched him out of the corner of her eye. Every movement he made appeared easy and relaxed, but he was nervous. His hand, too tight on the wheel, gave him away. He must be about forty, a man in his prime. A man strong enough to throw a drill bit into a window.

"I've been here almost a week," he said without looking at her. "I feel like I've eaten at every place in town twice, but the truck stop was too packed the first time I drove out there."

She looked again, but saw no deceit in his manner. His direct way of glancing at her told her he was either an honest man, or a man very good at lying.

"It's a popular place." Sidney frowned, hoping she followed the conversation. She had no idea what she was talking about, but she had to say something. "I like to cook, however, I've never quite gotten the hang of Mexican food."

He spread his hand out along the back of the seat, almost touching her shoulder. Was he relaxing or trying to look as if he were? "I

grew up cooking it. My mom had a house-
keeper who could make the best enchiladas
in town. By the time I was eight I was helping her."

"Really?" She found it hard to see him as
a boy or a cook. He looked like a businessman, but looks could fool people. She
couldn't forget the fact that he was in the oil
business and it had been a drilling bit that
flew through the window.

He turned in her direction and smiled. "If
I had a kitchen, I'd cook you the best chili
rellenos you've ever tasted."

"Since I've never had chili *rellenos,* that
wouldn't be hard."

He raised one dark eyebrow as if he
didn't believe her.

"I promise. My mother's idea of Mexican
food night was a TV dinner."

Sloan laughed and turned into the truck
stop. When he cut the engine, he said,
"Wait for me to get the door, Sidney. This
wind has a hell of a way of ripping it right
out of your hand."

She waited as he shoved on his hat and
rounded the cab. He'd called her Sidney,
this man she hardly knew. Somehow it
sounded natural. Despite trying to remain

distant, she found herself liking Sloan Mc-Cormick.

When she stepped down, the wind almost whirled her around. Out in the open land like this nothing slowed the wind as it blew sandy dirt so hard she felt the sting on her skin.

Sloan put his arm over her shoulder and guided her toward the café side of the truck stop while Sidney tried to hold both her hair and skirt in place.

They stepped out of the wind into a tiny waiting area. Sloan turned to put his hat on a rack with several others. Sidney looked around. The place had been busy, most of the tables were dirty, but the lunch run must be over.

"Welcome," a girl behind a counter said. "Two for lunch?"

Sloan glanced at Sidney. "Yes. Nonsmoking?"

She nodded slightly.

They followed the girl to one of the few clean tables. She handed them menus and disappeared.

"How'd you know I didn't smoke?"

He smiled. "You don't look like a woman who smokes. No ashtrays in your office. No smell of stale tobacco hanging around. It was an easy guess."

She made a mental note. Sloan Mc-Cormick was a man of details. Sidney thought of asking him about the reason he wanted the meeting, but she found herself enjoying this time before they had to get down to the reason he'd come to see her. For a few minutes, she felt like they were almost on a date. Almost friends.

If someone she knew from the college walked by, she'd introduce him as a friend. Let them think what they wanted to. She felt reckless today.

"What do you think is good here?" The menu made little sense to her. Each dinner was a mixture of words she'd heard, but had no idea if she liked, and items she couldn't pronounce.

He lowered his menu. "I'm sorry. You really don't eat Mexican food, do you? We should have gone somewhere else."

He did it again, reading her too easily. "No it's not that. I'm just not familiar with all the lunch specials."

She straightened, expecting McCormick to say something about how she must be one of those people who never liked to try anything new. The one man she'd dated seriously ten years ago had constantly teased her about not having an ounce of adventure in her soul. But, if he'd stayed around, she could have fooled him. She'd packed up everything she owned and moved to Clifton Creek because of a note on a recipe card.

"If you'd allow me, Professor, I'd be happy to order for you. Nothing too hot or spicy, of course."

She nodded.

When the waitress returned, Sloan told her what they both wanted, adding sopaipillas with the meals and *queso* for an appetizer.

"With or without onions on the lady's?" the waitress asked.

"Without," Sloan said not even looking at Sidney.

"And to drink?"

He hesitated.

"Tea," she answered, surprised he didn't know that about her, too. "With extra lemon, please."

As the waitress left, Sloan smiled. "If it were evening and you didn't have a meeting, I'd teach you to drink tequila with salt and lime."

"Why do you think I don't already know how?"

His eyebrows shot up and she knew she'd surprised him. "I don't," she admitted slowly.

Sidney unfolded her napkin and wiped her silverware with it.

"You don't?" he asked.

"I don't," she admitted.

The waitress brought the *con queso* and chips. When she was out of hearing distance, Sloan leaned across the table and whispered, "Professor Dickerson, you are a fascinating woman."

Sidney felt herself blush, something she hadn't done in years. She knew he probably only put on an act because he wanted something from her and the committee, but she couldn't help being flattered. It took a few minutes for reason to win out. "I don't believe we're here to talk about me, Mr. Mc-Cormick. You said you had information about the Altman house."

He straightened, but his eyes still studied her. "I've been digging up all I could and I thought something I found might help the committee." He pulled a folded paper from his jacket pocket. "But, first I should tell you that my company is willing to make a fair offer for the land the house sets on."

"You want the drilling rights?"

"More, I'm afraid. You see the house sets on the crest of the property. Finding oil is a long shot in an area that's virgin. The test hole would need to be drilled on the most likely spot."

"And that spot is where the Altman house sets." She stiffened.

Sloan nodded slowly. "My company's not heartless, Sidney, but we're not foolish either. It'll cost thousands, maybe hundreds of thousands to drill. We can't afford to take less than our best shot at finding the oil beneath."

"I understand," she whispered, suddenly not the least bit hungry.

"No you don't," he answered. He unfolded the paper. "I think before you make up your mind about me, or the Altman place, you should have all the facts."

"You mean the committee should have the facts?"

"No, you." He looked down at the paper. "I dig through the records of every public file I can. Two days ago I found something that might surprise you. I've got copies of all the documents, but I just brought one page in with me." He passed the paper toward her. "According to Rosa Lee's will, the house only went to the city if it was not claimed within a year by Minnie Jefferson of Chicago, Illinois."

Sidney felt the blood draining from her face. "Minnie Jefferson was my grandmother," she whispered.

"I know." Sloan looked down at the paper. "I looked up her name on the Internet. She died in an accident on her way here, didn't she?"

Sidney fought back tears. "My mother was with her. I didn't know where they were heading. I was teaching in a junior college north of Chicago and must have been in class when they left a message on my home phone saying they were off on a little trip. I thought it strange because my mother rarely left the city.

"The next time the phone rang, it was the state police saying they were killed in a pileup a hundred miles south of their home." She closed her eyes and tried to remember every detail of a day she'd often wished she could forget. "They were headed south, so this could have been their destination. My mother's last words were that she'd call me before dark and let me know where they were spending the night. So, they must have known the trip they were taking would be more than a one-day drive."

"She didn't drive at night." Sloan filled in the blank.

"None of us did," she whispered, fighting tears. "I still can't. When I teach a night class I always walk home even if the faculty parking lot is right by my classroom. I'd rather face the cold than chance not seeing one of the students out walking at night."

She stared at the paper in his folder. "This brings up a hundred questions."

"I've only a few answers," he whispered. "But, I'm willing to help."

The waitress circled by and Sloan asked for their orders to go. They sat in silence until she came back with the bags. Sloan walked beside her to his truck, but didn't close the door when she got in. He stood next to her, the meals in one hand and his arm on the frame of her door.

"I shouldn't have told you like that." He reached in awkwardly and took her hand.

The bag bumped against her knee. "I'm sorry."

Sidney managed to smile more at herself than him. How could she have been so foolish to even allow a tiny part of her mind think he'd asked her on a date? She should have known better. "It's all right. Thank you for being honest with me. Not that it will matter, since my grandmother never claimed the house I don't have any more say than anyone else on the committee."

"Yeah," he mumbled. "But, I shouldn't have blurted it out like that. I should have started with the little things I learned and not just handed you part of the will."

Sidney placed her free hand over both theirs. "I thank you. I've already mourned my mother's and grandmother's deaths. You've only given me a piece of the puzzle I couldn't understand. How about we go back to my office and look over all the papers while we eat our lunch?"

His eyes met hers. "I'd like that. Whether my oil company gets the property or not, I'd like to think that we can be friends."

Sidney nodded.

An hour later they were both reading through every detail Sloan had managed to dig up on the history of the Altman house. He had found records of the good Henry Altman had done for his community. How he'd donated money to just about every cause to better the community, and how he'd served on early education boards.

Sloan's work added to Sidney's research, but still offered little as to why Rosa Lee would have left a house to a woman she could only have met during the Depression. As far as Sidney knew, her grandmother had not been back to Texas since her mother had been born in Chicago.

"If your grandmother was in Clifton Creek, how would she have known Rosa Lee?"

Sidney raised her eyebrows. "Maybe from church? All my life my grandmother Minnie went to church every time the door was open. If she lived here in the Depression, I'm guessing she continued the habit."

Sloan shook his head. "Could be, but from all I read Rosa Lee never left the place. If she'd been active in a church, looks like it would have shown up in the newspaper at some time."

Sidney tried again. "Both my mother and grandmother were nurses?"

"Maybe," he guessed. "If Rosa Lee or her father needed home nursing, your grandmother could have been there. There are folks who feel mighty grateful to caretakers. I've worked a few oil rights where someone died and left everything to the nurse or doctor who took care of them during the last few years."

"I know during the Depression Granny Minnie worked to save enough money to join my grandfather in Chicago. She might have spent her time here as a nurse. I think they were separated for almost a year. She said the hardest part of the Depression was the year she spent away from him. She took the train up to visit him a few times, but I never asked if he came down to see her."

"Times must have been hard back then," Sloan agreed. "I think a lot of couples were separated like that. Men could find work in towns but couldn't afford to bring the family."

"Once Minnie was in Chicago, it wasn't long before my mother came along and I don't think my grandmother ever worked again. When my father died in 'Nam, Grandmother Minnie came to live with us. For as long as I can remember it's been the three of us."

Sloan circled to her side of the desk and read the will once more over her shoulder. "Maybe Rosa Lee and Minnie were friends. Maybe the old maid had no one else to leave her house to. Did your grandmother ever mention a friend in Texas?"

Sidney started to shake her head, then whispered, "Only once in a note on the back of a recipe card."

Sloan's starched shirt brushed her silk blouse as he straightened and checked his watch. "Looks like we missed lunch." He glanced at the meals still in the bag. "Cold Mexican food isn't much good anyway. How about I pick you up after your meeting and we try again? I've got some business to take care of, but I should be finished by six."

Reason told her to decline. Lunch was one thing, dinner another. But, he had been helpful. He'd also been honest about where he stood with the Altman property. He'd told her his company wanted the land, but he hadn't tried to talk her into anything.

"All right," she answered. "Only this time I buy."

He raised an eyebrow as if she were challenging him. "Fair enough," he said retrieving his coat from the rack. "Should I pick you up here, or at your place?"

She started to tell him that she'd pick him up, but an image of her knocking on doors at the town's only motel flashed in her brain. She didn't like the idea of meeting him at the restaurant, either. What if he was late? She'd be sitting alone like a woman waiting to be picked up. "Here," she finally said. "I'll leave my office door unlocked in case the committee meeting runs late."

"I'll wait."

Seventeen

Lora Whitman searched her desk for the yellow legal pad where she'd made notes and tried to ignore the loudspeaker calling one of the salesmen to the phone. She didn't want to be late to the committee meeting, but her summary of what Billy and she had found looked puny.

One sighting of someone with a flashlight in the house, evidence of an attempted fire and a dozen nail holes at the base of the stairs.

Lora frowned. Not exactly a conspiracy. Sidney said to collect all the information they could, but Lora didn't feel as if she had much.

She could almost see herself sitting on

the Rogers porch every night counting cars and writing down license-plate numbers. Maybe they'd make matching militia outfits with crocheted armbands.

As she pulled the legal pad from beneath a stack of papers, a rapid-fire knock sounded on the frame where her door should have been.

"Howdy, honey." Talon Graham stepped in without an invitation. "Glad to see me?" He looked every inch the young Texas oilman even though she knew he dropped by in his capacity as president of the rodeo association.

Since they'd met earlier in the week, Lora had, at least, done her homework on Talon Graham. He had a degree from the University of Texas, a rich grandfather who lived in the area and a powerful lawyer for a father. He was working for an oil company out of Austin. According to Dora, her father's secretary, Talon was back in Clifton Creek not just to put together an oil deal, but to start his career in politics.

Lora forced a smile. He was easy on the eyes but, she decided, he was a bother to the brain. She'd seen too many of his type. Men who knew they had it all. Men who got friendly too fast. Men who thought because she had blond hair she must like to be called honey.

She thought briefly of having him stuffed. Then he would be the perfect man. Good-looking, well dressed and silent. "Afternoon, Tal. I'm afraid I have a meeting in a few minutes and can't talk. Maybe you should call next time to save yourself a trip." Lora knew she couldn't afford to be rude, it might hurt business, but she'd do her best to put him in his place.

It crossed her mind that another time, another place, she might have been kinder. She almost wanted to warn him not to come back until her wounds had healed.

"Oh, I only need a minute. I brought you a surprise." He grinned, showing perfect teeth. "You're going to love this, honey."

Lora doubted she'd love anything any man had to offer, but she tried to be polite. "I'm not much on surprises." She wanted to add she'd slug him if he called her honey again but decided to concentrate on one fault at a time. First she had to make him stop thinking they could possibly be an item, even if he probably was the only single man her age in this zip code.

His granddaddy had miles of land and cattle, her father had reminded her twice. She'd heard so many people say "he might be governor someday" that she was starting to think of the tag as part of his name.

So, why didn't she like him . . . ? Use him to get over her broken heart? Maybe because sleaziness hung on him like a film, the way it does on lake water during a draught. It was so thin no one else seemed to notice, but as a recent veteran of the heartache wars, she knew he might be dangerous.

He retrieved a large package from behind himself and grinned at her. Without any care to the papers on her desk, he pulled several poster boards out and spread them across her work space. "I found these upstairs in the old bank's storage room. They're posters from some of Clifton Creek's early rodeos. I figured you'd want to see them."

Lora stared. To Tal's credit, he did surprise her. She loved them. While he talked about how he'd discovered them among files of his family's records, she sifted through the posters, visualizing next year's ads based on images from the thirties and forties.

"I thought you'd like them." He broke into

her thoughts. "The guys at the bank helped me get them in order by year. We're not missing a one until 1942. One of the men said he didn't think they even had a rodeo that year 'cause of the war." Tal had a blank look about him as if he wouldn't attempt to guess what war that might be.

"I love them. They'll be a great inspiration." She studied each poster, examined the details. The dates. The names. The artwork.

Tal leaned on the corner of her desk. "I thought you might see it that way. I figure if nothing else, we can plaster one wall of the community center with them, then staple letters running across announcing the rodeo dates and times. That way everyone who walks in the center will see what's coming."

"Not a bad idea," she answered without looking up. "But we'd use copies. I want to keep these originals in good condition. Look, most of the coloring hasn't even faded. They must have been stored in the dark." She couldn't take her eyes off the gray photos of bronc and bull riders providing the backdrop for all the information. Some of the best rodeo cowboys were listed. Names like Tex Riley, Jack Hampton and Mike Kirkland.

Lora suddenly sucked in a breath. On the 1933 poster, under bull riders, was the name Fuller Crane. "It can't be," she whispered. The note Sidney had read in a book to Rosa Lee came to mind. *It had to be just a coincidence.* She tried to remember the words in the note, but all she'd caught was the name. *Fuller.*

"What can't be?" Tal looked worried.

"Nothing," she answered, pulling the poster away from the rest. "I just thought how this treasure you've found is too good to be true." She could tell he waited for more praise. "You've done a fine job. I'll have to work hard if you keep bringing me ideas as good as this one. These are unbelievable."

Tal winked at her. "That's what I said. Who would have ever thought these would all be stuck in storage for years. There's no telling what else is up in that old place if you ever want to wander up there and look with me."

Lora ignored the invitation as she stuffed her legal pad in the side of her briefcase and picked up the poster from 1933. "Would you mind if I took one with me to study? I hate to leave, but I really do have a meeting at three."

He gave her the *little-boy-hurt* look before shrugging. "I'll let you go, but only if you agree to have dinner with me tonight."

Lora had too much on her mind to think of a quick reason to decline. "All right. I'll call you when I'm finished, but it may be late." Right now all she wanted to do was show her find to the committee. Sidney was going to love that she'd learned Fuller's full name.

Talon followed her to her car. "Wear something sexy. I know a place over in Wichita Falls where we can eat steaks as late as midnight, then dance until the sun comes up." He reached in and patted her shoulder as if she were a horse he planned to ride.

She fought the urge to slam her door on his hand. In her imagination, she might even pull the whole arm off when she sped away. And, how would that look, driving down Main with an arm flying from the window? For a moment, images of blood spattering on every passing car filled her thoughts. People would say, "Oh, it's only poor Lora

Whitman taking her anger out on a man because her husband left her flat."

Talon backed away as she pulled the door closed and stepped on the gas. He had the nerve to wave with the hand he'd never know how close he came to losing.

Eighteen

As Micah Parker sat in the quiet classroom at Clifton College, he found himself drawn into the meeting. He'd planned to come, check on everyone, and then make his excuses. He had a meeting, concerning next year's budget, starting at the church at four that he viewed as far more important. But the other members of the committee drew him in. They all seemed to have caught Sidney's madness about learning the history of the house. In Micah's mind, they might as well vote now. He wasn't sure he wanted to hear more about a woman who wasted her life waiting for a man who never showed.

The house was falling down, anyone could see that. It was no good to anyone.

But, he had to admit, the history of the Altmans read like a mystery.

The Rogers sisters gave detailed accounts of what they considered strange behavior with the skill of a fifth grader giving a book report. Unknown cars circling their street. Phone calls where the caller hung up. Noises that had no direction in the middle of the night. They'd even missed the opening of one of their garden club meetings because they'd circled the block several times to make sure they weren't being followed.

Micah could have written them off as eccentric, but Billy and Lora told a story of seeing someone in the house one night and catching others trying to burn the Altman place down the next evening. Micah couldn't deny the possibility that someone wanted the house and the committee to disappear. Lora said both accounts had been reported to the sheriff, which made them somehow more credible.

Sidney produced a page from a will and explained that her grandmother would have inherited the place if she'd lived. Micah thought this fact interesting, but probably just a coincidence. After all, Sidney's grandmother and Rosa Lee were around the same age. If Minnie Jefferson had lived in Clifton Creek in the midthirties, there was a real chance they'd known each other. The old maid had to leave the house to someone, and Sidney's grandmother seemed as likely as anyone.

He made a note to check the church record to see if Rosa Lee belonged to any of the churches. Since Sidney came every Sunday morning, maybe her grandmother had been Methodist, too. If so, there might be information still in the files.

The most interesting fact mentioned was an old poster Lora had found while digging through rodeo ads. Apparently, a man named Fuller Crane rode bulls in the 1933 rodeo. He must have been fairly well-known to be listed on the poster, but Lora said there was no record of him in any ads after that year.

"He probably left not only Clifton Creek, but the rodeo after Rosa Lee stood him up." Billy ended Lora's presentation. "She may have told him to get lost."

"Maybe." Lora shrugged. "I'm going to try to find out more about the cowboy. He might simply have the same name, or he might be Rosa Lee's love. If he was here in thirty-three, there must be a record of him somewhere."

Micah hated to be the one to do it, but someone had to get this committee back on track. Sidney seemed to have lost her focus. "Look," he stood. "All this is great history, but how does it really impact our decision? The mayor is waiting for a vote."

Sidney agreed, reluctantly. "He called me this morning to say they have begun taking bids on the oil rights as well as for the land itself. No one's ever been interested in Rosa Lee's property since it passed to the city, but when one company shows an interest, the others smell oil. The mayor says they're talking enough money to get the town out of debt. If oil is found, it could mean raises for all city workers, updated Christmas lights, maybe even a wing built onto the hospital."

"Christmas lights," Billy mumbled. "That makes me want to hurry. And a new wing. What'll that add, another ten beds?"

Lora frowned. "The town's dying. We all know it. But would the money be enough to rebuild—a shot in the arm? Or would selling the oil rights just prolong a death that is inevitable?"

"I don't think the town is dying." Beth Ann raised her hand. "It's just a little sleepy."

"That's right." For once Ada May agreed with her sister. "We got a new dollar store last year, and there's talk of a new hotel going in out by the interstate."

Billy laughed. "There's talk of a new hotel going in out there."

"I think the point is—" Sidney pulled the group back to order "—is the old place worth saving for future generations, or would the money do the town good? If we fight to keep the house and nothing is done to restore the place, it will crumble away and we've accomplished nothing. At least with oil money, we might give the town a chance."

"No sense having a historical marker in front of the house if the town dries up and blows away," Billy reasoned.

Ada May frowned at him. "And what is a town without a history?"

Micah loosened his tie. It looked as if they would be here till dark.

A little before six, the professor excused herself to walk a few doors down the hall and unlock her office. If anyone but Micah thought the action strange, none commented. During the three-hour session, Billy had left twice to get Cokes from the machine on the first floor, Micah had stepped out to call and notify the church he wouldn't be attending the budget meeting and to make sure Logan got home safely. Beth Ann had gone to the restroom four times.

In the end, all they agreed on was that they needed to take the weekend to think about what to do with the house. The sisters planned to cut clippings from some of the antique roses on the grounds for their garden club. Billy said he'd do a detailed walk-through of the house to determine how much damage existed and, he'd ask his boss to prepare an estimate of necessary repairs if they voted to save the old place. Micah planned to research church and county records for anything concerning the house. Sidney agreed to try to find the nurse who found Rosa Lee's body. Lora promised to get at least a ballpark figure on how much the town would stand to make if they sold the land.

Then, with all the information, they'd vote next Wednesday.

Micah watched the members march out of the meeting. All were determined, knowing that fighting for money to remodel would do no more good than spitting in the wind. But, all seemed unwilling to let go of possibilities and legends.

Sidney stopped him just before he walked out. She reached in her pocket and passed him a slip of paper. "Someone put this on the note board outside my office."

Micah looked at the words. "Let the house fall," he read aloud, then looked up at her. "What do you think it means?"

"I think someone is trying to frighten us into voting." She straightened. "I've decided they think I must be the weak link, the one who can be bullied."

Micah raised an eyebrow.

Sidney smiled. "You know what I think?"

"No." He had no idea.

"I think whoever it is better think again."

Nineteen

Sidney stepped into her office and closed the door, feeling as if she'd been listening to headphones playing different channels in each ear.

"I'm sorry I'm so late," she said to the dark shadow against her windows. Her voice sounded tired, but she'd been on an emotional roller coaster all day. Memories of her grandmother. Trouble at the Altman house. Information about oil deals and arson. Too many questions without answers.

She needed to be practical and cancel her dinner plans with Sloan McCormick. He'd understand. A hot bath, warm green tea and maybe mindless TV sounded like the right prescription for the headache that had been building since three.

Sloan turned, but with the office light shut off his face remained in shadow. "No problem." He shrugged. "I've been watching the clouds move in from the north. Looks as though we may be in for another storm late tonight." He crossed to the side of her desk. "I spent too many summers camping out with my grandfather not to know the signs."

Sidney put the committee notes on her desk and reached for her purse in the bottom drawer of her file cabinet. "It's later than I planned. We might be wise to . . ."

When she turned, Sloan was closer than she thought. She bumped into his chest. The man was as solid as a rock.

His hands brushed her shoulders, holding her steady.

"I'm sorry," she mumbled, embarrassed. "This office really isn't big enough to move around in."

He didn't let go. The warmth of his fingers held her gently in place.

She didn't know what to do. Part of her wanted him to keep a proper distance. But, another part, deep inside, wanted to hold this one moment, press it between all the lonely hours in her mind and keep it there forever. Her practical nature told her to stop being foolish. The dreamer whispered, *Just once let something happen.*

"Sidney." She felt his breath touch her hair. "Don't be afraid of me. Look at me."

"I'm not," she insisted, knowing that she'd been afraid of pretty near everything in her life since birth. Her cheeks warmed as she glanced up.

Before she had time to think, to react, he kissed her, soft and laced with promise, like a man who knew what he was doing.

When he pulled away, he smiled. "I've been wanting to do that since I first met you, Professor. I'm probably out of line, but I'll be damned if I'll say I'm sorry."

Sidney didn't trust words. She just stood there like some fifteen-year-old who'd never been kissed.

Sloan studied her. "Say something, Sidney. Slap me if you feel like it. Or say 'do it again,' but don't just stare at me."

Emotions double-timed through her veins. The fact that he seemed attracted to her put him on her list of insane people she'd met. Of course, if this was just some way to try and win her vote on the Altman house, she didn't want to be humiliated in the end. She'd fallen blindly for a man once and learned too late that she was simply more a convenience than a lover.

"I'll have to ask you not to do that again." She straightened, forcing herself not to react at all.

"All right." He smiled, as if seeing through her manner. "How about you let me know when you're ready."

"And if it's never?"

He picked up his hat and held the door for her. "Well, then I'll respect your wishes, of course." They walked halfway down the hall before he added, "Or get real good at apologizing."

Neither said a word as he helped her into his huge pickup and drove back to the truck stop.

The waitress looked surprised to see them again but didn't comment. She sat them at the same table. Sloan gave their order without looking at the menu.

When drinks and chips had been delivered, he leaned forward. "Want to talk about the meeting?" Before she could answer, he added, " 'Cause if you do, that's fine, and if you don't, that's fine, too. I didn't invite you to dinner to pump you for information. I want you to know that up front. We don't have to talk about it at all."

Sidney relaxed a little. If he was giving her all this attention just to find out about the committee vote, he was doing a good job of hiding it. "Mind if we talk about something else?"

"Not at all." He dipped a chip in the cheese sauce and handed it to her. "While we wait for our meal, I'll tell you about my grandfather. He was half Apache and half Irish. Lived along the South Fork of the Red River on a farm that mostly grew jackrab-bits."

Sidney listened to his stories of summers with his grandfather. The old man seemed a good sort, farming some, running a few cat-tle. Except, every Saturday night he drank himself senseless and howled at the moon, then got up Sunday morning and walked to church where he sang in the choir.

"He claimed his Irish blood made him drink, the Indian blood made him howl at the moon, and all of his ancestors' bad habits made him praise the Lord."

Sidney caught herself laughing at his story.

Sloan leaned across the table and took her hand as if he'd done so a thousand times. "You don't understand," he said, all serious. "My grandfather's people were all outlaws and thieves. Meanest folks who ever rode across West Texas. Most of them died in family feuds or from hanging by the neck. My grandfather decided early on if he didn't want to have to put up with them in the afterlife, he'd better sing in the choir every Sunday."

They were still laughing when the waitress brought their food. Sidney didn't notice the truck drivers and families with noisy children. To her, she was alone with Sloan and enjoying every minute. She relaxed and told him stories of her childhood, growing up with only women in the house.

She tasted his food. He ate off her plate complaining that she needed more hot sauce on everything. They drank coffee for so long that the third time the waitress came around, Sloan ordered sopaipillas so they wouldn't have to leave.

The fried bread tasted like refrigerator biscuits dropped in the fryer, but Sidney didn't complain.

He asked about her years in Chicago and

where she'd gone to school. His questions were easy to answer, nothing too personal. He talked about his college days at Texas Tech and the semester he forgot to go to one class. To his surprise, the instructor failed him, putting him on academic suspension.

When she looked shocked, he claimed it wasn't his fault, he couldn't find the classroom. She laughed until tears came when he told her his dad was so angry he made him drive a cattle truck back and forth from the feed lot to the packing house for an entire semester, hoping to teach him something about direction.

Finally, when the waitress refilled their coffee and told them it was closing time, he lifted his cup in salute. "I don't know when I've had such a fine dinner, Dr. Dickerson."

"Me, either," she admitted. "I'm still not crazy about Mexican food, but I enjoyed the company."

"You looking forward to the day off tomorrow?"

Sidney nodded. "I thought I'd drive over to Wichita Falls. There's a nurse in a retirement home over there who I'd like to visit with."

"The nurse who found Rosa Lee's body?"

She realized she'd said the comment casually, innocently, but he'd picked up on it.

A man of details, she reminded herself. Was he hunting for information, or only making conversation? It crossed her mind how little she knew about him despite all his tales.

"Yes," she said slowly.

He got the hint. "I wasn't trying to cross-examine you, Sidney. Only putting two and two together."

"I know," she answered, a bit too quickly.

He stood and dropped a few bills on the table, picked up the check and paid at the counter. They walked to his truck without saying a word.

The spell had been broken without either of them bringing up the vote to come. What hadn't been said hung between them like a declaration of war. He started the engine and flipped the radio on low, obviously uneasy with the silence.

He didn't ask where she lived, but drove to her bungalow beside the campus. Sloan managed to pick the right one in the row of ten even though her porch light wasn't on and he couldn't have seen the number.

When he reached her side of the truck, she'd already slid off the seat and stood with both feet firm on the ground. Where they should have been all evening, she reminded herself.

"Thank you for the dinner," she said as he walked her to her door.

"You're welcome," he answered formally.

When he reached the first step of her porch, he removed his hat and looked down. "I enjoyed the evening. That's the first meal I've had in two weeks where I could talk to someone."

She almost added, "Me, too." She usually ate in front of the TV watching the evening news. Somehow that made it seem as if she weren't eating alone.

He was halfway down the walk when she finally said, "Would you like to come with me to Wichita Falls tomorrow? I forgot to buy you that meal I said I'd buy." The old saying about keeping your friends close and your enemies closer came to mind.

He turned and smiled. "What time?"

"Nine."

"I'll be here."

She opened the screen door and pulled out her key. "Until then," she said, already worrying that she may have made a wrong move. But he had volunteered information about her grandmother and he'd been straightforward about his interest in the committee. The question remained, was he being honest about his interest in her?

"Until then," he echoed, then tipped his hat in farewell.

As she turned the knob and shoved the door, a yellow piece of paper fell out from where it had been slipped into the facing.

Sidney watched it float down to the porch without trying to catch it as Sloan's truck roared to life and he pulled away.

She'd already guessed what it would say. She didn't have to look.

Let the house fall.

Twenty

After the endless committee meeting, Billy Hatcher needed to work his muscles and let his brain relax. He changed clothes in the gym dressing room at the Y and caught the last half of a self-defense class for senior citizens. The best thing about being a member was that he could attend all classes. He might be sleeping on the back porch at Rosa Lee's house, but he had a place to shower and relax.

The sheriff had stepped in as the instructor for the night, so Billy knew he'd be welcomed in class.

By the time Billy walked on the mats offering to help, most of the citizens were tired and trying to ask questions about everything so Sheriff Farrington wouldn't give them any more exercises to do. Billy stretched using the breathing methods he'd learned in other classes as he listened to the sheriff try to fend off personal inquiries.

Granger Farrington explained that his wife was attending her baby shower and all husbands had been told to stay away. He complained about it, but everyone knew he went along with whatever Meredith asked him to do. He even admitted to volunteering for a night shift so Meredith and her friends could all go over and decorate the baby's room after the shower.

Twice, he tried to get the class back on track, but finally gave up ending with having them all yell "call 911" if they suspected trouble. While the seniors visited, the sheriff moved over to Billy. Having both been in the aikido classes together for a year, they moved easily into a workout.

Granger was stronger, more powerful, more advanced, but he wouldn't be for long. Billy had figured out within days of his first lesson in this art of self-defense that he learned more when practicing with someone better than himself. He could go through the steps, the breathing, the strength training alone, but he needed to practice with someone who challenged him.

When the sheriff easily twisted and knocked Billy to the mat, several of the senior citizens looked up in alarm. Farrington offered his hand and pulled Billy to his feet and smiled. Several in the class began to watch.

"Move through to conclusion the next time." Granger's order was kind. "Remember, once you set your course, no hesitation."

An hour later, both men were sweating and laughing. Billy had managed to knock the sheriff off his feet twice. Before long, he'd take every other fall.

"You're good, son."

"Thanks." Billy swung, almost tripping Granger. He liked it when the sheriff called him "son" even though Farrington wasn't old enough to be his father. He respected the man as much for what he didn't do when he could have as for what he did. If Sheriff Farrington had been a different kind of cop, Billy knew he'd be spending time in jail right now. But, without Billy saying a word in his own defense, Granger had sized up the situation and brought Billy in on a lesser charge when stolen goods were found in his father's garage. The deputy had assumed the worst but Granger had given Billy a chance without overwhelming him with lectures. He'd let the boy stand as a man.

Now, they were friends enough to tease. "Maybe it's not me, Sheriff." Billy laughed. "Maybe you're just getting old and slow."

Granger shifted, flattening Billy to the mat once more. "Not for a few years."

When the sheriff helped Billy up, he asked, "You doing anything tonight, Hatcher? Must not have a date if you're hanging around here."

"Typical Friday night on the wild side."

"How about riding along with me on rounds when we're cleaned up?"

Billy raised both eyebrows. "In the front seat?"

Granger laughed. "In the front seat."

Fifteen minutes later, Billy sat in the passenger side of Sheriff Farrington's squad car. Everything was in order and Granger was all business, even a little more bossy than usual. "Never drive the same route at the same time of day. Rounds are essential every night in a town this size, but never be predictable."

Billy was surprised the sheriff sounded as if he were still instructing a class.

"Never let down your guard, no matter how calm the night looks. One mistake could mean your life. A badge doesn't make you invisible. In fact, it could make you a target."

Billy shifted uneasily.

"It's wise to keep the tank at least half-full and all weapons loaded."

Billy twisted as far as he could in his seat belt. "All right. You can cut the instructor talk. I didn't know you invited me along to practice lecturing for your next recruit."

Granger smiled. "That is exactly what I'm doing. Only, I'm not practicing." He stopped the car in front of the station. "I'm asking, poorly I guess, if you'd be interested in working with me. You'd have to take several classes at the college, but I could put you on part-time on weekends, manning the office. Depending on how fast you can finish the classes, I'd like you to be a full deputy within two years, tops."

Billy couldn't form words. He figured he'd

be working for the lumberyard until he was as old as Sam Davis. He liked working with wood and didn't mind doing the jobs no one else wanted. He thought, with his record, he was lucky to have any job. If he kept his nose clean, maybe in a few years he'd save enough to buy a trailer and build on until it looked like a real house.

"You're offering me a job?" he finally managed to say.

"More than that, son," Granger said. "I'm offering you a career. One you'll never get rich doing. One where you'll hear far more complaints than praise. But one you can be proud doing. If money's a problem, I'll pay your first semester's tuition and then deduct it from your wages. For a while, you could still work at the lumberyard, take classes a few nights a week and work for me on weekends."

"That doesn't leave much time for getting in trouble."

Granger laughed. "True. What do you say?" The sheriff offered his hand.

Billy took it. "Thanks." He wanted to ask why, but didn't dare.

"It won't be easy, but like they say, nothing worth having ever is." Granger put the car in gear and continued on his rounds. "You'll have to find an apartment somewhere. You'll need an address on the application."

"How'd you know?" Billy only went home to his dad's house when he had to. He hadn't bothered to show up when Billy had been arrested and barely talked to him when his son came by. With the shower at the Y he planned to stay away until the weather made sleeping out impossible. "What about my record?"

"It'll give you headaches for a few years, but you'll outgrow it. The lumberyard says you never miss a day, and by the time you finish school you'll have enough experience to go anywhere you want and work on a force." Granger glanced at Billy. "But, you've got to keep your nose clean until then. No fights. No problems. You even show up at the wrong place at the wrong time, it won't look good."

"I understand." Billy had a feeling this was a onetime offer. "When do I start?"

Granger laughed. "Come by tomorrow morning. I'll be in the office working on paperwork. We'll get all the forms filled out and I'll show you around. If you survive six months and a semester of classes, I'll put you in uniform."

Billy was silent a long while. "Thanks isn't enough," he finally said, fully realizing the sheriff had just changed his life.

"You'll do the same one day for another," Granger said. "I just did."

Billy suddenly understood the sheriff and where he'd come from.

They rode in silence for a while then casually they began to talk. Billy had a million questions about the law. They turned onto Cemetery Road and headed back toward town.

With an unexpected jerk, Granger pulled his patrol car off the road into brown weeds as high as his window.

"Stay here." The sheriff cut the engine and rolled both front windows down a few inches. "Don't move until I get back. I didn't plan on this tonight."

As he climbed from the car, he kicked at a dried tumbleweed while he unbuckled his belt and laid his revolver over the seat. After putting his hat inside, he leaned down and ordered. "Lock the door and don't open it unless I say so. I don't want to scare the rustlers into thinking they're surrounded."

Billy could feel his heart in his throat. He thought of reaching for the gun. He'd feel better holding it. But the sheriff hadn't handed it to him, he'd left it in the seat.

He watched as the sheriff stepped through the barbed-wire fence that framed the sides of the cemetery. The lawman's shadow moved between the graves, but Billy couldn't hear or see much of anything else.

Finally, after endless minutes passed, voices drifted on the cold wind. "Get that one!"

"No don't cut there."

"Oh, you're doing it all wrong."

"Let me have the sharper knife."

Billy locked his fingers together. Part of him wanted to go help the sheriff. Pretty much all of him voted for picking up the gun, but he knew he'd better follow orders.

Maybe this was a test, he thought. If he moved, Granger would take back his job offer.

"Grab that one!" a woman's voice yelled.

"Don't tell me what to do!"

Billy tried to place the angry voices. He'd

heard them before. But then, he'd heard everyone in town before.

"Look at you. You've got mud all over your shoes," one said.

"How do you know that?" another asked. "I can't see a thing out here."

"Well, I can. I've got the sight of a cat in the dark."

"How do you know what a cat sees in the dark?"

Billy stared as two rounded shadows came into view and the voices registered in his mind. Both carried buckets and what looked like weapons. The Rogers sisters.

The sheriff's order came from somewhere in the darkness. "All right ladies, put down your shovels, knives and buckets. I'm taking you in this time."

One of the sisters swung her knife, looking like a samurai bobble doll. "We're not going in!"

The other bumped her with her shoulder. "Oh, stop it Ada May. You'll frighten the sheriff. He's not going to arrest us."

Granger moved from the shadows. "Oh, yes I am. I've warned you two for the last time."

Billy watched, feeling as though he were

in some kind of alternate universe where little old ladies fought the cops.

The sheriff herded them toward the patrol car. "You can't go around cutting branches off other people's plants. Not even those in a cemetery."

"But we're Rose Rustlers," Beth Ann answered. "Haven't you heard of our group? The first rule is to be polite and ask."

"And we did," Ada May interrupted. "Not a soul answered, so we figured it was all right."

"I've heard of your group, but nowhere does the Web site say you are allowed to steal roses from cemeteries that have No Trespassing signs posted after dark."

Beth Ann handed over her knife. "But no one will let us cut them during the day."

Ada May moved her bucket behind her. "Besides, we're not doing any harm. We're only taking a few clippings."

"Billy," Granger shouted. "Open the back doors. We're taking these women to jail."

Even Billy wanted to argue, but he thought it wise to keep his mouth closed. As he helped the old maids into the back, both thanked him and told him what a nice young man he was.

Granger locked their buckets and knives up in the trunk and drove toward town. The women complained all the way. Ada May insisted she knew her rights, but then couldn't list any when the sheriff asked, except the right to remain silent. Beth Ann worried about whether or not the sheriff got the mud off the knife because she feared it might dull the blade if it was allowed to dry. She wanted him to stop the car and check.

Granger helped them up the back stairs at the station. Billy watched as he handcuffed them together and pulled out a long piece of paper from his right desk drawer. If he was trying to frighten them, he had his work cut out for him.

Billy leaned against the counter and listened, wondering what this lawman he always thought had good sense planned to do with his latest two criminals.

"We get one phone call," Ada May demanded. "I know the law."

"Okay." Granger turned the phone around so she could reach it. "Who you going to wake up after midnight, Miss Rogers?"

Ada May thought a minute and turned to her sister. "You still got that card with the number on it?"

"Not him!" Beth Ann put her hand over her heart.

"He's already helped us once. After what we did, he probably couldn't think much lower of us. Maybe he'll help us again?"

"You threw up in his car," Beth Ann whispered.

"Well, you stripped," Ada May whispered back as the sheriff tried to act as if he didn't hear and Billy turned red.

Beth Ann passed her sister the card and Ada May dialed a number. "Hello, Reverend Parker. Did I wake you?"

Dumb question, Billy thought.

"It's Ada May Rogers and there's been a misunderstanding on Sheriff Granger's part. We need an angel of mercy to bail us out. Would you come down and tell the man that we are not criminals?"

Ada May waited a few seconds and hung up the phone.

"Is this angel of mercy coming?" Granger asked.

"I think so. He dropped the phone," she answered.

Beth Ann moved forward in her chair. "I get a phone call, too."

Granger's stern frown cracked. "Who do you want to wake up, Miss Beth Ann?"

"No one. I want to call Randi at the bar. I'm sure she's still awake."

Granger shoved the phone closer to the second sister in crime. "Go ahead. If nothing else, Randi will get a kick out of this."

After the second call, the sheriff tried to explain how dangerous it was for two women of their age to be tromping around in the mud at midnight. He didn't want to take legal action, but since they didn't seem to understand the word *stop,* he saw no other choice.

Both women dummied up.

"Look," Granger pleaded. "What if one of you fell and broke a leg?"

They didn't answer.

"This is the third time I've caught you out where you had no business being." He stared at them. "Empty your pockets."

They didn't move.

"Empty your pockets!"

Beth Ann pulled out several tissues and a half-full bag of M&M's. Ada May slowly laid a pair of wire cutters on the desk and then stared at them as if she'd never seen them before.

"Just as I thought. You cut the barbed wire on the cemetery fence."

"Well, you didn't expect us to jump over it, Granger. Honestly, what a foolish idea." Ada May looked at him as if he were not as bright as she gave him credit for being.

"Not only were you trespassing, you were damaging property."

"What property? The fence is down on the back side of the cemetery anyway and I didn't hear any of the residents complaining."

A sleepy-looking Reverend Parker and an angry Randi Howard rushed through the door at the same time. Micah tried to ask questions, but the redhead stormed Granger in full attack.

"Where do you get off arresting these two old dears, Granger? I swear, you've got oatmeal for brains."

"Now calm down, Randi." Granger stood.

Randi shoved a finger into his chest.

To Billy's surprise, the sheriff took a step back.

"Who's an old dear?" Ada May asked.

"We are," Beth Ann mumbled.

"How can I calm down when you've arrested them?" Randi took the time to smile at the sisters, then turned back to Granger. "You've put handcuffs on them! Take those things off of them right now."

Billy watched as Micah stepped between the sheriff and Randi Howard. "Calm down, Randi," he said as if he knew the bar owner. "Granger, what has happened here and what can we do to help?"

"Help!" Randi yelled moving forward, but letting Micah hold her back with one arm. "First you get my friend pregnant and now you're out arresting old ladies. I swear, if you don't straighten up I'm running against you next election."

Granger grinned. "Now, Randi, it's not like I tricked Meredith into sleeping with me after the prom. We've been married two years. And as for these two, I caught them stomping around a closed and gated cemetery in the dark carrying knives and buckets."

Randi and Micah both turned to the Rogers sisters.

When neither of them said anything, Randi asked, "Is that true?"

"Guilty as charged." Ada May squared

her shoulders. "We've been out saving antique roses. The sheriff will not let us do it in
daylight, so we've gone underground."

"Undercover," Beth Ann corrected. "We're
guilty, all right. We did the crime and we'll do
the time."

"Unbelievable." Micah rubbed his forehead.

"I'm willing to release them, in your custody, if they both promise not to break into
any place at night again." He thought about
it a moment and decided he needed to add,
"Or any other time, night or day."

Both sisters were silent.

Granger waited.

Beth Ann broke first. "If we don't promise,
do we have to spend the night in jail?"

"Yes," Granger answered without any hint
of a smile.

Micah opened his mouth to argue, but
Granger raised his hand for the preacher to
remain silent.

"We'd need to pack overnight bags," Ada
May said, her chin shaking slightly. "And put
the rose clippings in water."

"No bags. No water. You'll have to sleep
in your clothes and those clippings will stay

in my trunk where they're bound to dry up by morning. You'll get what every criminal gets. One phone call. One blanket. You've already had your call."

Both women looked horrified. Billy noticed Randi and Micah had moved behind the criminals' chairs and both were fighting to keep straight faces.

Beth Ann looked pitiful. "Do we have to sleep in our teeth, too?"

Granger nodded. "And without a pillow."

Beth Ann whispered, "I've heard the toilet is in the center of the cell."

Granger nodded.

She paled and broke. "Oh, all right. I promise."

Ada May snorted. "Well, I can't very well go rustling without you. You drive the getaway van." She glared at the sheriff. "I promise."

Granger leaned forward and unlocked the handcuffs. "All right ladies, you can go, but I don't want any more trouble. I need to be getting home to my wife, not driving around looking for you two."

They refused to speak to him as they marched out, heads held high.

When the room was silent, Granger

turned to Billy. "There's no such thing as a typical night. Sure you still want the job?"

"You bet." Billy straightened, feeling a pride grow in him. "No hesitation."

Twenty-One

Micah followed Randi Howard as she drove the Rogers sisters' old Suburban back from Cemetery Road. He swore the thing slung mud for half a mile, causing him to wonder where else the sisters might have been tonight. He and Randi had taken the criminals home, then dropped off Randi's car at the bar before going out to claim the sisters' van.

He pulled up as Randi parked in the old maids' drive and climbed out. He studied her as she moved toward his car. *A long-legged, spitfire of a woman,* he thought. The sheriff must have known she'd yell at him, but he didn't seem too bothered by it. Granger knew Randi and accepted her; it was obvious they were friends. Micah had never known a woman so full of life and energy. If she'd been a tent preacher, she'd have been *hellfire-and-brimstone.*

"What you smiling at?" Randi climbed in beside him.

"I was thinking that I'd want you on my side in a fight," he said as she twisted his mirror and scrubbed a line of mud off her cheek.

"You get in a lot of fights, Preacher?" She tossed her leather jacket between them and rolled down her window. The night wind caught her hair as he put the car in motion, but she didn't seem to mind.

When he didn't answer her question, she leaned her head against the headrest and closed her eyes. They drove back to her bar without a word. He pulled around back, but didn't cut the engine.

"I'd invite you in," she said in her midnight voice. "But you wouldn't come, would you?"

The words not said seemed a wall between them. They both knew he wanted to. They both knew he wouldn't.

"No," he answered. What was it about this woman that made him be so honest? It would have sounded so much better if he'd been polite. Thanked her. Claimed he was tired. Used any excuse. But what would it matter—anything else would be a lie.

"Fair enough." She was gone before he could even think of how to say goodbye.

He sat for a while, trying to decide what to do. He could use a friend. A real friend. And he had a feeling whether they saw each other or not, she'd be in his thoughts. Everything about this town reminded him of her. He couldn't run at night without circling by the bar, or eat breakfast without thinking of the steak and eggs they'd shared. A few times he'd heard someone say a word in just the way Randi, with her accent that belonged nowhere but Texas, would have said it. Micah caught himself thinking, *That's how Randi would have put it.* But he couldn't voice his observation because no one knew they were friends.

He gripped the wheel. It was time he admitted, at least to himself, that he was attracted to her. He knew he'd never do anything about it, but being honest helped. Just knowing a woman existed in this world who he might be attracted to if they spent time together made him realize he had to go on living.

As he threw the car in gear, he spotted her jacket folded next to him. He cut the engine and picked it up. He'd go in and give it back to her, then leave. Who knows, he thought, maybe they'd talk a few minutes and get back to that easy kidding they'd had before. He wouldn't say he'd call or come by, she wouldn't offer again, but they'd be more comfortable if fate, or the Rogers sisters, tossed them together again.

He climbed out of the car and headed for the back door. Reaching up, he flipped the latch above the rear entrance and stepped inside, guessing she'd see the light and know someone was coming in from the back door.

The kitchen was empty when he walked down the hallway and he saw no light coming from upstairs. He crossed to her office. All the lights were still on and music played, but no one was there. When he looked through the glass, only the twinkle lights greeted him in the empty bar beyond the one-way mirror. He smiled, remembering the days he'd worked in a place like this.

There was nothing quite as lonely as a bar after closing time.

He walked around the desk planning to drape her coat over the office chair when he saw her through the glass. For a moment he could only stare at the view through the mirror.

Randi moved across the tiny dance floor, dancing alone. Her arms were raised, as if she had an invisible partner guiding her around. Her steps were wide, bold as she circled, lost in the rhythm of an old country-western tune.

Something bumped against the wall near the hallway leading back to the kitchen. The bearded bartender Randi called Frankie banged his way in with a load of boxes.

Micah didn't know what to say. He nodded once toward the man.

"Evenin'." Frankie sat the load down. "That's it from the basement," he mumbled more to himself than Micah. "Tell Randi everything's locked up and I'm heading home."

Micah turned back to the mirror wondering why Frankie hadn't bothered to ask why he stood in Randi's office. Maybe Randi had told him where she had gone earlier. Maybe

Frankie figured she trusted him. Maybe a man hanging around after closing wasn't all that unusual.

Micah didn't want to think about it. He just wanted to watch her for a minute. "She's something, dancing like that."

Frankie moved a step closer to the mirror and joined Micah. "She does that sometimes, dances all alone. Before her husband died, she used to wear out half the cowboys in the place dancing with them. Her Jimmy wasn't much of a dancer, but he liked to watch her move. Since he died, I haven't seen her dance any way but like that. All alone. Like she's dancing with a ghost."

Micah couldn't take his eyes off her.

Frankie's footsteps sounded in the hallway, then the back door closed. Micah thought of what Lora had said about Rosa Lee waiting all her life to live and he realized that was what most people in the world do. They wait until they're older, richer, thinner—whatever—before they step out.

But not Randi. She'd dance even if she had to do it alone.

He placed her jacket on the desk and pushed through the swinging door. She didn't see him until he'd lifted the pass-through and stood at the edge of the dance floor.

Slowly, she lowered her arms. "You forget something?"

Micah smiled. "I thought I'd come back for a dance."

She smiled. "I'm surprised you two-step, Preacher."

"I don't. You'll have to teach me." He offered his hand.

She laughed. "You're either the dumbest man I ever met, or the smartest. I can't figure out which. All right, I'll give you the five-minute lesson."

Twenty minutes later she swore he must be brain-dead. He couldn't seem to get the idea that the two-step only had two steps. "I don't even want to try a waltz with you. My feet would never live through the lesson."

Then she laughed softly against his ear and they tried again.

When, finally, they were too tired to dance, they made breakfast and talked. He told her about the people at the church, the ones he loved, the ones who drove him crazy. He told her things he'd never told anyone about how he sometimes felt in his job. How he loved the teaching and never saw himself taking over the running of a church.

They drifted easily from dreams and hopes to a listing of their day as if they'd talked a thousand times.

After Micah had filled her in on the committee meeting, Randi told of the legends and stories of Clifton Creek. He listened carefully to the details about Henry Altman and his daughter Rosa Lee.

Finally, he told her about the decision the committee would have to make. It felt so good to talk to someone about it.

She had her own ideas about who might be causing trouble. She named a few of the oil companies, a group of wild kids who sometimes destroyed things around town, and to Micah's surprise, she mentioned an old rancher named Luther Oates. Luther and Henry Altman had been best of friends even though Luther was younger.

"Wouldn't a friend want the house to stand?" Micah asked.

"Probably," she said as she sat, her legs crossed under her. "But talk is some of the founding fathers had strong ideals back in the early years of Clifton Creek. Men who were leaders, men like Talon Graham's great-grandfather and Henry Altman were rumored to be linked to a murder, but no one could prove it."

"Really?"

Randi laughed. "I wouldn't be pulling your leg, Preacher. You might want to start dancing again."

Micah laughed and leaned back in his chair. "Well, thanks for listening to me rattle on."

"Anytime."

They both stood. She followed him to the back door and they said good-night without either of them realizing how little of the night was left.

Twenty-Two

Billy spread his bedroll on the back porch of Rosa Lee's house and slid inside. The night would probably be over before he could sleep. "You're not going to believe what happened, Miss Altman," he said into the shadows as if she were listening just on the other side. "The sheriff asked me if I wanted a job. Imagine that. Me."

He laid his head on his hands and looked out at the night. "Now that it's happened, I can see he's been watching me for a long time." Billy felt like a fool for talking to himself, but he had to tell someone, even a ghost. No one would see it, but Billy felt like he and Miss Rosa Lee were a lot alike. She didn't have much family. Folks didn't include her. She was a loner, living out here in this house all by herself.

He grinned. If he'd lived back years ago, he bet they would have been friends. She'd probably have him over to dinner or maybe they'd set on the porch and have lemonade. She couldn't have been a bad sort. After all, she gave Sam Davis a drink and Billy would bet a week's pay the man had been as much of a pain as a kid as he was now as an old man.

Maybe, if they'd known each other, he would have fixed up some of the things Rosa Lee let fall down. It was obvious no one had taken care of this place for years. Even the trellises for the roses looked as if she'd built them herself. The roof sagged in one place, most of the gutters were down, and vines must be growing into the mortar on all sides of the house.

Yes, sir. They'd have been friends. They would have talked.

Dried leaves rattled. Billy sat up listening. He'd protect her place now, he thought. It's something friends do.

The leaves rustled again. Billy stood on stockinged feet and moved to the corner of the porch where no one would see him. For

October, the night wasn't particularly cold, at least not sheltered on the porch, out of the wind, but there was a dampness to the air that made it seem colder.

"Billy?" came a whisper. "Billy Hatcher? You here?"

"Lora?" He relaxed. "What are you doing out here?" He moved to the edge of the porch where she stood in the pale moonlight. She looked as if she'd just left a party. High heels, short black dress, little jacket made of material that was almost see-through.

She shrugged. "Seems like this place draws me after dark." She laughed. "Maybe I'm a vampire here to suck your blood."

She didn't quite carry off her casual air. Something was wrong, he could hear it in her voice, see it in the way she moved.

"What's happened?" he asked.

She took a long breath and said, "Mind if I come in and sit down? I kind of need a friend right now."

He could smell the alcohol on her breath as he offered his hand. "Watch out for the second step. It's about to give way."

"If I broke the board, cut my leg and had to have it amputated, that would be on par with the evening for me." She stomped onto the second step. "Of course, then I could buy shoes at half price. My budget could use the break. Panty hose might be a problem."

He laughed as she continued to imagine life with one leg while they crossed to where his bedroll had been spread in the moonlight at the far end of the porch.

They sat cross-legged on his sleeping bag. Her face was in shadow, but he would almost bet she'd been crying. She tugged off her shoe, tried to pull her skirt down, then gave up and hugged her knees.

Billy grabbed his jacket and leaned forward to put it around her. "You okay, Whitman?"

"Yeah, just a little shaken. I've had a rough night. I had to walk from the interstate." She tossed her other shoe a few feet away. "When I passed here, I thought you might be sleeping on the porch keeping an eye on the place. I decided to stop by and get warm before walking the rest of the way home."

"Start from the beginning. Car trouble?" He found that hard to believe since her daddy ran the dealership, but maybe it was a case of the cobbler's children having no shoes.

She shook her head. "More like cowboy trouble. I think I've just had the worst date of my life."

Billy lay down a few feet away and waited. He figured she'd tell him all she wanted him to know. Even if she didn't tell him anything, it felt good to know that she came to him to talk. For as long as he could remember, he'd been thought of as the town drunk's kid and no one his age offered even casual friendship. He almost told her that the reason he watched her all those years ago was that she had never been rude to him. In his world, not being picked on by someone was a real plus. He wasn't sure, but he thought she'd even smiled at him once when he'd held a door for all the cheerleaders.

Lora pushed her hair back from her face. "I went over to Wichita Falls with Talon Graham. Man, was that a mistake."

"The guy who brought you the poster?"

"Right. I figured I owed him something."

Billy swore. "So you went out dressed like fresh meat."

She laughed. "I guess it did seem something like that. Anyway, we had dinner. He spent most of it telling me how important it was that his company get the Altman land. He drank way too much, then he wanted to go dancing out near North Scott Street. By midnight, he was in no shape to drive home so I asked him to give me the keys."

"Let me guess," Billy interrupted. "He said no."

"Right. In fact he gave me a choice. Let him drive home, or spend the night in Wichita Falls. He seemed to think I should be honored that he was even considering sleeping with me on our first date." She hugged her bare legs. "Like a fool, I'd left my purse at home thinking I'd be dancing and didn't want to worry about it. Dumb. I also abandoned my cell for fear my mother would call wanting updates on my first date since the divorce."

"Dumb," Billy agreed.

"I know, but I've been out of the dating pool for a few years." She pushed her toes beneath the edge of his sleeping bag. "Anyway I tried to talk it over with him, but got nowhere, so I walked out."

"Why didn't you call someone?"

"Who? You're pretty much the only friend

I have in town. My mother made a point of telling me they'd leave a door unlocked no matter how late I got in. She and Dad have been trying to match me up with Talon ever since they found out he's heir to the Graham ranch north of here. He plays the rich grandson to the hilt, but I've got the feeling his grandfather is making him prove himself in business before he turns over the running of a ranch. He mumbled on for half an hour about how important it was that we see it their way and give the Altman land over to them."

"So, how'd you get here?"

"I walked for a while after I left Talon. The place was out of town, but I noticed an all night café at the crossroad. I sat there for a while, telling the waitress my problems when some truckers hauling cattle came in to refill their Thermoses. One of the trucks had Wichita County Feed Lot on the side, so I asked the driver if he was heading anywhere near Clifton Creek."

"He gave you a ride." Billy couldn't believe anyone would turn her down.

"Yeah. Said he was on a tight schedule and had to drop me off at the turnoff, but he did ask me for a date."

Billy laughed. "You didn't say yes because you were beholden to him did you?"

"No. I've learned my lesson. I did tell him I'd give him a real good deal on a new car. That seemed to cheer him up."

"It's over two miles from the interstate."

"You're telling me. I had time to think of a dozen ways I'd probably be killed before I reached Main." She rubbed her feet. "Not the least of which was freezing to death. Whoever made that rule about women never wearing open toed shoes after Labor Day might have had a good idea. I can't seem to stop shivering."

"I could drive you home?"

"No thanks. I don't think I could face a cross-exam right now and knowing mother, she's waiting up. I thought she was determined to get me married off before, but this time I'm like damaged goods, and she's put me on the 'must go' table."

"Want to share my bedroll until you get warm or it gets late enough to be safe to go home?"

Lora looked up. "As a friend?"

"As a friend." Billy opened the old sleeping bag and slid as far as he could to the back half. He lay on his side, his arm extended.

She hesitantly slid in beside him, her back to him, and rested her head on his arm as he laid the top half over them both. They lay side by side for a few minutes until the warmth relaxed them.

"This is great," she whispered. "I'm starting to feel my toes again. Another block and I think they would have fallen off and started rolling down the street ahead of me."

He didn't answer.

"I hope Talon's out there looking for me, but more likely, he's passed out over the table. I could tell something was bothering him when he picked me up. I should have canceled the date right then. He must have taken a dozen cell calls during dinner. He'd leave the table for a while, then come back and order another drink. Something, besides me, was ruining his night."

She stretched and moved her hair above Billy's arm, then tucked the cover around her as if building a nest. Their bodies brushed lightly in several places as their combined warmth took the chill off the inside of the bag.

"Billy, what you thinking?"

He didn't answer.

"You asleep?" She rolled a few inches until her shoulder touched his.

"No," he finally whispered. "I'm just trying not to think about how you used to jump."

She stabbed him in the ribs with her elbow and he let out a groan.

"Thanks," he whispered out of breath. "That helped."

She giggled and cuddled next to him, spooning against him for warmth.

Billy closed his eyes and tried to give up thinking all together. This had been one hell of a night.

Twenty-Three

Micah let himself into his duplex and paused to listen, making sure all was calm. Mrs. Mac's TV still sounded through the open door. He checked on Logan. The boy had kicked off his cover, but was sound asleep. The kitten, curled on Logan's extra pillow, opened one eye, then went back to sleep. Micah pulled off his shoes and moved into Mrs. Mac's quarters. She snored away in her extended recliner. He turned down the TV and covered her with a blanket. He'd made the mistake of switching off the set once and she'd jumped with the shock of sudden silence.

When he moved down the hall to his bedroom, he fought the urge to practice the two-step. It had taken Randi an hour to teach him enough so that they moved smoothly. Then, they'd danced like he'd never thought he'd dance in his life, fluid and free, as if blowing in the breeze.

If anyone had seen them dancing, they would have thought it strange, the preacher and the bar owner. But, somehow they'd found the one thing they could do together. He told himself they could never be lovers. Dating was probably out of the question. Neither wanted any involvement.

But they could dance. He could hold her close, feel her heart beat. For a short time, he wouldn't be so alone and maybe she wouldn't either. He'd never danced with Amy, so Micah didn't feel as if he were replacing his wife. The feel of Randi in his arms took the edge off his loneliness. Maybe it did the same for her.

He pulled off his clothes and fell into bed, thankful tomorrow was Saturday and maybe Logan would let him sleep until nine. The boy's favorite thing to do on Saturday morning was to sneak the cereal and milk into Mrs. Mac's place. They'd eat together and watch cartoons until Micah awoke. It was their special time together.

Closing his eyes, he guessed Mrs. Mac would probably get her fill of cartoons and Cheerios tomorrow. Just before he fell asleep, he reached for his other pillow, pulling it against him. But tonight, it was Randi he pulled into his embrace, not Amy.

Twenty-Four

The phone rang as Sidney pulled her keys from her purse. She'd given up on waiting for Sloan McCormick and decided to drive over to Wichita Falls alone to visit with Dr. Eastland's old nurse. Sloan might have some reason for not showing up, or he could have changed his mind about wanting to go with her. Either way, talking to the person who'd found Rosa Lee's body had to take priority.

She caught the call on the third ring, already preparing to hear his excuse. "Hello," she almost shouted.

"Professor Dickerson?" The voice was definitely not Sloan McCormick's.

"Yes." She straightened, all business.

"This is Mayor Dunley. I hate to bother you so early on this Saturday morning, but I'm feeling some pressure to find an answer to the Altman house problem and I need to know if anything was decided yesterday." He hesitated. "I tried to phone last night, but you must have gone to bed early."

Sidney wasn't aware the house, or her private life, was a problem. The mayor had made serving on the committee sound like an honor only a few weeks ago. Now, it was a problem he felt he had to check on.

"What kind of pressure?" She knew offers were coming in to buy or lease the land, but the oil companies surely could wait a few days—after all, the oil, if it was down there, had been beneath the land for hundreds of thousands of years.

"I got a call about an hour ago from Howard Drilling. They're interested in placing a bid, even though they say they've got all they can handle right now. Normally, I'd want to give it to a local company, but Talon Graham's been in my office every day this week. He seems to think that since his grandfather owned a ranch north of town, he's local even if he did grow up in Austin. If you add those two offers to the one a man named McCormick set on my desk Friday afternoon, that's three."

Sidney remained silent. Sloan must have made his offer Friday while the committee was meeting, but true to his word, he hadn't mentioned it to her. He'd said any offer made would be between the mayor and him.

The mayor cleared his throat. "I told both Talon Graham and Howard Drilling that they'd have an answer as soon as possible."

"Can they lease the oil rights and not bother the house?"

"No. Both claim the house is on the crest and that's where the drilling needs to be. Talon suggested moving the house, but it would crumble for sure if we tried anything like that. Even the Harvey brothers, who moved picky Old Man Hamm's house to town, aren't up for a job like that." The mayor laughed. "I forget you're not from around here and don't know everyone, but you've probably seen Old Man Hamm. He's got six kids living in the county, not counting grandkids and greats, and far as I know not one of them speaks to him."

Sidney glanced out the window. She

really didn't have time to play the mayor's favorite game of who is related to whom in Wichita County. Since she had no roots here, he always took it on himself to go over local family trees with her.

The mayor grew silent for a minute. "I told Talon we'd have an answer in a few days. He's really in a hurry to know. He seems to think this job is vital to his career, even though we all know he's only in the oil business until he decides to run for election."

Sidney didn't want to get into another long discussion about someone she didn't know. "The committee meets again Wednesday, but I'll call everyone and tell them to be ready to vote. As far as Talon Graham goes, I've never met him, so his impatience isn't my concern."

"Oh, you'd know him if you saw him," the mayor told her. "Looks just like his father."

Sidney crossed her eyes in frustration. "I assure you, the committee is working, Mayor. We'll have a decision as soon as possible."

The mayor coughed into the phone. "I'm sure you are, and I want you to know I'm not trying to influence you in any way. Just let you know the facts. A group out of Dallas wrote saying they would take a look at the place to see if it qualified as a historical site, but they didn't much think it would. If the committee goes that direction, you'll make a lot of the older residents happy and I promise you we'll try to survive without the extra revenue."

"Thank you, Mayor. I'm glad you're not trying to influence me."

"You're welcome. It's the only fair way, but I got to tell you I don't know how the town will pay the bills this winter much less come up with any money for fixing up the house. I had to pull the money for the new window out of our snowplow budget. We'll just have to hope it doesn't snow bad enough to close the roads before Christmas."

"I understand." His not-so-subtle hints were growing stronger with each passing minute.

When he began telling her about the snow of 1970 that closed even the interstate, she leaned away from the phone enough to see out the window. Sloan pulled up in his pickup and stepped out. His long legs looked even longer in jeans. She had no idea what he'd been like as a young man, but she had a feeling he was in his prime in his forties. The slight gray at his temples suited him, as did the laugh lines.

"I have an appointment," Sidney interrupted the mayor. "I hate to leave, but I must if I plan to be ready for the vote Wednesday."

He mumbled something about telling her more later and hung up.

The doorbell rang just as she put the phone back in place.

"Morning," Sloan said when she opened the door. "Sorry, I'm late."

She waited for him to explain, but he didn't. After an awkward pause, she held up her hand for him to wait for her on the porch. Stepping back into the hallway, she grabbed her briefcase and purse. Sidney thought of telling him about the mayor's phone call, but wasn't sure how much she wanted him to know. A tiny part of her couldn't shake the feeling that he might be playing her for information. Maybe he even thought she'd swing the committee his direction if he flirted with her.

When she stepped outside and locked her door, she asked as casually as if they were simply going for a drive, "I forgot to of-fer to take my Jeep."

Sloan glanced over at the rusting Jeep parked in the carport beside her bungalow.

"If you'd like to drive?" He studied her car as if trying to decide if he'd fit into the thing. "We can take whatever you like."

"I hate to drive," she admitted. "And sometimes my Jeep hates to run."

He relaxed. "I guess living on campus you don't drive often."

"Right." She walked toward his pickup. "It does have its disadvantages. Students drop by without calling sometimes. Usually to turn in late papers as if shoving them under my door at 11:59 p.m. still counts." She thought of adding that sometimes anony-mous people dropped off yellow slips of pa-per telling her how to vote, but if he didn't know about the paper, she wasn't about to tell him.

"Everyone in town knows where you live," he added more as a statement than a ques-tion. He helped her into the truck.

"I wondered how you knew which place was mine last night."

He closed the door without commenting.

He seemed preoccupied, not fully in the conversation.

While he walked around to his side, she noticed he'd cleaned up his work space between the seats. His small laptop was off and folded into a pouch. The papers and notepads were all stuffed into a pocket. The cords to cell phones, computer or whatever he used were gone. Even the cups of half-finished coffee usually stuffed in his holders had disappeared.

When he climbed in, she noticed he'd dressed more casually today. Boots, jeans, pressed shirt. The shirt was a pale blue, not white, with snaps not buttons. The boots expensive, but worn.

"Ready?" He started the engine without waiting for an answer.

She wanted to ask him again how he knew where she lived. Another time, she decided. She only nodded and opened her briefcase. As he drove, she told him all the information about Rosa Lee that she had found in the county records. The woman had been born in 1910 and had died ninety-two years later. Her mother had died the day she was born with Rosa Lee being her first and only child.

Sidney glanced at Sloan. He didn't interrupt, in fact she wasn't even sure he was listening.

"Rosa Lee must have been friends with my grandmother Minnie during her short stay in Clifton Creek during the Depression," Sidney continued, needing to organize the facts whether he listened or not. "Minnie couldn't have lived here long for my mother's birth certificate was registered in Chicago on April 3, 1934."

"You have no proof they knew each other?" Sloan interrupted, finally interested.

She shook her head. "I remember Grandmother Minnie talking about how she and my grandfather married and worked the farm until fall. Then, she stayed in Texas while he went north to find work. He had family he stayed with and saved money until they had enough for her to join him."

"Times must have been hard then," he said, more to himself than her. "But, at least they had each other."

She knew without asking that no one waited for him.

Sidney flipped to Henry Altman. "Rosa Lee's father was born 1878, one record shows he died in 1964, the same year I was born."

"Me, too," Sloan added. "Sixty-four must have been a good year for everyone but old Henry."

"Strange thing is, everyone thought of him as the father of the town even though it had never been official. He established one of the first ranches in Wichita County, shipping cattle as soon as the railroads came in. He donated the land for the railroad station and the city hall. He was remembered as a kind man who did a great deal to help others." Sidney paused and lowered her voice. "But, the paper reported that he was buried next to his wife in the Wichita County cemetery without a funeral. Not even a graveside. Apparently, Rosa Lee refused all visitors."

"Strange."

"I read through the society notes from back then. She was never mentioned, not before or after her father died."

"Maybe she just didn't like people?" Sloan pulled around an eighteen-wheeler.

"Probably," Sidney said halfheartedly. "Rosa Lee never married. Fell on hard times in her later years and died penniless except for the forty acres she still owned where the house and her gardens stand. In her last few years some people said she kept her money hidden away in her house, but more likely, she'd been selling off first land and later furniture to live."

"You think there's more to the story than just a dislike of people?"

"Maybe, but we'll never know."

"Lonely life," Sloan said. "Maybe she was homely, or had a wart on her nose. Or bald. I had an aunt once. Head looked like a bowling ball. We all figured she'd be an old maid for sure, but one day she brought home the hairiest man you've ever seen. He was crazy in love with her and she said he kept her warm at night."

Sidney laughed. "You have an interesting family, Mr. McCormick, but Rosa Lee wasn't ugly. I have a picture of her." Sidney pulled a small framed picture out of her briefcase. "The librarians found it on a shelf among the books. It seemed she never gave away or sold a single book all her life. Books and roses were her loves, I guess."

Sloan took the picture. "She looks sad," he said handing it back. "She also could've been an ancestor of yours. Same strong chin."

Sidney smiled. "Not likely, my grandmother's people were from Tennessee. The few my father had were from Chicago. I've got a box of the most bored-looking ancestors you've ever seen. Mother's side in Confederate uniforms, Father's in Union. My grandmother Minnie used to laugh and say even though they married seventy years after the War Between the States, some of her relatives never forgave her for marrying a Yankee."

He laughed. "I come from a family like that. I'm not sure some to this day would be too fond of you. They'd still hear that hint of northern accent in your speech."

"I don't have an accent."

"I know, but I like you anyway."

She couldn't help herself, she had to say, "Why?"

He backed off the gas a little. "You have no idea, do you?"

"What?"

"How intelligent you are. Or what a fine-looking woman lies beneath that brain." He said it more as a statement than a compliment. "I guess with teaching eighteen-year-olds you must see yourself as older."

"And what do you see?"

"You probably don't want to know."

"I think I do." She didn't want to admit it but he was right about her looking at her students with their cute young bodies and trendy clothes. She feared she suffered in comparison.

"First, promise you won't get mad. I don't want to be out here in the middle of nowhere with an angry woman."

Sidney nodded, trying not to look as if anything he might say would affect her one way or the other.

Sloan winked at her before turning back to stare at the road. "When I look at you, I see a body that could offer heaven and pale blue eyes that promise honesty. It's a deadly combination."

She laughed knowing that he was teasing her. "We'd best get back to Rosa Lee's life. I brought a map of Wichita Falls that should help us locate the retirement home."

He caught her hand before she could pull the map out. "You don't believe me, do you, Sidney?"

"No, but I'm not angry."

She thought he might say something else, but he just held her hand a moment longer and then stared straight ahead. She wished she'd known him better—she might have joked with him. She might have admitted wishing his compliment could be true.

Two hours later they walked into the third retirement home. Sidney had been given the name of a developer who built and managed several facilities. Since it was Saturday, the main office was closed, so their only choice was to go to each building complex. The first one was more like apartments than a nursing home. A young girl at the desk didn't have a list with her, but swore there was no one by the name of Carter in the building. The second complex fell more under assisted living. Here, the nurses seemed well able to handle anything. They were professional but of no help in finding Rosa Lee's nurse.

The third try didn't look any more promising. Here most of the patients were in wheelchairs and the staff appeared bored and overworked. Their questions were passed along from one orderly to another over the blare of a TV in the lobby area.

Sidney hated the place. It smelled of urine

and dust. The front desk was cluttered with half-eaten breakfasts on trays.

Sloan leaned over the counter and shouted his question for the fourth time. A tired-looking woman glanced up and pointed toward the left hallway. "Carter's in there. Number three. She doesn't get many visitors."

As they headed toward the room, Sloan slid his arm across her shoulder and Sidney didn't move away. The comfort felt good as they slowly pushed the door open.

Annie Carter looked tiny in her chair by the window. Her room was orderly, but plain. One painting hung on the wall, a small depiction of an English garden done in shades of blue. Whoever had hung it hadn't considered that the person looking at it would be in a wheelchair.

"Miss Carter?" Sidney stepped into the room. "May we come in?"

The little woman's eyes widened in fear. "Are you real or spirit?"

Sidney was taken aback by the question, but Sloan simply knelt beside the tiny woman's chair. "I'm flesh and blood, Miss Carter. Would you like to pinch me to make sure?"

When she raised her fingers, he added, "Not too hard now, I tend to yell."

A wrinkled hand patted his arm. "No, thank you, I don't want to hurt you. I just have to ask now and then. When you're my age and close to crossing over, you need to be reminded which world you're in now and then."

"I understand," he said. "It won't be long before you're walking with the angels."

"Oh happy day," she nodded. "I'm ready with my bag packed whenever the good Lord decides to take me. Some of us leave too early, but most of us are forced to set at the station long after we're ready to go."

Sloan held her tiny hand and turned to Sidney. "Miss Carter, I'd like you to meet Sidney Dickerson. She teaches at the college in Clifton Creek."

"Oh," Miss Carter looked impressed. "She looks like someone I used to know, but I can't recall anyone named Dickerson."

To Sidney's surprise, Miss Carter giggled. "But then, these days everyone is someone I *used* to know. I've outlived two husbands, all my brothers and sisters, and most of my friends. If I hang around much longer I won't have anyone at my funeral."

"Maybe it's time you made a few new friends. Name's Sloan McCormick."

Dancing eyes darted from him to Sidney. "You her fellow?"

Before Sidney could answer, he said, "That I am. Fell for her at first sight."

Sidney couldn't believe it. Sloan had wrapped Miss Carter around his finger in less than a minute and proceeded to tell her lies. One dinner didn't make them a couple any more than one kiss did. But, now wasn't the time to straighten out the facts. She'd do that later. Right now she needed to find out as much as she could about Annie Carter and her last day in Rosa Lee's employ.

She sat down in the only other chair in the room and got out her notepad while Sloan complimented the old woman on the only personal item they could see in the room. "That's a mighty fine painting," he said.

"Thank you," Miss Carter answered. She watched Sidney carefully as if she didn't quite believe her real. "I've had it for years. A dear friend gave it to me. She could paint flowers so real you'd swear you could smell them."

"Miss Carter," Sidney began. "I'd like to

ask you a few questions about Rosa Lee Altman."

"Of course you would, my dear." The old woman leaned back in her chair. "After we talk, can we go down the hall to the kitchen and have ice cream? It'll make the day seem like a party. I have a weakness for chocolate ice cream. It keeps a little fat on my bones."

"I'll push you myself," Sloan said.

Sidney wondered how much of the old woman's mind was left. She didn't seem to grasp the idea that they were strangers.

"Where do you want me to start, dear?" She patted Sidney's hand.

"At the beginning."

Miss Carter closed her eyes for a minute, collected her thoughts. When she opened them once more, Sidney saw determination in her watery gaze. "I retired from being a school nurse over twenty years ago. My arthritis was bothering me too bad to keep working so hard, but I found a part-time job with Dr. Eastland. He wanted me to check on some of his older patients who couldn't, or wouldn't, come to the office. Miss Altman was one of them."

Miss Carter waited for Sidney to make

notes. "She must have been about eighty when I first knocked on her door. For a while she wouldn't let me in, so we visited on the porch. But slowly, she finally asked me inside. I felt quite honored to be invited. She might have been shy but she was a fine southern lady. I could tell just by looking. The place was like a library, books everywhere. She told me she ordered them from a bookstore in Dallas. I'll bet she had a hundred on gardening alone."

"What kind of health was she in?" Sidney moved closer hoping to keep Miss Carter on track.

"Good, strong as an ox. Worked out in those flower beds of hers from dawn tlll dark. Dr. Eastland said she had good bones but she worried about her mind failing. She always wanted me to question her to make sure she wasn't slipping mentally. I told her I wasn't all that far behind her in age and I might not notice, but she made me ask."

"What kind of questions?" Sloan leaned against the windowsill. He looked so totally out of place, both women smiled at him.

Miss Carter continued, "Made me ask her to recite her social-security number like if she accidentally forgot it I should put her to sleep right then. I thought it was a game, but she never missed, not one number of it, or the code."

"The code?" Sidney and Sloan both echoed.

"She had a rhyme she always said. Told me someone would ask me to repeat it one day after her death." The old woman frowned. "I didn't figure you'd wait years to come by. I'm not even sure I remember it now. In truth, I thought it was just a memory game she played."

Sidney knew Miss Carter's story had nothing to do with whether to save the house, but she was fascinated. "Try," she whispered.

After a few minutes the old woman shook her head. "I can't." Tears floated in her eyes. "It's been too long. I'd love to keep my promise to her, but I can't."

Sloan put his hand over hers and said, "It will come, Miss Carter. How about we go down for ice cream?"

They pushed her down the hallway to a large lunchroom and Miss Carter seemed to cheer up. "I usually only come here for dinner. They bring my breakfast and lunch to the room. I like the evening meal, lots of people, lots of noise. Only independent people eat here and my hands won't let me push myself three times a day."

Sloan walked over to an ice-cream machine at the corner of a bar cluttered with coffee and tea containers. "I'm surprised you don't come down for the ice cream." He pulled a cone from the box next to it. He glanced from her to the machine. "You can't reach the machine, can you?"

She shrugged. "Keeps me thin. Otherwise, I'd be a ball. Once in a while someone helps me and I sneak down here. One of the orderlies usually gets me one after dinner if he's not too busy."

Sloan made her an ice-cream cone Dairy Queen would be proud of, then without asking, made Sidney one. They ate over by the windows.

When they'd finished, Miss Carter put her hand on Sidney's arm. "I found her resting in her bed, like she'd passed in her sleep. I don't think she suffered, dear. I think she dreamed her way into heaven."

Sidney guessed the old woman must have thought she knew Rosa Lee. "I'm glad," Sidney said and was surprised how much she meant the words.

Miss Carter continued, "She left me a note about what to do with her clothes and such. She said she didn't want anyone in the house but me and the people who came to take her body out.

"I stayed right by her side until they carried her out, then I locked the door, like I knew she would have wanted me to. If she didn't want people wandering about when she was alive, she sure wouldn't want them doing so after she died."

"That was kind of you," Sidney said.

"I was her friend," Miss Carter answered with tears sparkling in her eyes.

Sloan pushed Miss Carter back to her room. When she was in her place by the window, he knelt down close to her chair. "I'll be back next week, Miss Carter, for another date if you've a mind to hit the ice-cream machine again."

"I'll be waiting."

Sidney hugged her goodbye. "I'd like to come again, too. Just for a visit. Not to talk about Rosa Lee."

Miss Carter let out a short cry. "I remember," she said. "I remember the line Miss Altman used to say. I thought she must have learned it when she was a child because it had her name in it."

Sidney and Sloan waited while the old woman took a deep breath and said, "Gone in thirty-four, a love forgotten nevermore. Look among roses ever bright for the key to unlock the secrets of Rosa Lee."

Miss Carter frowned. "There was another line, but I don't remember it."

Sidney scribbled the saying and glanced up. "Try," she whispered.

Miss Carter closed her eyes. "A mirror turns, blending old and young, to the chime of a tune that was never sung."

"What does it mean?" Sloan asked.

"I don't know. Maybe it was just a saying. She never would explain anything more about it." Miss Carter looked tired. "After she died, I looked among her roses for a key, but I never found anything. The garden was a maze. No matter which path you took, you returned to her back door. It must have been just a rhyme because what kind of rose is ever bright?" The old woman laughed. "She had lots of talents, but Rosa Lee wasn't much on poetry."

Miss Carter said her farewell and pulled the cord for the nurse.

Sloan offered to lift her into bed, but she said he needed to take care of his woman.

Sidney felt his arm go round her and pull her into the hallway. "Are you all right?" He sounded frightened.

"Why?" she managed to say, her thoughts still filled with the rhyme.

"Because you look like you're about to pass out."

Twenty-Five

Sloan slammed Sidney's door and ran through the rain to the other side of his truck. He flipped the driver's seat down and reached in the back for a flask. Without bothering to ask, he mixed the whiskey with what was left of her Coke and handed it to her. He had no idea if the whiskey would help, but it couldn't hurt. The professor looked as if she'd seen a ghost.

As she drank, he watched a little of the color return to her face. The rain pounded hard, closing out all the world but the pickup's cab. He started the engine wishing he understood what had upset her, surprising himself by how much he cared. "Do I need to drive to the hospital?" Maybe she was having one of those spells she'd had on Monday when the drill bit flew through the window at the Altman place. He was no doctor. He had no idea what would help.

"No. It's not another panic attack or whatever the doctors called it on Monday," she answered his unasked question and took a long drink. "I'll be all right in a minute."

"What did you have to eat today?" His mom's answer to everything from a cold to cancer was food. They had picked up Cokes on their way out of Clifton Creek but he hadn't thought to ask if she'd wanted anything else.

"I skipped breakfast."

"I was afraid of that. It's after one. How about we eat lunch and you tell me what shook you up back there?"

Sidney nodded. "Your bedside manner could use a little work, but thanks for getting me out of that place. If I'd had to breathe that air much longer I might truly have passed out."

He watched her closely, unsure she wasn't putting on an act of being brave. She looked healthy, but she might be one of those fragile women for all he knew. His mother had spent her entire marriage convincing Sloan's dad how fragile she was. She'd stayed in bed most of her three pregnancies and continued nap time long after her children had given it up because she had to rest. Strange thing was, she outlived Sloan's dad by almost twenty years.

Sidney broke into his thoughts. "I'm fine. Really."

He leaned across and tilted her face up with his hand. "You still look pale." His thumb brushed across her cheek as he studied her. Her skin was soft, warm and free of makeup. Most women her age wore so much they needed a separate piece of luggage just to carry it all.

"I promise, I'm all right," she insisted, reading his mind again. "But, you're right. I'm starving."

He relaxed and straightened back to his side of the seat. "I know just the place. Best chicken-fry in the state."

Fifteen minutes later they were shown to a booth in a crowded restaurant known as the Pioneer. He shook his head when the waitress tried to hand him a menu and ordered two chicken-fried steak specials.

"Specials?" Sidney asked when they were alone once more.

"Beans, fried okra, potatoes and steak covered in gravy."

She turned her head as if she were trying to understand another language. He liked that about her, he decided. She never acted as if she knew something when she didn't, but she was a woman no one would ever take for a fool.

When the food arrived he noticed he'd forgotten to mention rolls, corn bread and a salad. While they ate, the place began to clear. It finally got quiet enough to hear music in the background blending with the sound of the rain. Sloan listened to the voices around him and decided not to ask Sidney any questions here.

He ordered cobbler, but neither of them ate more than a few bites. She didn't try to make small talk. He needed to think, to replay again the last thing Miss Carter had said. Somewhere in the rhyme lay the answer and maybe even a key to understanding Sidney.

He paid the bill, took her hand as they left the booth and didn't turn loose of her until they were back in his truck. Something about her made him feel like a kid on his first date. He couldn't remember how many years it had been since he'd wanted to hold a woman's hand. Sloan wasn't sure he could explain his attraction to her if he tried.

"Better?" he asked, liking the color returning to her face. She had a kind of beauty that would still be there when she was eighty, he thought.

"Much better. How'd you find this place?"

"When you knock around all the oil fields in Texas you learn the towns. Or at least the hotels, cafés and bars."

"Bars?"

He nodded. "If you want to know about a town, you'll hear it all in the bars. The closer it gets to closing time, the more you learn."

"Where do you call home?" she asked.

He didn't miss the look in her eye. She was thinking the question might have been too personal. Had she gone too far? Had she been too bold?

"Nowhere," he answered. "I've got a place on Lake Travis where I go to fish, and an apartment in Houston that looks like a hotel room."

"No one waiting anywhere?"

There was the look again. She worried about her boldness. He almost told her how damn sexy he thought it was. Not the question, but the shyness behind it. She was a woman who spent her whole life thinking about everything she said. She'd never learned to play games.

"No one. Not for a long time," he answered. He could have told her of all the women he knew. Women who were dinner companions, company, even lovers. But none were home.

When she was silent for a while, he asked, "Any more questions?"

"I didn't mean to pry."

"You didn't. You've got a right to know."

She shook her head. "It's really none of my business."

Dear God, how he wanted to hold her. She sat so proper beside him, so remote. She would never assume . . . never push. Something had frightened her back at the retirement home, but she didn't seem to want to talk about it. He didn't know her well enough to ask. He really hadn't known her well enough to kiss her yesterday, either. Her politeness in asking him not to repeat the kiss stopped him cold. Too bad she hadn't asked him to stop thinking about it.

Not that the kiss had been all that great. Maybe she wasn't ready, or maybe no one had ever taken the time to teach her to kiss. He'd met a few women like that. Some who'd even been around, but they'd never taken the time between hello and bed to learn how to kiss. He had a feeling with the professor it would more likely be lack of practice or opportunity. A few personal questions he'd like to ask her came to mind.

He put the car in gear and drove toward the interstate. After a while, the silence got to him. "I liked Miss Carter," he said as if they had just been talking.

"I did, too." She didn't turn to look at him.

"I can see why Rosa Lee Altman must have trusted her." When she didn't comment, he added, "I'll bet they were great friends. Maybe your grandmother was that kind of friend to Rosa Lee. After all, your grandmother, Minnie, and Miss Carter were both nurses."

He didn't know how long he could go on talking to himself. He tried again. "We never did get around to asking her about cause of death. Though I guess when someone is ninety-two there's not much guessing to it."

Nothing from the other side of the car.

"I bet that was real hard on Miss Carter, finding her friend like that. But, maybe she found comfort in knowing Rosa Lee died in her sleep. She seemed to think telling you would help you for some reason."

A truck passed, splashing a wave of water at his pickup. Sloan slowed. "If this rain doesn't let up we might want to pull over."

He frowned. He felt as if he were traveling alone.

"Don't you think it's strange that she remembered that saying after all these years? I can understand the part about the social-security number. I've often been afraid I'd get Alzheimer's. A few of my relatives have it. I don't want to be walking around not remembering my own name. I've thought it might make sense to rig up a bomb. If you didn't punch in your phone number, driver's license number and social every week, it would blow you off the face of the earth. Then you wouldn't have to worry about ending up in a nursing home."

He laughed. "Except the other day at the bank I wrote down my cell-phone number as my account. It may already be too late for me."

Sidney didn't answer.

Sloan started to truly worry. He spotted a

roadside picnic area and pulled off the road. He twisted in the seat and waited for her to look at him.

When she turned, he swore he felt his heart miss a beat. Professor Sidney Dickerson was crying.

Without a word, he opened his arms and she moved toward him. He held her for a long while, feeling her sobs as she silently cried on the front of his shirt. He wished he could think of something to say, but he wasn't sure what was wrong and like most men over eighteen, he'd learned to keep his mouth closed and wait.

Finally, she pulled away and dug in the bottom of her briefcase for a tissue. "I'm sorry."

"Want to talk about it?"

"There's nothing to say. I know there's something in what Miss Carter said that may be a clue to understanding Rosa Lee, and why she was the way she was, but I've only got four days to figure it out. Even if I do learn something, it may not save a house."

"Is that what you want, to save the house?"

Sidney shook her head. "I don't know. I'm drawn to the place, but I need to think about what's best for the town." She blew her nose. "The money would make a difference. No one in the town seems to care about the house but me, and I'm an outsider."

She looked up at him and he saw the hesitation in her eyes. She wanted to tell him more, but she wasn't sure she could trust him.

Hell, he thought, he wasn't sure he could trust himself. If it got right down to finding something that would make that old dump worth saving, or making half his year's income on the sale, was he willing to help her? He'd been researching this deal for over a month. He had all the facts he needed and he hadn't felt this sure about the drilling site being good in a long time. The company he worked for stood to make a great deal of money, but the whole process couldn't start until he got at least a lease. The mayor had made it plain they were far more interested in selling than leasing the land so it looked as if the house would end up belonging to the oil company.

Sloan shifted, fighting the urge to touch her. Before they went any further, he had to decide if he would walk away with nothing just to keep her pale blue eyes from crying.

He told himself, at forty, he was too old to be that kind of fool, but in forty years he'd never met a woman like this one.

Twenty-Six

"It's about time you got here." Billy pulled a tool belt from his car parked directly behind the Altman house. "I thought we agreed last night to start our search at two. It's after three. Saturday's almost over, and we're keeping the ghosts waiting, Whitman."

Lora yawned and stretched like a bored runner preparing for a marathon. She'd left him sleeping just before dawn and walked the rest of the way home staying well in the shadows. The last thing her shredded reputation needed was to be seen dragging in at dawn.

She'd slipped into her parents' house knowing, come morning, she'd claim she hadn't bothered to glance at a clock when she arrived home. Her mother would never know the time she returned. Not that she cared, she told herself.

"I needed my beauty sleep," Lora answered without adding more.

Her cotton-lined jogging suit felt much more comfortable than the little black dress she'd worn last night. Though the day was gray, she felt grand, as if she'd somehow broken a few of the shackles her mother kept trying to bind around her. She'd even managed to avoid questions about Talon Graham at lunch, but couldn't help but wonder how long he'd wait before calling.

She grinned at Billy as he strapped on the belt. "You would think you'd be a little nicer to me, Billy Hatcher, after I slept with you last night."

He looked up and frowned. "Don't go spreading that around. You'll ruin *my* reputation."

She decided right there and then that she'd be Billy Hatcher's friend for the rest of her life. "Wouldn't want to do that, but is the offer to return still open? I can't remember when I've slept so soundly."

He smiled. "Whitman, you can curl into my sleeping bag anytime." Something in his eyes told her he wasn't quite as young as she thought he was, not in experience anyway.

He closed his trunk. "Grab that flashlight on the front seat, will you? I'm ready to go exploring. I've been in this house three times now and never climbed the stairs. It's time we see what the old place looks like."

Lora leaned into the car and followed orders. "Did you call the other committee members?"

"The professor isn't home, but I left a message." He jumped over the porch railing. "Micah has a picnic with his son, but he said he'd try to catch up with us later and see if we found anything interesting. The sisters said they were going on some kind of mission, but they'd report in when possible. I swear, they're starting to sound like militia."

As he unlocked the back door to the Altman place, he added, "Since we're a third of the committee, I think its okay to go in. The others will come when they can. If the deputy drops by, I'll turn you loose on him again. I swear, you make him nervous."

Lora nodded. If she could handle a drunk Talon Graham, she could manage Deputy

Adams. She followed close behind as they wound their way toward the stairs. She could almost hear the ghosts in the house whispering, planning how they would kill anyone who thought to explore. The damp air held the breath of danger as if they were tromping over memories and secrets, and not just dusty boards. The ghost of Rosa Lee would be pouring their blood over her roses by nightfall.

She bumped into Billy's back.

"Be careful," he whispered as if he sensed something, too.

"Sorry." She couldn't help but wonder why he whispered. If anyone had a right to be in the house it was them. "I'm staying close. They always get the one at the end of the line, you know."

He laughed. "There's only two of us. I think I'll notice if you disappear. Want to lead?"

"No, that's who always gets killed by a swinging ax or falling boulder."

"I'll be careful." He took her hand. The tape from his bandages felt rough reminding her of the harm that had found them the last time they were here.

"Wiggle your fingers now and then so I'll

know I'm not just holding a hand after some monster gobbles up the rest of you." He laughed. "I hate it when that happens to my dates."

"Very funny, and I'm not your date." They started up the stairs. "Dan always hated it when I let my imagination run wild, but it's hard not to in a place like this."

Billy stopped midway up the stairs and turned to face her. "Let's get something straight, Whitman." At almost the same height, his face was only an inch from hers. "No man is ever going to be Dan, again. You're rid of him. I'm not like him and neither is anyone else you meet. Don't go around figuring every male thinks like he does. The guy must have been a total jerk to leave you. Drop his memory in the dust and move on."

"Divorce counseling?"

Billy smiled. "No, just advice from a friend." His gray eyes studied her. "By the way, I like that imagination of yours. It's sexy as hell."

She doubled back her free fist to pound him in the ribs, but couldn't quite bring herself to hit a man for complimenting her. He was right about Dan. She'd given him too much time already to fret about him now. She should look at the bright side. She had no job to speak of, no home to call her own, and no friends but Billy Hatcher, but at least she didn't have to put up with Dan anymore. Things could only get better.

A creaking sound came from above them. Billy looked up as he squeezed her fingers. "Let's go meet our host."

Or maybe the worst was yet to come, she thought, wishing the creak didn't sound like a footstep. There was no telling what traps Rosa Lee might have left.

They took the stairs slowly, feeling for the give in the wood. Most steps were solid, but a few were bowed. When they reached the thirteenth, Billy dropped to his knee. "Once in a while, I've heard, builders put a hollow step for the thirteenth." He tugged at the board, but it didn't give. "It's kind of an extra safe. Someplace no one would think to look."

"Where did you learn that?"

"Hanging around old carpenters. A fellow told me rebels moving into Texas after the Civil War put them in along with several other hiding places because they'd lived through the Yankees looting their homes.

The carpenter said lots of the old houses have hidden spaces."

It made sense, Lora thought. She'd heard the professor say that she wasn't sure where old Henry Altman came from. Chances were fifty-fifty he'd come from a Southern state. Even though he'd been born years after the war, he might have known about putting hiding places in the stairs.

"Anything?" Lora asked when Billy stood.

"Nothing. Guess no one let old Henry Altman in on the practice."

They moved on up the stairs. The railing seemed solid, but the second story's floor had water damage in several places. The boards were uneven and creaked with each step.

"I'm going to bring my boss from the lumberyard in Monday to make a list of have-to repairs, but I kind of wanted to see the place first."

"Me, too." Lora wasn't sure what she'd expected, a scene out of Dickens's *Great Expectations* maybe, with mice eating a rotting wedding cake on the table. But what she got was nothing. No furniture, no rugs, no pictures on the walls. Only a dark hallway with the window at the end boarded over.

Billy shoved open the first door. It creaked as warped wood scarred the floor. They carefully stepped inside. Only the barest of furniture greeted them. A bed frame, a dresser with one drawer missing, a few wicker chairs with the bottoms decayed.

"It's like looking at the skeleton of a room," Lora whispered as she followed him around. "All the beauty, all the trappings are gone."

"Accurate description." He kicked at what looked like a rat's nest of rags cluttered up in one corner while Lora turned slowly around. The rods were still above the windows, but the curtains were gone. Heavy storm shutters like horizontal bars blocked out all but thin slices of light in this prison of a room. Dust and the smell of mold thickened the stale air.

Billy moved his fingers along the chair railing running on one wall. "This must have been grand once," he whispered. "Fine hardwood. Crown molding. Inlay in the floor." His fingers stopped and he leaned closer to the wall.

"What?" She knew he'd found something.

"Nothing," he answered. "Just more of
those nail holes in the wood. Something
was once nailed to this wall and removed
without care or skill."

Lora let her fingers follow his along the
wall, but had no answer. The markings were
too low to be pictures or mirrors, too high to
have been used to secure rugs.

They moved to the second room. More of
the same broken, abandoned furniture. Billy
explored each wall as though looking at a
map he couldn't read.

The third room, at the end of the hall, had
unbroken furniture, but little more. All the
bedding and curtains had been removed. At
first glance, the space reminded Lora of a
cheap hotel room. She opened the closet
door and found nothing but a few abandoned coat hangers. "This has to be her
room," Lora reasoned. "Someone must
have moved Rosa Lee's things out after she
died."

"Looks that way. If the will left all her
books to the library, maybe she gave some
charity her clothes." Billy opened a French
door leading to a balcony, but vines had

completely covered any view of the back. "I agree, she would have wanted the room with a view of her gardens."

Lora hugged herself. "It's as if she planned her death. Planned that nothing of her would be left." She noticed squares where the wall must have faded around picture frames. But the pictures, even the frames, were gone, leaving only a slight imprint that they'd once been there.

"Dying in her nineties doesn't sound as if she was in any hurry to commit suicide." He opened one of the dresser drawers and found a dead cockroach. "Maybe she was just a person who wanted everything to be in order when she died. Without any family, she probably didn't want strangers digging through her stuff."

"Makes sense. My guess is all the furniture we're finding was either too heavy to haul off, or too worthless to bother with."

They walked through the other rooms. Smaller rooms that must have been built for children, but never furnished.

"That's it." Lora turned around ready to get out of the dark hallways and into fresh air.

"Except for one," Billy mumbled as he felt

along the wall. "There's another door here at the end. Probably only a linen closet or one of those luggage rooms folks used to put on second floors to store out-of-season clothes and luggage." He shoved the door, unsure if it was locked or warped with time.

The door didn't move.

"Are you sure that's a door? Maybe it's only part of the paneling." She flashed the light into the dark end of the hallway.

Billy shoved again with more force. Something snapped, wood cracked and gave with his weight. Light rushed into the hall as they stepped into the last room. The space was small with windows running high along the ceiling. A storage room, she thought, where indirect light would be best.

"Look!" Lora laughed with delight.

In the center of the empty room, resting on a trunk, stood a child's dusty white rocking horse that looked as if it might belong on a miniature merry-go-round. The toy, with roses circling the horse's neck, must have been hand-painted.

Lora ran her hand over the finely carved wood and removed a layer of dust. "Can you believe this? It's just sitting here, waiting for us to find it."

"Probably no one noticed this door." He seemed more interested in the lock that had snapped than the wooden rocking horse. "I would have missed it if I hadn't noticed the hinges. It looks as if the door had been locked, but the nails holding the lock in place have rusted from a leak in the ceiling."

Lora looked up and laughed, "So, you're saying the house *let* us in this room? I think Rosa Lee left this for us. Look, she put it in the center, on a trunk so water wouldn't damage it." Lora leaned down to examine the toy's details. "Doesn't it strike you as odd that an old maid would buy a rocking horse? It must have cost her dearly, even years ago."

Billy shrugged. "I don't know, my grandmother collected little nude rubber dolls with wild, strange-colored hair. Always said they brought her good luck, but one night her cat knocked a few of them behind the TV and she took quite a shock trying to get them out."

Closing her eyes, Lora tried not to picture the scene he'd painted. "Why would an old lady buy such an expensive toy for no one? Why would she save it when it's obvious she had to sell almost everything she owned to live? Why hide it away behind a locked door?"

Lora had looked for anything that might reflect the woman who'd spent her entire life in this house and all she'd found were questions. Billy seemed more interested in the woodwork. He touched the molding and knelt to examine the floor where the wood buckled with age.

"Maybe we'd better take another look around. Go over every inch of this floor before we move on. If this got left behind, maybe we'll find something else."

Lora shrugged. She didn't like the idea, but if he hadn't been with her, she would have missed the rocking horse. She clicked on the flashlight. "All right, we'll go through the rooms again, but we're not separating."

He winked at her and led the way.

"Nothing," Lora mumbled after an hour of opening every door and drawer on the second floor, again.

"I wouldn't say that," Billy answered. "I found several things, none of which make sense."

He pointed toward the biggest bedroom. "This must be the master. Look, it has an old bolt, probably original to the house, on the inside of the door and another, the kind sold years ago at any hardware store, on the outside."

Lora touched the bolt. "Someone was locked in."

Billy nodded. "Maybe that's our answer as to why Rosa Lee never met Fuller. Maybe the old man locked his only daughter away."

Lora didn't like the images that came to mind. "Or maybe," she tried to find another reason. "Henry locked the master bedroom when his wife died because he loved her so much and he never wanted anyone to go in there."

Before Billy had time to consider her theory, she asked, "What else?"

"With one exception, the floor is most worn in the third bedroom, further confirming that was Rosa Lee's room. If I were guessing, I'd say it was her room all her life."

"Not a very impressive room for such a big house. You'd think, once she was living here all alone, she'd have spread her stuff out."

"Maybe that was the way she lived. It might also explain why she never answered the door." Billy blinked the flashlight along the baseboards. "I doubt she could have heard anyone from this far back in the house."

Lora walked out of the room and noticed Billy took the time to close Rosa Lee's bedroom door. "You said 'with one exception'?"

He walked back to the master. "The light's bad in here with no way to open the shutters from the inside, but I couldn't help seeing this." He pointed his beam of light in front of the windows. On the floorboards, a long, three-foot wide row from wall to wall was so worn, it looked as if it had been sanded.

"What could have made that?"

"I don't know. Maybe Rosa Lee walked the floor over the loss of her man."

Lora didn't like that image of Rosa Lee. Had she really been such a weak person to allow her father to run—no, to ruin—her life? She suddenly realized she'd allowed her parents to do the same thing. They'd always been crazy about Dan, even offered to help set him up in an office as soon as he married their only daughter. When Lora had voted for waiting a few years, she'd lost three-to-one and been idiot enough at twenty to think someone else could vote in her life. Isadore had been the one who had insisted on a huge wedding, inviting everyone in town. They hadn't used a chisel to mold her the way they wanted in what they saw as the perfect life, they'd used sand, one grain at a time. And the crime in it all was that she'd let them.

"Lora, you all right?" Billy moved closer, his hand resting on her shoulder. "Not lost in one of your fantasies are you?"

She smiled. "No, in reality this time. It's far more frightening."

"Let's get out of here." He slid his hand down her arm to her fingers.

"What next, the attic, or the basement?"

Before he could answer, they heard footsteps coming up the stairs.

"We're here!" someone sounding very much like one of the Rogers sisters shouted. "Did we miss anything?"

Lora crossed to the landing as the sisters reached the top of the stairs. Ada May carried a flashlight and her sister held a cane like a weapon. They both looked windblown.

Ada May clicked the flashlight on and off. "Any critters up here?"

"One dead cockroach," Billy answered.

"But you can check him if you like. He may have only been playing possum."

Beth Ann leaned against the banister. "We've been all over the garden. You wouldn't believe the variety of roses we've found. But her favorite was definitely a Portland Rose called the Marbree. They've been planted in several spots."

Everyone turned to explore the house, but Beth Ann kept chattering. "If we decide to have the city sell this land, Ada May and I will take more clippings. The sheriff and oil company might even let us move some of the plants. Ada May has started a list of places who could adopt plants but we'll need to check the soil before we move them."

Ada May shook with cold and talked over her sister as if Beth Ann were no more than a radio. "We just came in because it's starting to rain. Another hour and the trails out back will be rivers of mud."

As if on cue, thunder rumbled above them. A shutter somewhere flapped against the house, adding a tapping sound.

"I guess the attic is out," Billy said. "From the water on the second floor, the roof must have several holes."

"How about the basement?"

He looked at the Rogers sisters. "You two willing?"

They both nodded. Within five minutes they were all shivering in the damp basement. The rain was pouring down, splattering against cracked windows lining the top of the basement walls. Beth Ann refused to take the last step down to the dirt floor. She seemed positive she saw movement on the floor too big to be cockroaches.

Billy made a circle with his flashlight. He didn't catch anything in the beam, but he also felt movements just beyond the light. The basement had been used mostly for storage. The frame of an old-fashioned drying rack ran along one wall, a pressing machine lay on its side in one corner. Behind the stairs were stacks of old newspaper tied with twine.

"Snakes?" Beth Ann whispered.

Ada May jumped, almost tumbling into her sister. "Stop that," she shouted when she realized it was a false alarm. "You're scaring the willies out of me."

Billy leaned near Lora's ear. "How many willies you think she's got in her?"

Lora poked him, but laughed.

He acted as if he'd been hurt. "Pain always seems to factor into our conversations, Whitman. You really should have that temper of yours listed as a weapon."

Beth Ann lowered her foot to the floor, but kept her death grip on the railing. "What could be down here?"

"We're about to find out." Billy headed toward one corner. Slowly, the women joined in the search.

Lora fought the urge to follow behind Billy. She heard the Rogers sisters arguing about where to look. In truth, there wasn't much to explore. The remains of an old furnace took up most of the center space. A collection of years of bug traps were scattered along the back wall. Long boards were stacked neatly against another.

"Nothing," Lora sighed after twenty minutes of examining corners. The thunder and lightning gnawed at her nerves and, with the onset of evening, the basement shadows turned from gray to black. The sudden flashes across the broken windows in the basement made the damp air seem full of electricity.

Beth Ann took a few steps up the stairs. "We might as well forget about the basement. It's almost time to start supper." She glanced at Lora and Billy. "You two want to come home with us for meat loaf? We cooked enough for an army hoping you might come."

Before Lora could answer, Billy yelled. Everyone froze.

"I found something." He crawled from under the stairs carrying a long tube as if it were a sword. "It was stuffed on the back ledge of one of the steps."

Everyone gathered round as Billy pulled out the paper rolled inside the tube. As he held it up to the light, a poster was slowly revealed. The same rodeo poster Lora had shown the group.

"I don't believe it," she whispered as she leaned against his shoulder for a better look. "It's the same one that has Fuller Crane listed as one of the riders."

Billy passed the treasure to the Rogers sisters. "I guess that confirms it," he shrugged. "Our Rosa Lee and Fuller must have been an item."

Lora sat down on the steps. "But what happened and why would she hide the poster away?"

"Maybe these will explain it," Billy whispered as he lifted a small stack of letters tied together with ribbon.

"Explain what?" Sidney shouted down from the opening above.

Everyone jumped, then relaxed as they recognized the voice. Lora watched as the professor moved slowly down the stairs. A tall man followed her.

"Sorry to have startled you, but I got your message and came right over as soon as I could." Sidney pointed upward. "This is Sloan McCormick. He drove me to Wichita Falls today to talk to a woman who visited Rosa Lee."

Lora studied the man. He looked about forty, tall, broad shouldered and looking as if he'd been born in a Stetson. She was puzzled at the intrusion of a nonmember in committee business, but she didn't miss the way he watched Sidney, offering his hand for support as she moved down the stairs. He only gave Lora a quick nod when introduced, then turned his attention back to the professor. That kind of devotion would have been hard to miss.

Billy shook hands with Sloan when the couple reached the floor of the basement.

He seemed to accept the stranger, but the sisters had a few questions.

"Where are you from, Mr. McCormick? What brings you to Clifton Creek? Have you been a friend of our professor for some time?"

To Sloan's credit, he smiled. "I'm a good friend of Sidney's. I've been in Clifton Creek for almost two weeks and I'm doing research for a drilling company out of Houston. But, before you ask, I'm here as Sidney's friend, nothing more. Any business I have will be with the mayor, not this group."

Everyone looked at Sidney as if she'd brought a wolf among the lambs.

Sidney defended him. "Sloan has brought some interesting research to me and he did it knowing that it might influence the group to decide against his company."

No one appeared to believe her. Lora almost felt sorry for the professor. Sloan got the hint before Sidney had to say anything.

"Look," he said. "I didn't mean to interrupt the group. I just brought Sidney here because it's raining and she hates to drive."

No one commented.

He brushed the professor's arm with one hand while he pulled his cell from his pocket. "Take this and hit one, then the talk button when you need me to come back for you. I've got my other cell in the truck. I'll wait there."

Sidney shook her head and tried to give back the phone. "That's not necessary, Sloan. I can catch a ride home if it's still raining."

He brushed her shoulder. "Don't worry about it. I don't mind. I'll probably be out front in my truck checking my e-mail when you call."

Lora saw it again, that caring way he had of looking at the professor. Maybe she didn't consider herself a good judge of men, but Lora would have had to be blind not to see that McCormick cared for Sidney. She took a chance. "Don't feel like you have to leave, Mr. McCormick." Lora purposely didn't glance at the others. "You're welcome to stay as long as we have your word that you are here as a friend and not on business."

Sloan lifted his right hand as if ready to take an oath.

To her surprise Billy came to her aid. "Yeah. Maybe you can shed some light on our find." He handed Sloan the poster.

Sloan seemed to relax a fraction. "Sidney told me about this poster."

"Not that poster," Billy corrected. "One just like it. We found this one hidden down here."

Suddenly, everyone wanted to talk at once. Now that half the committee had decided to accept Sloan, he had to be filled in. The rain still pounded, lightning flashed across the windows, but Lora didn't feel the chill. She stood back and watched the others, hoping she'd done the right thing by inviting Sloan to join them. She hadn't done it for him, really, she'd done it for the professor.

They moved upstairs where the light was better and sat on the wide stairs. Sloan pulled a folding chair from the room where they'd held the first meeting. He offered it to Sidney and then stood behind her as she untied the ribbon around the letters Billy had found. Like a choir on risers, the sisters took the third step for seating. Lora moved up a few and dusted off a spot. Billy climbed higher and sat behind her, offering his leg as a backrest.

Lora leaned against him, feeling the now familiar sense of being accepted. He ran his hand over her shoulder almost absently as they waited for Sidney.

The professor looked at the first envelope. "It's a letter from Rosa Lee Altman to Fuller Crane." She flipped through the stack. "Six letters," she corrected. "All the same, addressed to Fuller in care of the Wichita Hospital." Sidney looked up. "They are all unopened and stamped Return to Sender."

Sidney passed the letters out.

While they talked about this twist, Lora noticed Sloan, with one of the letters in hand, walk out of the hallway and into the dining room. She guessed he needed more light, but doubted the streetlight would offer much.

"We should open them," Billy suggested.

"They're not addressed to us," Ada May pointed out the obvious. "If we open them wouldn't that be some kind of federal crime? Tampering with the mail."

"From September 1933?" Billy stared at the letter in his hand.

Beth Ann shook her head. "That doesn't change the fact that we're holding someone else's mail."

"From a dead woman," he mumbled.

Everyone remained silent for a few minutes, then the professor said, "Whether we open them or not doesn't really matter. They prove that Rosa Lee had a lover. Fuller and she are connected, but that still doesn't change any of the facts about this house."

The sisters talked at length about how all the stories of Rosa Lee never having a man caller must not be true. They even recounted a few they'd heard when they were young. They also agreed that the letters should be opened. Maybe Rosa Lee was telling him goodbye.

Sidney finally ended the long debate by repeating that whatever they learned probably wouldn't make any difference to the committee, or to the vote they would all have to make by Wednesday.

There was some talk of asking the mayor for more time, but no one could come up with a good reason apart from the fact that they had somehow all gotten into the secret Rosa Lee had managed to hide from the community all her life.

Sloan stepped back into the room, his cell in hand. "I just called the hospital and asked for records."

"How'd you know to do that?" Beth Ann wondered aloud.

"It's what I do for a living. Find people."

"Well?" Ada May waited.

"Well," he smiled. "There was a Fuller Crane admitted to the hospital in September of 1933. Injuries listed as critical from a rodeo accident."

"If he was at the hospital, why didn't he get the letters?" Sidney whispered.

Sloan rested his hand on her shoulder and knelt to eye level. "He died a few days after being admitted. He must have already been dead by the time they arrived."

Twenty-Seven

Micah joined the committee at the Rogers sisters' house after he put his son to bed. He'd spent the day entertaining Logan and Jimmy at the school picnic, which had turned inside to a noisy gym once the rain had started. Logan had played so hard, he'd fallen asleep in the car on the ride home. Micah had carried him inside and tucked him in bed, checked with Mrs. Mac and had headed back out in the rain.

When he saw the message on his phone, Micah knew he had to join the group. It might not be an official meeting at the Rogers sisters' home on Saturday night, but Micah had a feeling he needed to be there.

The others filled him in on their find, the poster, the rocking horse, the letters, while Ada May insisted he eat supper. Micah was surprised to learn they hadn't opened Rosa Lee's letters to Fuller.

"What do you think, morally, Reverend?" Beth Ann asked. "Is it all right to open mail to a dead person, from a dead person?"

Micah tried to swallow the driest meat loaf he'd ever had in his life. Ada May apologized, explaining that the others had finished off the gravy earlier. Micah understood why. He felt like he was eating grease-soaked sawdust.

"Well?" Beth Ann leaned forward, tired of waiting for him to finish chewing.

"I think it's all right," Micah managed to say as he grabbed his tea.

The tall man someone had introduced as Sloan McCormick grinned at Micah, then down at the empty plate. Micah swore he saw admiration in the man's eyes.

"Thanks for the meal." Micah handed over his plate.

"Would you like some more?" Ada May asked.

McCormick coughed down a laugh.

"No, thank you," Micah answered. "I don't think I could eat another bite."

While Beth Ann cleared the table and carefully wiped off the plastic tablecloth, the others gathered round. With all the committee present, they might as well have a meeting.

Somehow during the week they'd become a family, totally accepting of one another. Micah never ceased to be amazed at how fast folks in this part of the country bonded. Maybe it was the pioneer spirit still running in their blood.

Sloan, though he didn't join them at the table, had picked up a fax earlier that gave all the details of Fuller's death. He laid it on the table like an offering and walked back to the living area. Apparently, Fuller Crane had had no living relatives. Several other cowboys who'd rodeoed with him had covered the bill for his funeral. His saddle and horse had been auctioned off to pay the hospital.

"That's so sad." Beth Ann looked near tears. "When you think that he had Rosa Lee who loved him. She must have not known how badly he'd been hurt or surely she'd have made the trip to see him."

"We don't know that she loved him," Ada May pointed out.

"Then, why'd she keep the letters and the poster?" Beth Ann patted the pack. "She loved him. I'm sure of it."

"It's time," Sidney interrupted the argument. "We have to open the letters."

One by one she carefully slit the envelopes open with a dinner knife. Each letter looked as if it had been hastily written and they all said the same thing. *Come back for me.*

Sidney passed the yellowed paper. No *Dear Fuller.* No signature at the end. Only four words on a page. One letter each day he lived.

The members all fell silent, heartbroken over a love affair that had died seventy years before.

Finally, Billy pushed back his chair. "She stood him up once and then changed her mind."

"She must not have known how badly he was hurt," Beth Ann mumbled.

Lora walked to the edge of the living room and handed Sloan one of the letters.

Sloan thanked her. "It's possible Rosa Lee didn't know how bad the injuries were," he agreed with Beth Ann. "I rodeoed a few seasons in my wild and crazy days. I saw men with broken bones be helped to stand and limp out of the arena with the announcer yelling about how lucky they were not to be hurt. You *cowboy up* and take the pain, then you collapse behind the chutes."

"Even the paper probably listed him as recovering," Lora added. "They wouldn't have wanted bad press. It wouldn't have been good for the rodeo, or the town."

Micah nodded. He couldn't help but wonder if Fuller had lived, would he have followed Rosa Lee's request? Did he want her enough to fight whatever trouble kept her from being there the first time? Apparently, she offered no explanation. Did he love her enough to swallow his pride and come asking again?

"Well, we know what happened between them." Ada May rubbed at one eye. "Or what didn't. But that still doesn't explain why, as an old woman, she kept a rocking horse hidden away."

"I don't think we should have left it," Lora said suddenly. "I don't think it's safe."

"It's been there for years, dear," Beth Ann said, comforting her.

"I feel the same," Billy added. "I'm not sure one more storm wouldn't take the roof down. It might be wise to get it out of there."

"I could keep it at my house," Sidney suggested. "Until we decide what to do with it."

Billy stood. "The rain's slowed some. I'll go get it."

"I'll go with you," Sloan said. "We can put it in the back of my pickup. I've got a tarp and ropes to secure it."

"I don't need—" Billy started.

"You'll need someone to hold the light while you carry it down those dark stairs," Sloan offered.

Billy nodded once.

A second after Ada May stood and offered everyone pie, Micah decided he'd better accompany the other men. He'd had all he wanted of her cooking. He grabbed the old blankets Beth Ann offered to pad the horse and followed the others.

As the men walked to Sloan's truck, Billy kidded Micah about the meat loaf. By the time they were at the Altman place, all three were laughing at how many men Ada May must have poisoned before she perfected her recipe. She might not be just an old maid—she might be a serial killer.

Micah liked the way Sloan let Billy take the lead and didn't try to step in and run the show just because he was twice the kid's age. He wasn't sure how he felt about the stranger, but the man seemed to want to help. He hadn't said a word about what they should do with the house. If he planned to sway the committee, he was taking his time going about it.

Billy unlocked the house and the three men headed upstairs, their arms loaded down with supplies. A loud clap of thunder shook the house and they all slowed. The eaves creaked, teasing them all into worry.

"Storm doesn't sound like it's over." Sloan moved forward with the light. "Taking the rocking horse out is probably a good idea."

Billy shoved open the old door. "The house has withstood storms for years." The door protested as it had before, then opened.

Sloan flashed the beam of the flashlight on the toy. Micah was surprised at the size. He'd expected something small that a tod-dler would ride, but this white ghost horse stood three feet tall with bowed polished wood boards for rocking that made the toy almost five feet long.

Sloan moved the light slowly down the body of the animal in all its carved glory. "Even in the thirties this must have cost dearly," he said.

"Maybe it's older than that." Billy brushed his hand over the mane. "Maybe the old man bought it for Rosa Lee when she was born. That would explain why she couldn't part with it."

"If so, she never played on it," Micah guessed. "Not a chip of paint has been rubbed off."

"We'd better get it loaded before the next round of rain hits." Billy tossed one of the blankets Beth Ann had insisted on sending. "We'll wrap it up before heading downstairs. I'd hate to bump it against a wall and damage the toy after Rosa Lee took such good care of it all these years."

They wrapped the horse carefully, first in blankets and then a drop cloth spattered with dried paint. Finally, Billy sealed it with duct tape to hold everything together. Micah and Billy lifted the horse while Sloan walked backward shining the light just ahead of them.

They made it to the front door before another clap of thunder announced more rain. Sloan backed ahead of them. He'd pulled the pickup close, into the mud that had once been a yard. Micah and Billy took the steps one at a time, protective of their cargo.

The rain fell so fast it stung Micah's face, but he didn't dare hurry.

Lightning flashed as they slid the toy beneath the tarp in Sloan's truck. Micah thought he caught the blink of another pickup parked thirty feet away at the street. A moment later, a popping sound blended with the noise of the storm. Like short thunder, it came in rapid fire.

Sloan swung around, pointing the light toward the street before cutting it.

The popping sound came again, muted firecrackers in the rain.

Billy dropped behind the truck, then grabbed Micah, jerking him so hard, his side caught the corner of the pickup before he tumbled in the mud. "Get down!" Billy yelled. "That's gunfire."

Micah gripped his ribs in pain as he heard

the pickup door open and Sloan swear. The truck blocked his view of Sloan and Micah realized the tall man was without any barrier between himself and whoever fired.

In the silence between thunderclaps there was no mistaking the sound of a shotgun being racked, ready to fire. "Come on out and play, whoever you are!" Sloan shouted. "But you better be popping more than a twenty-two."

In the shadows, Micah looked over the bed of the pickup to see Sloan standing behind his open door with a shotgun raised to his shoulder.

The shadow of the pickup near the street backed up and burned rubber pulling into the rainy blackness.

Sloan didn't move. "You both all right?" he said as calmly as if they'd just slipped in the mud.

"We're fine," Billy answered. "You?"

"Looks like two or three bullet holes in my windshield." Sloan shoved his shotgun back in its place behind his seat. "First time I ever used that gun for anything but scaring coyotes and rattlesnakes around the drilling sites. Nothing better for getting someone's attention than racking a shotgun."

Micah tried to slow his breathing. He wished he could blame his troubled breathing on his throbbing side but, the truth was, he could never remember being so frightened. He hadn't been raised around guns. He didn't even know what the sound was when he was being fired on. God must have left out survival instincts in him for even when the other two men had hit the dirt, he'd stood watching.

"You all right, Reverend?" Billy patted him on the back. "Sorry I tossed you so hard. I panicked when I saw you standing there like a target."

"Apparently, I didn't panic. That was my problem."

Sloan rounded the back of the truck. "I'm guessing you don't hear many shots fired in your line of work. Those boys meant to bother us, not harm us. Otherwise, I find it hard to believe they missed me." Sloan closed the tailgate. "How about we get out of the rain, take this back to Sidney, and go turn in a report to the sheriff?"

Billy swung into the back. "I'll ride with the rocking horse. I don't mind the rain."

When Micah climbed into the truck, he noticed three holes about a quarter of an inch wide in the windshield. "Would you have shot at them?" he asked Sloan directly.

"Yes," Sloan answered. "I'm not interested in turning the other cheek when someone's firing at me." He drove the truck out of the mud. "My father used to say don't ever pick up a gun unless you're willing to use it."

"You've used one before," Micah said.

"After the Gulf War. I went in with one of the big oil companies to help get the fields up and running again. We were ambushed twice by terrorists."

Micah didn't ask for more details. He wouldn't judge a man when he hadn't walked in his shoes.

Sloan drove through the rain. "Whoever shot at us tonight was trying to frighten us off. The question is why?"

They drove back to the sisters' place in silence. As they walked up to the house, the three agreed the less said to Ada May and Beth Ann, the better. The two old ladies were frightened enough already. If they thought someone living in town meant them harm, they'd probably organize a house-to-house search.

So, Sloan related how someone shot a hole in his windshield while they were parked at the Altman place. He also said he thought it best if he got the horse out of the weather. Micah and Billy quickly agreed that it was time to call it a night.

Micah walked out with Sloan and Sidney. "I don't mind going with you to the station to file the report."

"No use. We'll file the paperwork and tell them you were there."

"I think it best if we leave out the rocking horse," Sidney whispered. "After all, it has nothing to do with the shooting."

"Agreed," Sloan said.

"Agreed," Micah echoed. He could hear the Rogers sisters behind him insisting that Billy remove his wet clothes. Micah knew he'd better make his escape while he had the chance. He shook hands with Sloan, said his goodbyes to the professor and ran for his car. He didn't miss the way Sloan put his arm around Sidney as they ran into the rain and toward his pickup.

Micah knew Sloan, as an oilman, had no business hanging around the committee. The mayor would probably be mad if he heard about it, but as far as Micah was concerned, Sloan came with Sidney, nothing more. The minute he crossed the line and tried to talk them into anything, not one person on the committee would hesitate to stop him.

Twenty-Eight

Inside the Rogers sisters' house, Lora couldn't stop laughing. Billy was red with embarrassment, but he couldn't fight both the sisters mothering him. In truth, he was soaked from riding in the back of the truck and muddy from where he had to have fallen while loading the truck.

Lora took pity on him and handed him a quilt as he stepped into the bathroom with both sisters waiting like vultures just outside the door for his clothes.

Minutes later, he passed out his jeans, then his shirt. The sisters hurried off on a mission.

"What about your underwear?" Lora giggled as she heard the shower running.

"I didn't wear any," he answered. "How about you?"

She rattled the door and wasn't surprised to find it locked. Giving up, she wandered back to the living room and sat so that she could see the bathroom door. She waited.

When he stepped out of the bathroom with the quilt wrapped around him, Lora walked over and poked him for being so personal. She didn't bother to explain, he got the point.

"Let me get this rule straight, Whitman. You can ask about my underwear, but I can't ask about yours?"

"Correct." She changed the subject. "You didn't wear Beth Ann's robe. She said you could."

"Very funny." Billy wrapped the quilt around his waist. "You could have helped me out."

"No way." She moved her hand over his finely sculpted shoulder muscles. "The sisters may have wanted you clean, but I want to see your body." She circled around him. "Very nice."

"Cut the cracks, Whitman." He smiled. "If we're going to be friends, you've got to keep it clean."

She let her hand brush the warm flesh of his chest, surprised at how good it felt. "Beth Ann said for us to make ourselves comfortable on the couch and she'd bring in hot cocoa."

He kept a tight grip on his quilt covering as he moved to the cluttered living area. She couldn't stop her laughter. What did he think she'd do, tug at the blanket? To her surprise, the thought had crossed her mind.

They fought over pillows on the couch for a while, than settled beside one another. In whispered tones, he filled her in on the shooting.

"My God, Billy," she cried. "One of you could have been killed."

He shook his head. "I don't think they were shooting at us. If they were, they were pretty poor shots. But why would anyone want to run us off?"

"Maybe they were just drunk kids out shooting at anything. Half the road signs outside of town have at least one bullet hole in them."

"I know," he reasoned. "But you'll not find many on Main—even at the end of it. Sloan's truck was pulled up close to the house, but I don't think they were shooting at the house because I didn't hear any glass breaking." He relaxed back. "I think they were trying to send us a message."

"What?"

He shook his head. "I don't know."

An hour later, while the sisters watched their favorite program about detectives who solve old crimes, Billy fell asleep on the couch. Lora closed her eyes and rested her head against his shoulder.

"What should we do?" Lora heard Beth Ann whisper a while later.

"Leave them, I guess. They're safe enough here and this is no night to go out in again so late."

"But he doesn't have any clothes on."

Ada May huffed. "Well, he doesn't seem to mind and they're not dry yet to put on anyway. I told you we shouldn't have pre-soaked them."

"Should we stay up and keep them company? After all, they are two single young people and sweet as Lora is, she is divorced and you know what that means."

"What?"

"It means she knows a thing or two."

Lora fought to keep from laughing. They

weren't worrying about Billy attacking her. The old dears were worried that she might corrupt him.

"They're not interested in each other that way." Ada May spoke as if she considered herself an expert on the subject. "Don't be foolish. They treat one another more like brother and sister. We can't stay up any later. We've got church in the morning."

With that, the sisters moved down the hall turning off lights as they went. Lora cuddled closer to Billy. He opened his arm and pulled her against him, his slow steady breathing warm against the top of her head.

Lora spread her hand across his chest. Even in the shadows, she could see that the blanket had slipped revealing one bare thigh.

There was nothing sisterly in the way she looked at Billy Hatcher. She told herself she must be cracking up. He was four years younger. They had nothing in common. Her mother would die if she brought him home. That thought made her smile, but she could never be so cruel as to lead him on just to aggravate her mother.

But he was, she had to admit, one fine-looking man.

Twenty-Nine

A few miles away, on the north side of Clifton College campus, Sloan McCormick carried the rocking horse into Sidney's house as she held the door. They'd spent an hour filling out forms and answering questions at the sheriff's office. Deputy Adams seemed more interested in what Sloan, Micah and Billy were doing in the house than in the fact they'd been shot at.

Sidney explained that as committee members Micah and Billy had every right to be there checking water damage, and Sloan was a personal friend of hers who just happened to be with her when she stopped by.

On the way to the station, Sidney and Sloan agreed not to mention anything they found in the house, so Sloan stuck to his story that they went by the place to check for water damage.

"Do you think Adams believed us?" Sidney asked as she closed her front door and relaxed. She was glad to be home. It seemed like days since she'd left this morning.

Sloan paused in the hallway just long enough to remove his muddy boots. Then, he followed her into the tidy little living room before answering. "The deputy may have believed us about the shooting, but not about why we were there." He carefully placed the rocking horse in the center of the room. "He might have pushed, but he didn't feel comfortable calling the preacher, or you, a liar. My guess is first chance he gets he'll ask Micah what he was doing at the Altman place just to make sure the story holds. As far as I go, he sees me as a stranger in town and, therefore, guilty of something."

Sloan knelt and carefully began removing the wrapping from around the horse. "Really, everyone had a reason for being there, except me. I was the piece the deputy couldn't figure out."

He looked back at her. "You've got a nice place here, Sidney. A real home."

"Thanks. I put together all the things I loved from my mother and grandmother's house. I like having memories around me. It makes me feel like I belong." She picked up the one photo on her desk. "I'd like you to meet my grandmother, Minnie, my mother, Marbree, and me."

Sloan tipped an imaginary hat. "Nice to meet the family."

Sidney knew she was being foolish, but she wanted him to see where she'd come from and, in a strange way, she wanted them to meet him, too.

He turned back to work. She crossed to the kitchen area and asked, "Would you like a cup of coffee?"

"I'd love one. The sisters' iced tea made me feel even colder in these damp clothes."

She'd been so worried about everything, Sidney hadn't noticed how wet he was. She'd walked to her house with an umbrella, but he'd carried the rocking horse through the rain. She reached for a towel and tossed it to him. "I'll turn up the heater."

"Just coffee will be fine." By the time he ran the cloth over his clothes and towel-dried his hair, she stood before him with the coffee. He downed half the cup and smiled. "Thanks," he said, handing back the cup so he could continue cutting the tape around their find.

She sat on the ottoman behind him, her knees almost bumping his back. "It frightens me to think that one of you could have been shot." Sidney reached out, almost touching him.

"We weren't. Someone just wanted to let us know we shouldn't be in the house."

"Why were you there, Sloan? Why'd you stay with me all day?" Like the deputy, she wanted the pieces to fit together and Sloan didn't fit. She didn't want to think that he might only be interested in the Altman house, but she couldn't help wondering how many times he'd have to prove otherwise before she believed him.

He forgot the rocking horse and relaxed on the carpet in front of her. He used one of his long legs as an arm rest. With his hair a mess, he looked younger. "Don't you know, Sidney?" His words came slowly, not with his usual confidence. "It has nothing to do with the house, or this horse." He ran his fingers through his hair, doing little to straighten it. "I'll tell you that a thousand times if you need to hear it. My company will get along just fine without the Altman deal. That has nothing to do with you and me, except that I wouldn't have met you if I hadn't been on the job."

He leaned nearer. "Truth of it is, I'd do whatever I had to do to be close to you."

"I'm not sure I believe you," she answered in the only way she could, honestly.

"I can understand." He took her hand in his. "You think it's all about the house, but it's not." His thumb rubbed across her palm. "I'm here on a job. A big job for me. And that's what brought us together at first. But now . . ."

"But now . . ." If he was going to lie to her, she wanted to hear it all. She was tired of being blindsided in life, thinking things were as important to others as they were to her. She'd had two relationships in her life with men and both of them had ended in the "let's be friends" speech. She didn't want to be a woman men loved, but couldn't be in love with.

"It's something else with you. I knew it the first day I stood outside your classroom and listened to you lecture. Something more.

Like when you see something you didn't know you wanted until the moment you spot it." He looked up at her. "And that scares the hell out of me."

He leaned closer and kissed her so softly it made her heart ache.

"I understand." She straightened, setting his cup aside. "You want to be friends. You think . . ."

"What do I think?" He leaned back a few inches, surprised.

She knew the lecture, she'd heard it before. "I'm the kind of woman who can be a good ally. A good friend. A cohort you could talk over mysteries with. Since we're both interested in the Altman house, we have something in common, that's all."

He smiled. "Like hell."

Before she could react, he raised to his knees and pulled her against him. "If you think all I want to be is your friend, Professor, you'd best think again."

This time he kissed her with a hunger like no one had ever kissed her before. He tasted of the cool rain and warm coffee as he pulled her against his damp shirt.

The proper part of Sidney wanted to push him away, to tell him to go, to lecture him on how they could never be. Sloan McCormick couldn't just drop into her life for less than a week and expect—expect what? She couldn't think with him kissing her. For a part of her, the part that felt she'd been waiting for this one kiss since puberty, couldn't resist. She wrapped her arms around him and kissed him back.

Without stopping to talk, he pulled her to her feet. They stood, wrapped in one another. His hands moved slowly over her back, pressing her closer.

When he finally broke the kiss, he whispered near her ear. "You feel so right in my arms, Sidney. I don't understand it. I can't explain it. You just feel so right."

She smiled, realizing his words were true. Ever since she'd been taller than her prom date in high school, she'd always felt awkward. Ever since, she'd always felt too tall for any man in her life. She was the kind of woman who commanded respect with her proper behavior, not the kind anyone thought of with words like *passion* or *desire*. Even in college, the girls in her dorm had called her Mother Dickerson because she'd seemed so much older than them.

But she was not too tall for Sloan, she realized as he held her. He breathed in deep, filling his lungs with her scent. When she laughed, he caught the sound in his mouth as he kissed her once more. There was no doubt he looked at her with different eyes.

When he broke the kiss once more, he pulled away roughly. "I have to stop, or I'll be spending the night and ruining your reputation, Professor Dickerson."

Sidney hadn't thought about it, but he was right. The faculty were like characters in a play. Everyone in town kept up with them and everyone who lived in the bungalows knew whenever anyone had company.

He grabbed her hand and pulled her along as he moved to the door. There, he put on his boots, leaned her against the hallway wall and kissed her once more with a hunger that surprised her.

"Before I go, I want to get one thing straight. I'm not interested in being just your friend. If you're not agreeable to the possibility of mattering a great deal more than a friend ever would, I need you to tell me now."

She felt too shocked to say anything. From what she knew of Sloan, he was a good man. Never, not even in her dreams, did she think such a man would ever say something like this to her. "I'm agreeable to the possibility," she repeated his words.

He took a deep breath and placed his hands on either side of her face. "I'm willing to wait. I don't want to hurry you or talk you into anything. But I'm forty years old and through playing games. I'm attracted to you, your quick mind, your tender heart and to that body I feel beneath those very correct clothes." He leaned closer until their bodies touched. "And if you've no objections, I'd like to get to know you better. Much better."

When she didn't speak, he tilted her face and kissed her once more. The heat of his kiss warmed her all the way to her toes. When senses completely replaced thought, he leaned away, kissed her lightly on the forehead and walked out the door.

Sidney closed her eyes, trying to keep hold of every feeling for one moment longer.

Sloan made it back to his hotel room before his cell phone rang. He'd felt it vibrate in his pocket several times since the shooting, but he'd ignored it. Once he left Sidney, he had meant to flip the volume back on.

"Yes," he said, guessing who would be on the other line.

"Did you get the message, McCormick?" a low male voice said in little more than a whisper.

"I got it." Sloan walked to the bathroom without turning on the hotel room's lights. "Now, you get this. Leave me alone."

The man on the other end laughed. "Stay away from the committee, McCormick. Stay away from the professor if you know what's good for you."

"Go to hell! My interest in Sidney has nothing to do with the oil deal," Sloan yelled as he flipped on the shower and turned it to hot.

"Sure it doesn't," the voice said with a laugh.

Sloan closed the phone and stripped off his clothes as steam filled the room.

He stood, letting hot water hit him full in the face when the phone rang again. He didn't move. He knew who it was.

The committee might believe Sloan was only interested in the professor. The mayor would probably not comment one way or the other. Sidney might even accept that his feelings for her were real . . . but Sloan knew other oilmen would never believe it.

And tonight, they'd made their point in the rain in front of the Altman house.

Thirty

Micah awoke with a start. The whole side of his body was in pain. He slowly stood up from the chair he'd fallen asleep in and walked to the kitchen. For a few minutes, he couldn't figure out what was wrong. Then, he remembered. The rain. The rocking horse. Being shoved into Sloan's truck by Billy. Falling in the mud. It all seemed more like some old movie he'd been watching, not real life.

He'd taken aspirin when he'd gotten home, thinking it was just muscle aches. He must need more by now.

When he reached for the bottle, he glanced out the window. The rain had finally stopped. The street looked as though it sparkled in diamonds in the streetlight's glow. This time, just after the rain, was always his favorite time to run. Everything was newborn.

Maybe walking would stretch out a little of the soreness. He needed to think and he did it best when he was on the move. This committee he thought would be so simple was proving to be a mystery. Everyone agreed the house was falling down on itself, but something about Rosa Lee's story drew them all. It was almost as if they had to hold the house up for a little while longer so the secrets could come out. The stories of her never having a lover hadn't been true. The committee knew that much. But what else had happened in the house that no one knew? What other secrets did it hold? Would they be smart to learn them, or let them stay buried?

Micah opened the connecting door to Mrs. Mac's apartment and grabbed his jacket. Within minutes he was walking the silent streets thinking about the house, the rocking horse, the poem the old nurse had told Sidney. Fuller had died without returning for Rosa Lee. Somehow, Micah felt tied to Rosa Lee. They'd both known the loss of a loved one. And, as of now, they'd both chosen never to get over it.

As he passed Cemetery Road and turned back toward town, he told himself he wouldn't stop in at Randi's place tonight. After Saturday night's crowd, she would be tired. She was probably already asleep.

But, when he passed, he noticed the back downstairs light on. It had to be well after closing time, but she must still be awake.

He decided to knock on the back door. If she were in the front of the bar, she wouldn't hear him and he'd move on without bothering her.

She answered the knock. "Looking for another dance lesson?" she said as she opened the door.

He stepped inside. "I just dropped by." He didn't know what else to say. "I didn't mean to bother you."

Randi headed down the hallway toward the kitchen. "You didn't bother me. I was making chili, want some?"

"No thanks." He followed her.

She didn't seem to hear him. "Chili always sounds good on a night like this. The rain kept away most of the business." She moved about the kitchen, returning to what she'd been doing. "Have you heard from the Rogers sisters?"

"They went over to the Altman house looking at the roses this afternoon." He pulled off his jacket and relaxed. "Then, I dropped by their place for supper about eight. I don't think the sheriff's warning slowed them down any. We'd probably be wise to keep extra money around for bail."

Randi laughed in the low way she had that made him think she laughed at the world. "So, Preacher, you're dropping by all the single women in town hoping for a meal."

"Something like that."

"Aren't the Rogers sisters a little old for you?"

"They're fine, but Ada May's meat loaf almost killed me." Micah pulled up a chair and watched Randi cook. "We had a committee meeting about the old Altman place since we were all together but, as usual, we didn't make any progress."

"Couldn't the six of you come up with a decision?" Like everyone in town, Randi followed the progress of a committee no one had wanted to be on when it had started.

"Not yet. What's the bet going in the bar?" Micah knew the locals were betting on which way the committee would vote, but then, folks in bars bet on everything.

Randi sat a bowl of chili in front of him. "Most think you'll let one of the oil companies have it. I've heard there are a few fighting over it, so the money they pay may be good. No one really cares about the house. They see it as another falling down property in town. Probably the only people around who can even remember Henry Altman are Old Man Hamm and maybe Luther Oates. As for Rosa Lee, I'm not sure anyone really knew her to start with."

Randi filled her bowl and joined him. They talked about the sisters, the sheriff and his pregnant wife and what the committee had learned. It felt good to turn over ideas with someone. Randi poured him coffee and encouraged him to at least taste her chili. She told him about growing up in Clifton Creek and finally about the oil-rig accident that took her husband's life. Something about the foggy night made secrets safe to tell.

"I came into a little money and figured if I didn't want to work at the factory for the rest of my life I'd better invest in something. A bar seemed like a good idea."

"You could open a café," he mumbled between bites.

Randi shook her head. "Once I dreamed of being a singer, but it's not easy to make it. In the end, I knew I was just a small-town girl and I needed to go back to where I belonged."

"Do you still sing?"

She shook her head. "Not much. Once in a while I write a song down in a book I keep behind the bar. That kind of makes me feel as if I've still got my finger in the business. It was just a wild, crazy dream I had, but dreams, no matter how impractical, die hard."

"I know how you feel."

She laughed. "I doubt it. I have a hard time ever believing you were wild or crazy."

"Probably not." He realized by her standards he'd never done anything. "When I was a kid though, I wanted to raise horses. We moved around a lot, but in one town I got to take riding lessons. From then on I dreamed of having a horse ranch, raising horses."

"Your parents farmed?"

"No. My dad was an interim preacher. A minister who fills in at churches when they are between ministers. When I was twelve he got assigned to this church that had problems. We moved to East Texas thinking we'd only be there a year. But the church was in a crisis my folks never bothered to explain to me, so I guess I thought we were finally settling. It turned out we stayed four years trying to help the church."

Micah leaned back in his chair, but his words betrayed any hint of being relaxed. "I met my wife when we were in middle school in that little town in East Texas. When my parents moved on to the next church, I stayed behind with friends to finish out my senior year, then we both got scholarships to Harden Simmons. I don't remember ever thinking about being anything else but a minister. Amy wanted it. My parents wanted it. My professors in college said I was a natural at problem solving like my father. My strength wasn't in the pulpit, but in meetings." He hesitated. "I wanted to make things run more smoothly, make the world better, I guess."

Randi's eyes looked into his very soul.

"Did you ever tell Amy about wanting to raise horses?"

The question shocked him, but he answered honestly. "No." He would have sworn he'd told Amy everything he'd thought or felt from the time he was in the eighth grade. But he'd never told her about the dream. Maybe because he'd known it was only a child's dream and nothing more. He knew little about horses, nothing about taking care of them and had no money to buy land even if he did have the knowledge.

"Well." She smiled. "It's a nice dream."

Without either of them saying a word, they stood and cleaned up the dishes. When he dried his hands, he said, "I'd better get back. I didn't mean to take up so much of your time. I guess I just needed to talk to someone."

"Wouldn't the sisters listen?"

He smiled, caught in his lie. "Correction," he said. "I needed to talk to you."

She walked toward her office. "Have you time for one dance before you go? I want to make sure you haven't forgotten everything I taught you. You look like one of those slow learners/fast forgetters to me."

He followed. "I've time and I haven't forgotten a thing."

"Then pull off those running shoes and let's circle round the floor one time."

He tugged off the shoes while she put on the music. When they walked onto the floor, she stepped easily into his arms and he fought to keep from saying *welcome home.*

They danced an easy two-step, then when the music slowed, she melted against him and they moved unhurried and easy. He closed his eyes and let his mind drift with the music, drinking in the nearness of her with all his other senses. He could feel her heart pounding against his, smell the spices from the chili on her skin and in her hair. She softly sang the words to the song against his ear.

He let go of her fingers and crushed a handful of her wild hair, needing the feel of it in his memory. He might never hold her except to dance, but he planned to remember everything.

She wrapped both arms around his neck and swayed with him, her body fluid and warm against his as she whispered the words to the song so low he felt them against his throat more than heard them.

He would have been happy if the music had played on forever, but it ended. They separated and headed off the floor, staying close to one another as if the room were crowded. She flipped off the twinkle lights as she moved behind the bar.

He grabbed his shoes and followed not knowing what to say and unsure if he could form words even if he tried. They walked in silence to the back door. They were so close their clothes brushed as they moved.

"Take care," she whispered and kissed him on the cheek. "Drop by anytime you see the lights on."

She patted his side and he winced with sudden pain.

"What is it?" Worry pulled her from the slow waltz dream they'd both been floating in.

"Nothing," he answered. "I just fell against a pickup in the rain." He didn't want to worry her about the shooting earlier at the Altman house.

She flipped on the light and tugged at his jacket and shirt. "Let me see."

Micah had a feeling there was no use in arguing with her, so he lifted his shirt. "It's just bruised." He'd tried to look at it in the mirror at home, but most of the bruising had been on his back where he couldn't see anything.

Randi pulled him toward the kitchen. "It's also scraped. Didn't you clean this up?"

"I wiped the mud off it." Micah didn't know how to take the mothering. He didn't want to admit how much it hurt and his usual remedy of ignoring pain until it went away would probably work fine.

"Pull off your jacket and shirt."

He thought of arguing, but she disappeared. A few moments later, she returned with a towel and medicine kit. "I'm cleaning that scrape up and disinfecting it, even if I have to knock you senseless to do so."

He laughed and pulled off his jogging jacket and raised his T-shirt to his shoulders. "Nice bedside manner."

"Shut up and stand still." She pulled a chair up and sat while she cleaned the scrape that ran from his side to his spine.

"This is deeper than you think, Micah," she said. "If it got infected, it would be a mess."

He didn't tell her that pain, physical or emotional, was something he'd learned to disconnect from a long time ago. Her hands moved over his skin warming him. He tried not to think about how long it had been since a woman had touched him.

She leaned forward, softly blowing where she'd doctored along his back. The feel of her breath moving along his skin almost buckled his knees. "I think you'll live," she whispered, "but I want to take another look next week."

"Sure, doc." He started to pull down his shirt, but she stood, so close he could feel the heat of her.

"I have to take care of you," she whispered. "Friends aren't that easy to come by." She helped him lower his shirt.

When they said goodbye for the second time at the back door, he turned when she leaned to kiss his cheek just as she had before. The kiss was light, friendly and on the lips.

"Thanks," he said as he stepped outside and she vanished into shadow. For a moment he stood in the darkness, then knelt and tied his shoes.

She closed the door and he heard the bolt sliding across. The last thing she did each night before climbing the stairs, he remembered her saying. The light went out in the hallway. One came on upstairs. He thought he heard her singing the words to one of the songs they'd danced to.

Micah walked home trying to hold the memory of her near for as long as possible. Somewhere between the talk, the dancing and the chili, he'd become someone she cared about.

Thirty-One

Billy blinked away the bright sunlight. It had to be morning, he thought, Sunday morning. The only day in his week that he had free.

He straightened and felt a warm lump beside him.

"Lora," he mumbled as he pushed hair away from her face. "You'd better wake up or I'm having some kind of nightmare that I've slept all night in the Rogers sisters' house."

She didn't look interested in the idea. She pulled the afghan she'd been using for cover over her head. "We are at the Rogers sisters' house," she mumbled. "Go back to sleep."

"Lora," he laughed. "It's dawn and you've slept with me again."

She poked him in the side. "Shut up. I'm trying to sleep."

He tugged his blanket away from where she was lying on it and stood. "I've got to find my clothes. You do whatever you like."

"I don't want to go home," she mumbled, sounding like a five-year-old. "I never want to go home."

"I understand," he answered as he moved through the kitchen. "I've felt that way all my life."

When Billy got back from the laundry room on the sisters' back porch, Lora was sitting upright, but didn't look happy about it. "You all right, babe?" He grinned. She still pouted.

"I'm not your babe," she corrected.

He snapped his jeans and pulled on his shirt. "For a woman who loves to cuddle, you sure do wake up cross. I think bears come out of hibernation in friendlier moods."

"I wasn't cuddling. I was freezing and you were warm." She rubbed the back of her neck. "I've got a headache and this conversation isn't helping."

"Suit yourself, Whitman. You think you could get your butt off the couch long enough to drive me back to my car?"

She reached for her shoes. "I guess. I'll never get warm if you leave."

"Don't do me any favors. I can walk."

"Now who's testy?" She tried to shove her foot into the shoe and stand at the same time and tumbled back into the mass of pillows.

Billy laughed and offered a hand. "All right. I'll go easy on you. I guess morning isn't really your time."

"You got that right." She accepted his help. "But then, lately, neither is afternoon, evening, or night. I've got an emotional disability. I keep getting up on the wrong side of the bed." She looked behind her. "Or couch."

"I'll buy you a cup of coffee if you can manage to get that hair of yours under control."

She flung it over her shoulder and looked for her other shoe. "We'd better hurry or Ada May will cook us breakfast."

Suddenly, it was a game. They giggled their way through finding clothes and dressing, then tiptoed out of the house like two kids. Lora pitched Billy the keys to her Audi and they were off.

She tried to comb her hair while he drove, but the effort was pretty much hopeless. They headed out to the only places open on Sunday mornings, the truck stops on the interstate. Billy found one that had a breakfast buffet and they stuffed themselves with courses of fruit, pancakes, sausage, hash browns and grits. When they finished, the stack of plates looked like a family had eaten in the booth.

Billy offered to refill their coffee cups while Lora leaned back. Her headache had been replaced by a stomachache, but she wouldn't have missed the fun of pigging out. After last night's dinner at the sisters' she deserved a real meal and Ada May made even truck stop food look good.

A shadow crossed between her and the light. "Lora?"

She looked up into the face of a shocked Talon Graham. He hadn't changed, the oilman dressed as a cowboy. Perfect ironed shirt, hat shoved back on his perfect hair. A smile that never moved to his perfect blue eyes. Only this morning, he didn't have whiskey on his breath and his hands were in his pockets, not on her.

"Is that you?" He cocked his head to one side as if not believing what he was seeing. "I thought I saw your Audi in the parking lot, so I stopped. You haven't returned any of my calls."

She didn't bother to glance down at the wrinkled jogging suit. "It's me. And I haven't been home much to take calls. Glad to see you made it back from Wichita Falls. You were pretty far under the table when I left."

"I woke up yesterday morning in my car with you nowhere in sight." He raised an eyebrow. "How'd you get home? You know I would have taken you if you'd insisted. I'd just had a rough day Friday and wanted to get lost in the bottle for a few hours."

While she thought about answering, Billy appeared. He wasn't as tall as Talon and his clothes were stained and wrinkled, but Lora decided he was about a thousand times better to look up at than the cowboy. Billy Hatcher had never let her down.

He handed her a coffee and slid into the seat across from her. His gray eyes watched the stranger closely over his coffee mug, but he seemed calm, almost totally relaxed, as if he'd spent years learning not to show emotion.

For a moment, both men waited, staring at her. "Talon Graham, I'd like you to meet a friend of mine, Billy Hatcher."

Talon didn't look as if he believed her but, to his credit, he offered his hand. Neither bothered to say they were happy to meet the other. Lora didn't offer Talon a seat.

"Well," he finally said. "I guess I'll see you later, Lora. Maybe we can try dinner again sometime?"

Billy watched her. She knew all she had to say was one word and he'd clobber Talon Graham. She'd told Billy all the details of the date, so Billy knew what a slug the guy was. But, she didn't want to make a scene any more than she wanted Talon to think there would be any possibility of a second date.

She slid her hand across the table and laced her fingers with Billy's. After the initial shock, he played along. "I don't think there will be another date, Talon. I'm seeing someone."

The oilman looked confused. He obviously hadn't considered Billy in the game, not with Lora Whitman. "Isn't he a little young for you, Lora?"

"You're four years older than me, why can't I be four years older than him?" She winked at Billy. "Maybe I like robbing the cradle."

Talon nodded once. "I see. Well, have a good day." He walked away.

Billy pulled his hand away. "I wouldn't mind punching that guy a few times, but I'm not into fighting old men."

"Who, Talon?" She laughed. "You just beat him without raising a hand and he knows it. If you're wise, stay away for a while, I'd hate to see my new boyfriend hurt."

"I can take care of myself."

"After a close look at your body last night, I've no doubt of that, but knowing Talon, I'd guess he wouldn't face you alone. He's more the type to get someone else to do his fighting for him."

Billy frowned. "Are you trying to tell me that being your new boyfriend comes with a downside?"

She laughed. "Of course it does. I just told Talon we're dating. It'll be all over town by noon. Billy Hatcher and Lora Whitman." She winked at him again. "And you haven't met the downside until you meet my mother."

"There goes my reputation," Billy mumbled as he sipped his coffee. "And stop winking at me. You're giving me the creeps being so nice."

"You want to break up?"

"No, I'm too used to sleeping with you now." He grinned. "Any chance I can call you babe?"

"No."

"How about the odds of getting lucky?"

"None."

"Damn, Whitman, being your steady sounds like great fun."

They paid out and headed toward the parking lot. "You get to drive my car. Dating me is not all bad."

He walked beside her, their strides matching easily. "I usually get a little more out of a relationship than car keys," he complained. "But, it's a start."

She swung back to slug him, when she caught sight of Talon sitting in his Cadillac watching.

"All right, one kiss." She swung her arms around him and pressed her lips hard against his, then stepped away and slipped into the passenger side of her car.

She watched Talon slam his car into Reverse as Billy climbed behind the wheel of her Audi. He rubbed his mouth. "Where'd you learn to kiss, prison?"

Before she could explain, he leaned over and pressed her against the seat with a kiss that took her breath away.

When he settled back in his seat, he said, "The next time you kiss me just to piss another guy off, try to remember how."

She tried to tell if he was angry about her show for Talon. She couldn't tell, but one thing she knew. Anger hadn't kissed her, passion had.

When he turned in at the Altman house, he left the car running as he climbed out. Lora opened her door and walked to the other side. "Still friends?" she asked knowing that she'd used him back in the truck stop.

He winked. "Always, Whitman, always."

Then, before she could answer, he was gone. Jumping over the railing of the porch and vanishing into the back of the house. She smiled. He was too young for her and she had a feeling that if they'd been the same age he would be too much of a man for her to handle.

"Friends," she said as she drove away.

Thirty-Two

The First United Methodist Church of Clifton Creek had their monthly covered-dish luncheon after the eleven o'clock service. Micah loved the time. Everyone who stayed ate together, then the kids played in the basement while the younger couples visited and the older members played dominoes. The blending of generations always made him feel grounded.

By two in the afternoon, one of the ladies' groups had set up a quilting corner and guitar lessons were running nonstop in one corner of the activity hall. Micah suspected their popularity was due to the teacher who'd made a name for himself in clubs as far away as Dallas. In the summers, families moved out on the lawn behind the church and cranked up ice-cream freezers, but in the fall lots of coffee and an endless supply of desserts seemed to help pass the afternoon in what Reverend Milburn called country fellowship.

Today, Micah had begged out of a domino game in favor of digging through the old church files while he had the time. If Rosa Lee Altman had ever attended church, there was a good chance she'd come here. The Baptist church hadn't been founded until after World War II, so most folks, Methodist or not, must have attended here during the early years.

Unfortunately, the records weren't in great order. Every ten years or so the files were cleaned out upstairs, stuffed together in boxes and placed in a closet that also held extra folding chairs. Every time Micah tried a new box, he had to move chairs.

After half an hour of work, he hadn't even managed to find a single record of Rosa Lee Altman ever setting foot in the church. Maybe, if her mother had died when Rosa Lee was born, her father might have been too heartbroken to register her birth in the church record. Micah checked the next twenty years. Nothing.

Nancy, the church secretary, poked her head in. "Would you like a dessert, Reverend Parker? We're about to close down the kitchen."

He didn't bother to ask how she'd found him. The woman had radar for knowing where everyone in the church was at any one moment. "No thanks." He smiled. "Could I ask a favor of you when you have time?"

"Sure," she answered, enjoying being inside the circle for once.

"Would you see if you can find any listing of Rosa Lee Altman in our records? I hate to ask, it may take hours."

"I'll have hospitality start on it first thing Monday morning. If it's here, we'll find it before your next committee meeting with the professor."

Micah frowned, then realized, of course Nancy would know of his next meeting. It was on his calendar. He wondered if her habit had always irritated him, or if the fact that he now had a midnight friend made him aware folks might be watching. He told himself he didn't care. He'd visit Randi even if the whole town knew about their break-fasts.

The hospitality committee Nancy had vol-unteered was a group of older ladies who prepared meals for funerals and set up for weddings. They met every Monday morning to plan. Micah figured a lady had to be sweet for at least fifty years to get on hospi-tality. He'd never heard one of them say a cross word. Not even when the oven had gone out and the usual funeral brisket hadn't gotten cooked, or when the bakery had forgotten to make a groom cake and it hadn't been discovered until two hours be-fore a wedding. Hospitality had simply gone to work and done the best they could.

"Thanks, Nancy," he said, dusting off his hands and feeling grateful she'd agreed to take over the task.

"Anytime." She smiled.

Micah knew Nancy wanted to be friends, not just co-workers. She'd invited him over for dinner with her and her husband a dozen times over the years. But he'd never gone. He told himself a single minister had to be careful against rumors, but it was more than that. He just didn't have much to say to Nancy and even less to say to her husband, who worked at the grain elevator and lived with a wad of tobacco in his mouth all waking hours except while he was in church. Micah suspected he reached for a pinch during the final prayer.

When she closed the door, he stacked a few boxes back in place and then sat down in one of the chairs. He'd lost sleep three nights this week visiting Randi and probably more time thinking about her. How could he have so much to say to a bar owner and nothing to say to the nice lady who worked in his office, or the older minister who loved his church more than Micah ever would? How could they be strangers and Randi be his friend?

He knew he could talk to Randi about anything, and he didn't really know her at all. Maybe it was the way she treated him. Maybe it was her quick wit and even quicker temper. Or maybe it was the way she let him dance with her, heart-to-heart without asking questions as to why he came around.

Micah closed his eyes. He wished she were here now. He wanted to talk to someone about why, in all the years he'd been with Amy, he'd never told her his childhood dream. Yet he'd told Randi.

He'd acted as though the dream had passed, but sometimes at night when he couldn't sleep he remembered. Once in a while when he'd be driving past a ranch, the dream returned to slam against his reality. He'd pull over and watch the horses run. He wasn't a cowboy. He couldn't even ride all that well, but part of the little boy in him had never outgrown the dream of horses.

The dream didn't matter, he decided, but the fact he'd never told Amy did. Why hadn't he told her? Did he think she'd somehow love him less? If he hadn't wanted to be a minister, would he have been the perfect fit for her? Did he love her so much he was willing to erase a dream, or did she love him so little that it would have made a difference?

Micah leaned forward, his head in his hands. He'd lived with the loss of perfection when he'd lost his Amy. Now to see a crack made him grieve all over again.

"Dad?" Logan yelled from the doorway. "Are you in here?"

"I'm here," he answered and stepped

back into the role that had become his life. "Ready to head home, son?"

The boy came closer. He had a cookie in one hand and a paper butterfly with a Bible verse typed on it in the other. "I was wondering." Logan made the butterfly fly as he neared. "If I could go home with Jimmy and play. His mom said she wouldn't mind at all. She says she owes you big-time for yesterday, whatever that means."

"Tell her yesterday was my pleasure, but if you want to go home with Jimmy and his parents, I'll pick you up later."

"Wait until after supper, would you, Dad? Me and Jimmy got some talking to do. Tomorrow's school and we don't get to talk much then."

"All right. After supper if it's okay with Jimmy's mom." Micah knew it would be. The boys spent so much time together, Logan kept a toothbrush at Jimmy's house and Micah always bought a box of Jimmy's favorite cereal when he shopped.

He straightened Logan's hair and smiled.

With that his son was gone, running as always. Micah finished up, helping several elderly to their cars and locking doors. He crossed into his office where all was quiet.

Without really thinking about it, he dialed Randi's number.

"Hello," she answered on the first ring.

"Hello." He couldn't think of anything else to say. He couldn't very well just blurt out that he wanted to see her. And, if he suggested they talk, she might ask what about and he'd be stuck. Maybe he was safer to stop with hello.

She laughed. "This is the most boring obscene call I've ever had."

Micah relaxed. "I just thought I'd call before dark so you'll know I do come out when it's light."

The other end of the phone was dead for so long, Micah thought she'd hung up on him. "Micah," she finally said. "It's been four years this week since my husband and four others were in that oil-rig accident."

He already knew that, the whole town talked about it from time to time. The worst thing that had ever happened in Clifton Creek. An oil rig blew, killing four and leaving one crippled.

Micah felt like a fool. He shouldn't have called.

Before he could say anything, Randi continued, "Some of us are going out to the site this afternoon to kind of pay our respects. We're leaving in a few minutes."

"I'm sorry." He felt bad for calling. "I didn't mean to interrupt you."

"No, it's okay," she answered. "I thought of calling you to see if you'd go with me. I don't really want to go alone this year."

"Are you sure you want me along?"

"I could use a friend."

"I'm on my way."

Ten minutes later, he drove into the bar parking lot. The sheriff and his pregnant wife were waiting with Randi. Granger didn't seem the least surprised to see Micah and greeted him with a nod. Meredith, who'd never met Micah, greeted him warmly. She waddled a few steps and Granger frowned and followed as if ready to catch her if she tumbled.

Before the introductions were over, another car arrived with a beautiful woman dressed in wealth and a man leaning heavily on a cane. Randi introduced them as Crystal and Shelby Howard. She didn't add, the one survivor, but Micah figured it out. Though the man was scarred and moved in slow steps, there was no doubt he loved his wife. Micah had heard more than one person in town say that Crystal had worked miracles taking care of Shelby and running an oil company.

They greeted Micah formally. The men shook hands, the women hugged one another. They all spoke of a widow who'd died soon after her husband and how much they missed her. Micah tried to follow the conversation, but these were old friends used to finishing one another's thoughts. Finally, everyone climbed back into their cars and the sheriff's car led the caravan out to the site.

Randi seemed quieter than usual as Micah drove. Micah knew ways to draw her out, get her to talk about things she kept locked away. The tricks of the trade in counseling, he thought, but he used none of them on her. He wanted her to tell him when she was ready, if she ever felt ready.

He laid his hand over hers. She turned her palm up and gripped his hand, but didn't look at him. He drove on in silence.

The final woman widowed four years ago was waiting for the caravan at her ranch gate. She was striking atop a beautiful black mare. When she opened the gate, she introduced herself as Anna and to Micah's surprise, she winked at him. "Randi tells me you ride. I brought along an extra mount. We can cross to the site by the time everyone drives around along the road if you want to ride with me."

Micah couldn't believe it. In his best dress pants, he swung up on a horse just as he had as a child. Anna kicked her animal into action. Randi smiled at him then slid over to the driver's seat of his car and followed the other vehicles. Micah was left at the gate trying to remember a skill he hadn't practiced in twenty years. Luckily, the horse seemed to want to follow Anna, so Micah's main task came down to hanging on.

He could see the beautiful woman riding as if she'd been born on a horse, while he bumped along behind. But the wind in his face was the same, and Micah laughed, remembering how dearly he loved riding even if he couldn't quite master the skill.

Anna slowed as a skeleton of an oil rig came into sight. She walked her mount until Micah caught up. "We meet here every year to remember. This is the first time Randi's ever brought a friend." She smiled at him. "I'm glad you could come."

By the time they got to the rig, the cars

had pulled in close to the ashes. Randi held his horse's reins while he climbed off. "Enjoy the ride, cowboy?"

He fought a smile. "I'm a long way from that and you know it, but yes. Thank you."

"Hey, you're closer than you think. You can ride and two-step. There's not all that much more to it."

Anna kissed a lean man standing by the cars and handed him the reins to her horse. Randi told Micah the rancher was Anna's husband, but she didn't take the time to introduce the men.

They joined the others, all silent now as they began the ritual. The women each collected flowers from the trunk of Crystal's car and scattered them on the burned pile that had once been a rig. The sheriff, Anna's husband and Micah stood back where Crystal had parked the car so that her Shelby could see without having to stand.

Micah was very much aware that each man watched his wife. The men were silent and it took Micah a minute to realize why they all frowned. They all realized that if the accident hadn't happened—if the men hadn't died—they wouldn't have their women now. They wouldn't have the life they had.

He looked toward the women. They must have suffered greatly, but they'd survived and somehow each must be stronger because of it. Crystal opened a bottle of wine and all but the sheriff's pregnant wife drank a toast. Then, they threw their glasses into the rubble.

Finally, the women turned one by one and walked back to their cars, tears streaming down their cheeks. Micah was glad he'd come. He wondered if Randi usually did this alone with no one to hold her after the odd ceremony.

For a few minutes, they let the men who waited wrap them in caring arms, then, nervously, they laughed as tissues were passed.

Anna invited them back to the house. Crystal said Shelby wasn't feeling well, but the others agreed. Anna's husband Zack swung his wife onto her saddle and said he'd meet her back at the house.

Randi looked up at Micah. "Can you stay a while?"

"Sure." He grinned. "You don't want to help me up in the saddle?"

She shook her head and jingled the car keys. "No, but I'll race you back."

He climbed back on the horse thinking he was getting the hang of it now. He even managed to stay up with Anna on the mile ride to their barn. In the afternoon sun, the place looked like what Micah had always dreamed a working ranch would be. It felt good to know that somewhere, for someone, his dream was real.

When they reached the corral, Anna handed her animal over to one of the hands, but Micah wanted to see the barn. He promised to catch up with Anna soon and then turned to ask the hand questions. Micah wanted to see more, smell more, feel more, while he had the chance.

An hour later Randi found him bottle-feeding a young colt, his Sunday pants covered in dirt.

"Anna sent me to tell you they've got barbecue ready if you're interested."

He nodded and gave the bottle to the ranch hand who had been answering questions. As Micah walked beside Randi to the main house, he whispered, "You have no idea how much I needed this. The past hour has been like stepping into a dream."

"Anna's invited us out next week. Maybe you can bring Logan along. I'd like to meet him." The second the words were out of her mouth, she bit her lip. She'd gone too far. Made it seem like they were a couple. Presumed.

He understood. An invisible line crossed between them, keeping them both apart, even when they were close to one another. The past. Her husband. His wife. Their lives. Reality. He decided if she could play hopscotch with the line, he could, too, even if it were just pretend for tonight and they'd go back to the real world tomorrow. "I'd like that," he said simply and took her hand as they walked toward the house.

It couldn't be this simple, Micah thought an hour later when they were sitting around laughing and talking horses. He couldn't step so easily into being with Randi, but somehow, if only for today, he had. She teased him, even showing the others how he first danced. He laughed so hard when Granger told the group about having to arrest the Rogers sisters, Micah felt tears come to his eyes.

Micah had never seen the sheriff relaxed. Granger and Zack were friendly with one another, but not like the women. Randi, Meredith and Anna seemed more like sisters even though they were very different women.

The phone rang somewhere in the kitchen and they lowered their voices. A moment later Zack called Granger back. Everyone continued to talk, but the tone was low now.

Granger returned, pulling on his uniform jacket. "Randi, can you see Meredith gets home?"

Randi nodded but the sheriff wasn't looking. He strapped on the gun he'd removed when he'd walked in the door. Glancing up at his wife, he ordered, "I want you to call me if anything happens. Don't wait because you think I'm busy. Call me if you feel anything."

"I promise. What is it? What's happened?" Meredith asked and everyone else waited.

Granger hesitated. "It's Billy Hatcher. He's been beat up bad. Lora Whitman found him out behind the Altman place. They're taking him to the hospital now. I told them I'd meet them there."

Meredith straightened, as a sheriff's wife she'd learned not to ask for more.

"We'll get her home," Micah said wishing he were already at Billy's side. "Tell him—"

Granger turned to Micah. "Tell him yourself," he said. "You're going with me."

Something in Granger's eyes made Micah nod without arguing.

They were running by the time they reached the police car. Granger threw it into gear before Micah got his door closed. They were off, sailing down a dirt road with lights flashing.

"He may need you," Granger said.

"I'll phone Jimmy's mom and let her know I may be late picking up Logan." He pulled out his cell phone. "Thanks for letting me ride along. I want to be there if Billy's hurt. I'm his friend."

Granger shook his head slowly. "You're the closest thing he's got to a priest. I don't know how bad it is."

Thirty-Three

Lora Whitman curled into one of the hospital blankets in the waiting room and tried to get warm. She hadn't stopped shaking for two hours. Closing her eyes, she tried to piece together her day.

She'd woken up in the sisters' living room with Billy beside her. They'd eaten breakfast, then she'd dropped him off at the Altman place where his car had been parked behind the house. He'd told her he was going over to the professor's to get Sidney to help him fill out forms so he could take some classes. Then he'd planned to spend a few hours working out at the Y. He'd tried to tease her into joining him.

She'd laughed and driven off yelling

something about why should she work out
when she could already whip him.

Lora had gone home to flowers from
Talon and questions from her mother. The
flowers must have been delivered on Saturday, before he'd seen her at the truck stop
Sunday morning, because the card asked
for a second date. Since they'd only had
half of the first one, she didn't see how that
could be possible. She wouldn't go out with
Talon again if he bought half the cars on her
father's lot. He might be model handsome,
but being with him made her feel strange,
as if she were only a bit player in the play
that framed *his* life.

Lora finally got rid of her mother by claiming she had a headache. She spent the rest
of the day trying not to be accidentally in the
same room with Isadore. About sunset, she
decided to go for a drive and when she saw
Billy's car back at the Altman place, she
thought she'd offer to buy him a hamburger
if he'd ride along.

But, the house was locked up and Billy, or
his bedroll, was nowhere in sight. She
walked around the gardens, until it grew too
dark to see the path, remembering how she
used to hate the grounds when she was a

kid. She'd always thought of it as a haunted place. She even remembered hearing stories about a madman who roamed in the dark. But now she saw the gardens for what they were. A lonely old woman's passion. Rosa Lee Altman had cared and tended to them all her life and they'd ended up just like Rosa Lee, dead.

Lora walked back to her car, watching for a light in the house and telling herself Billy was probably down at the café having supper. She knew he never went home unless he had to and couldn't help but wonder how much of his life he'd spent roaming about the town, sleeping wherever he found a place. People always thought of street kids as being in big cities. She told herself he must have some place to call home, but she wasn't so sure. His car was here, so he'd be returning sometime, but she wasn't about to wait for him in the dark.

When she swung her car around to leave, her lights crossed over the pile of bricks and trash at the end of the back porch.

Something moved.

Her imagination went wild. Zombie animals crawling out to roam the streets at dusk. Rats the size of cats.

The car light reflected off something black and shiny—a leather jacket.

Lora froze. She clicked the lights to bright and saw an arm shoving from the rubble.

From then on, everything happened at once. She jumped from her car and ran down the beam of light. She pulled at Billy's arm, crying, screaming for him to stop scaring her. She clawed at the mud as she jerked him free, her hands red with his blood, her ears hurting at the volume of her own cries.

She didn't remember what she screamed into the cell phone, but it only took a few minutes before the ambulance pulled up. For a moment, she wouldn't turn loose of him. He seemed a rag doll made of mud and blood, but his hand gripped hers as if holding on to life. When they'd gotten to the hospital, the nurse had had to pry her away. Then they'd forced her into the hell of the waiting room and had left her alone.

"Lora?"

She looked up as Micah ran toward her.

"Are you all right?"

She shook her head. It seemed a dozen people had passed by and asked her the same question, then drifted away. Micah sat down and pulled her into a hug.

She thought of crying, but she wasn't sure she had any more tears. She'd asked the others how Billy was, but none of them told her. She didn't bother to ask Micah.

"At first." Her voice sounded hoarse, strange to her. "I thought the house had fallen on him. But the wall was still there. Whoever hurt him tried to bury him."

Micah didn't say anything. He just held her tightly for a while. She leaned into him, trying not to think as she listened to his heart beating.

Finally, Micah whispered, "Do you want me to call someone? Your folks?"

"No, but we need to call the professor. Billy had planned a meeting with her. I don't know if he made it there or not. I don't know how long he lay in the mud before I found him. It could have been a few minutes. It might have been all day."

Micah nodded and dialed Sidney's number. In low tones, he told the professor what had happened, then lowered his phone without saying goodbye. "She's on her way," he said.

Lora curled back into the blanket and

they waited. Sidney arrived with questions and, to Lora's surprise, it helped her focus to tell the story again. The first time with the deputy, she hadn't been able to stop crying. The sisters rushed in a few minutes later and she repeated every detail, forcing herself to remember.

"What did the doctor say?" Ada May demanded the same thing the professor had.

"Nothing, yet," Micah answered. "They said it may be hours. The sheriff told me there was a bad cut on his head. Maybe some internal injuries. He's lost a lot of blood."

Beth Ann pulled out her crochet. "Then we wait."

Ada May agreed. "We wait. No matter how long." Only she wasn't as good at sitting still as her sister. She paced. Organized the magazines. Got everyone coffee. And finally, started pestering anyone who walked by for news.

The sheriff came out from behind the doors marked Authorized Personnel Only and said Billy hadn't regained consciousness yet. Old Doc Hamilton had been on backup call, since it was Sunday night. He'd taken one look at Billy's head and had called his grandson, who was a specialist on brain injuries in Wichita Falls.

"That's right, Doc Hamilton had three children, two of them are doctors, and eight grandchildren, four of them are finished with med school and two are still in," Ada May added as if testing her memory. "They believe in passing down the family business. If the doc told them to come, my guess is they jump to."

The sheriff didn't look as if he needed to know the details of Hamilton lineage. He continued looking at Lora and Micah. "They'll let us know something as soon as they finish working on him. All I got out of Hamilton was that it looked like Billy was in one hell of a fight. Bruises everywhere, probably some cracked ribs, and a blow to the head that must have knocked him out cold."

Lora nodded. "When I held his hand, his knuckles were bloody. The bandage he still wore from the glass cuts was soaked in blood."

Granger got out his notepad. "I'll need to know every detail you can remember, Lora. If it was a fight, Billy didn't go down easy."

He looked up at the sisters and Sidney as if he were going to ask them to leave.

"Don't even think about it, Granger," Ada May said. "We're all staying right here until the boy is out of danger. Anything you need to say to one of us can be said to all."

Granger groaned in frustration, but began writing. "Start at the beginning, Lora. Tell me everything you remember."

Before Lora could say anything, Sidney answered. "The beginning might be the drill bit through the window, or someone starting a fire, or the gunshots last night."

Granger's head jerked up. "What gunshots?"

"The ones made at Sloan McCormick's truck while he was over at the house with Micah and Billy."

The sheriff looked at Micah. "Is that true? In the city limits? You were shot at."

Micah nodded. "We filled out a report, or Sloan and Sidney did."

"Deputy Adams said he'd see to it that you were notified this morning," Sidney added.

Anger molded Granger's face into worry. "Anyone know where Sloan McCormick is?"

"I do," Sidney answered. "He's got a room at the motel."

"Would you see if he'd come up here? I need to talk to him as soon as I take Lora's statement. Gunfire in town should have been looked into before now."

Sidney nodded and moved across the room to the pay phone.

Granger wrote down everything Lora said. When she finished, he asked, "Did you tell the deputy all this?"

"Yes."

"Have you seen him?"

"No, he said he was going back to the office to write up his report."

Granger pulled his cell from his belt and punched a number. "Adams is on call. If he's not at the station, he'll pick up on his mobile." He waited.

There was no answer.

Lora watched the sheriff try to hide his frustration. He was a man of order, of rules. Everyone in town knew it. The deputy was either breaking the number-one rule, or he'd disappeared.

Lora was too tired and spent to even let her imagination think about where he might be.

"Sheriff?" the professor whispered as she returned from the phone.

"Yes," Granger answered.

"Sloan McCormick's on his way, but there's something else I need to tell you. It may not be important, but I'd planned to drop by your office tomorrow with these." She opened her hand revealing three yellow slips of paper. "Someone keeps leaving me notes."

Granger unfolded the first. Then the second. Then the third.

They all said the same thing. *Let the house fall.*

Thirty-Four

Sidney figured the hospital would probably send her a bill for wearing out the tile on the waiting room floor, but she couldn't sit down. Somehow, all the things that had happened at Rosa Lee's house were linked. She could no longer accept the first theory that the drill bit flying through the window had simply been a prank. She felt like a general who didn't know which way to turn to fight. The violence didn't make sense.

She walked back to the windows. Sloan McCormick and the sheriff were talking out by his truck, which was now illegally parked in the handicap slot. She guessed the light was best there, for the sheriff had wanted to look at the holes in Sloan's windshield.

Sheriff Granger Farrington was a good man—he'd figure out something. He had to.

She turned away and walked to the other end of the room where her committee waited. Beth Ann had been asleep for an hour and Lora looked to be dozing on Micah's shoulder. Ada May thumbed through the notes she'd made on unusual behavior happening in Clifton Creek this week. Micah had his hands folded and his eyes closed. He might have been praying or sleeping.

Sidney sat down next to him. He shifted and opened his eyes. Though he smiled at her, as always, there was a sadness in his smile. "You all right?" he asked.

"I'm fine, just frustrated. Do you think someone attacked Billy because of the house?"

He shrugged. "Maybe, but I doubt it. Most folks I know like Billy. He hasn't had it easy with his dad, but I think he's giving it his best shot. Lora thinks the guy she had one date with might have hired someone to beat Billy up, but I tend to think maybe he just walked in on someone in the house."

"He came by to see me earlier." Sidney tried to relax. "We're working on getting him into the criminal justice program at the college. He said the sheriff wants to offer him a job that could work into a career."

Micah looked surprised but didn't say anything.

Sidney needed to keep talking. "His grades are surprisingly good. I think we can get him not only a grant but maybe a scholarship to cover some living expenses." She lowered her voice. "You know what he told me?"

"What?"

She leaned closer. "He said he's saved almost eight thousand dollars since he got out of high school. He said he was waiting for his break."

Leaning back, Sidney tried not to cry. Seeing Billy made her aware of how hard it was for some people. She'd gone eight years to college with her mother picking up the bills for everything but spending money. She'd had her mother and grandmother backing her all the way, encouraging her, helping her.

Billy had no one. Even when the sheriff called his father a few hours ago, the man said he already had plans tonight, but he'd try to stop in and see Billy after work tomorrow.

"He's going to be all right," Micah whispered.

"Power of prayer?"

"No. Intuition. He's too much of a fighter."

She nodded, wanting to believe. "It's my fault he's hurt. I told him to keep an eye on the house. If I hadn't, he would not have gone inside and surprised whoever beat him up."

"We don't know that," Micah whispered.

The doors to the operating room opened and retired Dr. Hamilton walked out with a younger version of himself at his side. Micah woke Lora; Ada May woke Beth Ann. They all stood.

"How is he, Doc?" Ada May couldn't wait any longer.

The older doctor smiled. "He's going to be fine, Miss Rogers. We patched him up and stitched him up until he looks like one of your quilts, but he'll pull through."

Everyone let out a breath at once. The doctor continued, "He's got four cracked ribs, scrapes and cuts everywhere. He took a blow to the head from behind. We figure that's what took him out of the fight."

Granger came through the sliding front doors with McCormick at his side. They caught the last sentence. The sheriff turned to the doctors. "How soon till I can see him?"

"Wait a while. He's full of painkillers." The younger Hamilton stepped up and shook hands with the sheriff. "I've worked the emergency-room crowd in Wichita Falls for three years and treated my share of fight victims. Whoever hurt Hatcher wasn't trying to kill him, they seemed to be doling out as much punishment as possible." He lowered his voice. "They were going for as much pain as the kid would take, but not murder."

"Until one got tired of the fight and hit him in the back of the head," Sloan guessed.

Hamilton nodded. "Looks that way." He glanced at the others. "Are you all family?"

"Yes," Ada May answered and dared the sheriff to argue.

"Well," Hamilton continued. "I'd suggest all of you go home for the night. It's unlikely he'll wake up before morning and when he does he'll be weak from a loss of blood. One of you can stay to call the others if there is any change. In a town this size you all can be back here in five minutes if we see any change."

The young doctor turned to his grandfather. "I'm heading home, but if you need me, call me."

The old man rested his hand on his grandson's shoulder. "You did a good job in there. I'm proud of you."

The younger Hamilton smiled. He had just been given all the pay he needed for the night's work.

Suddenly, everyone talked at once, arguing over who would stay. Finally, youth won and Lora wrote down everyone's numbers so she could call if anything happened. The tired warriors picked up their belongings and headed home.

Sidney gave Lora a few last instructions, then watched her disappear with the doctor behind the doors. She glanced up to see Sloan watching her with a smile. She raised an eyebrow, wondering what was so funny.

He crossed to her side and said, "Time to go home, General."

Surprised, she realized he'd seen what she'd felt when the group was together. They were a unit and, like it or not, she was their leader.

They walked to his truck and he drove her home without talking. She relaxed, happy not to be alone. When he parked the truck, she asked, "Do you want to come in?"

"It's late," he answered.

"I know, but I'm not sleepy."

He cut the engine. "Me either. How about some cocoa?"

"Sure," she answered as they climbed out of the pickup. Tonight she didn't want to wonder about what he might think she meant by inviting him in. Her offer represented so much more than her not wanting to be alone.

They walked through the darkness to her door. "Sorry I forgot to leave the light on," she commented.

The shrubs up close to the porch moved in the wind, casting shadows back and forth. It occurred to her that someone could easily hide behind them and wait for her in the dark. She'd never worried about it before, but after tonight—after one of the committee had been beaten—she thought about it.

Sloan seemed to sense her nervousness. He put his arm around her protectively.

She pulled her keys from her purse and

fought to keep from running the last few steps.

When Sidney was safely inside, she called herself a fool for panicking. "Have a seat, I'll make the cocoa."

Sloan shrugged off his jacket, but didn't sit down. He leaned against the door frame leading into the tiny kitchen and watched her. "Do you have any idea who beat Billy up?"

"None," she answered. "Logic tells me if it was someone wanting us to decide on what to do with the house that they would have let us know. Right now the only message the beating seems to say was that Billy should stay away from the house."

"Or stay away from Lora." Sloan didn't meet Sidney's stare.

"What do you know?" she asked.

"Nothing yet." Sloan accepted his cocoa. "Want to go over what we do know?"

She shook her head.

"Want me to leave?"

She moved her head back and forth again. How could she tell a man she'd only known a few days how dearly she needed him to stay? She didn't want to talk. She just needed to know someone was near.

"Maybe we better have a seat." He walked to the couch and sat down.

She followed, taking the other end of the couch. For a few minutes, they drank their cocoa in silence.

"I like those paintings," he said pointing with his cup to the dozen small paintings grouped together on one wall. "How many do you have?"

"About thirty, I guess. There is another grouping in the bedroom. They were my mother's and before her, Grandmother Minnie's. I always thought they were the reason I loved plants. Even in the dead of winter, with the paintings, the house always seems full of flowers. That's one of the things that drew me to the Altman place, I guess. My mother and grandmother also loved flowers. My mother was named after a flower."

"These paintings kind of remind me of the one in Miss Carter's room back at the retirement home."

Sidney nodded. "Maybe some local artist. I'm not sure where Grandmother Minnie got them from. She wouldn't have bought them while she lived here back in the thirties, not when she was saving every penny. But, she might have ordered them. I remember my mother saying once that when she was a child every now and then, another painting would appear."

Sloan lifted his leg and rested it on the coffee table, then thought better of it and lowered the boot back to the floor.

Sidney laughed. "How about a compromise? Take off those boots and you can put your feet on the coffee table."

He grinned. "Fair enough."

Sidney looked around her place guessing what he must see. Flowered couch, plants everywhere, sewing basket, books on top of books. Nothing about the room looked as if it would make a man feel comfortable. The room seemed to scream that there was no man in her life and no room for one.

She wanted to talk to Sloan about Billy and what the sheriff had said, and the parts of Rosa Lee's life they'd managed to put together. But it was late and they'd been over every detail before. He might try to kiss her. She'd liked that last night, but that wasn't why she'd invited him in. Maybe she needed to explain to him that she wasn't the type of woman given to love affairs. A man should know that from the first, she thought, so he doesn't get any ideas.

She jumped up. "Would you like a refill?"

He caught her hand when she reached for his cup. "Sit down, Sidney," he said. "There's no need to be nervous."

She perched on the edge of the couch beside him. "I'm not."

He waited, knowing she was lying.

"I just don't know what to do. I don't want to talk, but I don't want you to go."

He covered her hand with his. "It's all right, Sidney. You're just worried about Billy and keyed up about what happened. We don't have to talk."

She frowned, surprised at how easily he'd read her mind.

"You also don't need a lover, tonight, Professor, you need a friend."

If she'd ever worried about the kind of man Sloan McCormick was, her doubts were laid to rest. She smiled and relaxed next to him. They talked about nothing, and everything. Sometime after midnight they made popcorn, and she watched Sloan eat it by the handful. By then, they'd moved on to talking of family and places they'd dreamed of living. The conversation was easy without awkward pauses. She told him how dearly she loved teaching and he admitted that he hated his job traveling. He said no one was living on his grandfather's farm, but without a little money, he'd never be able to make the place go. So, he kept working, hoping one day to save enough money to quit.

A little after one, he yawned, "I'd better say good-night." He stood and carried his bowl to the kitchen.

"Me, too. In a few hours I'll be teaching a class wishing I could have slept late." She walked him to the door.

"Good night," he whispered as he kissed her lightly, the taste of salt still on his lips.

"Good night." She smiled thinking of how much she'd enjoyed the last few hours. If they were never meant to be lovers, she'd settle for friends with this man. "I'll call you if I hear anything from the hospital."

"You do that." He stepped outside, turning his collar up against the sudden cold. "And by the way, Professor. I think I'm falling in love with you."

Before Sidney could think of an answer, he was gone.

Sloan tried not to hurry, but he was speeding by the time he reached the bar out near Cemetery Road. He parked by the front door and stormed in like a winter wind.

He wasn't surprised to see Talon Graham drinking at the back table. Sloan had run into the younger man a few times before. Once Talon had stolen oil rights out from under him by passing money under the table to make sure the landowners never saw Sloan's company's bid. Another time, in Oklahoma, a farmer had backed away from Sloan claiming he'd heard Sloan's company was about to go bankrupt. Before Sloan could prove the rumor a lie, Talon had sealed the deal.

To say he hated Talon Graham would have been too strong. But he did avoid him whenever possible. But, since they were in the same business, it was impossible never to cross paths.

Talon stood as Sloan neared. So did the two other men at the table. "Evening, Mc-Cormick," Talon said without smiling. "Join us for a drink?"

Sloan wanted to see Talon's face when he lost this deal, but tonight wasn't about oil rights. "I'm here to ask you straight out if you had anything to do with that boy being hurt."

"What boy?" Talon raised his eyebrows.

"Billy Hatcher was beat up tonight at the Altman place."

Talon smiled. "Wish I could say different, but I had nothing to do with it."

Sloan hesitated. He'd seen surprise flicker in Talon's eyes. If he was lying, he was doing a good job of it. Talon was the kind of man who liked to take credit for what he did, good or bad.

"If I find you're lying," Sloan breathed, "I'll be back and it won't have anything to do with business, Graham. It will be personal."

A hairy old bartender pushed his way between them and picked up empty bottles. "You boys talking or drinking?"

Sloan turned away. "We're finished . . . for now."

He didn't look back as he walked to the door. But he knew Talon Graham would be watching him.

Thirty-Five

The sheriff offered Micah a ride as they walked out of the hospital's sliding doors. "Your car is probably parked in front of my house. Randi should have driven Meredith home hours ago. Knowing them, they're still up talking."

Micah followed Granger to the parking lot, surprised at how easy Granger talked to him. The sheriff had always seemed so formal.

"Of course, there is a detour Randi is bad about taking. She likes to stop for ice cream." He shook his head. "I don't know how the woman stays so thin."

Micah didn't comment. He just climbed into the police car.

Granger started the car and drove out of the parking lot before he turned serious. "Any ideas on who might have done that to Billy?"

"None." Micah let out a breath thankful Granger wanted to talk about the crime and not what kind of relationship he had with Randi. The sheriff seemed to genuinely like her, but with Granger it was hard to tell. "Strange things have been happening all week."

"There's something I need to tell you," the sheriff said without looking in his direction. "But, I'd rather the rest of the committee not know it until I've got some proof."

"All right."

"A few of those plates the sisters collected from people driving by their house were for rental cars, which we don't see a lot of in Clifton Creek. I ran a check. They were all rented in Wichita Falls to a man named Jeter."

When the sheriff paused, Micah shook his head. "I don't think I know anyone by that name."

"Me either, so I had the office in Wichita Falls do some checking." Granger turned to Micah, ignoring the fact that the town's one light had turned green. "Jeter works for an oil company."

Micah wasn't surprised.

The sheriff added, "The same oil company Sloan McCormick said he worked for."

"Sloan has a partner in town?"

The sheriff shook his head. "I may be wrong, but I don't think Sloan McCormick knows about the man. When I asked him, he said he worked alone."

"So, you think this man named Jeter is here to watch the committee?"

Granger shook his head. "No. I think Jeter is here to watch Sloan McCormick."

Thirty-Six

Lora Whitman stretched and pulled her hand away from where she'd rested it on Billy's arm between the bandages. She'd found a few inches of skin that weren't bruised, bloody or wrapped. The warmth of it calmed her. She glanced at the clock, six-fifteen in the morning. She settled back in the chair so that she could be comfortable and still touch Billy.

"Hi, babe," he whispered.

Lora looked up into sleepy gray eyes watching her. "Don't call me babe," she whispered back, but she couldn't hide the smile.

"What are you doing here?" he asked, ignoring her demand. "Hell, what am I doing here?"

She leaned closer. "I found you hurt and buried in the rubble behind Rosa Lee's house. Coming here seemed the logical choice."

"I knew you'd come." He started to smile, then groaned. "Can't stay away from me, can you?"

"You got it," she answered. "Do you remember what happened?"

Billy closed his eyes. "They were in the house when I unlocked the door. I remember hearing something as I turned the key, but I thought it might be mice." He reached for something, but Lora caught his hand.

"Don't." She held his hand in both of hers. "You're all plugged up to machines."

A nurse rushed in before she could say more. She waved Lora aside and turned up the light over Billy's bed.

"Water," he said, staring at the nurse as if she were an alien. "I just wanted a drink."

"How about a little ice?" The nurse sounded far too cheery. "Very glad to see you awake, Mr. Hatcher. Everyone's been worried about you."

She spooned him a few slivers of ice,

then checked all the bandages as if she were afraid he might have bothered one of them. When she was satisfied, she turned to Lora. "He can have more ice and a little water. Nothing else until the doctor comes in. The sheriff wanted to be called the minute he woke up. I've got his number at the desk."

Lora nodded and was thankful when the nurse hurried back out.

"Who is she?" Billy asked, not liking her any more than Lora did.

"She's the nurse. She told me her name, but I can't remember it." Lora spooned him more ice. "But, you'd better do everything she tells you."

"Yes, ma'am." He sounded tired. "What are you here for other than to boss me around?"

"I'm sitting up with you. You're my boyfriend, remember." Lora ate the ice she'd spooned for him. "It was either me or Beth Ann Rogers and we thought the constant clicking of her needles would keep you awake."

"Some guard you are." He managed a grin even with his bruised jawline and black eye. "I've been watching you sleep for half an hour."

She gave him the next spoonful. "I can't help it, something about being with you puts me to sleep."

"Give me a few days and I'll wake you up, babe."

She doubled up a fist. "If you call me babe one more time, I'll have to hit you. It won't be easy finding a spot on you that isn't already bruised."

The nurse poked her head in. "Sheriff says he's on his way."

Lora fought the urge to question Billy ahead of time. He didn't look as if he had the energy but for one telling. The strong, tough guy she'd been half-afraid of when she'd first seen him didn't look all that tough right now. His ribs were wrapped, one arm in a sling, a cut on the back of his head and both hands covered in bandages.

"Need to use the bedpan?" she asked.

"No."

She swore he reddened beneath the bruises.

"Well, I have to go. If I leave you for a minute, promise not to fall out of bed or anything."

"I promise." He frowned at her.

She ran across the hall to the ladies' room. The moment the door closed, she leaned against the wall and began to cry. Silent sobs at first, then little hiccups between laughter. He was going to be all right, she told herself over and over. She hadn't believed it until she saw his eyes watching her. It was stupid to fall apart now that the fears that had been with her since the moment she'd found him were finally laid to rest.

By the time the sheriff got to the hospital, Lora had washed away her tears and combed her hair. She stood silently next to Billy's bed as he described every detail he remembered.

"I walked in, more alert than I would have been if I hadn't heard the noise first. I noticed Lora's car parked out front, so I thought she might be in the house even though I didn't remember her having a key.

"The sun had already gone down, but there was still enough light to look around the entry. I'm guessing it was between seven-thirty and eight."

Lora gave him a drink while the sheriff wrote on his pad.

Billy closed his eyes as if reliving the attack. "The first one came at me from the shadows behind the stairs. I saw him coming and had a few seconds to get ready for him. By the time he hit the floor, another one was rushing down the stairs."

"Did you recognize them?"

"No. They were big, thick like some of those oil-field workers you see in town. A third man rushed in. He had a pipe, or cane in his hand." Billy smiled. "Until then, I was giving more than I took. I don't remember much after that. Only for a minute after I went down, it felt like they were all three using me for a punching bag."

Granger glanced up with a question in his stare.

Billy continued, "If they wanted me dead, they could have used the pipe again. A few more blows to the head would have done it. But, they took the slow method. I think they just wanted me hurt."

The sheriff nodded. "I figured out the same thing, but don't see how it makes any sense. Are you sure you didn't know them?"

Billy shook his head. "No, it wasn't personal. I'm not even sure they knew my name. It wasn't like any fight I've ever been in. No one yelled, or cussed."

"Did they say anything?"

Billy glanced at Lora. "The last thing I heard was something the guy with a pipe said when I fell. He said, strike one."

Granger wrote in his pad.

Lora could stand the silence no longer. "What does that mean?"

The sheriff shook his head. "He could have been swinging, playing an imaginary game. Some bad types are like that. Hitting a man doesn't mean any more to them than swinging at a ball."

Billy added. "Only they were using my head as a ball. It's possible. He didn't even sound angry."

"Or—" Lora fought to breathe "—he could have meant the first one is down. Strike one like there was going to be a strike two and three."

No one said a word. The machines hummed in the background, pulsing like a heartbeat.

Finally, the sheriff turned to Lora. "Maybe you'd better call the committee and have them come up here."

"What are you going to do?" Billy asked.

"Tell them to be careful. Lock their doors. Don't walk alone. Until we find these guys, we can't be sure what they meant, but I'm not taking chances."

"One should be easy to find," Billy whispered. "I think I broke his nose."

The sheriff made one last note.

An hour later, the committee assembled around Billy Hatcher's hospital bed. The sisters brought doughnuts and coffee. Everyone looked tired.

"I know we don't have much time, most of you have jobs you need to get to," the sheriff began. "But I wanted to talk to you all as a group. At this point, we don't know if the attack on Billy had anything to do with the Altman house." Before everyone could argue, he hurried on, "We must assume, however, that it did, so I'd like to have your cooperation on a few precautions."

Lora listened to the sheriff's rules. Lock your doors, tell someone where you are going at all times. Be home safely locked inside by sundown. It all made sense, Lora thought, but not for this group. She didn't want someone keeping tabs on her. The professor was alone most of the time, the sisters weren't able to protect themselves.

Everyone in town knew the preacher ran at night. The sheriff was trying to talk a group of loners into changing their habits.

"I've only got two deputies," Granger continued. "But I'll put one here at the hospital until the doctor says Billy can go home. If any of you see, or even feel anything that looks out of the ordinary, I'd like you to call me. If someone is trying to tamper with this committee they are sure going about it in a strange way."

Micah stepped forward. "What if whoever got to Billy wasn't interested in the committee or in our vote? What if they were looking for something in the house and he just got in the way?"

Ada May nodded her head. "The millions Rosa Lee supposedly hid away. After all she sold off her land piece by piece and never seemed to spend a dime of it."

"That's only a rumor." Beth Ann jumped into the conversation. "Don't you think if she had any money she would have spent some of it fixing the place up? And if anyone really believed the stories, they would have looked for it long before now."

Billy whispered, "We searched and didn't find any money and my guess is neither did the men who met me at the door. If they'd found what they were looking for, they'd have run out the back door."

The sheriff agreed.

"When I get out, I'll look again."

Everyone in the room opened their mouth to argue, but it was Lora who spoke first. "We'll all go," she said as she put her hand on his shoulder.

A few minutes later, Micah walked out with the sheriff. "Did you find your deputy last night?"

Granger nodded. "He said he had a call that there had been an accident out by the interstate, but when he got there he found nothing. He went in to one of the truck stops to ask and when he returned to his car, he had a flat."

Micah didn't say anything, but the sheriff added, "He knew he should have called me, but he said he forgot."

Both men glanced at one another, but neither said a word.

Thirty-Seven

Micah tried to concentrate all morning on Monday's paperwork for the church. Tomorrow he'd have couples coming in for counseling and he would have no time for budget planning. He had to work today. But it was no use. He couldn't stop worrying about what had happened to Billy.

The boy could have died. The doctor had said if the blow had been a little to the right, it might have paralyzed him, or had it been harder it could have killed him, or if Lora hadn't found him he could have bled to death. Micah couldn't believe someone would hurt him so badly over a house. There had to be another reason someone didn't want them in the house. But what? The place was empty.

Nancy dropped by to ask if he planned to go to lunch and he realized he hadn't even thought about it. He nodded and grabbed his jacket. Once Micah was in his car, it occurred to him that he had nowhere he needed to be. The sheriff's warning about not going anywhere alone would be impractical. Except for when he was with Logan, Micah went everywhere alone. Most days he even ate lunch alone.

He droved past the Altman place fighting the urge to go in. They must be overlooking something in the old house. What they'd found so far had been interesting, but not worth fighting over.

He settled for grabbing a hamburger at the drivethrough and parking out on Cemetery Road where he could watch the town. From his vantage point, he could see the bar and wondered what Randi would be doing this time of day. She might still be asleep. He knew he had no right, but he wished he could have taken her home after he'd ridden home with the sheriff and picked up his car last night. But he'd only stopped at the sheriff's place long enough to collect his keys.

Randi had been asleep on the couch. The sheriff had said he'd drive her home when she woke.

Micah couldn't keep showing up asking her to dance. He couldn't help but think about how Sunday evening would have ended if Granger hadn't got the call that Billy had been hurt.

Shoving his half-eaten burger into the bag, Micah started the car. He might as well go back to work. He could do nothing just as easily in his office and it was warm back at the church.

Just as he put the car in gear, he noticed Sloan McCormick's big pickup pull into the parking lot of the bar.

Micah frowned. It was too far away to see anything, but there was no mistaking the truck. Another older, smaller pickup pulled in behind Sloan. They seemed to be talking for a minute, then Sloan pulled away.

Micah started down the hill toward town. The second pickup turned out of the parking lot in his direction. As he passed, he noticed the passenger looked like he had a bandage over his nose.

Fumbling for his cell phone, Micah was almost back to the church before he got Granger. He told him what he saw, knowing the truck would probably be in the next county before Granger could catch up with it. And he could have been wrong about the bandage. The guy might have been blowing his nose, or wiping his mouth. Micah didn't get that clear a look.

"Thanks," Granger said. "I'll let you know."

Micah clicked the phone closed and walked into the church office feeling as if he'd helped in some small way.

When he walked past Nancy, she looked up. "You're back early," she commented, always keeping track of everyone.

He didn't answer.

"Oh." She lifted a paper. "We checked in the files. There was no record of any Altman ever attending this church. I called Sally, the secretary over at First Baptist. They have their records on computer, which we really should have but there's no time to think of that now."

Micah tried to be patient. For Nancy, the grass was always greener on the Baptist side.

"Anyway," she continued. "Sally was able to tell me within minutes that no Henry, or Rosa Lee Altman ever came through their doors."

He thanked her, but wasn't surprised. It had been a long shot even to look.

"But," Nancy smiled and hesitated. "One of the hospitality ladies, Miss Martha, remembered that early on in Clifton Creek's days there used to be a little Catholic church up by the cemetery. I don't think anything remains but part of the foundation. She said she can remember Old Man Hamm and his string of kids always walking past her place to go to mass."

Nancy glanced up at Micah and added, "Miss Martha said the last she heard the Hamm family had to go all the way to Wichita Falls for service. Quite a few families used to make the journey every Sunday. She said if you wanted to check with any of the grandkids, Charlie at the repair shop is Hamm's grandson. Dale Wilbur over at the fire station or Randi Howard who owns the bar out by Cemetery Road would probably know. They're all related to him."

He took a step toward the door no longer thinking about Rosa Lee. Of course, Randi had said she'd grown up here. It made sense she'd have family in town. She had to be someone's granddaughter.

Nancy always raised her voice when she thought he might not be listening. "So, I called Wichita Falls and they had records going all the way back to 1917."

Too late to record Rosa Lee's birth or her mother's death in childbirth, Micah thought, forcing his mind back to the problem at hand.

Nancy turned up the volume once more. "All they had was one baptism in 1934."

Micah retraced his steps. Nancy had his attention.

Nancy smiled and handed him the paper. "I had them fax over the record. It appears our town's oldest old maid had a child."

"Thanks," Micah managed to say as he stared at the paper.

He still had the fax in his hand when he walked into Sidney's office a few minutes later. She looked tired, but glad to see him.

They both stared at the record. It took Sidney time to read down each line, but when it came to the place left for godparents, there was only one name. Minnie Jefferson.

"They did know one another," Micah said. "Your grandmother was there with Rosa Lee when Rosa Lee had her child baptized. You now have proof. They must have been good friends if Rosa Lee named her as god-mother and very close if Minnie was the only one to sign." Micah smiled. "There's your answer, Sidney. There's the tie to the house you've been looking for."

"Or more questions?" Sidney shook her head. "What happened to Rosa Lee's baby? According to this it would have been two weeks older than my mother, Marbree." Sidney looked up. "That would make Rosa Lee's baby seventy years old. She could still be alive. But where and how could it be possible that no one in town ever knew she lived?"

"Do you have any old letters that belonged to your grandmother Minnie? Maybe, since she was named godmother, she kept up with the baby."

Sidney shook her head. "Nothing. When Granny Minnie moved in with us most of her things were given away. She was widowed early as was my mom. Neither of them were collectors or savers. They combined what they had in our small house. I'm sure if there had been letters I would have found them. As far as I remember, Granny only brought her favorite chair and her paintings when she came to live with us. Maybe some kitchen stuff. She loved to cook. But our house was so small, there wasn't much room for private things."

Micah looked out the window of Sidney's second-floor office. "Maybe that explains why they were friends. They must have both been pregnant at the same time."

"I'm surprised my grandmother traveled all the way to Chicago that far along in the pregnancy. This shows her in Clifton Creek two weeks before her own child was born. She must have wanted to be with my grandfather when her baby came. I thought in those days women were put to bed when they got close. Why would my grand-mother take such a risk and travel that far along?"

"Maybe she waited here to help deliver Rosa Lee's baby," Micah suggested. "If they were friends and for some reason Rosa Lee kept the baby a secret, Minnie might have been the only person she trusted to deliver it."

"Granny Minnie would do something like

that. Several times over her nursing career she acted as a midwife. She never judged anyone. I can see in the thirties why Rosa Lee would keep the baby a secret. An unwed mother in those days would have been ostracized, her family shunned."

Micah watched the professor carefully. There seemed to be something she wasn't saying and he didn't want to pry. "I saw Sloan's truck at Randi's bar parking lot." He felt like a tattletale, but knew they needed to share all information. "One of the men he was talking to looked like he had a bandage over his nose."

Micah didn't need to say more. Sidney would figure it out. They were silent for a while. He watched leaves whirl on the street below in pointless circles and thought of his life and Rosa Lee's. What had she done to protect her name? What would he do to protect his?

Micah knew, if he continued seeing Randi, it would only be a matter of time before the town caught on. He didn't want to be a man folks whispered about. And more than that, he didn't want Randi to have a secret that everyone knew and talked about when she couldn't hear.

"I think I trust Sloan McCormick, Micah," Sidney said, finally breaking the silence. "If he was there, he had his reasons."

"I agree." Micah had always considered himself a good judge of people. He could be wrong about little things from time to time, but not that wrong. "Sloan's probably just trying to help. He's crazy about you."

"We're becoming friends," Sidney answered the unasked question. "Just friends."

"Friendship can turn on a dime to something more." Micah smiled, wishing it would for Sloan and Sidney.

"Maybe," she answered honestly. "When the vote is in and all this is over, we'll see."

"Has he tried to talk you into going with his oil company?" Micah saw no hint of a con in Sloan's actions toward Sidney, but anyone could be fooled.

"Not one word," Sidney answered. "The mayor, on the other hand, can't wait to get this over with. Every day he calls reminding me how badly the town needs the money from the sale. Sloan's company out of Houston put in a bid, as did Talon Graham's company from Austin. Even a local company made an offer. They all seem interested, but not chomping at the bit."

"Makes you wonder why the mayor bothered with a committee if he'd already made up his mind."

Sidney agreed. "He chose people with whom no one in town would argue. We were a safe bet. He'd get what he wanted and people wouldn't yell at us. He'd walk away smelling like a rose."

"He had no idea how much trouble we'd get into."

She laughed. "Right. But, one way or the other, it will all be over Wednesday. I have to turn in the final vote then."

Micah left her office feeling the cold more than usual. He told himself he needed to get back to work, but he drove past the bar anyway. Randi had been thick in his mind all day. Maybe he just wanted to talk to someone, he thought. But he knew it was a lie. He wanted—needed—to see her.

Micah left work early and picked up Logan. They bundled up and played in the front yard, racing leaves in the wind. Then they talked Mrs. Mac into going out for dinner. A rare thing that could never have been accomplished without Micah agreeing to tape her shows while they were gone.

The three of them went to the pizza place.

They seemed a strange family among all the normal ones, but Logan didn't notice. He hit the old pinball machine with three quarters and thought he was in heaven. While he played, Micah filled Mrs. Mac in on what had happened last night. To his surprise, she grew worried.

"I got a bad feeling about this, Micah. I don't like it at all."

"The sheriff will—"

She interrupted. "Granger's a good man, but I've lived in this town long enough to know that when trouble comes, a few men with badges can't always stop it."

Micah had no doubt she was right. He'd heard about the wild twenties when the oil business was young. He could tell himself those days and those people were gone, but if Rosa Lee's place was in the middle of some kind of oil fight, he wasn't so sure. Would companies fight over a small plot of land?

"Maybe you should take a little vacation," she said. "Go visit some of your friends down in Tyler."

"I've lost track of most of them," Micah admitted. "Besides, I can't leave. Logan has school." He didn't add that he wouldn't leave the committee.

She looked relieved and he realized that if he ran, he would have been leaving her alone. "We'll be more careful, just like the sheriff says. I'll call Fred across the street and ask him to watch our house. If he sees anyone even driving slowly, he'll report in."

Micah smiled. The neighbors in Clifton Creek kept an eye on one another. Maybe he was overreacting. Nothing ever happened. Nothing would happen now.

After pizza, he stopped by and visited with Billy while Mrs. Mac and Logan talked with the Rogers sisters in the waiting room. To his surprise, Mrs. Mac joined their militia, agreeing to phone in if she saw anything. Micah couldn't help but smile. If they got all the gray hair in this town together, they'd have an army. Maybe he should stop worrying.

That night when he ran, he watched any cars that passed by. He stayed on the main streets where the light was better, and he didn't go all the way out to Cemetery Road. He didn't run near Randi's place either.

But when he'd showered and crawled

into bed, he couldn't help but think about her and wish he'd stopped. Reason told him not to. If there was trouble coming, he didn't need to involve her in any of it. But he couldn't sleep. The need to hold her was a phantom ache within him he couldn't heal.

The next morning, after Logan left for school, he stopped by the café for breakfast. He wasn't surprised to see Lora Whitman at the counter. It was Tuesday after all.

"Time for your weekly dose of grease and chocolate?" he asked as he slid onto the stool next to her.

She smiled, much more at ease with him than she had been last week. "You can't beat chocolate-covered cinnamon rolls." She raised her hand. "Polly, a roll for my friend."

Polly groaned her usual greeting. "This ain't no fast-service place and I ain't asking if you want fries with that, so just wait your turn."

Lora split her roll with him and they ate hers while waiting for his to arrive.

"Where are you headed?" he asked between bites.

"The hospital. Billy gets out today. The professor and I got him a room at the dorm. We knew he wouldn't take it if we offered charity, so he'll work off his room and board as the handyman. He'll be taking a full load and working twenty hours a week at the sheriff's office. His boss at the lumberyard said he can work there on Saturdays and breaks if he needs extra money."

She leaned closer. "You know his family."

"I met his dad once when I went by his house to ask where I could find Billy."

Lora stabbed a piece of roll. "The old guy lives within walking distance of the hospital and hasn't even stopped by to check on his son."

"We can't pick our parents."

She nodded. "Yeah, but it makes me take a look at my own. I complain all the time about them, but they'd both die for me. It's no wonder Billy got into trouble when he was a kid. He must have had no one looking out for him."

"You like him, don't you?" Micah felt strange even asking. It seemed like something a middle-school kid would say.

She grinned. "We're friends."

There was that word again, he thought. That word that could turn on a dime.

They talked, their heads almost touching while people walked by, glancing in their direction when Lora laughed, or when Polly griped about them ordering more coffee and a third roll.

Micah finally forced himself to say goodbye and rushed to his office, barely making it before his first couple came in for counseling. For the next few hours he worked unaware of the storm building outside. About two, Nancy brought him a cup of coffee and told him it was snowing. Micah hadn't even had time to look out his window.

"Early, this year," Nancy commented. "Usually we don't see snow till after Halloween. Maybe we'll have an early spring, as well."

Micah watched the magic. Snow, covering everything, making the world newborn one more time.

He wasn't surprised Logan called to ask if he could go over to Jimmy's and make snow ice cream. Micah looked at the light dusting of snow and suggested they might have to settle for making cookies. Logan didn't seem to mind. Micah promised to pick him up as soon as he could get away from the church.

Micah finished up the paperwork thinking how dark the day looked. As if the earth hugged the clouds close for warmth. Randi had crossed his mind several times and he'd thought of calling her. The day might seem a little less gloomy if he could hear her voice.

Finally, after everyone had left, he picked up the phone and dialed.

She answered on the first ring.

"Afternoon," he said already smiling.

"I heard about Hatcher. How are you?" she asked, worry touching her words.

"I'm fine." She'd known his voice, he realized. "How are you?"

"I'm missing seeing you."

She didn't mess around, this woman who didn't belong in his world. She went straight to the truth. He'd thought their conversation would be small talk, casual. He should have known better.

He closed his eyes and let out a long breath he felt he'd been holding in since he'd seen her last. "Me, too."

He could hear her breathing on the other end of the line. He didn't have to say more. Neither did she. It was enough to know she was there.

Thirty-Eight

Sidney built a fire in the fireplace of her bungalow and put on her warm flannel pajamas. She'd been cold all day. It wasn't late, but she was ready to call it a night. After teaching her classes, she'd helped move Billy into the dorm as the day grew colder. She'd tried to call Sloan, thinking his truck would help them get all Lora had brought home from the store, but he hadn't answered his cell.

He'd probably gone, she decided. Maybe the men Micah had seen him talking to in the bar parking lot had scared Sloan into giving up. Or maybe he'd been taken off this job and gone on to another without letting her know. After all, she didn't exactly have a bond with Sloan. For him it was probably little more than a flirtation. He didn't owe her reasons. He'd told her from the beginning that he had no home, so why was she surprised he turned out to be a tumbleweed? She'd let him get too close.

She made cocoa, flipped through the channels for something to watch and settled on watching the fire as she thumbed through a book she'd already read twice. Sidney was determined not to feel sorry for herself, but today was her birthday and no one had known, or noticed. Not that it mattered, but she was now forty. Now, officially an old maid. She might as well move in with the Rogers sisters and start playing for who turns out the lights.

Since her mother and grandmother had died, she'd felt alone, but never quite so much as she did tonight. Closing her eyes, she tried to think what life would have been like if they'd lived. Her Minnie would have baked a cake, a red velvet with coconut icing. And her mother, who always seemed to know what she wanted, would have brought presents. Little things like socks and books. They would have driven up before dark to her place north of Chicago, and been waiting to eat dinner when she got in from work. Then they'd all laugh as she opened the gifts. Minnie, her grandmother, would tell the story of the year Sidney was five and bought all the things she wanted to play with as gifts for them. Marbree, Sidney's mother, would say what she said every year about how proud Sidney's father would have been of her if he'd lived to see her all grown-up. Then, they'd settle in for the night. Sidney wouldn't have to ask, she'd know they'd stay a few days.

The three of them had been so much alike, not in looks, but in temperament. Through three generations, they could read each other's thoughts and moods.

A tear fought its way down Sidney's cheek. If she'd known them so well, why hadn't her grandmother told her about knowing Rosa Lee? In all the thousands of hours they must have talked, why hadn't she told of living in Clifton Creek? Sidney had to wonder if her grandmother had kept the secret from just her, or from her mother, as well.

They'd been her stable ground all her life and now they were gone. She hadn't even been able to say goodbye. In one car wreck all her family had died. And now, she'd have the rest of her birthdays alone with only memories for company. She'd never be able to ask Minnie her questions or find out if her mother knew the secrets of Rosa Lee that her grandmother had written about. She'd probably never know for sure if it was Clifton Creek they'd been heading to the day they'd both been killed.

Sidney jumped when the doorbell rang. The sudden jolt back to reality shook her. She glanced out at the snow-covered yard and saw Sloan's truck parked in front.

For a moment, she thought of not answering. After all it was late, probably close to nine. She was ready for bed. He hadn't called. She hadn't dated enough in the past few years to know what the rules were anymore, but surely just dropping by when they'd only gone out on one real date wasn't acceptable.

But none of that really mattered. He was here, standing on her doorstep, freezing.

She opened the door.

The sight that greeted her made her laugh. He stood there, all six foot four of him, his hair and shoulders dusted in snow, with a cake box in one hand and a bottle of wine in the other.

"May I come in?" he asked. "The guy at the store said this wine doesn't need to be chilled."

"And, if I say no?"

He frowned as if he feared she might. "I'm not moving, Sidney. If you don't let me in I'll freeze and you'll have the largest yard elf in town."

She giggled as she backed out of the way and he walked straight to her kitchen. He sat the cake and wine down and turned toward her. "Happy birthday!"

He flipped open the top of the box. The cake was decorated with red icing roses. Happy Birthday Sidney Elizabeth was printed in bright green icing.

Sidney laughed. "My middle name is Lee, not Elizabeth."

Sloan ran his finger across a few of the letters and ate part of the *e* and *l.* "I was afraid of that. I had no idea what it would be so I picked the longest name I could think of hoping for more icing." He took another finger full. "I love this stuff." He offered her a taste.

Sidney smiled, her melancholy mood forgotten. "What kind of wine goes with cake?"

"The man at the gas service recommended red. I've always had the feeling wine should be reserved for communion and cooking, but I thought a bottle of whiskey might look just a little strange to give a lady like yourself, Professor."

"Wise choice."

While Sloan opened the wine, Sidney found plates. She considered asking him where he'd been all day, but wasn't sure she wanted to know. She liked him, a deep down kind of like that would forgive much, she decided.

They drank wine in front of the fire. He pulled off his boots and stretched out, his long legs crossing half the space in her living area. "So your middle name is Lee," he said.

She nodded. "My mother was Marbree Lee, so I'm Sidney Lee."

He studied her closely before adding, "Like Rosa Lee."

The possibility that had been nagging in her mind since the preacher had told her about the baptism record filled her thoughts. She knew Sloan probably wasn't the one to talk to, but there didn't seem to be anyone else.

"I've had a wild thought haunting me," she said trying to make her words sound casual. She laid out all the facts. The note on the recipe card her grandmother kept in a safety deposit box, the baptism her grandmother attended two weeks before her mother was born, the fact that Rosa Lee left her house to Minnie if claimed within a year, and now Lee being her middle name.

"Your grandmother Minnie could have used the middle name of Lee with her daughter because she was such good friends with Rosa Lee."

"But wouldn't Minnie have mentioned it sometime? Wouldn't she have said, 'I named you Marbree Lee after an old friend'? To my knowledge, Minnie never mentioned Rosa Lee or the house or even Clifton Creek to me or my mother."

"Strange," Sloan agreed.

Sidney turned toward him needing to talk to someone about her theory. "It adds up to only a slight possibility, but I have the feeling that Rosa Lee Altman could have been my real grandmother. My birth grandmother."

"But, what about the birth record of your mother being born in Chicago?"

"I remember hearing Granny Minnie say that she delivered at home. My grandfather lived for several years but they had no more children. Knowing Minnie's love for children, if she could have had more, she would have. Since she said she delivered my mother at home, there was no one to say that my mother wasn't born in Chicago."

"What name was on the baptism record Micah found?"

"That's the strange part. None. I thought priests had to have a name before they baptized. Maybe he thought Rosa Lee would fill it in later."

Sloan shook his head. "I don't know about the name, but the idea is too outrageous. You're suggesting that your grandmother took Rosa Lee's baby and raised it as her own."

"Think about it. If she'd kept the baby, she would have been an unwed mother. Back then people didn't accept babies born out of wedlock. Fuller was dead. He couldn't marry her and make it right. She'd have no chance of ever getting married with a bastard baby. Again and again folks have mentioned how Henry Altman was a fine and proper man. Having an unwed daughter with a child wouldn't have been very proper back then."

Sloan shook his head. "I don't know. I somehow would have guessed Rosa Lee stronger than that."

"Me, too. It was just a wild thought. But, maybe there was another reason she couldn't keep the baby. Maybe she had to make a choice."

"But what?"

Sidney tried to think of a reason Rosa Lee would give the baby up besides how people would look at an unwed mother.

Sloan stood and walked to the door. Without stepping outside, he grabbed a sack he'd left on the porch. "I brought you something."

"You didn't have to do that." Sidney laced her fingers to keep from jumping to get the present. "We've only known one another a few days."

"Yeah, but we're going to know one another for a long time and I wanted to start something." He handed her the sack. "I got to tell you, Professor, I've had a few one-night stands in my life, but I don't plan on you being one of them. We may not be teenagers, but we might as well get started on a few traditions that'll last the years we have left."

She carefully pulled an aluminum-wrapped tamale out and looked up. "A tamale?"

"Two dozen," he corrected with pride. "You think that will be enough for the party?"

"What party?"

"The one we're having in about ten minutes. It's your birthday and you should have a party. I told everyone to be here by a quarter after nine."

Sidney looked up in shock. "You're kidding."

He shook his head.

She jumped up and ran to the bedroom.

"I kind of liked the pajamas. Don't feel like you have to change. I told everyone it was come as you are."

"I'm going to kill you, Sloan McCormick, when this night is over," she yelled from the bedroom. "I swear I'll kill you."

"I kind of figured you liked surprise parties."

Before she could say more, the doorbell

rang. By the time she'd dressed and combed her hair, everyone had arrived.

"You shouldn't have come," she said after they all yelled happy birthday. "It's too cold and late. The roads are bad."

No one appeared to be listening.

Billy stood with his arm around Lora's shoulder. He looked pale, but happy. "We all wanted to come," he said.

"We needed a reason to celebrate," Micah added as he handed her a book tied in ribbon. "I didn't have a chance to buy the right book, so I'm giving you my copy."

Sidney turned over what had to be a treasured book, a first edition of *The Lion, the Witch and the Wardrobe*.

"Thank you."

The Rogers sisters organized the party, telling everyone where to sit and passing out food. Their gifts were crocheted house shoes that looked as if they could double as long pot holders, and a lap quilt in Easter-egg bright yarn.

Lora gave Sidney a book on gardening and several hand tools.

Billy gave her a sketch of a bench that would fit beneath her window. "I drew it after you helped me with my schedule. I fig-

ured I'd make it for you when I had time."
He lifted his bandaged arm. "I had no idea
I'd be taking a vacation so soon."

Everyone laughed, releasing a little of the
worry they'd held for him over the past two
days. While they sat around the coffee table
eating chips dipped in the sisters' special
hot-sauce mixture they'd made last summer
and devouring Sloan's tamales he swore he
bought from a roadside vendor out by the
interstate, Sidney related her theory of Rosa
Lee having a baby.

Everyone liked the idea, but didn't quite
buy into it. Her story seemed more a list of
coincidences than facts pointing to ancestors. Sidney realized they all knew the vote
was tomorrow, yet none mentioned the
meeting. It was as if they didn't want the
committee to disband.

She felt the same. Despite the trouble,
they'd all hung together. She leaned back
and watched the group. Sloan and Lora
were arguing over the wine. She'd declared
it the worst she'd ever tasted and he
seemed to be trying to make the point that
there was no such thing as good wine.

The preacher and Billy were looking over
his sketch for the window bench and the

Rogers sisters were thumbing through the gardening book. Sidney smiled. Maybe there was no such thing as a perfect fortieth birthday, but this one came close.

Sloan took her hand and she turned toward him.

"Thank you," she whispered.

"You are welcome." He smiled. "An hour ago, after having one hell of a day, I made it back here and remembered this was your birthday. I wasn't sure I could pull a party off."

"Bad day?" She didn't want to outright ask, but he'd given her the opening.

"Until now." He squeezed her fingers gently. "You've got icing on your face."

"Where?" She touched her lips.

"Right here." He leaned over and kissed her on the cheek.

Sidney blushed, but before she could see if anyone watched them, Ada May screamed, "Oh, my goodness! Look at this."

Everyone turned to where she was pointing in the gardening book. Sidney could see what they were looking at and she was thankful it wasn't her.

Ada May held the book up. "I can't believe it. I just can't believe it."

"What?" Lora asked from too far away to see the book's pictures.

"Right here, under Portland Roses. There's one that grows as an upright shrub. A red blend." She held the book toward Sidney and added, "It's called a Marbree."

Beth Ann pulled the book so she could see better. "That's the one we saw growing all over Rosa Lee's garden."

"Didn't you say your mother's name was Marbree Lee?" Lora asked as she looked from the book to Sidney.

Sidney straightened, trying to remember to breathe. Sloan's arm went round her shoulder as all the others stared at her.

The wild thought had just become a possibility.

Thirty-Nine

Micah told himself he wasn't going to circle by Randi's place when he left the professor's party. After all, it was after ten on a weeknight. He had to work tomorrow and the bar would probably still be open tonight.

The snow continued to fall. Within a few hours it would be hazardous as he headed out toward Cemetery Road. Even though Logan was asleep, Micah needed to get home. The committee had agreed to meet at three o'clock tomorrow to take the final vote and, as near as he could tell, not one member knew how to vote.

Even if Sidney was Rosa Lee's granddaughter, she had no claim to the house. The old place was still about to crumble in on itself. Three oil companies were making good offers. The town needed the money to stay alive.

Micah tried to get his heater to work as he circled Randi's bar. Even if Sidney's mother's name had been on the baptism document, he decided, it wouldn't change anything.

Bad luck had followed the committee this past week. Maybe if they voted, that would end.

Micah found himself in the bar parking lot wondering when he'd turned off the main road. The lights to Randi's place were on, but not a car sat in the lot. Apparently, everyone but him had sense enough to stay off the roads tonight.

He parked at the front door and ran in before he changed his mind. He'd just say hello, ask how she was, check to make sure all was well.

An old country song greeted him through the blink of twinkle lights. The chairs were turned over on the tables, all the pool cues were racked.

She stood behind the bar, cleaning up for the night. "I was just about to close," she said before he stepped into enough light for her to recognize him.

Micah shook the snow from his hair and walked across the empty bar. He pulled off his coat and loosened his tie knowing he must look out of place. He wished he had something clever to say. Something about the night and the storm and why he stopped by.

But, there was nothing he could say that would be the truth. He raised his hand. She stepped around the bar and took it, her eyes as full of need as he knew his heart was.

They walked to the worn dance floor. He turned toward her and Randi melted against him. She laid her head on his shoulder, he held her with one arm around her waist and they danced, moving slowly across the floor, as smooth as leaves drifting in lazy water.

He closed his eyes, loving the feel of her breath against his throat, loving the smell of her hair against his cheek, loving Randi. He didn't know when it had happened, he didn't care, but he knew he loved her.

Neither said a word as the song changed

from one to another on her favorite mix of tunes. She lifted her arms and wrapped them around his neck, molding so close against him he could feel her heart pounding.

He spread his hand across the warm skin at her waist and let his fingers glide back and forth along her spine. Circling, like she'd taught him to do, he laughed at the way she followed as if she'd read his mind. He didn't care if knowing her was right or wrong. It had become a part of him.

They danced to one song after another, without any need to talk. He moved his hands along her body, learning every curve. There was no hesitance on his part, no shyness on hers. He'd never felt about a woman the way he felt about Randi, not even his wife. Amy had been his partner. But Randi, whether they ever married or not, was his mate. There was something primitive about it. In the beat of the music. In the beat of his heart. Something drew him to her and had from the first.

Finally, when the songs had circled back to where he walked in, Randi pulled away. "Go home," she said the words, but her eyes seemed to say so much more. "It's late."

He nodded and turned to pick up the jacket he'd let fall over a table. He was afraid if he started talking he might never stop. He'd probably frighten her to death. He had a hole of need so deep he didn't know if anyone but her would ever fill it. He pulled on his coat and took a step toward the door.

Randi's touch stopped him.

When he turned, she moved closer, turning his collar up as her body leaned into him. "Be careful," she whispered as her arms circled inside his coat. Her hug was so tight, he couldn't breathe. He wrapped her against him and held on, wishing he never had to let her go.

She pulled away and walked to the door.

When he passed her, he leaned and kissed her lightly on the mouth as he had before. Her lips were warm and slightly open. Then, he stepped out into the cold. A moment later the door locked behind him.

Micah drove home with Randi still close. He could feel the warmth of her against him. The scent of her lay thick in his lungs. The taste of her lips lingered on his mouth.

He checked on Logan, then fell into bed after removing only his coat. Lying in the dark, Micah stared out at the night. The snow had begun to blow and circle. *Dancing,* he thought.

Nothing made sense anymore. His life. His attraction to Randi. He knew all the rules, he taught them to couples about to marry. Look for someone with the same background, same religion, same values, same goals in life.

People don't pick a mate by how she smells or how she feels. There had to be more to it than that. Amy and he had been mirror images of one another. Both only children raised by religious parents with strict values. Both educated the same, both loving the same things. How could he have not loved Amy from the first day he met her? It had been as natural, as reasonable, as breathing.

He stared into the night. How could he love Randi now?

Maybe he was starved to have a woman near?

No, that made no sense. There were plenty of women around and he had no desire to hold any of them close the way he held Randi. Women at the church were always hugging him. It never crossed his mind to pull one close enough so that he could feel her heart. Surely he would have noticed if he'd developed the habit of smelling a woman's hair.

He tried to concentrate. Had he ever smelled a woman's hair?

No. Not one.

So, that eliminated the possibility that he'd changed into some kind of sex-starved maniac.

He didn't want a woman. He wanted Randi.

He wanted her in his life. He wanted to laugh with her and fight with her. He wanted to feel all the mess that comes from caring about another. He wanted to worry about her and have her worry about him. He wanted to fall asleep with her in his arms and wake up with her warmth beside him.

The strangest thing about this relationship, if he could call it that, was that she seemed to feel the same way. What had Frankie said? *She only dances alone.* Yet, she'd danced with him.

He didn't have to ask if she felt the same

about him. He knew it all the way to his marrow. Just as he knew she was lying awake across town right now wishing they'd danced one more dance.

Forty

After everyone had left for the night, Sloan helped Sidney pick up from the party. "Have fun?" he asked like a kid who needed to be told that he'd done something right one more time.

She yawned. "I wish I didn't have to get up early in the morning, but I had a great time."

"I think everyone did." He shoved aluminum-foil wrappers into the trash. "Only next year I'm buying three dozen tamales. Those Rogers sisters can put them away."

Sidney laughed. "They had to have something to cut the fire of their hot sauce. When I heard Beth Ann tell Billy she called it her 'death-wish special,' I thought she was kidding until I tasted it."

"It was a little warm," he said as he bumped into her pulling the bag out of the trash can. "You ever think of getting a bigger place? I feel like I've been walking around in a dollhouse all night."

"I could just get a smaller friend," she countered.

He sat the bag down and gently pulled her to the couch. "I wanted to talk to you about that."

"About trading you in for someone smaller? Maybe I could get two guys half your size. Or maybe if I left you out in the rain, you'd shrink."

"No." He looked serious. "I want to talk about becoming more than friends."

He sat beside her without touching. "I'm tired of tiptoeing around and not asking personal questions, and trying to act like you are just someone I've met in passing. But, it's not working."

"We've only known one another a week." She knew she could argue the point but, in truth, she felt as if they'd known each other longer, too.

"I know." He took her hand. "I'm too old to be your boyfriend and it's probably too soon to be lovers, but there needs to be someplace in between. Some place where we can be comfortable."

He reached into his pocket. "I got you something. It's not really a gift, so I didn't want to give it to you in front of everyone."

"Thank you." She stared down at the box wrapped in what looked like a grocery sack.

"I didn't have any ribbon." He frowned looking very much like he wished he could take the gift back.

Carefully she opened the box as if it were something special.

Sloan rubbed his hands together and watched.

Sidney pushed the lid off and pulled out a set of keys. She looked up, having no idea what to say.

He tried to explain. "That red one is the key to the lock box on the back of my truck where I keep my tools. The blue one will get you in the back door of my place on Lake Travis. The silver one is my apartment in Houston. The biggest one is to my truck. That funny-looking one unlocks any door on my family's old place outside of Tyler. No one lives there anymore, but I keep it locked."

"I don't understand."

Sloan leaned back looking as if he believed this might be the dumbest thing he'd ever done. "I wanted you to have them. You should know that I want you in my life. In all of my life." He pulled out his keys. "There's not a key on this ring that isn't on that one. I want you to feel free to walk around."

"You're saying no locked doors. Nothing I can't ask." She didn't look as if she believed him.

He breathed. She got the point. "That's what I'm saying. There are things in my past that I may not volunteer unless you ask but, if you want the truth, you got the right to know."

Sidney frowned. "And what are you asking in return?"

"Nothing," he said. "This was my gift to you. You take your time about unlocking your doors. I've just spent too many years closed away. I want to know I allowed someone in even if it may be the first and only time in my life. I allowed you in."

She circled her fingers around the keys. "Thank you."

He closed his eyes thinking this idea

hadn't seemed near as crazy when he'd thought of it. Maybe he should have just written her a letter saying how special he thought she was and how he wanted her to feel comfortable around him and not worry that she might say the wrong thing or ask something too personal. She wasn't the type to laugh at him behind his back, but he wouldn't blame her if she did. A set of keys! What kind of gift is that?

Her lips brushing his surprised him. He opened his eyes as she leaned forward again and kissed him lightly.

"Anything else you have to say, Sloan?"

He smiled. "Yeah, come a little closer. There's something I'd like to teach you."

For the next several minutes, he kissed her. Either he was getting rusty, or she was a fast learner because Sloan finally broke the kiss and swore that kissing her was about as good as kissing gets. Everything about the professor surprised him. Why shouldn't this?

"You wouldn't want to change back into those cute flannel pajamas, would you?"

She shook her head. "It's time for bed."

"That was my thinking exactly," he grinned.

"No. I mean it's late."

"I know. It's time for me to go."

"Right."

The good news, he thought, was that she didn't look any happier about it than he did. He stood, offering his hand to her. "Before you toss me out in the cold, I want to tell you about an idea I have. When the Rogers sisters were looking through your new gardening book, I remembered the line from Miss Carter's poem. The roses in a book are ever bright."

Sidney whispered, "Look among roses ever bright for the key to unlocking the secrets of Rosa Lee. But what book? Where? All the books she had were donated to the library."

He nodded. "What time can you get away tomorrow? I'll pick you up and we'll visit the library."

"But Miss Carter said she had hundreds of books on gardening."

He tugged on his boots. "Then we've got our work cut out for us. I'll be waiting when you get out of class. It might not be a bad idea to call the committee and ask if they could help us out before the big meeting tomorrow. Maybe some of them could meet us at the library. Ada May and Beth Ann know all about roses so they'd probably be the most help. We might not find anything, but if we did, you'd all know it before you vote."

When they stood at the door, she asked, "Why are you doing all this, Sloan? Why help me find out about the house and Rosa Lee? Don't you realize that if I find something it might sway my vote toward not letting the town sell the house?"

He shrugged. "Can't you tell why I'm helping you, Sidney?"

She shook her head, not accepting his answer.

"From the first time I saw you, I've been crazy about you. I should probably play it cool, but I've spent too much of my life playing my hand too close to the chest. You matter to me whether you believe it or not. I meant what I said about those keys." He kissed her cheek. "I'm helping you because it matters to you. I'll help you any way I can."

Sidney crossed her arms, accepting the challenge. "All right. Who were those men you talked to in the parking lot of Randi's bar this morning?"

"How'd—" He stopped and faced her square. "They were local men I hired to keep me informed about what's going on concerning the bidding on the Altman land. One works for Talon Graham, but he's hoping to get on with us. The other has lived here for generations and knows pretty much everyone in town. His last name is Hamm, I think. He must be kin to that crazy old man I've almost rear-ended twice."

She nodded. "Fair enough. But you could have asked me about the bids."

He fought the urge to touch her. "What's between us has nothing to do with my job. I'll never take advantage of that. I told you that from the first. As far as I'm concerned my business is with the mayor, no one else."

She had to admit he'd kept his word so far.

He put on his hat and buttoned up his coat. "I'll be waiting for you when you get out of class tomorrow."

She touched his arm and waited for him to lean down so she could brush her lips against his. "Be careful driving tonight."

He grinned. "I'm growing on you, Professor."

She laughed. "That you are."

She was still smiling when she met him the next morning. As he drove to the library, she told him the sisters were already looking through Rosa Lee's old books. Billy, Lora and Micah had plans, but they'd said they'd join them as soon as they could get away.

"I've been thinking about the part of the poem that goes, *Gone in thirty-four, a love forgotten nevermore.* She must be talking about Fuller dying, but he died late in thirty-three."

Sloan pulled into the library parking lot. "Maybe it didn't rhyme with *more* so she changed the date?"

"A man might do that, but a woman never would."

"A man would have remembered the secret and passed it on, not made up a rhyme."

She didn't argue as they walked to the library. Today was the day, she thought. The day she'd promised to let the mayor know what would be done with the Altman house.

In a few hours they'd all meet and vote. She had no idea how it would go. Sidney wasn't even sure how she'd vote.

"Sloan?" she asked as they walked toward the tiny library that had been added on to the back of the courthouse. "Where were you yesterday?"

"I went over to Wichita Falls to get a new windshield put in. I stopped by for a visit with Miss Carter. I'd mentioned that I might come back and I thought yesterday would be a good time." He hesitated. "I also spent a few hours after lunch talking to my boss who is working on a site near Midland. He wants me there as soon as I'm finished here."

Sidney didn't want to think about Sloan going on to the next job. They were just getting to know one another. But, she couldn't help but wonder how many times he'd said goodbye before he had time to form a bond. "Did Miss Carter tell you any more about Rosa Lee?" she asked, shoving thoughts of him leaving aside.

"Not really. Only that the old doctor who treated Henry and then Rosa Lee has a widow who is still alive. She talked on and on about how the old doc thought Henry was a fine man. Said he'd never met a man who walked his religion the way Henry Altman did. I don't see that could be much help to you."

"Seems strange that, if he were religious, Rosa Lee wouldn't have had a wake and a funeral for him."

"Maybe he didn't want it." Sloan opened the library door.

"Maybe she was such a recluse she couldn't go through with it. With no other family, when he died she was all alone. Surely she had a priest come in."

Sloan shook his head. "Miss Carter said Rosa Lee had nothing that she knew of."

The Rogers sisters waved, drawing Sidney's attention. They were at a massive table surrounded by gardening books.

"I guess it's time we go to work." Sloan winked at Sidney, then joined the sisters.

All four thumbed through book after book looking for anything written in the margins. Nothing.

After a while, Sidney's eyes began to blur. Time was running out. At three, they'd meet at the old house and vote. She glanced at the clock. Three more hours. It wasn't the house that drew her, but the secret. She felt as if Rosa Lee had kept something secret all her life and now, for some reason, was trying to tell her. If the house fell, the secret might forever be lost. She had to find it.

She leaned over to Sloan. "Have you got your phone?"

He handed her his cell without asking questions.

She dialed the mayor's number and leaned back, waiting.

On the fourth ring, the mayor picked up.

"This is Professor Dickerson, Mayor. I'd like to let you know the committee will not be making their final decision on the house until tomorrow."

She held the phone away from her ear. Sloan looked up hearing the complaining from across the table.

"All right," she said when he paused. "We'll vote at nine o'clock in the morning. Have everyone who is interested in the outcome at the house. We'll vote and announce our recommendation."

She paused, listened, then added, "I'm

aware of that . . . yes . . . see you in the morning."

Sidney handed Sloan back his phone. "I guess I'm off the mayor's Christmas list."

"What did he feel he needed to make you aware of?" Sloan asked.

"That only two people have filed letters about the historical importance of the house. One was mine. The other was old Mr. Hamm. He claims he'd never remember how to find Cemetery Road if the house wasn't there to remind him."

"You thought more people would care, didn't you?" He hit her problem with a bull's-eye.

"I did. Yet, I seem to be the only one. I'm sure whoever buys the land will put up a sign for Old Man Hamm. Not that he'll read it any more than he does the stop signs around town."

Sloan's big hand covered hers. "Did you ever think that maybe this house holds your history and not the town's? The walls are whispering to you, not future generations from Clifton Creek."

"You believe she was my grandmother?"

He winked at her. "I just found a book you

might want to take a look at." He passed
her a small book entitled *The Portland Rose.*
"Page fifty-seven."

Sidney held her breath as she opened the
book. She knew before she found the page
he'd named that there would be a picture of
a small red-pink rose spotted with white.
The Marbree rose.

For a moment she just looked at the picture of the rose her mother had been named
after. Her mother had never mentioned
where her name came from, but Minnie had
planted Portland roses in the garden of
every house she'd lived. Most of the time
the zone wasn't right and the shrub died,
but once, when they'd had a courtyard, it
had thrived.

"One more clue," Sloan whispered from
close behind her. "One more link between
your family and Rosa Lee. How many do
you need, Sidney, to believe?"

Sidney brushed her thumb across the
rose and felt the imprint in the paper. She
turned the page and saw writing in the mar-
gin of the next page. *Beneath the wooden
rose. RL.*

Sidney shook her head. "I don't remember a wooden rose."

"We'll go look. There's bound to be one in the woodwork of that house somewhere."

Ada May and Beth Ann agreed it was time for another search, providing they all stop for lunch first.

Forty-One

Lora dragged herself into work Wednesday morning bundled up like an Eskimo and trying to rub her headache away. She was getting too old for this, she decided. After Sidney's party, Billy and she had stayed up half the night talking in his dorm room. They'd watched the snow fall outside his window and listened to the noises of dorm life. She hadn't told so many stories about herself since she'd been a teenager at slumber parties.

He'd finally fallen asleep on the futon that doubled as his bed and she'd driven home trying to figure out why she liked being around him so much. He was a good listener. She talked his ears off. Anyone would think they had nothing in common, unless you counted the committee. But she could be herself around him. He was there as a friend right when she needed one. He didn't seem to want anything from her and he never tried to make her into someone else.

That was it, she thought. He liked her just the way she was and no one had ever done that before.

"Morning," Lora said as she passed the center desk in the showroom of her father's dealership. "Going to be a slow day, I'm guessing." No one wanted to buy a car on snowy days.

Dora Smithee smiled as she was paid to do. "Your father left a message that he wants to see you when you come in. And . . ." She leaned over the counter and added in a whisper, "That good-looking Mr. Hunk is back in your office looking ever so fine and holding flowers. Everyone says he'll be our governor in twenty years. If you play your cards right you could be sitting beside him in the governor's mansion."

Lora groaned. "Thanks for the warning." Dora's definition of character involved a sentence that always had something to do with how a man filled out his jeans. To her, *looking deeper* meant checking out how much cash he carried. The woman had been test-driven more than any car on the lot.

Lora pulled off her sunglasses and stared through the glass wall at Talon Graham propped on the corner of her desk. She'd hoped not to have to face him again. At least not until after the vote. She knew what he wanted and, despite his protests, it wasn't her. He was far more interested in the pending deal with the mayor.

He flashed her a perfect smile as she stepped into her glass-walled office. "Morning, honey." Talon grinned.

"What is this obsession men have with pet names?" she mumbled as she passed him and stored her purse behind her desk.

He looked downright sensitive. "I'm terribly sorry if I offended you. I thought we knew each other well enough for endearments."

Not in this lifetime, Lora thought as she rolled her eyes. "How can I help you today, Talon?"

He handed her the flowers, the most expensive spray the grocer carried. "I just had to come by and say how deeply sorry I am

about the other night. I've been under a lot
of pressure from the office in Austin to wrap
up the Altman deal and I guess I tried to
drink my troubles away. I hope I didn't talk
too much about business."

He'd only had two topics, business and
sex, as she remembered. "I've told you before, Talon, I can't talk with you about how
the committee plans to vote. First of all, I
don't know and second, it wouldn't be eth-
ical." Her actions with Billy at the truck stop
Sunday morning surely made it plain there
wouldn't be any sex between her and Mr.
Hunk.

Now, he looked hurt. The man was a
chameleon. "How can you even think I'm
here because of that? I wouldn't play you
like that land man from Houston is playing
the professor. Every time I see him in town,
he's either near the house, or someone on
the committee. I'd never do that."

For once, he had her attention. "Are you
talking about Sloan McCormick?" She knew
Sloan was in oil, but she'd never thought
that he might just be using the professor.

Talon smiled. "He's smooth, isn't he? I'll
bet that old maid has no idea what hit her. I
almost feel sorry for him. He may have to

sleep with her to get the vote he wants out of your committee, but if I know Sloan Mc-Cormick, he'll do whatever it takes."

Lora didn't like what he was implying. Sloan seemed a straight-up guy. She hadn't noticed him trying to talk Sidney into any-thing. And the professor was no starry-eyed girl. She'd keep her head about her. "What makes you think he's playing her?"

Talon smiled that perfect smile she was learning to hate. "It's his job, Lora. Part of the game. You've been in the big leagues before. You know. Deals get done in more places than boardrooms. Business is a game and you do whatever you have to do to win."

That was it, she thought. She did know. Never, not for one moment, had she be-lieved that Talon was interested in her. Even the flowers he'd brought and sent to the house were simply a business expense. It occurred to her that he'd finally realized he couldn't play her so his next move would be to make sure Sloan, his competition, made no progress with the chairman. Classic strategy for the game.

But Sloan *had* fooled her, Lora thought. She'd believed he truly cared about the professor. Part of her still believed it, or wanted to anyway. She had to give McCormick credit, he was either telling the truth, or he was the best at playing people she'd ever seen.

Kicking Talon out of her office took about as much effort as emptying the trash. Lora thought of tossing the flowers as well, but decided to give them to Dora at the front desk. She even wrote Dora's name on the card and claimed Talon was only delivering them for a friend. Maybe the mystery man who sometimes sent Dora daisies would think the woman had another suitor.

"Your father still wants to see you," Dora said after she gushed over the flowers.

"Tell him I'm going to the library," Lora yelled on her way out.

Dora shrugged as if expecting the answer. She probably figured as long as Lora worked for her father, she had job security as the messenger.

Lora drove twice the speed limit to the library, but couldn't find any of the committee. She asked at the desk and wasn't surprised to learn that the librarian on duty had heard every word. She even knew all their names, except Sloan, whom she referred to as "the noncardholder."

"They're meeting Reverend Parker for lunch at the downtown café and then they plan to go search for something at the Altman place." The librarian thought a moment. "I'm sorry, that's all I heard. Someone phoned and I had to step into my office."

"That's great." Lora headed for the door thinking Clifton Creek's librarian could go straight into the FBI without further training. "Do you happen to know if they found what they were looking for here?"

She nodded once. "I believe they did. Professor Dickerson checked out one book on Portland roses."

When Lora left the library, she wasn't surprised to see Talon Graham's car parked across the street. He'd leaned back in his seat as if taking a nap, but she knew he was watching her. When she pulled out of the parking place, she noticed he also started his engine. He must have nothing else to do before he learned of the vote, so he might as well follow her and see what trouble he'd stirred up by telling her about Sloan McCormick. Only Lora decided not to play the game anymore.

Three blocks later, they took the last two spaces left in front of the café, but he made no effort to go in. As she walked to the door, she noticed Billy carefully climbing out of his car. He still had on his worn leather jacket, but his clothes now looked more like he belonged in college than on the streets. Lora knew he hadn't had time to shop, so he must be wearing his Sunday best, tailored khaki pants and a white button-down shirt.

"You shouldn't be driving!" she yelled as she hurried toward him.

"The Rogers sisters called and invited me to lunch. When I found out we were eating out, I couldn't say no." He lifted his one good arm around her shoulder. "How you doing, babe?" His words were light, but his eyes told her he cared about her answer.

She glanced back and noticed Talon watching. "I'm fine. Aren't you going to give me a hello kiss?"

He raised an eyebrow. "Are you serious?"

"Sure. Lay one on me."

His arm tightened, drawing her to him as he lowered his mouth to hers.

The kiss wasn't as long as Lora would

have liked to display to Talon, but it was very pleasant just the same.

"I got a feeling there's going to be pain somewhere in this greeting," Billy whispered. "But it was worth it."

She wrapped an arm around his waist and walked with him toward the door. "I've decided to stop beating you up. There's too many people in line ahead of me."

Two farmers walked out as she opened the door. They'd probably passed the morning with coffee and talk. One removed his hat. "Morning, Lora," he said politely.

"Morning, Jake," she said.

Both men looked at Billy. "Mornin'," Jake said to Billy and moved out of the way. "Glad to see you getting around so good. We was worried about you. Ain't right, someone jumping you like that when you was just doing your duty watching over that old Altman place."

The other farmer agreed and leaned forward to pat Billy on the shoulder in awkward comfort.

Once she and Billy were inside, he laughed. "That's the first time either of them have ever said a word to me. I would have sworn they didn't know I existed."

Billy didn't comment on how the men knew about his beating.

Lora waved at the Rogers sisters. As they moved across the room, she felt every set of eyes on her, watching. Several people spoke to her, a few to Billy. The town was keeping up with what had happened at the Altman place.

He slid into the booth beside Lora and across from the Rogers sisters. "Am I in the right town?"

Lora laughed. "I know what you mean. People smiled at me without the usual *poor thing* kind of look in their eyes. Nothing like stepping into another crisis to get you out of the one you think you're living in."

Ada May interrupted. "Of course, they stare at you. The committee is the talk of the town today. I'm starting to feel like a rock star."

"How do you know what a rock star feels like, Ada May? Have you ever been a rock star? I don't think so," Beth Ann said.

"I was just guessing."

"Well, not me. I'm not saying I feel like something when I don't have any idea what that feels like and neither do you. You've never even been near a rock star in your whole life."

"Yes, I have," Ada May corrected. "I touched Willie Nelson's car once when he was in Amarillo. I went right up to it and touched the door where he probably put his hand before he got in."

"Hope I'm not interrupting something," Micah Parker said as he took the last seat in the long booth. He waved away a menu and lifted one finger, indicating he wanted the special, which was what anyone with sense ordered if they wanted to be served before two o'clock.

Billy grinned. "Hopefully, you are interrupting." He pointed with his head toward the sisters. "They're already into round two."

Both sisters looked as if they had no idea what he was talking about. After giving their order, they rejoined the group.

Ada May leaned close to Micah. "The professor stood right up to the mayor and told him we needed more time. This afternoon, we're heading over to the house to do more investigating."

Micah glanced at Sidney.

"Actually, I asked if we could have one

more day. There are a few things we have to settle. I promised we'd have the answer by tomorrow morning at nine."

Micah waited as Sidney explained. She ended by saying, "Sloan and I plan to go visit the widow of Dr. Eastland. We're hoping she might remember something about Rosa Lee."

"Good. I've got my own lead. I'm going out to Luther Oates's place and see if I can find out what he remembers," Micah said. "A friend of mine told me about a religious group that called themselves the Brotherhood. She said Oates and Altman might have been in it. I've been dying to hear if any of the stories are true. And if he knows anything, he might know if the house was used as their meeting place."

Sloan shook his head. "I don't know. The road's unpaved and bound to be bad, plus the Oateses aren't known for welcoming company. We've got a few rigs near there and some of the men swear they've been shot at taking shortcuts across Oates's land to get to our rigs. Maybe you should wait until I can go with you. We'll be back from Eastland's by three."

Lora looked around Ada May and almost

shouted, "I'll go with Sidney to see the widow. Sloan, you take Micah." She didn't miss Sloan's doubt. "Then we can cover ground twice as fast. We're running out of time. We'll meet back here in two hours for coffee, then go out to the house."

Sloan nodded, but obviously wasn't happy with leaving Sidney. He even insisted on giving her his extra cell phone. Lora couldn't help but wonder why. Was he doing his job and didn't want to miss anything, or was he being a caring friend? Talon Graham might be worthless, but he'd opened her eyes to watching Sloan and if Sloan McCormick stepped out of line, Lora planned to be there.

"I could go over to the house and look for the wooden rose while everyone else is out visiting," Billy offered.

Everyone at the table said no at the same time.

Billy shrugged. "It was an idea."

Beth Ann patted his bandaged hand. "Ada May and I will go with you. While they are interviewing everyone, we can start with the grounds before it gets any colder. A cold front is on its way in."

"Then—" Ada May picked up the plan

"—we'll come back here for dessert and warm up while we learn what Sidney and Micah found out."

Sidney glanced at her watch. "All right, we meet back here no later than four and go back to the house for a final search."

Her troops were too busy getting their hamburgers to answer, but finally, between bites, Ada May mumbled, "I don't know about anyone else, but when we go back to the old place tonight I'm going armed."

Forty-Two

Sloan McCormick pulled his truck off the paved road and hoped the ground was still frozen enough not to have turned to mud. The day had held to below freezing with a cloudy enough sky to keep the few inches of snow from melting, but he knew West Texas. An hour of sunshine and the road to Luther Oates's place might be impossible to travel.

"What are we looking for, Preacher?"

"I don't know. I think I may be chasing something that is little more than a legend. The story goes that once, when only a few Anglos settled this area, most of the people here were Catholic."

Sloan laughed. "That's no legend, Micah.

That's fact. When Texas belonged to Mexico the only people allowed to settle here were Catholics, or at least they had to claim to be."

Micah shrugged. "I was thinking about a little later than the revolution. From about the turn of the century until the thirties or so. Legends in Clifton Creek talk of a group of Catholics who broke away from the church. They called themselves the Brotherhood. They believed in suffering for their sins. I don't know what it would have to do with the Altman place, but the time period was when Henry Altman would have been an important man. It's just a hunch I've had ever since I found out that Rosa Lee had her baby baptized in the Catholic church."

"It's a lead anyway." Sloan laughed. "I know how they must have felt back then. I think I've suffered for every sin I've ever enjoyed. My ex-wife made sure of that."

"You were married?" Micah wanted to change the subject. The parts of the legend he had heard frightened him. Clifton Creek was a calm little town where nothing bad happened. He didn't like the idea that someone might have died in town and no one knew why.

"I married once, about ten years ago. She was a knockout who made me chase her until she caught me. I should have spent some time talking to her before we ended up married. She made my life such hell even the oil field half a world away looked good. I swore I'd never fall for a woman again."

"And?"

Sloan smiled. "I kept my word, until I stood outside a classroom and watched Dr. Sidney Dickerson lecture. I've never met a woman like her, all brains and caring. She's innocent and irresistible at the same time. I think it will take me a lifetime to figure her out if I can convince her to let me stay around."

"You fear she might not."

"I worry about it. She doesn't know how far I'm willing to go to make sure I stay out of the way of her committee vote." The oilman hesitated only a moment. "I'm willing to step aside. Quit if I have to. My company's already got another man ready to step in and take my place."

Micah tried not to show his surprise.

Sloan glanced at the preacher. "You ever had love slam into you, Preacher?"

"Once," he answered.

"Did you do anything about it?"

"Not yet," Micah said.

Sloan nodded, lost in his own thoughts. "That's the thing, when it hits you hard and fast. You worry that it might not be real, but then, you figure, what if it is real and I let it get away? What if I let my one-in-a-million chance at happiness walk out of my life because I'm too much of a coward to hold on?"

Both men watched the road without talking for a few minutes.

The echo of three rounds being fired reached them. Sloan slowed and rolled the window down a few inches.

"Is someone shooting at us?" Micah leaned forward staring out into open plains. "From where?" The land was flat and endless.

"I'm guessing those were warning shots." Sloan reached for his shotgun. "You know how to shoot?"

Micah hadn't touched a gun since he'd been in Boy Scouts and fired a .22. "I can fire, but I doubt I could hit anything."

"That's fine," Sloan laughed. "We're not planning on killing anything. Just stick that barrel out the window so they'll know we're not scared."

Micah carefully twisted the rifle until the barrel pointed out the window.

"You don't like guns, do you?" Sloan leaned forward, watching as he continued down the road. "But I need to know, one way or the other, in case this is more trouble than I think. If it came down to life or death, could you fire? Will you cover my back if we drive into harm's way?"

Micah had never been asked such a question. Never even given it any thought. He remembered his mother saying once that thank God there was no longer a draft because she couldn't imagine her son carrying a gun.

Then he recalled the stories he'd heard about the Brotherhood. Stories about how they'd taken their religion too far and left a man dead after he'd suffered for their sins. Micah told himself he didn't believe it, but was he willing to bet his life on it? "I can fire if I have to."

Sloan laughed nervously. "We're probably only going to find an old man living on this place who shoots at the crows."

They bumped across the hard road until

they finally saw a windmill to the left. Sloan turned at the first gate. After a half mile, he said, "I'm not even sure we're on the road anymore. I don't have any tracks to follow and the ground is covered." He paused. "When we get there, let me do the talking. We can't go in asking about some secret society or they'll shoot us for sure."

Micah nodded. He had no idea how he would bring the subject up anyway. Where could he start? All he had were a few rumors to base his theory on and the fact that everyone in town thought Luther Oates and Henry Altman had been friends seventy years ago.

They drove up to the house and saw three men standing on a long porch that ran the length of the front. One was old and shriveled into his coat like a turtle. Another had to be in his sixties, but stood straight and tall, a big man even without the boots and hat. The third stranger didn't look long out of his teens. All three had guns within reach.

Sloan told Micah to stay put and stepped out of his truck, slow and easy. "Howdy." He held his hands wide and didn't bother to close the truck door. "I was hoping to have a few words with Luther Oates."

"You the law?"

"No. I'm just here to ask him a few questions about Henry Altman. His granddaughter asked me to come by."

The big man shook his head. "Henry Altman didn't have but one daughter and she was an old maid. So, either you're lying, or you've been lied to which makes you a fool."

Sloan raised his hands higher and took another step. "That may be true, I've fallen for lies a few times in my life, but I saw a picture of Rosa Lee Altman and my lady friend is close to a mirror image."

"Maybe she's a distant cousin or something."

"Did you know Rosa Lee?" Sloan asked.

"I did." The big man answered. "But I've nothing to say."

"Well, her picture was in black-and-white so I couldn't see the color of her eyes, but my friend has light blue. You wouldn't remember what color Rosa Lee's were, would you?"

The older man shifted, but didn't say a word.

Sloan took another step. "Look, I'm not

here to cause any trouble. My friend doesn't have a relative in this world and she'd like to know a little about the people she came from."

The big man in the middle raised his voice as if he thought Sloan must be hard of hearing. "I told you—"

The older man lifted his hand. "It's all right. I'll talk to him. I knew Henry Altman. He was older than me, but I was proud to call him a friend. A finer man never lived."

Micah left the rifle in the truck and stepped out. "You're Luther Oates, aren't you?"

The old man nodded.

"I'm Reverend Micah Parker." Micah took a few steps. "We'd like to ask a few questions about Henry Altman."

"He loved his daughter and she loved him. I'll say that."

"Did he ever lock her away in that house?" Sloan asked.

The old man shook his head and spoke to Micah. "He loved her and she proved she loved him. That's all I'm planning to say."

Sloan leaned closer, now standing just off the porch. "Why? What is the secret that circles around that house like a moat? What is it that no one will tell?"

The old man's eyes floated with tears. "It ain't for me to say. But, best I remember Rosa Lee did have light blue eyes."

Sloan's gaze met Micah's for a second and Micah knew to be ready as Sloan lowered his voice slightly and asked, "Mr. Oates, did Henry Altman have something he wanted to hide? Maybe an organization he belonged to, or something he did he wouldn't want anyone to know about."

Luther glared at Sloan, then shook his head and turned. Without another word the old man considered the meeting over.

Sloan started back to the truck. "Well, then, I guess we're wasting your time."

Micah didn't move, or take his gaze off the old man's back. Sloan was playing him, but Micah guessed Luther would be too smart to fall.

Sloan turned, as if thinking of one last question. "Mr. Oates, how do you feel about the house being demolished?"

Luther glanced over his shoulder. "I say let it fall, there's nothing left but bad memories."

Micah almost echoed the words from the note, *let the house fall.* He knew the old man couldn't have been strong enough to throw the drill bit, but his son or grandson could have.

Sloan agreed. "I'm guessing it'll be torn down in a few days. We're going through it one more time tonight to look for anything."

"You won't find nothing," the kid on the end of the porch mumbled and then seemed embarrassed that he'd said the words aloud.

"Because you've looked," Sloan said before the boy's father or grandfather could speak.

"Maybe," the kid said. "There ain't no crime in walking through a vacant house. I didn't do any damage."

Sloan appeared to agree. "Maybe we'll have better luck," he mumbled continuing his journey to the truck. "Rosa Lee left us a map, written in a book, as to where she kept secrets hidden."

Micah knew Sloan was stretching the truth, but didn't mention it as he watched all three men on the porch stiffen.

"We've reason to believe Henry belonged

to a secret organization," Micah said. "We'd like to find out if it's only a legend, or if it could have been fact."

Finally the old man answered, "If the sheriff were standing here, I'd swear I never heard of such a group. It ain't healthy to mention them."

Sloan nodded then asked, "Mind telling me why? I'm not from around here."

The old man looked as if he questioned just how bright Sloan was. Finally, he said, "From what I hear, they were a group of very religious men. It's rumored one of the ceremonies got out of hand one night in the early thirties and men died. After that, the group broke up."

"You have any idea if Henry Altman belonged to that group?" Micah asked, already seeing the answer in the old man's eyes.

"If he did a thing like that it would weigh heavy on him." Oates looked tired, a lifetime of tired. "I heard there was a list, a role of the members. If it were found, it could destroy whole families around here."

Luther Oates took a deep breath. "If this woman friend of yours is kin to Henry Alt-

man, and he was a member of the Brotherhood, maybe it's better she never knows."

"One last question, Mr. Oates," Sloan
said. "Do you have any idea why Henry's
daughter didn't have a service for her father?"

The old man looked Sloan straight in the
eyes. "Maybe she did."

Sloan thanked Oates and backed to the
open door of his pickup. Micah did the
same. When they were far enough away
from the house to be safe, Sloan punched in
a number on his cell.

"Sidney," he said with a snap. "Have you
seen Dr. Eastland's widow yet?"

He listened then added, "Try to get a
copy of the death certificate."

He clicked the phone closed without saying goodbye.

"What is it?" Micah asked as he braced
himself for the bumps Sloan took at top
speed.

Sloan rubbed his forehead. "I don't know,
more a feeling than anything, but I got the
idea that maybe Henry didn't die when
everyone thinks he did. Luther knows more
than he's telling. Maybe there was no funeral in 1950 because Henry didn't die then.

You said you found a record listing his death in 1964."

"But it must have been wrong. Why would a man fake his own death?"

"Maybe he didn't. Maybe Rosa Lee did?"

Forty-Three

Lora Whitman and Sidney Dickerson waited in the tiny front room of Dr. Eastland's widow's home. The room could be called nothing else but a sitting room, just like the ones Sidney had seen in museums. In the fifties, families had tried to revive them, calling them formal living rooms, but their usefulness was gone, thanks probably to telephones. There was no need for guests to arrive and wait until someone was ready to receive them—they could simply call first.

When Mrs. Eastland walked in, or more accurately shuffled in, she looked as if she belonged in sitting-room surroundings. The dress she wore could have been bought thirty or more years ago. "Welcome." Her smile was framed by a thousand wrinkles. "How may I help you, Dr. Dickerson? I read your articles in the paper so I feel we are already friends."

She offered her hand to Sidney then turned to Lora. "Hello, child." Her tiny hand patted Lora's. "You've grown up to be a real lady. I know your parents must be proud. I saw where you graduated from the University of Texas a few years back."

Lora smiled and thanked her. Mrs. Eastland might be one of the town's oldest residents but her mind was still razor sharp.

"Thanks for seeing us on such short notice, Mrs. Eastland," Lora said, knowing that Sidney was dying to get to the questions but Mrs. Eastland would expect conversation first.

So, Lora asked about the grandchildren and Mrs. Eastland showed pictures of the great-grandchildren, taking the time to point out the parents of each child. Then Sidney mentioned the committee she chaired and Mrs. Eastland inquired who was on it and how the meetings were going.

Finally, after twenty minutes, she turned to Sidney and asked how she could help.

Sidney reached for her notes and

glasses. "First, we'd like to ask if you still have Dr. Eastland's records available, and a copy of Henry Altman's death certificate?"

"Of course I do," she said. "His office was next door for almost fifty years." Mrs. Eastland led them down an enclosed passageway leading from her home into her husband's offices.

The office looked exactly as it must have twenty years before. Sidney wasn't surprised.

"The doctor kept detailed files. I was his office manager when we first met and helped out here now and then even after the children came." She crossed the room to an old filing cabinet. "The records are closed except to family, but I think the committee would qualify. I rented out this office to the new doctors when they first came to Clifton Creek, but last year they finally got a new place. I kept the files of patients who'd passed on. Active files were moved to the new doctor's office."

Lora glanced at Sidney. The professor was fighting to keep from reaching across the old lady and grabbing the records.

"Here is Rosa Lee's." Mrs. Eastland pulled out a thin folder. "She was healthy, but given to depression, I think, for my husband sent medicine to her place every month, but he never talked about it with me. Dr. Eastland prided himself in keeping confidences, but now I guess it no longer matters." She handed the folder to Sidney. "I'll have to go out to storage for Henry's file. Will you excuse me, please?"

Lora offered to help, but Mrs. Eastland insisted they wait. When she was gone, Sidney opened Rosa Lee's file. An orderly telling of her life spread before them. The doctors changed from time to time, recording all illnesses. The flu, pneumonia, a twisted ankle X-rayed in the sixties, pills for high blood pressure in the eighties, pills for sleeping in the nineties.

"Any record of a child?" Lora whispered.

"No. But 1934 was the year she had pneumonia. It says the doctor left orders for a nurse to check on her twice a week until she recovered. The dates of the house calls are listed with initials beside them."

Lora leaned close. "M.J."

"Minnie Jefferson. My grandmother was there. The dates are the months before my mother's birth. But there is no record of Rosa Lee giving birth. Maybe my grandmother just had my mother early but wanted to record her birth in Chicago. We still have no proof."

Lora didn't answer. She knew neither of them believed that. "We may never know the truth if the doctor didn't record it in his files."

Sidney shook her head. "I don't know why it matters. They are all dead anyway. If Rosa Lee was my grandmother, she must not have loved my mother or me. She never tried to keep in touch. Maybe the notes someone keeps sending me are right. Maybe the committee should just let the house fall and forget the past. If Rosa Lee had been my grandmother wouldn't it make sense that she would have kept in touch?"

"I found Henry Altman's file," Mrs. Eastland said as she moved slowly back into the room. "It's a little dusty I'm afraid. Probably no one has opened it since he died."

"Do you remember when he died?"

Mrs. Eastland nodded. "I was busy with little ones then, but I remember. My husband had been over at the house several times. He said he'd tried everything to get Henry to go to the hospital, but the old man wouldn't hear of it. They didn't have a funeral, which everyone thought was unusual, but Rosa Lee was so shy. She likely wasn't up to having one."

Lora nodded as the old lady continued, "Henry died in 1950 and Rosa Lee took over the running of the ranch. Just in time from what I heard. The place was losing money. She had to sell off pieces of it to live and if the old man had been alive he never would have allowed that. They would have lost everything if she hadn't cut back and saved what she could."

"She must have felt so alone after her father died." Sidney knew what it was like to lose all relatives.

"Her father had a few good friends. Luther Oates and Earl Hamm, I believe. As long as Rosa Lee was alive, they checked on her now and then."

Mrs. Eastland turned through the pages of the file to the end. "This is strange," she said as she pulled out two documents.

"What?"

"Henry Altman has two death certificates."

"Copies?"

Mrs. Eastland shook her head. "No, one is dated November 1950. The other is October of 1964. There must be some mistake," Mrs. Eastland whispered. "But I never knew my husband to be careless. He took pride in always having his files in order."

Lora looked at the two death certificates. The one in 1950 had been filed and notarized. The one in 1964 had been filled out by the same hand, but not stamped. Her imagination went wild. "Maybe this explains why there was no funeral."

"Why?" Sidney studied the documents.

"Because, Henry was listed as dead in 1950, but didn't really die until 1964. Maybe he faked his own death."

"Whatever for?"

Lora shook her head. "I have no idea, but if the doctor and Rosa Lee knew about it, so did others."

"What if he faked his death and continued to live in the old house?" Sidney guessed.

"But, why?" Mrs. Eastland questioned.

"Insurance money?" Lora guessed.

Mrs. Eastland shook her head. "If Rosa Lee had gotten money, she wouldn't have had to sell land."

The phone Sloan had given Sidney jingled in her pocket. She answered it, said a few words and hung up.

Sidney was pale as she faced Lora. "You may be right," she whispered. "Sloan just told me to bring copies of the death certificate. He also has a question about when Henry died."

Forty-Four

Micah left Sloan promising to meet everyone at the Main Street Café at four. He
drove straight to Randi's bar knowing he
had to talk to her before he allowed any
more time to slip by. He parked in the empty
lot and fought the wind as he walked to the
front door.

The hairy old biker who acted as bartender stood behind the bar. Micah swore
the man growled at him when he fought to
close the door against the cold.

"I need to see Randi," Micah said.

Frankie shrugged.

Micah put his hand on the pass-through
opening. "Maybe I should say I'm going to
see Randi." He guessed the bartender

would make about double his own weight and, from the tattoos and scars, the man could probably flatten him with his breath, but Micah had to try. "Are you going to try and stop me?"

Frankie shook his head. "Not me, but she will. You're getting too close, Preacher, and Randi don't let no one close."

Micah stepped behind the bar and opened the office door. "Thanks for the warning."

Randi sat at the desk, a pencil stuck behind one ear and papers scattered everywhere. When she looked up, she smiled. "Micah. Is something wrong?"

He closed the door and moved around the desk. "Nothing's wrong." He took her hand and led her to the hallway behind her office. "I just didn't want to wait any longer to do this."

He leaned against her, cupping her face with his hands, and kissed her.

For a moment, he felt surprise, shock, hesitance, then he felt surrender. She wrapped her arms around his neck and held on tight as their world began to spin. He kissed her long and hard and hungry as he'd ached to do since she'd first touched him.

He'd lied to himself thinking friendship would be enough, or holding her while they danced was all he needed. He needed Randi, all of her.

When neither of them could breathe, they broke the kiss laughing, but their hands still moved over one another, learning every part of the other.

"We better go upstairs, Micah," she whispered. "The hallway's really not a good place to do what I plan to do with you."

He whispered in her ear as his hand gripped her hip. "I think you're right." He kissed her lightly. "I need you so much."

"It took you long enough to figure that out." She laughed. "You could have had me that first night after we put the sisters to bed."

He held her tight, closed his eyes and took a long breath. If she kept talking, kept melting against him, it was going to be hard to say all he'd come to say. "No, Randi, I need you with me. All the time."

"We could keep it like it is. You could come by at night. We could spend time every night."

He pulled an inch away. "No, Randi. If we're going to be together, we're together in daylight and darkness."

He felt her pull away even though he knew she hadn't moved. "You don't know what that would be like, Micah. It could be the end of your job. People would talk. People always talk."

"Then, we'd face them together."

She shook her head, her wild hair brushing the side of his face. "I can't."

He wasn't ready to give up. He held her tighter. "Randi. I need you, not just in my bed, but by my side. Randi, stand with me."

"No," she whispered. "I can't."

He kissed her long and tender then, and she let him, but she no longer kissed him back.

When he pulled away, he said, "Today I realized love slammed into me when I met you. I wasn't looking for it. I'm not even sure I know how to react to it. But I know that life with you has got to be better than life without you." He dug his fists into her hair. "I love you."

A tear rolled down her cheek. "I love you, too," she answered.

"Then walk with me, Randi. Walk out of

here and let's go for coffee, or just stroll down the street together. I don't want to hide what I feel for you. If you want me, you got to take all of me, just like I want all of you. I'm not a man who can come to you in pieces, so step out on my arm and we'll face the town."

"I can't."

He straightened, afraid if he said more he'd be begging her to love him. She said the words, but she didn't mean them. She wasn't willing to take a chance and the sad thing was, he knew her well enough to understand why. She'd been broken too many times to believe.

"Love doesn't slam into a person more than once in a lifetime. We need to hold on to it."

"I can't." She turned away hugging herself. "I won't."

"I never took you for a coward," he whispered. He straightened, memorizing the lines of her face as he moved away and stepped out the back door.

Micah didn't notice the cold as he walked. The years of running had left him with a sense of where things were in the town. Before he knew it, he'd walked to the back of Cemetery Road where his shoes began to slip on the icy snow. He'd been so angry, so confused, so afraid that he couldn't survive more pain in his life, that he hadn't thought of the cold or where he'd been heading.

The first love in his life had come so easily, it had never occurred to Micah that love might be hard to give. No matter what their problems were, they could work them out together. But, Randi had been hurt one too many times in her life. She didn't believe in love, in him. Micah couldn't figure out if he was being naive in believing they could work, or if she was being cynical.

The weak sun he'd seen earlier was gone and the cloudy air now hung thick with moisture. He wished he had his running shoes, or better yet, his boots. Climbing up the incline folks in town laughingly called "the hill" had been easy, but now, with the half-melted snow freezing, it became treacherous.

Micah checked his watch. It was almost time to pick Logan up. Today was his day to do the carpool. He couldn't be late. He'd have just enough time to see everyone home safely, get Logan settled with Mrs.

Mac, and make it back to the café for the meeting. *He would have had just enough time, if he were standing by his car right now, and not at the top of the hill on Cemetery Road.*

With quick steps, he started down the hill. Just as the sight of Randi's place came into view, a piece of ice gave way and his foot slipped. Micah fell, rolling into the ditch, landing against one of the barbed-wire poles that ran along the border of the cemetery.

The pain in his knee was crippling. Micah lay in the mud for a few minutes wondering how he could have been such a fool. All his life he'd been a careful runner. One of those people who always stretched before he ran, made sure his shoes were right, checked for traffic patterns. In the past week, he'd become an idiot.

He tried to get up, but found he couldn't put very much pressure on the knee. It's not broken, he told himself, only twisted. He'd twisted his ankle a few times. He knew what to do.

Micah almost laughed as he said out loud, "Put ice on it."

He stretched in the mud and tried to relax. Maybe if he let it relax a few minutes it would feel better. The only problem was, the back of his jacket that had been wet from the water in the ditch was now freezing solid. He held to the pole and pulled himself to his feet. Or foot. Maybe he could hop along the fence line for a while. Surely, someone would come along soon.

Forty-Five

"I say we go over and start looking without him. We said we'd all meet here at four and go on to the Altman house," Ada May said. "Everyone is here but the preacher."

"We'll have another cup of coffee and give him a few more minutes. He has to pick up his son. Maybe something is delaying him." Sidney picked up the papers she'd spread across the table. They'd all looked at the two death certificates, but no one had come up with an answer, except that this might be the secret of Rosa Lee.

Sidney didn't think so. Why would her granny Minnie write a note on the back of a card that concerned when a man had died?

What did it matter to anyone except maybe Rosa Lee and Henry Altman?

Sloan stood beside Sidney's chair. "I left Micah at his car right out front. He said he had to make a stop before he picked up his son." Sloan was thinking out loud and pretty much talking to himself. "It would probably be the store, or the church. I'll run over there and look for him. Maybe he's had car trouble. If I'm not back soon take the others and go on over to the Altman Place."

Sidney agreed. "We'll go inside and start the search."

After Sloan left, everyone had another cup of coffee, but no one settled down. Sidney felt the same. She wanted one last look at the house before the vote. Even if she found no answers, she planned to take the time memorizing all she could of the old place.

At ten till five, she collected the cups and told everyone to bundle up. They all marched out into thick fog. Billy rode with Lora. Sidney rode with the sisters. Everyone had flashlights.

When they pulled up in front of the house, Sheriff Granger Farrington was waiting for them.

She didn't miss the worried look the sheriff gave her. While the others went inside, she asked Granger, "You think something may have happened to Micah?" The memory of Billy's beaten body flashed in her thoughts.

Granger nodded once. "Sloan's already called me. Micah is probably fine, but just to be safe, I'll make a few calls and get back to you. He shouldn't be too hard to find." He tried to smile.

Sidney followed the others into the house. They needed to look before it got dark, but with the cold no one would want to stay long.

Once inside, she organized everyone into search groups. "Look everywhere for a wooden rose."

They all pointed their flashlights and parted to their separate rooms.

The sheriff was back before Sidney had left the entry. "I called the church. Nancy said he hadn't been there but the school called saying he didn't show up for the carpool. She said she went over and got the boys and took Logan to Jimmy's house. She sounded worried. Micah's never late."

"Where could he be?" Sidney frowned

knowing this meeting would have been important to Micah.

"I've got an idea." The sheriff punched in his cell and stepped out on the porch. After a minute, he stepped back in. "We've found his car. Maybe he just had trouble getting it started. He's probably walking this way now."

Forty-Six

Micah decided he might very likely freeze to death. He could have made it home limping if there had been no snow, but he couldn't slip across the ice on one good leg. His only hope was that someone would come along Cemetery Road and in the past hour it hadn't happened. His leg was no longer hurting, it was frozen and the fog had moved in until he couldn't see any part of Randi's place down the hill.

He thought of yelling for help, but knew there were no houses close enough for anyone to hear even if someone was standing outside.

In the fog, he heard a car and tried to make it the three feet to the road. But the ditch was just steep enough not to allow much progress.

The car drove up the road, inching its way over the ice.

Micah grabbed a rock and threw it at the car. He heard it hit metal.

He tossed another handful of mud and rock against the side of the car before it could pass.

He heard the car stop and said her name. Then, Randi was there, running toward him with her arms open wide. They almost tumbled back into the ditch, but her footing held more solid than his.

She hugged him tightly and he felt the warmth of her spread through him.

Then she pulled away, all fire and anger. "What in the hell do you think you're doing out here! I've been crazy with worry."

He laughed, pulling her back to him. "I was taking a walk. Do you think you could save yelling at me until we get in the car where, I hope, your heater works."

She helped him into the passenger side.

He carefully lifted his leg, trying not to bend it at the knee.

"What happened?" she cried. "You're hurt."

He laughed. "I'll be fine if I don't freeze."

She ran around to her side and turned up the heater.

For a long minute, he let the warm air blow over him, feeling his blood thaw. She helped him remove his wet coat and wrapped him in an old blanket she pulled from the back seat. Through it all and despite the cold, he noticed her touching him, reassuring herself that he was with her and safe.

"Thanks," he said, then leaned back and closed his eyes. "Before you start telling me what a fool I am, let me assure you I already know. First, I try to force you into loving me, then I think I can walk my problems off without paying any attention to the weather." He took a long breath. "I don't have any defense, except to say that until today I've never considered myself an idiot, so it's a relatively new illness."

"Logan's at Jimmy's house," she said calmly, her anger gone as fast as it came.

He smiled. "I knew he'd be smart enough to call Jimmy's mother or the church. He's got more brains than his old man."

"And you didn't try to force me into loving you. I already did. I've loved you from that

first night when you looked so helpless trying to get the sisters home."

He looked at her then. Wishing he understood her.

She laughed. "You've got mud on your
face." She leaned over and rubbed it off
with her thumb. "You're a mess, Preacher."

"That I am."

"When I was out looking for you in this
mess, I realized something." She smiled. "I
thought you wanted me because you saw
me as a project, someone to help, someone
to save. Now, I think maybe it's the other
way around. You may not be all perfect. You
might just need me."

He brushed his thumb along her cheek.
"More than you know."

Forty-Seven

Sidney and the others had been through every inch of the house. Her nerves were on edge. A thick fog blanketed the town and seemed to seep through the walls of the old place. The wind howled outside telling them to go away.

To make matters worse, they found nothing. Not one rose had been carved into the woodwork.

Sloan returned and told of finding Micah's car at the bar out near Cemetery Road. Once the sheriff had gotten there, they'd organized a search, knowing that without a car Micah could not have gone far.

He said it had taken them half an hour, but Randi had found him. Micah had taken a fall on the ice and Randi had driven him to the hospital to have his knee checked.

Sloan had brought two lanterns big enough to light up a whole room while he talked. Then with all questions answered about Micah, Lora and he went up to the attic to do a final search. They returned shortly with no news.

A few minutes later, Micah arrived on crutches and with a woman in blue jeans at his side. He introduced the woman as Randi Howard. Sidney was so glad to see Micah safe, she hugged him and the redhead who'd found him on the road. The Rogers sisters knew the woman and greeted her warmly. The committee seemed to be growing.

Billy and Micah compared injuries, then everyone resumed the search. Sidney could hear Micah filling Randi in on details. "Rosa Lee left a line in a book for us to look beneath a wooden rose."

"For you?" Randi asked.

Sidney interrupted. "No. For me, I think. I may be the granddaughter of Rosa Lee. We seem to have lots of clues pointing to it, but nothing solid. She baptized a baby here in Clifton Creek two weeks before my mother's birth was recorded in Chicago. My grandmother was her nurse and was with her at the baptism."

Randi raised an eyebrow. "Couldn't they both have been pregnant?"

"They could have, only my grandmother never had other children and she named my mother Marbree Lee. The name of a rose, and Rosa Lee's middle name."

Randi nodded, but didn't look like she fully believed. Then, she faced Sidney and smiled. "My great-grandfather used to say he knew Henry and Rosa Lee. He told me once that she had light blue eyes. Would that help?"

"That's what Sam said at work," Billy yelled from the next room. "He met her when he was a kid. He called them ghost eyes."

Everyone looked at Sidney.

Ada May pushed Lora aside and stood almost nose to nose with Sidney. "Yep. Light blue eyes if I've ever seen them."

"Only one more clue," Sidney whispered.

"When is one more going to be enough?" Sloan asked. "We've got the copy of the baptism of a child Rosa Lee had in thirty-four."

"But no name was on it," Sidney protested.

"The note from your grandmother saying never forget the secrets of Rosa Lee. What else could it be but that Rosa Lee gave your mother up to your grandmother Minnie to raise?"

Sidney shook her head. "Minnie could have been talking about Henry's death. Maybe the secret is that he didn't die in 1950?"

"Minnie wasn't in Clifton Creek at that time. She was here when your mother was born. The secret must have happened in 1934." Sloan tried again.

Sidney shook her head. "My mother's birth certificate says she was born in Chicago, not Clifton Creek."

Sloan kept trying. "Minnie named your mother after a rose that Rosa Lee planted all over these grounds so Rosa Lee must have known about your mother and later you."

"Maybe they both loved the same rose. Maybe it was one they discovered when they both were here."

Sloan gave up. "You won't accept it, will you, Sidney?"

"Even light blue eyes aren't that uncommon." She needed facts. "When I'm sure," she whispered, "I'll let you know. Otherwise this is just an old house and I'm chasing a secret I'll never find the answer to."

Sidney raised her voice and turned to the others. "Now, everyone stop looking at my eyes and start searching for a wooden rose." She didn't want to say that in her heart she hoped it wasn't true. She'd always belonged to her mother and Granny Minnie. She wasn't sure she wanted to belong to Rosa Lee, a woman who had given her mother up so quickly so she could live in a big house all alone and have her books and her garden without the worry of a child to complicate her life.

They moved to the second floor. Everyone tried to talk Micah into staying downstairs, but he leaned on Randi and hopped his way up. Like everyone else on the committee, he wouldn't be satisfied until he had checked every room for himself.

On the second floor, the wind seemed to howl louder as a winter storm blew in. Sidney knew, if they were smart, they'd all go home, but tonight was the last night before the vote. The committee's decision would be made tomorrow.

"Repeat the poem," Billy asked. "Maybe there is a clue in it that we overlooked."

Sidney pulled it from her pocket. "Gone in thirty-four, a love forgotten nevermore. Look among the roses ever bright for the key to unlock the secrets of Rosa Lee."

"We've looked everywhere," Lora said. "There is no rose carved into this house."

"What about outside?" Sloan asked.

"Beth Ann and I checked there this morning. We went around the house three times." Ada May hugged herself.

A rattling came from below as if the wind had kicked the door in. No one moved.

"Sloan McCormick!" someone shouted. "Are you up there?"

Sloan motioned for everyone to be quiet as he walked a few feet to the banister so that he could see below. "Who wants to know?" he shouted.

Three shadows stood in the darkness of the entryway.

"It's Luther Oates," another voice said. "I've got my son and grandson with me. We mean no harm. I've been thinking about it

and I want to say something to the committee about this place."

Sloan walked down the stairs carrying his
work lantern at his side. When he reached
the ground floor, he put the light between
them. "Did you boys come armed?"

"No," Luther said. "You have my word."

Sloan nodded and looked up. "Luther
Oates, I'd like you to meet the committee."

Slowly, they came to the stairs. Sidney in
front. Billy and Lora just behind her. Micah
leaning on Randi, and the Rogers sisters in
the back.

Sidney squared her shoulders. "I'm the
chairman. Say what you've come to say, Mr.
Oates."

He nodded and moved to face her. "I
knew Henry Altman. What I'm about to tell
you, I don't want to go beyond this house. It
never has."

"All right," Sidney said. "You have my
word."

"Before I tell you, Dr. Dickerson, I'd like to
see you up close."

Sidney hesitated, then walked down the
stairs. The old man moved closer, then nodded at Sloan. "You didn't lie, McCormick."

Sidney wanted to ask about what, but decided to hear Luther Oates out first.

The old man looked so tired, she wasn't sure he was strong enough to do the telling. "Henry Altman was a proud man. An honorable man. We were in a religious group together. There was an accident one night and a man died. It wasn't anyone's fault. Just an accident, but it bothered Henry. After a while, it began to play with his mind, this guilt he had. None of us could convince him it wasn't his fault. He had a spell one night where his private nightmares took over his mind. Rosa Lee was planning to leave, but she said she'd delay her plans because she feared what he'd do if he were left alone. He got worse a little at a time after that. There was nothing anyone could do, not even the doctor."

The committee moved silently down the stairs not wanting to miss a word of the old man's confession.

"As the years went by, his mind slipped more and more. Rosa Lee had the garden walk built so that if he got out of the house and wandered off, he'd eventually come right back to the house.

"By 1950 we knew he couldn't handle any

part of the ranch and she couldn't cover for him. We all knew his pride would never allow anyone to know, so we decided to act like he died. She took care of both the ranch and him after that. Sometimes having to lock him away when he had his bad spells. Other times, he'd be happy to sit and listen to her read for hours or sit in the garden and watch her paint little paintings of those flowers she loved."

Tears bubbled over Luther's eyes and fought their way down his wrinkled face. "We kept the secret. The doc, Earl Hamm and me. We kept it till the end, then buried him in a grave that already had his headstone on it.

"I thought when I died, the secret would die, too, but Sloan said you all were coming out here to find proof of a secret Rosa Lee kept. It wouldn't be fair if everyone knew it now. Not after all she sacrificed to keep her father's memory strong. Not after the way we all suffered knowing we couldn't help him out of his own hell.

"Henry Altman was a fine man. He'd be proud to think the sale of his land would go to help the town. Don't try to keep the house. Let the secret die."

Luther Oates's grandson put his arm around his grandfather. "I didn't want him to come, but he couldn't rest fearing what you might find. I threw the drill bit that first morning. I meant it to hit the porch, but my aim was off. I'm sorry for the trouble it caused but I didn't have anything to do with what happened to Hatcher the other night. I was just thinking of my grandfather when I threw the bit, not hurting anyone."

Sidney took Luther's hands in hers. "It's all right. Your secret is safe with us. We didn't find anything anyway and we've all been through the house several times. Now that we know what we'd find, maybe it's best left hidden away."

She looked at the committee. "Why don't we call it a night. We'll meet tomorrow and vote."

Everyone was too cold to argue.

They watched Luther Oates and his son and grandson leave, then one by one each said goodbye to the old house.

"Thanks," Billy shouted and everyone listened to his voice echo down the halls. "It was nice knowing you, Rosa Lee." He brushed the wood along the wall.

"You were stronger than we all thought," Lora added as she moved out the door.

Ada May laughed. "You gave us quite an adventure." She followed her sister out.

Micah leaned on his crutches and listened for a minute as if expecting the house to call out for them not to leave. Then, he smiled at the cowgirl at his side and said, "If you'll take me home, there's someone I'd like you to meet."

Randi nodded and followed him.

Sidney stood alone for one last moment while Sloan turned off the lanterns and the rooms went black. She knew the secret now, but she didn't understand her part in it.

Forty-Eight

Sloan started a fire in Sidney's little fireplace while she made coffee.

"Do you want anything to eat?" she asked absently.

"No. I'm still recovering from the chili burger I had at lunch." He stood and tripped over the coffee table as he backed away from the fire. "Did I ever tell you this place is too small?"

She laughed. "About a hundred times."

"How about next weekend, we take off for my place on Lake Travis. It's got a fireplace you could stand up in and a kitchen we could move around in while we cook. We could catch our dinner, then cook it up with hush puppies and fries."

"I'd like that." She tried to sound positive, but this was a big step for her. She had no idea how to act around Sloan. He was too old to be a boyfriend and, in truth, he was already far more to her than a friend.

Sloan circled one hand around her waist. "I've got two bedrooms at the place, Sidney. I'm not trying to talk you into anything more than spending some time with me."

She wanted to say she needed some time away from Clifton Creek but she didn't want him to think she was just going to get away. "What about your next job?"

"I've got a month of vacation planned. Or, if you have to finish out the semester, I could travel over on weekends till then and we could spend Christmas at the lake house."

She didn't answer. She was afraid to. She'd been alone. She knew what that was like. Being with him was stepping into uncharted territory.

"If the weather's bad," he continued as he stood behind her holding her gently, "we could read by the fire or pop popcorn and watch old movies. I've got about a hundred."

"Any on how to fish?"

"I can teach you that, but you have to clean what you catch."

"Maybe I'll bring soup and look through your movies."

They talked about what movies they liked as they filled their coffee and moved back into the living room. She knew he was purposely not mentioning the Altman house, or the vote. He was proving himself a man of his word. She mattered. Not the house or his company.

When the phone rang, Sidney settled in for a long talk with Ada May who wanted to know exactly the order of what would happen tomorrow morning and what Sidney thought they should wear. After the vote, the mayor planned an announcement. The whole thing probably wouldn't take half an hour, but Ada May would be up all night making a list of what had to be done.

Sidney finally hung up and turned to find Sloan examining the old rocking horse they'd found in Rosa Lee's house. "We'll have to decide what to do with this tomorrow," she said as she knelt beside him. "It's the only thing of value in the house, but it doesn't belong to me."

"Doesn't it?" Sloan touched an oval of

metal on the horse's bridle. The metal turned, reflecting a portrait on one side and a mirror on the other. "I've figured out this metal winds a music box inside the horse, but I can't seem to make it start playing. Look closely, Sidney."

She leaned near and saw a picture of Rosa Lee painted on one side of the metal and a mirror on the other.

"What were the last lines of the poem Miss Carter told us in the nursing home? *The mirror turns blending old and young to the chime of a tune that was never sung.*"

He looked at the painting, flipping the metal back and forth. "Old and young, almost the same face. You could have sat for the painting, Sidney." He leaned back and pushed his hand on the horse's head so the rocking horse began to rock.

A melody began to play. "Rock-a-bye Baby."

"To a tune that was never sung," Sloan repeated.

Sidney sat back trying to put all the pieces together. She didn't know what to believe. If Rosa Lee had been her mother's mother, Sidney now knew the reason she'd given her up. Not because of selfishness,

but because of love. Rosa Lee had lov
her father. She couldn't abandon him. She
given her baby to someone whom she kne
would love her so that she could stay witl
Henry.

Sidney reached to stop the rocking horse.
The melody was slowly breaking her heart.
Rosa Lee had never rocked her child.

Her fingers brushed against one of the
wooden roses carved into the lei of flowers
around the horse's neck.

Wooden roses!

Sidney gasped.

Sloan moved closer and put his fingers
over hers. "Wooden roses," he whispered
as he gently pushed her fingers against the
wood.

The rose shifted, giving to their touch and
sliding sideways. Letters tumbled out.

Sidney picked one up, then another, then
another. "They're all from Minnie Jefferson
to Rosa Lee. They're all from my grandmother."

Sloan laughed. "To your grandmother,
you mean. This looks like the one clue you
can't ignore. This looks like the secret Rosa
Lee left for you."

They spread the letters out by postmark

an Sidney opened them one by one. All contained pictures of her granny Minnie and mother and later of her. Each letter told detailed listing of Marbree's life. As the years passed there were newspaper clippings of when Minnie's husband died and when Marbree married. And pictures, more pictures than Sidney had ever seen. In each letter Minnie called Marbree, "our girl," and when Sidney was born, Minnie wrote in big letters. *We have a granddaughter.*

Sidney wasn't sure when she began to cry, but she couldn't seem to stop. Her life, her mother's life, Minnie's life were all spread out before her, told in loving letters to Rosa Lee. The family she'd loved so dearly and lost came back to her, treasured and kept for a lifetime by Rosa Lee.

She looked up to see that Sloan had moved to a chair and studied one of the last letters written. "What is it?"

"It doesn't sound like Rosa Lee ever wrote back. There is not one reference about Minnie knowing anything about Rosa Lee's life except here."

Sidney moved closer and leaned on his knee as he read.

"Minnie writes that the garden looks

beautiful this year. How would she kno, that if Rosa Lee never wrote or sent pi tures?"

Sidney shook her head. "I was aroun Minnie all the time growing up. I think I would have noticed pictures coming. I can't even remember her ever getting anything but bills except maybe the paintings she ordered."

They both turned to the collection of paintings on Sidney's wall. Small eight-by-tens, all of flowers.

Sloan stood and offered Sidney his hand. They walked slowly toward the paintings. "These weren't just paintings your grandmother collected. They were scenes from Rosa Lee's garden. Her life couldn't have been good, taking care of her father all the time, but she sent what beauty there was in it. She sent paintings of her garden here in Clifton Creek."

This time, Sidney believed. She smiled as she looked at the beautiful paintings she'd loved all her life. "My mother was the love gone in thirty-four," Sidney whispered. "A love forgotten nevermore."

"How many of these did you say you had?"

Thirty, maybe more. I asked my grandmother Minnie why she had so many and she told me because she loved them so dearly. Now, I understand why." Sidney brushed one of the frames, remembering how she'd studied them when she'd been small thinking that they were her special place where all was beautiful.

They spent most of the night looking at the paintings and rereading the letters. Sloan laughed at all the pictures of Sidney growing up. Finally, she fell asleep on his shoulder as they cuddled on the couch. The fire had died down and the wind outside had settled finally. All the world seemed silent.

As she closed her eyes, Sidney remembered thinking she was surrounded with family. She pushed her foot against the rocking horse and listened one more time to her grandmother Rosa Lee sing her to sleep.

Forty-Nine

Sidney stood on the front porch of her great-grandfather's home and faced the small crowd brave enough to ignore the weather and come out for the committee's report. The mayor wanted to have the meeting in the courthouse, but Sidney thought it more appropriate here.

The town's newspaper reporter was present, with his notepad and camera, as well as all three oil companies. Talon Graham didn't look happy. Sidney guessed the mayor had already given him the results even though the vote hadn't been announced officially.

Crystal Howard, of Howard Drilling, walked from her car where her husband watched to the edge of the porch. She greeted several in the crowd warmly.

Sloan stood back near his truck. True to his word, he'd never tried to sway Sidney's vote. He'd been gone by the time she woke at dawn, but he'd left a note promising to cook her the best Mexican food in Texas for dinner tonight, no matter what happened this morning. Micah had told Sidney that Sloan had told his boss he'd quit before he'd break his word to Sidney and interfere with the vote.

Old Earl Hamm sat in his rusty pickup waiting. He didn't seem so mean now that Sidney knew he'd been a true friend to Henry.

"Has the committee reached a decision?" the mayor yelled as if someone might not hear him.

"We have," Sidney said. "We recommend that the Altman house and the land be sold to the oil company that will agree to two demands."

Everyone but the committee and the mayor looked surprised that Sidney would place demands on the sale.

"First, the oil company offering the highest price will agree to fence off a section of the land for a park to be named after Clinton Creek's founding father Henry Altman. Second, Rosa Lee's roses will be removed the company's expense and moved to th library where a rose garden will be built."

Everyone applauded.

Sidney stepped back among the other committee members as the mayor moved forward. "Thank you, Dr. Dickerson, for serving on the committee. The city owes you and your tireless group many thanks." He unfolded a piece of paper. "Now, I have the honor of announcing that though the bidding was close, one oil company came up with not only the best price, but a bonus offer. They agreed to the committee's terms and would like to donate up to half the funds needed to build a new room onto the library to be dedicated to books on gardening."

The mayor smiled at the Rogers sisters. "The other half has already been matched by an anonymous offer that came in an hour ago. The wing will be called the Rosa Lee Altman Room and a percentage of the oil rights will make sure it houses the best books on gardening in the country."

veryone applauded.

he mayor paused for the newspaper re-
ter to take a shot, then continued, "The
le of the Altman property goes to Howard
illing."

Crystal Howard, representing her husband's company, stepped onto the porch to
shake the mayor's hand.

Sidney tried to hide her shock. She
glanced at Sloan, but he was gone. Somehow during the mayor's talk, she'd looked
away and he'd disappeared. Before she had
time to think, everyone around her started
talking at once.

People wanted to shake her hand and tell
her what a great job she'd done. Sidney
tried to follow the conversation, but in the
back of her mind, she couldn't understand.
Why had Sloan left?

Crystal Howard took her hand. "Thank
you, Dr. Dickerson, for suggesting the library room for Rosa Lee. I thought it was
touching. We didn't like the idea of destroy-
ing a part of Clifton Creek's history any
more than anyone. Now, we'll always have a
part of her with us."

Sidney smiled. "Who told you about my

idea?" She tried to sound casual, as if the idea had been hers.

"Sloan McCormick called us early this morning. He said he thought his company could meet our offer on the land, but he knew they'd never agree to the bonus of the library and the percentage to keep it up." Crystal tilted her head. "He knew we might care, since we're from here, and he was right. I admire his honesty. If you see him tell him, if he's ever looking, Howard Drilling could use a man like him."

"I will."

Sidney had no time to say more; Crystal was surrounded by the Rogers sisters who wanted to talk about the rose garden. Sidney stepped away, trying to understand why Sloan would talk to Crystal.

She watched Lora Whitman drag Billy Hatcher off the porch. "Come on," she protested. "You have to meet my mother sometime and a public place is far safer. She rarely kills with an audience watching."

"But I'm not sure I've built my blood count up enough yet," Billy complained.

"She's not going to eat you." Lora laughed. "Just kill you. But don't worry, I'll pick out a nice coffin for you and I'll visit your grave regularly."

"Slow that imagination down, babe. I'm not planning on leaving you anytime soon no matter what your mother does."

Sidney watched as Lora introduced Billy to her very proper mother. Before Mrs. Whitman could even think of being rude, the sheriff stepped beside Billy. Sidney wasn't sure if Granger was there for support or protection, but Mrs. Whitman seemed to get the point. She smiled and extended her gloved hand to Billy.

Micah, who'd been standing beside Randi, walked over to the group to lend his support to Billy. Somehow, they were family and if Mrs. Whitman planned to pick on one of them, she'd better watch out for them all.

Sidney noticed Micah's son, Logan, walk up to Randi. "Hi," he said in a shy little voice.

Randi folded down to his level. "You must be Micah's son," she said. "You look just like your father. I came by to meet you last night, but you were already asleep."

"I got my mother's eyes," the boy said.

"And they are very handsome eyes,"

Randi added. "I'll bet she was beautiful, wasn't she?"

"I don't remember much, but I think she was. She died when I was little."

"I know." Randi touched the boy's shoulder. "Your father told me."

"You like cats?"

"Yes. I do."

"I got a cat. His name's Baptist, but I think he's Methodist."

Randi smiled.

Logan looked up at her. "You my dad's girlfriend?"

She looked like she might bolt, but she held her ground. "I guess so. Is that all right with you?"

The boy took her hand. "Mrs. Mac and I saw you standing next to him and thought you might be. He's never had one before. We think it's 'cause he doesn't know how to talk to women. Except for Mrs. Mac. He talks to her fine. We're real worried about him. I think he's been waiting for you to show up for a long time."

"You think so?"

The boy nodded. "He needs someone to look after him. Mrs. Mac and I can't do it all."

Randi laughed. "I'd like to meet this Mrs. Mac."

Logan pulled on her hand. "She's over in the car. She says she's not standing outside again until spring." He pulled Randi along.

Sidney watched them move to a parked car and laughed. The boy was right, Micah needed someone to care about him.

She walked over to the side of the porch and placed her hand on the worn wood by the steps. Sidney couldn't help but wonder how many thousand times Rosa Lee must have stood in the same place and looked out on a town she'd never joined.

She touched the place Rosa Lee had touched and somehow she felt close to her, this grandmother she never knew. The house could fall. It didn't matter. Everything Rosa Lee had loved would live on. In Sidney, in memory, and in the rose garden.

As the crowd cleared, Sidney walked to her Jeep and climbed inside. As she waited for the heater to kick in, she pulled the old recipe card from her briefcase and read the back one last time.

Never forget the secrets of Rosa Lee.

Smiling, she put her Jeep in gear. She had classes to teach and a life to get busy living. It would be late before she made it back to her little bungalow, but she knew she'd have the best Mexican food in Texas waiting.